Ruins Extraterrestrial

Ruins

Extraterrestrial

Edited by Eric T. Reynolds

Hadley Rille Books
PO Box 25466
Overland Park, KS 66225
USA
http://www.hadleyrillebooks.com
info@hadleyrillebooks.com

RUINS EXTRATERRESTRIAL
Copyright © 2007 by Eric T. Reynolds

ISBN-13 978-0-9785148-6-0

To Santos "Joe" Jaimez
1923-2007

Acknowledgments

"Flies" copyright © 2007 by Paul L. Bates.

"Charybdis" copyright © 2007 by Sue Blalock.

"Borrowed Time" copyright © 2007 by Gustavo Bondoni.

"Heartcry" copyright © 2007 by Willis Couvillier.

"Among the Shards of Heaven" copyright © 2007 by Jennifer Crow.

"The Price of Peace" copyright © 2007 by Tristan S. Davenport.

"Planetfall" copyright © 2007 by Jack Hillman.

"Combustible Eden" appeared in the July 2003 issue of *Jupiter*, Issue #1,
    copyright © 2003 by Davin Ireland, reprinted by permission of the author.

"Memories" copyright © 2007 by Robert B. Marcus, Jr.

"When All Is Known" copyright © 2007 by Cheryl McCreary.

"The Empty Utopia" copyright © 2007 by Christopher McKitterick.

"Inclusions" copyright © 2007 by A. Camille Renwick.

"Introduction" copyright © 2007 by Eric T. Reynolds.

"Red City" copyright © 2007 by Rob Riel.

"Song of the Child-Prophet" copyright © 2007 by Jonathan Shipley.

"Jigsaw" appeared in *Odyssey* (Fitzhenry & Whiteside Press , Canada),
    copyright © 2004 by Douglas Smith, reprinted by permission of the author.

"Beyond the Wall" copyright © 2007 by Justin Stanchfield.

"I, Fixit" copyright © 2007 by Ted Stetson.

"Introduction to the Findings of Team 150B-T.2U by Raiden Mesc
    Gerarti" copyright © 2007 by Elizabeth Kate Switaj.

"The Fateful Voyage of *Dame La Liberté*" copyright © 2007 by Lavie Tidhar.

"Inheritance" copyright © 2007 by Trent Walters.

"Stonework" appeared in *InterZone*, Issue #207, copyright © 2006
    by Wendy Waring, reprinted by permission of the author.

"Watcher in the Dark" copyright © 2007 by Suanne Warr.

"The Dam" copyright © 2007 by Harvey Welles and Philip Raines.

Front Cover Art copyright © by Guillaume Le Tual, used by permission
    of the artist.

Editorial assistance by Rose Reynolds and Laura Reynolds is appreciated.

Invaluable advice over the years from Terry Bisson, James Gunn,
    Paul E. Martens, Mike Resnick, Lawrence M. Schoen,
    Justin Stanchfield and Trent Walters, and many others is greatly
    acknowledged.

Contents

Introduction by Eric T. Reynolds   13

Stonework by Wendy Waring   15

Beyond the Wall by Justin Stanchfield   25

The Empty Utopia by Christopher McKitterick   49

Borrowed Time by Gustavo Bondoni   73

Charybdis by Sue Blalock   85

Introduction to the Findings of Team
   150B-T.2U by Raiden Mesc Gerarti
      by Elizabeth Kate Switaj   105

The Dam by Harvey Welles and Philip Raines   115

The Fateful Voyage of *Dame La Liberté* by Lavie Tidhar   141

Memories by Robert B. Marcus, Jr.   147

Watcher in the Dark by Suanne Warr   175

Jigsaw by Douglas Smith   187

Heartcry by Willis Couvillier   203

When All Is Known by Cheryl McCreary   215

Red City by Rob Riel   227

Combustible Eden by Davin Ireland   229

The Price of Peace by Tristan S. Davenport   249

Song of the Child-Prophet by Jonathan Shipley   253

Flies by Paul L. Bates   261

Planetfall by Jack Hillman   267

Inheritance by Trent Walters   283

Inclusions by Camille Alexa   293

I, Fixit by Ted Stetson   309

Among the Shards of Heaven by Jennifer Crow   329

Introduction

We've landed and across the valley, standing sharply against the distant gray range, are the blocky white ruins. The early probes had only provided us low-resolution glimpses of their alien architecture. We are eager to explore, but we must be careful. Kicking around in an abandoned extraterrestrial complex could be analogous to a curious Cro-Magnon poking around an abandoned twentieth century steel mill. One wrong move and we could encounter disastrous results. Even the best trained future archaeologist, intrigued by the towering spires on a moon of Epsilon Eridani's fourth planet, must first perform careful analysis by remote sensing to determine the properties of the structures. Best to have an idea of what's there before treading on grounds that last had activity when our ancestors first discovered fire.

We have long been fascinated with ruins. Even people who lived during ancient times were interested in the artifacts left by even more ancient cultures. Ruins hold so much mystery that even the best analysis can give only an impression of a long-vanished culture. Whether future ruins of Earth or those found on distant worlds, their artifacts are small pieces to larger puzzles that can never be absolutely complete. To study them we have to think beyond our present world experience. This is true of earthly ruins as well as those of non-human origin.

Cultures that evolved independently of us will have developed societies far beyond our imagination. And yet, that's what carries us forward and motivates us to take those long trips across the void, confronting unknown obstacles in order to bring back knowledge from the remnants of a vanished civilization. How safe the visits will be will vary. Exploring alien ruins can be dangerous, both unintentionally on the part of those who left them, as well as by design. Some might still have a presence that can be triggered by the arrival of an unsuspecting archaeological team. Others will be completely dead.

Ruins can take many forms. Sometimes they consist of massive crumbling edifices that still preserve their alien design; sometimes they are "softer," barely there, more abstract. At times they still have inhabitants and are a part of a larger complex, their features integrated into a newer metropolis. Ruins are often left to the excavators, but they can also be rebuilt.

In *Ruins Extraterrestrial* you'll follow the teams who explore the ruins of the Universe. Some ruins are alien, some are of Earth. They will vary in their willingness to give up their secrets.

Sometimes it'll be worth the risk.

Eric T. Reynolds
Chaco Canyon, New Mexico, USA
May 2007

Wendy Waring grew up in Canada and emigrated to Australia in 1990. She is currently wrestling a big fat fantasy to the ground, and creeping up on a skinny SF/fantastique/litfic crossover novel set in a post-apocalyptic Paris. You can find out more at: http://wendy-waring.livejournal.com/profile.

Stonework
by Wendy Waring

I arise and unbuild it again.

I walk through a stutter of shadow and light, taking in the building's construction, layout, state of repair. Above me, the broken ribs of parabolic arches jut into a white sky. The dressed stone is white too, as if the improbable heat of this place has bleached its surface. The vault of the ceiling has collapsed, but my eye is still drawn upward, following the arches' jagged fingers where they point at the startled sky.

What was done here, in the cool shade of this hall? Was it a palace? A forum? A temple?

That's why they send in cultuRecon. To make educated guesses—about what happened, and about what might happen. The planet's environment might support life, but will its history?

I tug the collar of my landing suit tighter against the dust and kneel to examine the exposed face of a massive block fissured by—tremor? battle? shoddy engineering? I want to take measurements, samples, but I'm still waiting for the safety seal to release on the equipment locker. Typical Recon. They'll let me risk a suit-walk, but the machines wait for full environment clearance. My eyes and this handheld will have to do till the seal pops.

The building's entry juts into the desert like a ship's prow. I shoulder one door open, and stand on the terrace, my back to the settlement below, shielding my eyes from the grit-blasted plain as I gaze at the immense curve of unblemished stone. From the sky, the building was barely a shape, a stark white promise in an endless stretch of red. As the shuttle set down, it resolved from promise to problem, became an egg stretched like taffy at both ends. An egg for me to crack.

Below, roughly 600 two-story dwellings, modest but sturdy, cluster around the massive hall. The settlement supported a population of, I would guess, more than three thousand. An open space for a market place, what looks to be communal ovens, although why you would need ovens here . . . . In this heat, you could bake bread in the open air.

In itself, the settlement is unremarkable. Yet beyond the monumental building and the rummage of houses, there are no rivers, no roads, no obvious landing pads. Climate change? Some unknown transport technology? Who knows. It's as if the houses have sprung up from the very bedrock.

My first proper site visit. I open my pack and take out instruments. Data handscreen, loaded up with seismic and survey, a little trowel and brush. The trowel isn't quite an affectation. I used it uncovering the ceracomm artifacts on Galatia. But I suspect it's the Total Data Station and the offworld databases I'll be relying on here.

I want good answers fast. The rudimentary settlement won't give up much quick information, so I'm focusing on the grand structure I've taken to calling the temple. Its shape is perfect—parabola arches echo the ellipse of the building itself.

I take the preliminary measurements, sending TDS data-load to the geodome at regular intervals. I walk through the empty cavern of the temple, looking for impact marks, signs of wear, inscriptions, smoke smudge, water damage, traces of pigment. I record my impressions as I go. I'll add them to my first notes and organize them when I get back to the dome.

At the entrance to the cavernous hall, I find an inscription engraved in the stone. Curious. I didn't notice it on my first walk-around. Perhaps it's only visible under certain conditions. I photograph it: the text, the scribing surface, and its placement. Sometimes where an inscription is located speaks louder than the text itself: *Non omnis moriar* or *Arbeit macht frei.*

I run my fingers over the incisions. Are they new laws, the edicts of some divinity, the self-laudatory record of the master of the works? The lettering is still sharp, though the place sleeps in ancient abandonment. At some point, the chiseled text was painted red, and faded paint still shows in the deepest crevasses of the letters, like a scar. The alien alphabet reminds me vaguely of hieroglyphics. Stretched hieroglyphics. Beautiful, but meaningless. I need only find my own Rosetta stone. And become Champollion.

The echo of my laughter comes back to me as a lonely snort. Some sort of bird is singing in the broken space where the roof once was. This will be a good site to work.

I tell myself not to pace. Particularly as, in a three-square geodome, there's no room. Still, I'm managing to wear a track from cot to desk and back. From the pool of light isolating my handscreen on the long table, past the TDS and comms mobile, and on to the narrow comfort of the cot, it's all of four steps. But it's still pacing.

My fault or not, the screw-up on DP-Prime stuck to me. And as much as I had nothing to do with the massacre on Eli Lamii, it was my name that the Threads picked up. Sure, cultuRecon knows I wasn't responsible, and down the line, Gyorg does too. It'd be hard to work for him if he didn't. But failure has a strong odor, it clings to your clothes. Enter a room after spending time with it, and people sidle away, their noses wrinkling.

Some of the analysis will be tricky handling solo, but at least I won't have to worry about other people's baggage. Or politics. Jealousy. Or war.

I haven't located a quarry for the temple yet. Strange. Even though the dressed white stone is unlike the friable rock under the settlement, the quarry can't be far. The settlement is small, with no evidence of technology adequate to move large blocks of stone long distances. Maybe it was filled in. Or perhaps the settlement is older than I think. After enough time, excavations can escape a satellite lens. Accurate dating has been difficult, and the dust here is certainly persistent. Perhaps two races built it, a servant race, and another, the ones responsible for the mind-bending mathematics of its incredible architecture.

I know better than to touch anything, but I can't help but brush an ungloved hand against the walls as I leave at night. What could my fingers do to its impregnable grandeur? The temple is magnificent.

I've been working up some equations from the Total Data Station readings. Even with the help of TDS, $y(x)=K^*ch(C3^*x)$ is the best I've come up with so far for the arches. And it's a crude approximation. I wish I could walk through these numbers with Mel.

How long did it take us on Porrentruy to work out that peculiar symbiosis of dormancy and feeding? Ten standard days, non-stop, sleeping in turn, feeding every scrap of data into a jerry-rigged Massive. Nothing like avoiding being something's dinner to spur you on. And we cracked it. That algorithm rolled up the screen and we were grinning like idiots and slapping each other on the back.

I stop, arrested by the sudden memory of Mel's hands in the el-Lamian vice. I cover my eyes, but she's still hanging in front of me, blood seeping down her forearms. I kick the cot and it collapses. Why didn't she just stick to the work?

I must be more careful. My initial measurements are incorrect. In my first TDS readings, I measured the arches to calculate whether they were as well made as my eye said they were. Yesterday, I re-measured them. They are almost thirty-seven centimeters longer than I had originally calculated. How could I have made such an error? And yet, the calculations that I made of the shape of the arches, the catenary formula, are correct. I've checked and rechecked the transit. The instruments are fine.

It is as if, overnight, thirty-seven centimeters of dressed stone grew out from the shattered ends of the arches.

The alien building reminds me, in feeling if not in form, of a medieval monastery. And this is what puzzles me. There *is* no formal similarity. The terraces that surround the building are clearly not, and never have been, gardens, or places for silent contemplation and prayer. These soaring arches owe nothing to the stolid half-circles of the cloisters of Terran monks. If anything, I should be reminded of Gaudí. But I'm not. It's not like me to let fancy imprint the evidence of my senses. Why this feeling of familiarity?

Gellia would laugh. She always said I was unable to analyze even the simplest of feelings. "Only your work is real for you." Perhaps she was right. But it matters little, for I'm no longer accountable to Gellia. In fact, this is the first time in almost a year I've thought of her. But I am answerable to cultuRecon, and I can't give Gyorg a report which I know is complete, but which feels to me partial. I want to have something for him by next synch-loop.

I've retreated to the dome, though it doesn't offer much shelter. Hard to fathom any race living in this heat. But even in ruins, the cool of the temple is delicious. Perhaps that's the secret of the huddle of houses around the massive building.

Or perhaps, like me, the inhabitants of the place worshipped the perfection of calculation. Even with its gaping ceiling, I admire its aura of inviolable strength. If the temple were whole, it could stand in sublime perfection, and need no worshippers.

I call up the floor plan of the structure on the handscreen. Horizontal and vertical axes of the building mimic each other. Shaped like a zero pointed at both ends, it stretches to north and south. And it rises as if it were tipped like an egg into the soil, the arches stretching toward the sky.

Every time I look at the plan I have drawn, I have the unshakeable conviction that something eludes me. But what? I walk through the space, experience with my feet and eyes what I believe is here, what I *know* is here. I walk through the middle of the building, turning to pace down one bowing side and up the next. Even shattered by who knows what cataclysm, the form is perfect, elegant and complete at once.

I walk out onto the eastern terrace. Bright light bleaches my handscreen. I fiddle with the controls until I render the thick black lines visible again. The plan rotating on the screen mimics precisely the temple and terraces I have paced out.

There's an invitation here, a call. I answer the only way I know how. I send another packet through the handheld to the TDS.

At second moonrise, handscreen ready, I walk through the hall under one full moon and one gibbous. The double moonlight drenches the pillars in bone-white light. One hand flat against a pillar, I can feel the folded stone within. What alien technology created this? Until I am sure, I will not give the all-clear to the surface team. Even abandoned gods, and truant worshippers, have unpleasant secrets.

While examining the ribs of the temple, I'm reminded suddenly of a VR tour I took when I was student on Kilik Segund. It was a walk-through of the Thoronet abbey on old Terra. Its lines were so simple, the stonework abrupt and compelling, a rare combination of utility and majesty. I was fascinated—and I was a callous young know-it-all then—and later I dug out that architect's account of the abbey's construction. What was his name? Bouillon? Poulon? Something like that.

The Cistercians went where nature was wildest, away from the cities, and worked together. Like wasps building a nest from mud, they built up a cloister.

I stop pacing and squint into the shadow around me. Arch follows arch follows arch, steepled hands cup me, lost here in a forest of pillars.

What does this building want of me?

I couldn't sleep last night. Probably the heat. I got up and turned on the desk lamp, the geodome's only light. I sat and calculated shearing force and core sample compression, matching hypothesis to observation. The temple plan, its secret still elusive, rotated on my handscreen. After a while, I started pacing again. On my twentieth circuit, I sagged into the jumble of my cot and stared at the pool of light over my work. At the edges of its circle of light were a scatter of rock sample and a slide of smoke smudge. Memories of Gellia ambushed me.

Gellia.

Her hands always smelled of something—freshly crushed garlic, mountain sage, old leather. Mornings would leave the trace of her caress on my skin. I don't know. In the end, when I left for the five T-years duty I had signed on for at cultuRecon, an echo of cinnamon filmed my cheeks where her two hands had stroked them and then slid away.

I was in Eli Lamii when she communicated that I had given her a daughter, and when I could not find words to say how I felt, I heard no more from her. The child would be seven now. I wonder if she looks like me. I hope for the girl's sake she looks like her mother.

I will not think of her again. I have work to do.

This morning I walked through the settlement to its outer edge. Cloying dust leached the breath from my throat. Odd, I remember the town as much larger, more sprawling, on my first walk-through. And where is the graffiti? I was sure I saw some my first trip down, but now I can't find any of the stretched hieroglyphics.

And why would five hundred beings settle here in the first place? Nothing grows here, nothing has ever grown here, nothing but rock.

I have taken to sitting in the temple, trying to piece together the mystery of its collapse. The catenary arches are near perfect, and the pillars have an internal structure of folded reinforcement resistant to shearing. It's unique, unlike anything I've seen before. It's as if within the columns, the stone has folded itself up like corrugated cardboard. Solid, secure, unassailable. There is no engineering fault, no architectural reason for this temple to be open to the skies. And according to the orbital seismic telemetry Gyorg sent, no geological reason either. Even if the devout have decamped, the stone should've held. So was there war? There's no sign of it.

And where's the stone that fell from the ceilings? Some has been used in the village, although I can't comprehend why. Who would take the stone away and build those squat dwellings? With that fallen stone, I would complete this work.

Gyorg's latest transmission was incomprehensible. I couldn't decipher it. It was like an alien language. Probably a compression problem. I've patched transmission through to my handheld. I'll try to get the ship live on the next loop.

The birds twitter above me. I still haven't seen one at close quarters.

*   *   *

It was hot again today. It was hot yesterday and it'll be hot tomorrow. Only the arches cast shadow. Earlier today, overcome by the heat, I lay down in the temple hall, eager for the relief the stone gives. Under my face and outstretched arms the blocks were magnificently cool. Prostrate, I listened to the birds—which I'm calling swallows though I'm sure they're not—chatter and weave above me as they sought the safety of their nests. I must have fallen asleep.

I felt the birds enter their nests.

I don't mean that I heard their muted chirps, or felt the air empty of their hunting swoops.

No. I felt the whirr of wings against my body, a plump down squeezing against my cold solidity. Unbroken stone breached by spike of beak, imperceptible breath and beat of heart. I awoke with a start, slapping at my chest, convinced that swallows would fly out of me.

Outside, the sun had fallen midway to the horizon.

A dream, a strange one, or a touch of sunstroke.

I couldn't put it off any longer. I sent in my preliminary report. I tried to make it clear to Gyorg that while there seems to be no threat here, there is mystery, one I have not yet run to ground. He has given me more time. Was it hesitation I heard in his voice? I think he still trusts my judgement. This is the first time, though, that I've asked him to trust my instincts. As I cross the empty plain, skirling vortices of grit punctuate the moaning wind's long monotone.

As I was leaving the temple this evening, I noticed a formula inscribed in the stone just outside the massive bivalve doors: (1') $y'(x)=dy/dx=C2*mlgl/C1+C2*mwy/C1$. I was struck with an overpowering sense of *déjà lu*. Back in the dome, I open my notes, and there's my own little ditty for the column fill, that strange corrugated stone, the formula that I worked out after I finished the one for the arches. How could I have missed the inscription the first time? Wasn't there something else there? I can't recall. In any event, the temple's formula is an improvement on mine. Like working with Mel, but better.

*   *   *

I've left the geodome. The scant dozen dwellings of the settlement watched mutely as I shuffled at dawn through the stone-dumb alley. I left behind the cot, the table, and the rest of my instruments, although I still have the handheld. I don't entirely trust the relay from the comms unit so there's a chance I might miss Gyorg's transmission, but it's worth it to be close to this. In the temple's cool emptiness, I can feel the stone speaking to me. It's so much easier to think. The mathematical perfection of the arches fills me with awe. I dream of them unbroken.

Who could have thought sleeping on stone could be a delight? The heat is nothing to me now. I lie on my back and watch the moons bathe the arches where they meet. I feel in my bones the long, slow congress of stone.

Behind the tight vacuum seal of the dome's flaps, my handheld, the TDS and the comms module sit mute. The TDS is too crude to calculate the sublime mathematics of this delicate ribcage.

On my hardening flesh is written: $y(x)=K^*ch(C3^*x)$ and then these alien symbols I do not understand: gyorg eli lamii gellia . . . . Beautiful, but meaningless. Through the narrowing gap in the vault, I watch the constellations spin.

My mouth is calcium. Skin puckers against cool night stone. Stone fingers steeple. The work goes on until our vaulting is complete. I am taken in. Inch by inch, the stars disappear. The darkness is perfect.

Justin Stanchfield is a full-time rancher, part-time snowplow driver, occasional musician and, in his spare time, writer. His fiction has appeared in magazines including Boys' Life, Black Gate and InterZone, as well as The Year's Best Science Fiction, #24. He lives with his wife and children on a Montana cattle ranch, a stone's throw from the Continental Divide. His first novel, Space Cowboys, is due out in spring 2008 from Usborne Books.

Beyond the Wall
by Justin Stanchfield

From two hundred kilometers out the Wall seemed an impossibility, the scale too large to comprehend. Jenine Toole checked her descent rate against the radar, her own senses unreliable as she guided the lander downward. Outcrops of pitted stone vied with undulating lines of drifted, tarry snow until the surface seemed zebra-striped in the wan light. As the craft dropped lower she saw its shadows racing beneath them. Twin shadows, one diffuse, cast by Saturn's milky glow, the other sharper but faint, the sun a mere point in the carbon haze. She had landed on Titan before, and each time the oddness of the landscape threatened to overwhelm her. Small wonder, she thought, that whoever had built the Wall had chosen this moon to build it on.

"Four-Eight November, do you still have the intruder on screen?"

The clipped, male voice over the com-circuits startled her. Normally, she made a drop like this in silence. No sense letting the pot-hunters know they were being followed. Frowning, she thumbed the transmit switch.

"That's affirm, Control."

"Four-Eight November," the voice repeated. "Do you still have the target on your tracking screen?"

"Roger that." Annoyed, she double-checked the screen nestled near the top of the padded console. The intruder's ship sat a kilometer from the base of the Wall, its thermal signature bright after the hot-stick landing. Whoever the pilot was, she decided, they had balls to pull off a drop like that. She hit the transmit switch again. "I'm showing the target ninety klicks downrange."

"Four-eight November? If you can read this, be advised, we can not see the target."

"Wonderful." Jenine cursed under her breath, then flipped the radio to intercom. "Paul? You guys better strap in. I'm about to hit the brakes. And, just so you know, we're out of commo with the orbiter. I can hear them, but they can't hear us."

"Got it." Paul Tsing sounded calm despite the bad news. Jenine's lips curled in a half-smile. She was never sure if he was as confident as he seemed, or if he simply didn't understand how dangerous it was dropping ten tons of lander onto a haze-covered snowball. Still, she would rather have him in charge of a mission like this than any of the other inspectors she had flown with over the last nine years. Saturn and its entourage of moons was a harsh place, harsher still since the Wall had been discovered. Nothing brought out the worst in people—and nations—than the promise of alien technology waiting to be salvaged a billion kilometers from Earth.

The lander shuddered as she gave the braking jets another shot. She forced herself to relax while they bled off airspeed, the craft bucking in the thick atmosphere. Falling more than gliding, Jenine split her attention between the instruments and the view outside the narrow window. Already, the Wall dominated the view, its stark angles framed by Saturn, the gas-giant a monstrous rubber ball cut neatly in half by shadow.

"Can you see the ship?" Tsing asked.

"Yeah." Jenine could just make out a tiny, silver speck against the rust-brown terrain. "I've got 'em on visual."

She fired the thrusters again, slowed to a drifting hover and extended the landing gear. The radar showed them forty meters above the surface. Thirty meters. Gently, she eased back the throttle. Twenty meters.

Without warning, they struck. Jenine's head hit the low ceiling. "What the hell?"

The lander bounced, struck again and threatened to tip over. Moving on instinct, she chopped the thrust and let the craft settle ingloriously to the surface. A dozen alarms screamed inside the cockpit. She cut them off, made a fast inspection of the board to confirm they were still in one piece, then shut down the engines completely. Sweat trickled off her forehead as she thumbed the intercom.

"Sorry about the landing, fellas. The radar must have gone wonky on me."

"Never mind that," Tsing said. "Are you sure you set us down next to the right ship?"

"Of course I'm sure. It's the only one besides us on planet. Why?"

"Look out the side window."

She did. Annoyance changed to incredibility, and then to a cold, gripping fear. The ship she had tracked from orbit, the same ship that had glowed with the full heat of landing only seconds before, lay tipped on its nose gear, a rusted hulk half buried in the methane snow. Jenine stared at it, unbelieving.

The pot hunter's ship looked as if it had been here for centuries.

Nine years.

Absently, Jenine fingered the hem of her jacket sleeve, the cuff as worn and tattered as herself. She smiled at the thought. When was the last time she had gone on vacation, provided you could call two weeks on the U.N. research station on Iapetus a vacation. Still, it beat the hell out of Titan Control, the cramped, overcrowded orbiter and its wartime mind set more than most people could stand for a single tour, let alone three of them.

"Stop it," she chided herself. Her voice echoed in her headset. Lately, Jenine had found her mind dwelling on the choices she had made, the opportunities lost. It was a bad sign, another indication that it was time go home. She snorted. As if she could still call Earth home.

To distract herself, Jenine looked out the narrow window at the frigid, primordial atmosphere. Snow flurries danced, swirling in the floodlights that bathed the area. She watched as four figures, each in a different color E-suit, spread out around the crippled ship. Paul Tsing, wearing a dark blue suit with a white helmet, stopped at the base of the craft's extended landing ramp and looked up into the darkened airlock.

"Any sign of the pot-hunters?" she asked over the comm.

"Negative. Not a damn thing. Unless they have a safe room inside, this ship is cold. Deep cold. I doubt anyone has been here for years." Even Tsing's normal calm seemed stretched to the limit. "Are you certain we couldn't have missed their landing site?"

"Not a chance." Jenine had already played back the landing records. The ship was the only craft besides their own sitting on Titan's ice-choked surface. "Could it have been dead in orbit and came down on auto-pilot?"

"Doubt it." Tsing's breath cut in and out of the circuit. The man was nervous. "We're going inside. Let Control know, will you?"

"Okay. Be careful."

"We will."

Jenine watched a moment longer, then flipped over to the surface-to-orbit frequency. "Titan Control, Four-Eight November, come in." She waited, but heard only static in her earphones. She tried again. "Titan Control, this is landing craft Four-Eight November, come in."

The frequency remained empty, silent but for the irregular hiss and pop of lightning. A cold shudder ran down her back. In a system as active as Saturn's, communication problems were hardly uncommon, the background radiation at times so intense it could distort the strongest signal. But, in the dozens of drops she had made, she had never spent this long out of contact with the orbiting facility. Then again, she never set down this close to the Wall before.

The Wall. Her gaze drifted to the dark rampart half a kilometer off their nose. The massive structure was so tall she had to crane around until her nose nearly touched the window to see the top of it. Hundreds of tiny, rectangular portals dotted its face, spaced at seemingly random intervals along its length, the far ends so distant they stretched to either horizon until they were lost in the mist. Small wonder dozens of automated probes had passed it off as a geologic feature. Not until a manned mission arrived did anyone realize the thing was an artifact. Within hours, the powers that be had set the greatest discovery in archeological history off-limits until jurisdiction was established.

Jenine snorted in disgust. That had been a decade ago, and still the U.N argued over who had the right to set foot inside first. It had seemed a good place to escape a failed marriage and stalled career, to volunteer for a tour guarding the structure which had, by all evidence done perfectly well on its own for more than half a million years. Now, in retrospect, she could hardly imagine she had ever been that naïve. Her eyes began to sting, and she realized she hadn't blinked once as she stared at the Wall. She shook herself out of the dark reverie and reached for the transmit switch.

"Paul? What do you have inside?"

"Just what we thought." Tsing's voice crackled, the ship's hull hampering his signal. "This puppy has been down a long time. Not a drop of power in the system. No sign of crew. Oh, crap . . . "

"What's wrong?" Jenine tensed, instantly alert. Booby traps were the greatest threat any patrol faced. Few of the high-tech pirates that periodically attempted to break the prohibition would risk a physical fight, but nearly all of them were willing to leave a surprise or two aboard their ships for anyone who came poking around. "Talk to me, Paul. What's wrong?"

"We're okay." He sounded out of breath, clearly shaken. "I was wrong about that crew, that's all. The pilot is still aboard."

"Alive?"

"Neg on that. She's inside her suit, but frozen solid. Looks like the body's been here for ages. And you're not going to like this part. The suit is a GenDyn Six."

"You're kidding?" Jenine's eyebrows furrowed together. The General Dynamics Mark Six was standard issue for U.N. troops assigned to deep space missions and not available to the public. She glanced over her shoulder at the locker where her own suit hung ready should she need it, then turned once more to the window. "Must be stolen. Can you see the ID patch?"

"Stand by. We're checking now."

Jenine waited, her heartbeat practically the only sound other than computer fans and the soft moan of wind around the hull. She zipped her jacket tighter against the chill in the cabin. Impatient for news, her hand moved toward the transmit switch when Tsing's voice returned.

"We've got an ident." Another long pause.

"And?"

"Jenine . . . " Tsing's voice sounded small, as if he was fighting the urge to vomit. "According to the patch, the corpse sitting in this chair is you."

They faced each other across the fold-down table in the passenger compartment. Out of his suit, Paul Tsing was a short man, with a thick shock of black hair and boyish eyes that belied the deep wrinkles carved around them. Normally, he was a rock. But not today. His face was pale, almost waxen, and like his three teammates, the scent of cold sweat hung around him.

"There's a rational explanation," Jenine said. She looked around the cramped chamber. None of the others would meet her gaze. Two of them, Morrisy and Kvas, were new replacements. The fourth inspector was a dour, pinched-faced man named Bruner who had been transferred up from Jupiter two years earlier, no doubt a reprimand for something. Only two ways, she thought glumly, to wind up at Titan. Volunteer or screw up. She took a sip from her coffee bulb then continued, uncomfortable with the silence.

"The suit was stolen, that's all. There must be dozens of Mark Sixes unaccounted for."

"Fine," Tsing said quietly. "What about the ID patch?"

"Someone hacked my records. It happens."

"Maybe." Tsing took a drink, scowled, then pushed his own coffee aside. "We'll know more once we get the DNA back from the tissue we cored."

"Christ, you don't think it's me in that suit, do you?" Jenine's eyes widened in mock horror. Nervous laughter spread around the table. Even Bruner managed a weak grin. "Come on, guys. There's a logical explanation. We just have to find it."

Tsing's eyes locked on hers. "You weren't over there."

A low rumble coursed through the hull, strong enough to feel through the padded benches. The sound built into an undulating wail, then faded. One of the newbies, Kvas, practically jumped out of his skin.

"What was that?"

"The thing that goes bump in the night." Jenine motioned him to sit back down. "It's just our fuel—still bleeding off the methane into the main tank. You'll get used to it after a while."

"How long until the tanks are full enough to break ground?" Bruner asked, practically the first thing he had said since returning from the pot-hunter's ship.

"Three hours, maybe four." Jenine shrugged. "It doesn't really matter. We won't have a launch window for seventeen hours. And that's only if I can reestablish commo. I don't like the idea of launching blind."

"Any idea what's wrong with the radio?" Tsing asked.

Again, Jenine shrugged. "I think it's background noise. I'm running a full diagnostic now, but it takes a while."

"Well then . . . " Tsing spread his hands. "We've got a few hours to kill. Might as well get some rack time."

"What about the intruders, sir?" Morrissy asked. He sounded so young Jenine had to stifle a grin. "Shouldn't we do something about them?"

"We are." Tsing sank back onto his narrow couch. "In case you haven't noticed, there are only two ships in walking range. One of them is dead, and we're sitting in the other one. They're stranded without us. When they knock on our airlock, we'll arrest them. Until then, I'm going to get some sleep."

Frost built on the inner surface of the window. Despite the heaters, it was cold inside the cockpit. Jenine wrapped her arms around herself. The muted snores from the passenger cabin were somehow reassuring, a human touch on an indifferent world.

No, she reminded herself. Titan was not indifferent. It was dead. A void, smog-shrouded chunk of ice and rock whirling about a gas giant so far from the sun it might as well have been in interstellar space. Almost against her will, she turned to the narrow window and stared at the enormous structure outside.

"It's still hard to believe, isn't it?"

Startled, Jenine spun around in her chair. Tsing stood in the narrow doorway, a blanket wrapped around his shoulders. He glanced at the empty co-pilot's chair.

"Mind if I sit down?" He eased into the high-backed seat. "Why here? Of all the places in the solar system, why would any race build something like that here?"

"A message, maybe?" She shrugged. "They wanted to see if we became a space-faring race and left it as a marker."

"You know, I've never bought that explanation." His eyes traveled down the length of the enigmatic artifact. Titan was still on the sunward side of Saturn, but the feeble light that penetrated the haze revealed few details. "If they really were interested in our technological advances there are better ways to do it than this."

"All right, then, maybe the aliens landed here for the same reason we do. Titan's a perfect re-fuel point."

Tsing nodded thoughtfully. "That makes sense. But, it still doesn't explain our friends out there."

He tipped his head toward the other ship. Floodlights from the lander bathed it in a bright pool of light, accentuating the sharp angles. Unlike most pot-hunters who relied on stealth technology, this ship had simply blazed in-system along a standard approach path, almost as if they didn't care if they were spotted. Methane snow flitted back and forth in the wind before finally falling to ground. Skeptical as she was, Jenine couldn't help but notice how deep the accumulations around the machine were. If she hadn't seen it land, she would have sworn it had been sitting in the same spot for decades.

"How long has it been?" Tsing asked.

"Nearly five hours." She knew what the question meant. Whoever the pot-hunters were, they couldn't have been this long from their ship without carrying spare oxygen and batteries, and if they were using thrust packs, which seemed likely given the lack of footprints, their range would be limited. Six hours, seven at the most, she estimated, before the crew had to return or die of asphyxia. Unless, of course, they were already as dead as the frozen corpse they had discovered. A cold thought hammered against her, and she swung around to face Tsing.

"What if this is a decoy? What if there never was a crew, and that ship was just sent down to distract us while the real potters land somewhere else?"

"I thought of that," he admitted. "Seems like an awful lot of trouble to go to."

"Given what a single artifact from inside the Wall would be worth . . . " She let her voice trail off.

The creases around his eyes deepened. After a moment, he changed the subject. "Any luck with the commo?"

"No. I've run the diagnostics twice and can't find a damn thing. Has to be outside interference. I'm running a new scan on the tracking dish now, but . . . " Something out the corner of her eye struck her wrong, and she leaned closer to the window. "What the hell?"

"What's wrong?"

"The ship's gone." Shaken, Jenine looked again. To her amazement, the derelict was back, snow swirling around its hull. She shivered. "Wonderful. Now my eyes are playing tricks on me."

"Never mind that," Tsing said, an urgent tone in his voice. He pointed toward the Wall. "Look up near the top tier of portals. Our friends are back."

High above the red-hued snowdrifts, barely visible through the haze, a light glowed in one of the rectangular openings. Even as they watched, it brightened, then faded, as if someone holding a lamp had turned to face them then quickly swung away. Eyes locked on the wall, Jenine asked, "What now?"

"Now?" Tsing stood up. "I wake up the guys and suit up. Looks like we finally get to see what's inside that son of a bitch."

Time slipped to a crawl. Jenine sat alone inside the lander and watched the team march across the barren expanse toward the Wall. By regulation, she had donned her excursion suit, the stiff, bright green fabric uncomfortably snug around her chest and waist. She hated this part, the waiting, the feeling of utter uselessness while the rest of the team took on the real risk. Protocols had been in place for years, contingencies by which a team might actually enter the Wall should the structure be at risk. Under perfect circumstances they would have been in constant contact with the orbiter before such a decision was made, but with the commo down and clear evidence that someone had already penetrated the Wall, Tsing had made the only real choice he could.

Jenine shifted in the padded chair and tried to get comfortable. The waiting tore at her, the sensation that she was little more than a glorified chauffeur. Too much time on her hands, too much time to think. Think about why she stayed out here, and why she was reluctant to go back to Earth. So many missed opportunities, all the bright promise of her life dwindled to this odd little corner of the solar system. She had been running from herself so long she sometimes wondered if she could ever catch up.

The speaker crackled. "Are you reading us all right?" Tsing sounded slightly out of breath.

"Roger that." She glanced at the center screen, now split into four separate views, one for each of the team members. "A-V and telemetry all five by five. You got any tracks yet?"

"Nothing."

Jenine leaned closer to the screen. She couldn't imagine how the pot-hunters had entered the Wall without disturbing the snow around it. Even with thrust-packs there should have been marks. Nothing about this mission made sense, and not for the first time since they landed she felt the fear twisting within her stomach. She tried again unsuccessfully to contact the orbiter, then let her eyes drift back to the center screen. Already, details from the Wall were visible, the surface a mottled, pitted gray, cracked and worn by the harsh environment. If she had expected something high-tech she was disappointed. The material looked like any of hundreds of terrestrial ruins.

A dark rectangle came into view, the nearest of the portals on screen as Tsing's helmet lamp played across the opening, revealing a narrow hallway within. "Here we go." No mistaking the tension in his voice.

"Roger that," Jenine replied, her own voice barely a whisper. Like most of humanity, she had seen the old footage relayed back by the robot probes the initial teams had sent inside. Rough, skittering images of twisting, intertwined passages and stairwells, most so steep the probes had been unable to ascend. No artifacts had been found, no inscriptions or murals, nothing to indicate who or what had left the enormous monument. She tensed as Tsing's camera view darkened, then stabilized once he ducked under the lintel.

"Do you see anything?" she asked.

"Not much. It's pretty tight in here. Barely enough room to squeeze by. Lots of snow piled up . . . damn it!"

"What's wrong?" Jenine's fingers tightened around the armrests.

"Nothing. I tripped in the dark, that's all. Missed seeing a step down."

The view from Tsing's camera flickered, returned, then darkened once more, the signal weakened by the heavy stone. One by one, the others in the team followed him inside. Jenine looked out the cockpit window and tried to spot the door they had used, but the details were lost in the snow squall. High above the surface, nearly at the top of the Wall, she saw another flash of light.

"Paul? I just caught sight of the intruders again. They're above you and to the west." She waited, but Tsing didn't reply. "Paul? Are you reading me?"

"Yes. Stand by . . . " Tsing's transmission was almost unreadable. The video feed flickered then cut out. The other cameras did as well. Within seconds, the center screen was blank. Jenine stared at it while a wave of dizziness passed through her, as if the cabin had suddenly tilted then just as quickly righted itself. She glanced once more at the ship a hundred meters to her left.

It was gone.

"This isn't happening," she whispered, barely able to breathe. Her fingers flew across the control panel as she scanned the area around the lander. To her dismay, the instruments found nothing, no heat signature, no radar return, certainly nothing on the video feed. She stabbed the transmit button.

"Paul? Get out of there, now." She knew she was letting panic sway her, but couldn't stop. "If you can hear me, we have a situation out here. Return to the lander. Repeat, return to the lander."

She boosted the gain and listened. No voices replied, no pings from any of their trackers. Quickly, she switched to the orbiter's frequency and tried once more to reestablish contact. "Titan Control, this is landing craft Four-Eight November. Please come in." She waited without reply. Frustrated, she let the dish scan the southern horizon, hoping the computer might locate another radio source. "Any station, this is United

Nations landing craft Four-Eight November. Please come in."

She frowned. Somewhere, buried in the blanketing white hiss of Saturn, she heard a faint trill. The sound built, then faded only to return a few seconds later. Jenine narrowed the scanning range, but the electronic warble remained damningly obscure. Less than thirty seconds after it began, the transmission vanished.

"What the hell?" Her voice echoed softly in her earphones, the words clipped by the intercom while she waited for the ship's navigation library to identify the source. Seconds dragged into minutes as the computer searched through thousands of samples before it finally found a match. Jenine's jaw fell open. The only object that could have created the brief, passing signal was an early space probe that had gone non-functional over two hundred and sixty years earlier.

"This is impossible." She flicked back to the ground-to-ship channel. "Paul, this is the lander. If you can hear me, please return to the ship. Do you read me?"

Without warning, as if to answer her call, a loud bang ran through the hull. Jenine jumped and struck her helmet against the cockpit ceiling, then steadied herself against the back of her chair and listened. Another thud followed the first, and then another, all centered near the small airlock at the rear of the passenger compartment. Someone was knocking at the door.

"Paul?"

Hopeful, Jenine switched on the fish-eye camera mounted inside the lock. Blood roared in her ears as the camera focused on a lone figure in a bright green excursion suit framed in the outer hatchway. She squeezed her eyes shut and looked again, but the figure was gone, nothing visible but swirls of dull red snow. Certain that she was losing her mind, she replayed the video. The dizziness and nausea she had felt earlier returned, so strong she nearly vomited inside her helmet, all doubt removed.

The person who had been banging against the airlock was herself.

Seventeen minutes. Jenine watched the clock on her visor, clinging to the passage of time as a drowning dog might grasp a log between its front legs as it was swept downstream. "Come on, think . . . " The sound of her own voice helped her regain her calm. "Got to be a rational explanation for all this."

The obvious answer was the one she liked least. She was hallucinating.

"All right, then, why am I seeing things? Anoxia? My suit air is fouled." To test her theory, she carefully unlocked her visor and swung it up into her helmet. The smell of her own sour breath washed away, replaced by the colder, musty cabin air. She filled her lungs, exhaled and filled them again. A breath cloud hung around her face as she let the air out. She glanced at her bio-monitor, but the readout showed no change.

"Okay," she said out loud. "Go to plan B. What the hell is Plan B?"

Her eyes drifted around the cockpit and fell at last on the Emergency Medkit. She remembered it contained sedatives, but quickly rejected the idea. While a tranq patch might steady her nerves, it would also dull her senses. Until Tsing and the others returned, she had to remain sharp, even if she mistrusted what her mind reported. Still, the kit might contain something useful. Slowly, hampered by her suit, she reached for it but stopped as the radio unexpectedly burst to life.

"Four-Eight November? This is Tsing. Come in. Please come in."

"Paul? Go ahead."

"Thank God." Tsing's voice was raw. "We've been trying to contact you for hours."

"Hours?" The statement confused her. The team had been inside the ancient structure less than seventy minutes, but she passed it off as nerves. "It's the Wall. It's blocking your signal. What's your location?"

"I'm sitting in one of the portals. I think it's on the upper tier, but I can't really tell."

Through the murk she could just make out a faint glow near the rim of the massive artifact. "Okay, I've got you. I think you're in the same doorway the pot-hunters used. What's your situation?"

"Not good. Bruner is down. He panicked when his air got low and jumped through one of the doors to the ground. Kvass and Morrissy went to find him, but I can't raise them on the radio. Listen, Jenine, we're all short on power and air. My reserve is down to thirty minutes."

"Thirty minutes?" She leaned forward, certain Tsing was mistaken, and found his bio-read. Now that he was back on-line, the telemetry functioned again. She stiffened. Instead of the seven hours he should have had available, his air supply registered thirty-four minutes of usable oxygen. "What happened out there?"

"Got lost . . . wandered around inside the . . . " The signal, diamond bright only seconds ago, now began to break up. "Found the bodies . . . can't . . . "

"Say again? What bodies?"

"The pot-hunters. They're dead." He spoke more slowly, but the signal continued to weaken. "No chance to retrieve them. Not now."

"You found them?" Jenine blinked. "Paul, their ship is gone. Some of them must have made it out."

"What are you talking about? That ship is still on the ground." For a moment, Tsing's voice came in clear again. "I can see it from here."

Another wave of vertigo struck her. What should have been a routine mission had suddenly become impossibly complicated. One team member missing and most likely dead, three others on the verge of suffocation, her own mental health questionable. She took a deep breath, then spoke slowly, "Paul, what are the weather conditions where you are?"

"Huh?" He sounded perplexed. "What do you mean? They're the same as what you have. Overcast sky, visibility fair out to five klicks. Wind conditions calm."

She glanced out the window at the heavy snow driving past, the wind a howl. The Wall was nothing but a dark, blocky shadow through the haze, Tsing's lamp the only discernable feature. Even as she watched, that light faded, then was gone.

"Paul?"

Static answered. She slumped back into her seat and began to shiver, chilled to the core. She tried again to raise Tsing without success, then, moving stiffly, rose and wandered toward the back of the craft. A small locker was built into the wall behind the couches. From it, she withdrew three oxygen canisters and put them inside a carry sack, then added as many charged batteries as she could find. She picked up the bundle. In Titan's weak gravity the weight wouldn't be a factor, but the sack was bulky and would hamper her movements. She sighed, unable to think of any other way to carry the emergency supplies. Bundle in hand, she shuffled to the airlock, pulled on her gauntlets then resealed her visor. A row of tiny green lights popped into view along the rim. She reached for the airlock controls, but paused.

"This is insane," Jenine told herself. While she had been busy gathering supplies, the weirdness of the situation had been pushed to the back of her mind. Now, it returned with a vengeance. Regulations insisted she remain with the lander. So did common sense.

Unfortunately, that meant leaving a friend to die.

More frightened than she had ever been, she slapped the broad red button beside the door and waited for the airlock to slide open. Before she could change her mind, stepped through.

Jenine leaned forward, fighting the quartering headwind, the bulky pack of spare oxygen cylinders slapping her leg with every step. The surface felt spongy underfoot, the methane slush sticking to her insulated boots. She paused a moment to rest, and turned to look behind. The lander remained an oasis of light, its rotating beacon painting the swirling snow a garish orange. A fast glance at her clock showed that fifteen minutes had elapsed since she had spoken with Tsing. With time running out, she hefted the sack and pressed on.

The Wall stretched from horizon to horizon, its top lost in the blizzard. She could just make out the individual portals, coffin-sized openings spaced irregularly across the structure's stone face. She picked up her pace toward the nearest of them and hoped it was the one Tsing and the others had used. If she didn't pick up their trail soon, all of this was for nothing.

Something lay at the foot of the monument. Jenine jogged toward it, her gait hampered by the odd gravity. From the color of his suit, she knew it was Bruner. Her headlamp threw his body into an almost surrealistic accuracy. His visor was rimed in frost, a thin, diagonal crack across it. She didn't need to touch him to know he was dead. She swept the area with her lamp. Heavy footprints, half-filled with drifted snow, led away.

"Thank you," she said, blessing her luck at finding the tracks. She followed them to the portal, then stopped. The vertigo she had felt earlier returned, as if the moon's orbit had suddenly gone mad. She fought down the sensation, then ducked inside.

A narrow passage lay in front of her, the stone rough-hewn. Her mind flashed back to a school field trip when she was ten or eleven, a sim-tour of Egypt's Great Pyramid. The corridor could have been left by the same builders. Dragging the pack behind her, she continued down the passage. Twenty paces inside, the corridor turned left into a narrow flight of steps. Two more bodies sat upon them, unmoving.

"Morrissy?" Jenine knelt beside the nearer of the pair. "Can you hear me?"

The man stirred. Jenine bent closer, desperate to find an angle where her suit lamp didn't blind him. His eyes fluttered open.

"How . . . how'd you find us?" His words were thick, barely coherent.

"Just hang on, okay?" She pulled out one of the cylinders and exchanged it with one of the empties on his power unit. After she made certain the seal was tight, she did the same with his spent battery. "Take a deep breath, okay?"

Morrissy nodded weakly. She stepped over him and repeated the operation with Kvass's pack. Even with the fresh cylinder and battery, she couldn't tell if he was breathing.

"Thanks for coming back," Morrissy said, his voice stronger.

A cold finger skipped down Jenine's spine. "What do you mean, 'come back?'"

"The lander," Morrissy said. "When we got down, it was gone. We thought you'd abandoned us."

She thought about explaining, but decided against it. She still had to find Tsing. Dreading the thought of penetrating deeper into the structure by herself, she let her light play over the rough-cut stairs.

"Where's Paul?" she asked.

"We hoped he was with you."

"No. I talked to him from the lander, but he was on one of the upper tiers. Did you leave marker tabs?" Jenine helped Kvass sit up. The man groaned incoherently, the sound a muted roar in her headphones. She waited until the channel cleared, then asked again, "Did you tab a trail back to where you and Paul split up?"

"We . . . " Morrissy sounded on the edge of hysteria. "We ran out tabs hours ago. Doesn't matter anyway. They don't work in here."

"What do you mean they don't work?" The hair on the back of her neck stiffened. Standard practice was to drop a trail of the reflective tabs behind to leave a path for following teams, or to track your way back out. Unless the laws of physics were somehow violated, the system was practically foolproof. "Morrissy, how do I reach Paul?"

"Go up," was all he said.

Annoyed and more than a little frightened, she squeezed past Kvass and started up the constricting stairwell, then paused. "Can you two reach the lander?"

"I think so," Morrissy replied.

"Good. I'll meet you back there as soon as I can." She wondered if she was making a mistake. Given how frightened Morrissy sounded, she hoped he didn't try to launch without her. She pushed the thought out of her mind and started climbing.

A small landing lay at the top of the stairs, another corridor branching past it. To her left, the passage emptied into blackness, obviously one of the doors she had seen from the lander. At the other end of the passage she saw a small circle glowing pale yellow. She smiled to herself. Despite what Morrissy had said, the marker tabs were obviously working as promised. She hurried toward it.

The corridor turned sharply to the left. A second marker tab glowed at the far end, twenty meters away. Leaning forward to avoid brushing the ceiling, Jenine shuffled to the tab, then stopped, confused. Instead of another corner, she found a blank stone wall.

"Wonderful." Angry at the wasted time, she retraced her steps to the stairwell, then went past it toward the doorway. She steadied herself with a hand against the wall and carefully looked out. Far below she saw the lander, still bathed in the glow of its flood lights, the pot-hunter's ship beside it. She forced herself to look down, but quickly pulled back inside, the view dizzying. Odd, she thought? She hadn't noticed she had climbed so high. Again, she moved back toward the stairwell and dropped the carry sack beside it, then stared into the passage, utterly confused.

The descending corridor she had climbed only moments before was gone. Another stairwell lay in its place, the rough-cut steps beckoning upward.

"No. No, no, no . . . " she whispered. Over the frequency, she said, "Morrissy, can you hear me?" She listened, but her radio remained silent, nothing in her headphones but her own rapid breath.

"Slow down," she scolded herself, fully aware how much time she was wasting. By now, if Tsing's estimate had been correct, his tanks were dry. If he was alive, he was living on whatever his scrubber salvaged from inside his suit. She needed to find him and find him fast.

"Just calm down," she said out loud. "Don't lose your head."

Back and forth she moved along the corridor, each trip a dead end, every return bringing her not to her starting point, but to a new junction. Sweat poured down her back, her heart pounding furiously as the minutes trickled off. Unable to find her way back to the ground floor, she continued to take the ascending stairs.

She paused at the top of the next flight, blinded by the sheen of breathe condensed inside her visor. She waited for it to clear, then looked around. Her lamp lit the far end of the corridor with a pale, blueish glow. Unsure what she might find, Jenine shuffled toward it. As she neared the end of the passage, she saw that the glow came from reflected snow. Cautiously, she edged toward the opening and looked out, but nothing was visible, the blizzard impenetrable. Had the lander been directly beneath her she couldn't have seen it. Dismayed, she slowly turned around.

"Hello, Jenine."

"Paul?" Her jaw dropped open. Five paces behind her, his visor open to the frigid, toxic atmosphere, Paul Tsing stood, one arm propped casually against the stone wall. He smiled at her.

"I think you should follow me." His voice was calm and edged with regret. "You need to see what I've found."

Her head spun. Nothing made sense, not the man in front of her, nor the side passage Paul Tsing led her down. How had she missed seeing it before?

"Where are you taking me?"

"Home." Tsing turned and smiled at her, his face still exposed to Titan's atmosphere. "I know it doesn't make any sense, but believe me, everything is going to be fine."

"Paul, don't you understand, this is impossible?"

"Yes. I understand it. But I don't think that really matters anymore."

A faint glow lit the corridor, not the reflected gleam of helmet lamps against methane slush, but a softer, more subtle illumination. Confused, she followed Tsing into a small, vaulted chamber. Though it was constructed from the same rough gray stone as the rest of the Wall, the surface was smooth, almost polished, the floor patterned like marble. Tsing edged aside and let her step past toward a broad portico, slender columns supporting a trio of arched doorways. She shuddered as she crept beneath the middle arch onto a narrow ledge, an elegant stone handrail barring her from the precipice. Hands shaking, she leaned against it.

A city spread out below, high towers lit bright as candle flame. Helicopters and mag-rails flitted between the angular structures, little more than flashing red lights from her high vantage, while further beneath an endless swath of roofed streets covered the ground like a network of capillaries, their translucent surfaces adding a pleasant yellow wash to the base of the skyscrapers. Lazy clouds drifted along the steel canyons, as if a gentle rain might recently have fallen.

"That's Chicago," she whispered, unable to pull her eyes away. Tsing stepped beside her and nodded.

"That's where you grew up, isn't it?" His smile broadened. "I told you I was taking you home." Before she could stop him, Tsing put his hands against his helmet, gave it a sharp twist, then lifted the bulky headgear off and tucked it under his arm. His dark hair was damp with sweat.

"Have you lost your mind?"

"Maybe." He grinned. "Probably. Does it really matter? Open your visor, Jenine. Stop denying yourself. Admit it. This is what you've been searching for. Everything can be different this time. Anything you want, yours for the taking."

She felt the dream sweep through her, the sweetness of the moment palpable. Tsing was right, wasn't he? What good did it do to deny what she saw, whether it made sense or not? How long had she been running from herself? Slowly, her hands rose to her helmet. She placed her fingers firmly against the hard plastic, took a long swallow of the rubber-tinged air, then closed her eyes. Her forearms tensed as she started to twist.

"No." She let her hands drop to her sides. "This isn't right."

Her eyes fluttered open. Gone was city and the elegantly carved chamber, the narrow corridor replacing it, the only light the harsh white burn from her helmet lamp. At her feet a body in a heavy excursion suit lay sprawled on the rough stone floor.

"Paul?" She crouched beside the body and rolled it over. Tsing's visor was closed, but she had no way of knowing if he was alive or dead. Frantically, she groped for the carry-sack, but found nothing. She rose stiffly to her feet and looked back the way she had came. The sack lay crumpled at the top of the stairs leading downward. She rushed to it, gathered it in her cold fingers, then hurried back to Tsing. Shaking, she changed his oxygen cannister and battery, then shook him. "Can you hear me?"

A muffled groan answered in her speakers. She forced herself not to cry in sheer relief. Still hampered by the tight space, Jenine pulled the woozy Tsing to his feet, and holding him under the shoulders, guided him toward the stairs.

Snow met her head lamp, Titan's cold surface just outside the rectangular doorway. Too narrow to walk abreast, Jenine kept one hand on Tsing's arm as she led him toward the exit.

"Almost there," she said, coaxing him along.

"No . . ." His breath was labored. "Need to go back."

"We are going back. Just a little farther to the ship." Her boot brushed against something, and she glanced down, relieved to see the oxygen tanks she had exchanged from Kvass and Morrissy lying where she had left them. Somehow they vindicated her memory. "Come on, Paul. We can do this."

"Can't leave." He tried to pull away. "Not yet."

"Listen to me. We're both low on air. We need to get back to the ship." The wind forced a swirling tongue of snow into the passage. Tiny pellets struck her helmet as she ducked under the lintel back into the world outside the Wall. Night was falling as Titan slid into Saturn's shadow, the gas giant a hazy crescent stretching from ground to zenith.

In the deepening shadows, the lights from the lander played hypnotically against the ice. She paused a moment to stretch the kinks from her back, grateful to finally be free of the enigmatic structure. A flash of light at the lander brought her up cold.

"What the hell are they doing?" Horrified, she watched the attitude jets flash in sequence. Suddenly, she understood. Morrissy was pre-flighting the craft for launch. She twisted around so fast she nearly lost her balance, and grabbed Tsing's wrist. "Come on! They're going to leave without us."

She broke into a slow jog, hampered by the odd gravity and the still woozy Tsing. He pulled against her, dragging her back toward the doorway.

"We can't leave. Not now. Not after I've found the way home." With a twist, he broke free. Jenine tried to grab him, but he was already out of reach.

"Damn it, Paul!" She stood, torn by indecision, and watched his stumbling, retreating form. Two hundred meters still lay between herself and the lander. Even if she could stop Tsing, she couldn't physically drag him to the ship. Her only hope now lay in stopping Morrissy from launching. A pounding, throbbing pain built inside her skull. A quick glance at her suit monitor confirmed her suspicion. Her own oxygen supply was nearly gone. Decision made, she turned toward the lander, calling frantically over the radio as she skip-walked across the frozen ground.

"Four-Eight November, come in." The effort of speaking cost her, stealing precious gulps of air. "Morrissy, please, respond."

A red glow built beneath the craft, a shimmering blush as the engines came on line. Daring the blast that would certainly scorch her to cinders should Morrissy launch while she stood outside, she threw herself against the airlock's outer door and pounded her fists on the heavy plate, desperate to get the panicked deputy's attention.

"Morrissy! Listen to me!"

Her chest ached, the fear and lack of air overwhelming. Jenine felt as if she was drowning inside her helmet. A rhythmic shudder pulsed through the hull. An image of herself engulfed in flames as the craft broke ground flashed through her mind. Desperate, she looked for shelter, but saw only the pot-hunter's derelict ship fifty meters away. Out of options, she dashed toward the gaping hatchway.

The craft was dark within, the walls rimed with ice. Jenine fell on the ramp, bruised her knee, but staggered to her feet and blundered down short corridor toward the cockpit. Like the rest of the ship, the control panel was frosted, the systems long dead. She fell more than sat into the pilot's chair. Out the corner of her eye she saw blue-white flame spread beneath her own ship, the lander quivering as Morrissy powered up.

"You bastard," she shouted over the radio. "Damn you, you stupid, stupid bastard."

The chair felt rock hard beneath her, the padding frozen solid. Her headache had worsened, her air supply nearly gone. Silently, she laughed at the irony. At least she understood how the frozen corpse wearing her excursion suit wound up inside the abandoned ship. She clenched her fists in frustration and shut her eyes.

"No. I refuse to believe this is happening."

Jenine took a long, slow breath, the air sour as it wheezed in and out of the helmet's overworked regulator, then opened her eyes once more. A grim smile crept across her face. She was still inside the Wall, less than a meter from the exit. Paul Tsing stood behind her, weaving drunkenly on his feet. Outside, past the narrow opening, the lander sat alone, the pot-hunter's ship vanished. She took Tsing by the wrist.

"Let's get back to the lander."

"But ... "

"No," she said firmly and led him outside. Wind tore at her, driving her sideways as she struggled toward the craft. Snow swirled, at times so heavy it blinded her, but she held to the flashing orange strobe and trudged on. A vague shape took form, the lander a slumbering dragon in the gloom. Tsing said nothing as they reached the airlock, but stood complacently beside her as she raised her arm and pounded three sharp knocks against the hatch.

"Captain Tsing?" A nervous voice blared inside her helmet. Jenine breathed a sigh of relief.

"It's me, Morrissy. I've got Paul. Cycle us through, okay?"

The airlock slid open. Jenine helped Tsing inside, then followed him into the cramped chamber. The effort was nearly beyond her. The outer door resealed. Air whistled around her as the lock emptied then refilled with fresh oxygen. Finally, the inner door slid aside. Morrissy and Kvass stood just inside, waiting for them. Jenine pushed Tsing through the hatchway, then popped her helmet off. The musty, recycled air tasted sweeter than springtime. Feeling stronger, she nodded at Tsing.

"Help him. He's suffering from hypoxia."

Together, they removed Tsing's helmet, then led him to the nearest couch and eased him down. His hair was matted, his skin pale, but his eyes looked clearer.

"Thank God you came back when you did," Kvass said. Jenine thought she heard a note of guilt in his reedy voice. "Control's been calling for over an hour. They want to know if we need another ship to come down?"

"No." Jenine shook her head firmly. "Tell them we're okay. No, wait. I'll tell them myself in a minute." Somehow, she wasn't surprised that communication had returned.

"Ma'am?" Morrissy shuffled his boots nervously. "What about Bruner? Shouldn't we go back outside and retrieve . . . " He hesitated. "Retrieve his body?"

Jenine glanced across the narrow aisle at Tsing. He caught her eye and gave his head an almost imperceptible shake. He understood. So did she. Somewhere inside that labyrinth, somehow, Bruner was still alive, still contemplating whether to jump from the high doorway or die from asphyxiation. All she had to do was find him. The thought sent a chill through her. The memory of that city-scape glimpsed from the hidden balcony was still too fresh, too seductive. Anything that could be contemplated could be found there, but only at a price. Madness lay in that direction. She turned back to face Morrissy.

"We can bring the body back later, before the next launch window. But not tonight."

"Ma'am . . . " Again, Morrissy paused. He chewed on his lip, as if he couldn't bring himself to frame the question. "What is that place?"

"You mean the Wall?" She thought about the question. She could have told him that it was Hell. She almost said it was Heaven. Instead, she shrugged her shoulders. "I don't know. I wish I did, but I don't."

"What do we tell them when they ask what happened down here?"

Kvass inched closer. Jenine looked up at him and held his gaze, then smiled.

"The truth," she said. "We just tell them the truth."

Christopher McKitterick is an author, editor, technical writer, teacher, amateur astronomer and backyard engineer. Chris' short fiction has appeared in Analog, Artemis, Captain Proton, Extrapolation, Synergy SF, Tomorrow SF *and elsewhere. He teaches writing at the University of Kansas and is Associate Director of the Center for the Study of Science Fiction (http://www2.ku.edu/~sfcenter). He recently finished a far-future novel,* Empire Ship; *this and another novel,* Transcendence, *are looking for a home. For more, check out his website: www.sff.net/people/mckitterick and blog: mckitterick.livejournal.com.*

The Empty Utopia
by Christopher McKitterick

Happiness is death; death, happiness. Only in dissatisfaction does life exist.
—from *The Joy Makers*, by James Gunn

On a pleasant morning at humanity's twilight, Presque-Mourir and her mate Rajeunir flew home from a friend's funeral, the last they would ever attend together. The time had come for them to consider their future.

It was a quiet flight, their floater humming along an automated path toward the landing-niche on the balcony outside Rajeunir's 80th floor apartment. Though they kept separate residences, they had long shared his single unit. They had lived together for nearly two centuries because they felt the perverse urge to, yet did not wish to face the social ostracism of applying for a double unit. Of course, as their peers died, social pressure died as well, but one cannot easily overcome a lifetime of socialization. Presque-Mourir only used her residence—in another city on the other side of what was once called the United States of America, back when nations mattered—when she felt the need to be alone. She kept her antique hand-loom there. Sometimes, when the pressure or loneliness of being one of the last women living on Earth became too much for her to bear, she wove rugs and wall-hangings feverishly for weeks at a time.

Neither of them had spoken since they woke earlier this morning. Wind rushed across the canopy of the floater, a soothing sound. They passed over the end of a vast mechanized field, perfectly cultivated in kilometer-long rows of lustrous, late spring green; down there, the breeze was light and changed directions often. As the floater gently slowed to urban velocity, the voice of the wind quieted. Presque-Mourir's looked toward the city.

What had Raj said this place was once named? Minneapolis? she wondered. It did not matter. The bones of the men who had named it had turned to dust thousands of years ago, and bones do not care about designations given by the living.

The city stretched a few kilometers across rolling hills and river gouges. At its edges, where the rich soil of the fields met permastone walls, hints of ruins lay like puzzles, fragmented mazes beneath the narrow strip of dusty, unturned ground. A cultivator, its stainless steel hull glinting in the sun, treaded over the buried foundation of a near-vanished building without taking notice. It held no interest in the human history that had produced the building and later razed it. The machine performed its job flawlessly but its thoughts, if they could be considered thoughts in the human sense, walked the narrow path programmed into its neural network.

The floater hummed past a cylindrical residence tower that reached a kilometer toward the clouds and stars and spanned two hundred meters at its base. It contained three hundred levels, stacked with residences that served every human need and whim. Twenty-four thousand residences filled this single building. Presque-Mourir saw it anew today and marveled at what had once been a bustling honeycomb of life. She pictured how such towers had appeared in vids from the previous centuries: smiling, busy people greeting one another in the public balcony at the center of each floor, talking and laughing; elevators fading and re-materializing many floors up or down in their transfer-shafts. Genart-designed trees still filled the hollow core beyond the railing of the central balcony, their branches reaching into the airspace above each public area, lending the air a fresh scent and reminding people of their roots as animals in nature while machines carted food and beverages to their tables.

Presque-Mourir craned her neck to watch the building hush past, but the spell faded when her muscles tightened—when she felt her body. That massive residence tower, that grounded spike that so neared the sky, looked like a coffin to her. Less than that; not a single human inhabited it any longer. Gone was the old bustle. Only the trees survived within. Those and the machines that maintained the building and its residences, powered in part by the presserg—the differential generator—upon which it stood, quietly producing the power required by twenty-four thousand inhabitants and their electronic servants for as long as the architecture stood. Gravity provided its neverending crush, and the atmosphere maintained an ionic imbalance from ground to rooftop.

She faced forward again, all the dozens of towers sparkling sun from their windows—vast structures designed and built with cyclopean effort and a single plan over centuries. Now empty and hollow. The city suddenly looked to her like a necropolis, an Egyptian Thebes with its echoing temples and burial valleys, a city of the dead. More than empty: *emptied*.

For many years, she preserved the hope that these buildings would once again contain life, that once again the cities would become hubs of humanity. But, this morning, she and Rajeunir had witnessed Karemashita's funeral. They watched two funeral machines lower her cellophane coffin into a cemetery shaft, watched it slowly descend under its own power until it disappeared into the shadowy depths where human bodies were whisked away. The funeral machines tossed two shovelfuls of dirt after the woman, and patiently waited until Presque-Mourir and Rajeunir turned to leave before sliding the shaft's lid back into place. Presque-Mourir winced when she heard the ring of metal upon metal, the grate of sand and dirt caught between. And then there was no sound except the muffled whines and hums of the funeral machines returning to their keeping places.

That sound signaled the end of her delusion. As if some unseen fist had shattered the window through which she had watched the world, revealing that the window had not been made of glass but of some vid display material, and beyond only death was visible. She realized the cities would never be reborn.

That was when her thoughts returned to the interface she had programmed into her room, the simple way for her and her beloved to be free of all this.

She didn't have the energy to express her emotions. She hadn't even been able to cry at the funeral.

High above Earth, Hoffen disengaged the long-range freighter's flight program and unbuckled the crashbelts. He rose from his pilot's seat, pushing off with just the right thrust to cross the little cabin that smelled of his sweat, and avoided rebound by grabbing hold of a handgrip. He slid aside the radiation-blind and looked out *Walang Maipapalit*'s viewport. Pragmatic as he was, Hoffen gasped.

"Oh, Maputi, she is beautiful . . . and frightening," he murmured, looking down upon the Earth. As always when he was alone, he spoke to his wife.

Hoffen simply watched for a while. Below him, a great globe rotated slowly as his ship orbited. Vast green continents alternated with blue oceans that each appeared as broad as all of his native Mars.

"How can a world be so perfect?" he wondered aloud. His breath momentarily fogged the viewport. Vivid blues, greens, browns, white—alien and amazing to eyes used to reds and browns and the metal of spacecraft and burrow. This world looked like the glass ornament he gave his wife when they were newly pledged. Fragile, as she had been.

"Computer," he said gruffly, "establish comm link."

Many months alone in the freighter had taken their toll. His mind wasn't as strong as it had been before he left Burrow Hogar, where his family and comrades lived and worked. The memories flooded over him.

Maputi . . . .

No. He would fight the memory. He thought of the message.

When Mars first received the signal from Earth, Mars' elders argued long and hard about how to respond. Earth wanted to reconnect with its long-abandoned colony. They requested Mars send people to live in its grand, easy cities and send ships to collect whatever goods a far-flung colony might need after centuries of abandonment. Apparently those who sent the message to Mars hadn't considered that Isolationists would have become the dominant force in Martian politics. Even idlers and dreamers were leery of friendly gestures from Earth, the world that isolated itself from the rest of the Solar System long ago. The last Mars freighter to carry supplies from Earth had returned to port more than two hundred years ago—supplies given, not sold, by a patronizing Earth that no longer required trade. Well, Martians had more dignity than that.

But time had been brutal to the Martian burrows. Trade with the asteroids ended abruptly after a vicious solar storm ravaged their electronics. No one had heard from the rock-miners in eighty years, except for occasional bursts of static carrying senseless voices. The burrows knew they could not safely return to the asteroids, not even metropolitan Pallas.

Without trade, Mars had to provide for itself. But it was a world poor in just about everything humans need. Mere subsistence in the burrows grew increasingly more difficult; population steadily declined. So the Earth message—a flash of hope in a dark world—was seriously considered. Indeed, secret factions repeatedly tried to contact Earth. Hoffen, once content with life in Burrow Hogar, expressed interest.

That was after Maputi. Try as he might, he could not forget his pledged. Even as he looked out upon the riches of Earth, he could see only Maputi:

He loved to watch her prepare dinner in their rooms. The walls were decorated with strands of colored cloth and her beloved glass decorations. Fiber optics carried the sun's glow into their rooms, illuminating the bare surfaces that Maputi had painted with bright pigments.

He had just returned from a long day on the pipeline, resealing the burrow's water lines beneath the floorplates. Or maybe he had spent the hours wedged between a hallway collector and the sandy rock surrounding the burrow, crawling along the copper pipes, scraping his cold hands against stone and metal until he found the life-threatening leak. Now the work was done, and he watched as the woman he loved boiled potatoes and carrots. Today she had managed to obtain a slice of vat-grown chicken to flavor the stew. Yes, and spices, those precious flakes she kept sealed in bottles protected inside screw-top cans. Oh, how their rooms smelled like home when she cooked.

Hoffen could still smell Maputi's pungent stew. He could still see her dark features come to life as she welcomed him home with a quick kiss. She was the only woman he had ever known who could work all day in the burrows and still smile at day's end. His fingers remembered the soft, warm skin beneath her clothes. When the two of them found the energy to make love, her strong hands didn't feel rough on his back.

But the vision was fleeting: He remembered how she looked at the end. Her body lay on the tunnel floor, but the most important part of her had fled. Her face pale from suffocation, her tongue swollen, her usually well-groomed hair tossed over her face like black sand as she lay in the collapsed tunnel . . . .

"I would trade this whole world for one more day with you," he whispered, quietly so he would not burst into tears. Mercifully, at the sound of his voice, the vision began to fade. *I have been alone in this tin can far too long.*

"Navigation link established," the freighter's computer told him. The calm voice erased the image of a woman who had lost the intangible everything that made her *her*, who had disappeared while leaving behind the architecture of her flesh.

Hoffen drew a deep breath and pushed off the wall back to his acceleration couch. He re-fastened the crashbelt, and it pressed him against the threadbare cushions.

"Lock onto landing signals," he ordered. Somewhere behind him, Hoffen heard rusty machines creak to life. A small directional rocket fired a few times like gunshots, then the main engines began to roar.

Presque-Mourir watched empty buildings breeze past one by one. She shivered. *I can never return to our residence.* Without the heat of human bodies near one another, the buildings could never truly banish the cold of death. *Death,* she thought. *The long sleep, the endless dream.*

That's where all my friends have gone, to dream.

Presque-Mourir considered the ways to die. No guns or other manufactured weapons could be found anywhere but in the museums, and the museums' machines would never allow a person near a weapon from the barbarous days.

Yet people were still able to kill themselves and others quite efficiently. That is, they had been able to do so when they existed. Karemashita finally died last night from wounds sustained at the hands and knives of a gang a year prior, when the last gangs—primitive attempts at reorganizing humans into groups—had still been a threat. Eventually, enforcement machines rooted out and eliminated the perpetrators. Many of the last humans died at the devices of enforcement machines. Presque-Mourir remembered witnessing too much of that anarchy from the tenth-floor balcony outside Rajeunir's apartment. Those who moved to the country to escape the sudden violence were rounded up and returned to the melee: Humans must not face danger, the guardians' programming said, and where cities end, danger begins.

The hospital machines were unable to repair Karemashita's heart and other organs sufficiently; she died with many machines attempting to operate her body. Rajeunir said he suspected those machines would have kept the woman alive for many years had she not fallen into the abyss of depression. There was no such thing as a psychologist-machine, and there were no more psychologists. Presque-Mourir had never even heard the word; the profession became extinct nearly a millennium ago, when humans had perfected the science of neurochemistry.

"This is what a generation of writers at the end of the Nineteenth Century had called 'utopia,'" Rajeunir blurted. The sound of his voice startled her to the present. Raj fancied himself a historian, especially interested in vanished civilizations.

"Yes, I know," Presque-Mourir answered, mildly irritated. His words had become predictable over the years as acquaintances disappeared or dissociated themselves before their individual extinctions. Presque-Mourir and Rajeunir had lived together for so long with no outside interaction that they could predict the course of entire conversations. What was there to talk about?

"But this utopia is an empty one," she continued, adding new words to the familiar dialogue, pushing it onto a new path. "Though the city architects perfected our environment, they forgot or were unable to change human nature. What good is an empty utopia?"

Rajeunir turned a surprised face toward his mate. Presque-Mourir looked at him. He was still an attractive man, but his eyes had grown old, and his skin formed curves beneath his eyes. Despite incomparable medical care, he lacked anything resembling vitality.

Still, she was struck with a pleasant memory. Once, long ago, they considered having a child together. Not the traditional way: spending time in a fertility booth at a hospital where their sexual organs would be temporarily reawakened for the first time since pre-adolescence, their regenerative cells groomed, the genes sifted and perfected—perhaps rejected and transplanted with other genes from the sperm and ovum bank—then combined into a fertilized egg that would one day turn into a child handed over by the hospital, a child that maybe looked like them, only less flawed. Yet bringing a sterile child—as were all groomed children—into a sterile world would be the ultimate insult.

So Rajeunir and Presque-Mourir considered having themselves disarranged in order to impregnate her in the ancient tradition. She would suffer the pains of pregnancy and birth to bring into the world a child who was truly theirs. They had been careful not to talk about this unnatural bond with their friends. They had always been unique among their contemporaries. Perhaps that is what kept them lingering so long into this twilight of the world.

She still remembered how it felt to love him, the adrenalin rush, the heady excitement, the longing quenched only by nearness and touching and being loved back. The memory was distant, yet real, kinesthetic.

To have had a child when civilization was still alive would have required administrative approval. But peer pressure made them wait too long until no administrators remained. There was no such thing as an administrator-machine. So they had walked sub-legal channels in pursuit of a human doctor whom they could convince to assist them. Presque-Mourir allowed herself to dream about giving birth to a new tribe of humans and repopulating the world. But their risky search proved fruitless: Like the administrators, by the time they sought a doctor, there were no human medical professionals left on Earth. At that last failure, her body had felt as emptied as the city.

Now she sensed why they had always been considered strange, even perverse by the account of some of their acquaintances. Who but misfits would linger until curtain's close, and then remain? The last thousands had chosen to leave the performance as the human drama dwindled over the past few decades; the last millions before them had dragged one another from the theater during the final acts during the prior century. And then there had been the billions who had erased one another even before the play had gotten fully underway, unleashing long-nascent phage-weapons and nanite swarms to devour people from the inside. Had it been hatred that destroyed the race? Or accumulated boredom and fear?

Presque-Mourir turned her eyes from her mate to watch the cloudless sky. Again she thought of the lesser worlds. Beyond this blanket of blue, the universe was even colder, even emptier of life. Entropy and the inevitable mishaps of frontier life, coupled with the ease and comfort of life on Earth—and the disinterest of its inhabitants—gradually eroded humanity's presence beyond the atmosphere. The speed of light fenced humans in their little set of globes orbiting a yellow sun. Why leave a perfect world to struggle and die in untamed places?

So though human seed had been scattered over other worlds, it had not been cast far enough to guarantee human persistence should cataclysm destroy the homeworld. But the end had not come with a bang, as those who had once pressed for colonization warned, but with a long sigh. Extinction lay upon humankind like a shadow.

Was anyone out there alive to have heard her plea for help? Surely not, for several years had passed since she transmitted the outbound cry that now embarrassed her. She never told Rajeunir she had sent the message. More than a year had passed since she last looked for a response. She grew unable to endure the continued silence, imagining world upon world encrusted with ruins, her message falling across the dead like a hollow prayer.

Death everywhere—worse, absence of life, void, vacuum. Entropy was winning. She could bear the image no longer.

"I'm ready," Presque-Mourir declared, her eyes following the arc of what looked to be a stratospheric craft transporting materials from some mining or manufacturing plant to machines that needed repair in order to continue performing pointless tasks. She was certain the craft supplied no human, no living thing more sentient than a chimpanzee in a zoo. She knew because Rajeunir had called the cities in search of a doctor when Karemashita was dying. No flesh and blood person responded. Every tower computer save theirs reported zero residency.

What is one small death in the grand performance of the universe? What is one fewer warm body, and a skinny one at that? Somehow, the thought made her decision easier.

She thought perhaps the chimpanzee's line, perhaps the dolphin's, might rise to sentience as the machines eventually broke down—as they most likely would without human monitoring—over the ages it would take for primates to walk the path toward civilization. This was not a sad thing.

There was a long quiet before Rajeunir responded to her words. She watched his residence tower grow taller and nearer and heard the floater slow for landing.

"Ready for what?" he asked. She heard a note of false joviality in his voice. He knew full well what she meant.

"To join the rest of our people. We're fools to go quiet into our good night. I don't want to wait. I'm cold."

Rajeunir placed his hand on her thigh as if to warm her and made nervous noises, clearing his throat, beginning abortive words. The tower grew taller. Presque-Mourir grew nervous. *I won't go back into a residence tower. If only there were humans alive in there, if only there were a way to bring back all the people . . . but I'd rather ride this floater until it falls powerless from the sky than enter a coffin while blood still pumps through my brain. I won't.*

She heard Rajeunir's foot tapping the padded floor, his fingers patting a pattern on his armrests. When she looked at him, she noticed redness spreading across his balding forehead, panic in his eyes. Her stomach tightened. It pained her to see him so disturbed. She hadn't intended that. She simply wanted to end her aimless shuffle toward a meaningless future.

I'm sorry, she said within. *I just don't have any more answers.*

*   *   *

Hoffen sat at the end of the ramp, beneath the shadow of the Martian freighter. His heart clattered against his ribs, not simply from the exertion of standing upright against a full *g*, he admitted.

Earth's landing signal had taken him down to a quiet but vast—by Martian terms—spaceport. He was not bothered that no trade representatives greeted him. *This is an alien culture*, he reminded himself. Still, his mental image of a quick trade-and-return was crumbling, and that part disturbed him.

Clean gray concrete stretched nearly a kilometer to a gleaming wall; he assumed that was the terminal, although no windows faced the landing area. A few silent craft stood widely spaced across the field, pointed at the sky, poised as if to blast off, but caked with dust. Not far beyond the wall rose the towers of a city.

His mind couldn't quite grasp the proportions of his surroundings. The Martian spaceport where *Walang Maipapalit* had rested was little more than baked dirt.

He tried to draw a deep breath, but his body refused. Although his lungs were in fine condition for a hard-working burrow-dweller, he couldn't break through the mental barrier: *The Open is danger! Stay in the burrows if you don't have a viable suit! If your suit fails while you're in the Open, exhale slowly and run to an entrance. Don't inhale!*

Hoffen laughed at himself and rose to his feet. He had not crossed millions of kilometers of hungry vacuum to quiver in fear once he reached his destination. He had a job to do. This time he managed to draw a full breath.

"Maputi, how you would have loved this."

He savored the alien scents: growing things, unfamiliar dust, wafts of something sweet, oily odors, and many other unfamiliar smells. The air was thick, humid, and warm. The rich scent of soil capable of supporting open agriculture was omnipresent. In the direction opposite the city, beyond a fence at the edge of the concrete landing pad, green fields stretched to the horizons, tended by rotund robots. Hidden sprinklers sprayed water in great arcs over the plants. He couldn't even comprehend the wealth needed to throw water around like that.

"Sir Hoffen," his earplug said, "a car has been dispatched to pick you up. Welcome to Earth."

"Are you the trader who contacted us?" he asked. "My wares are aboard my vessel."

"I am the automated spaceport greeter," the voice said. "You have not been authorized to engage in interplanetary trade. Enjoy your visit."

Hoffen was stunned. He heard a distant whine and took a few steps out onto the pad and looked around. The robotic voice disturbed him, especially the bureaucracy it suggested; did this mean Earth shunning him after all his people had done to send him here? How would Hoffen's comrades feel if he returned to Mars still bearing the trinkets and disks he had taken along to trade? No, he would not leave Earth without something to show for their expenditure in sending him here. Martians were known for many traits, and one of those was stubbornness.

Hoffen watched a chrome ball grow gradually larger as it approached him across the concrete. As sunlight glinted off its hull, he was struck with the realization that he was standing in the Open beneath a naked sky. For just a moment he held his breath again, then released it and inhaled deeply. He marveled at how quickly his concerns faded.

A slow smile crept across Hoffen's scarred face. It hurt to smile. Still. . . .

"Welcome to Earth, my Maputi."

"Darling," Rajeunir finally spoke, "perhaps the problem wasn't human nature. Perhaps it was our cultural environment."

"I thought you said the city is a utopia," she contended.

"That's only our physical environment," he said. "I'm talking about cultural evolution. If you look at human history, you'll see we evolved through long ages of barbarism. But that barbarism was necessitated by a desperate need to survive, to eliminate dangerous foes, to live day by day with the sure knowledge that a lion or dragon or plague-bearing rat, or even another human being was lurking just past the portcullis or on the other side of the wall. I won't accept that human nature is evil. The problem was that we never evolved beyond that once those survival tools became senseless. What does one do in utopia? Humans need the struggle. What must be our struggle? We must change our struggle for survival into the struggle for rationality. We must eliminate rather than displace aggression."

His eyes began to glow, and what had been panic turned to something verging on insanity. Presque-Mourir grew embarrassed for him, uncomfortable in her soft seat. *Who must struggle, my dear?* she thought. *Us? What can two people do? And against what shall we struggle?*

"If only we could start a new cultural evolution whose roots rested in the rich soil of utopia rather than the past, the human animal could achieve its potential to be something grand, something brilliant and gentle and curious and without fear. If only . . ."

But then his speech faltered. Though this sounded more a lecture than part of a conversation, these were, at least, new thoughts. She felt herself warming to this man. She wanted to add: *Yes, we could do something. If only we could get disarranged, have our bodies altered in order to make children.* But the machines would not allow a human to be disarranged without administrative approval, and the machines ran the hospitals, and there were no other humans to perform the operation. They had gone through all this many years ago.

But Presque-Mourir desperately wanted to comfort him. He had done his best to comfort her until his energy ran down, his knowledge reached its edge. She realized that, through these words, he had declared his love for her. He wanted to tell her that all was not lost.

Something was still alive in the city. The old chemicals began to boil in her body. She needed to show him love in return, at least one last time before the end. She would tell him about the interface she had installed for them. The interface that would grant them every wish as they were painlessly stripped of their mortal coils. That would be quick. Now, when they felt love for one another again, when they finally felt alive, was the right time.

"Raj-" she began.

But before she could speak, the floater's computer interrupted.

"Citizen Presque-Mourir, your guest has arrived. He has just left Spaceport B23."

"Guest?" she said. Rajeunir echoed her question.

Then she remembered. *This is it! The greatest gift I can give my mate.* She broke through the wall of embarrassed silence.

"Raj, four years ago I sent a message to the colonies."

"You sent . . . ?" His words trailed off and an unreadable expression crossed his face.

"Yes, but I was afraid to say anything that might raise false hopes. I wanted to do what I could to avert the end. I—"

"Why didn't you tell me someone had responded?" he asked.

Presque-Mourir's heart fluttered with excitement; Rajeunir's entire demeanor had changed; he looked so alive. "I didn't know. I haven't checked for some time." She changed her pitch. "Computer, has anyone yet responded to my, um," she thought hard for a moment, quickly booting up her link and searching her private data-file icons, "comm number 457409?"

"Yes, citizen," a smooth alto voice responded from a speaker in the floater's dash. "Three hundred forty-seven days, five hours, and twelve minutes ago, you received a message from an uncertified station on Mars. The sender does not have identity authentication. This is the message." The voice changed to that of a hoarse-sounding man:

"Earth, this is Hoffen, Hogar Burrow, Mars. I will lift off aboard the freighter *Walang Maipapalit*, registration MCLRF0021, in two hours. I am coming alone. We appreciate your generous offer to resume trade. Over."

"Gods," Rajeunir said. Though his face showed fear, his eyes sparkled. Presque-Mourir thought that look, alone, was worth the effort.

"Computer, is this the same Hoffen who has just landed at Spaceport B23?"

"Yes."

"Oh. Um, where shall we meet him?" She was amazed, terrified, excited, dazed.

"Sir Hoffen is now en route to Tower 3860, as per your standing invitation."

"That's our tower," Rajeunir said, a moment later. "We're no longer alone."

Hoffen stepped out of the car onto a public landing platform near the base of the sky-touching building. Everything on this world was so large. He still sensed a mighty gravitational pull, a fatiguing weight dragging him down, but paid little attention now. Too many novelties tugged harder at his senses.

Quiet machines rode cushions of air and soft wheels across the steel cave, larger than Burrow Hogar's assembly room. A dozen other saucer-shaped cars were parked neatly along white lines painted on the floor, waiting. A small, wheeled robot rolled whisper-quiet about the wide space, cleaning and polishing the metal and plastic hulls. Behind Hoffen, the entrance gaped wide, providing a half-circle view of buildings and sidewalks. Before him, several archways opened to halls leading into the building's center. Hoffen felt at home here—sheltered rather than exposed to the open sky—even though Mars had nothing to compare with this architecture.

"Hello?" he said, noticing no one had come to greet him.

"Sir Hoffen," his earplug answered, "your hosts will join you soon. Please come to the gallery on this floor. We will provide refreshments."

I don't have any Earth money, he thought, unsure. Not only was he alone on a strange world, but he had no means to survive besides the ship's few hundred kilos of items. What would he eat and drink? Would he be charged for breathing the air? Suddenly, the expedition began to seem an adolescent folly. *Where's the trader who sounded so eager in her message? Was she angry about how long it took us to get here?*

When the elders decided they would not bar anyone from responding to that message, they scoffed at his volunteering to go to Earth. "You're not some fool boy," Elder Jank had said. "We need you here. You've got good brains and sense, too. You'd never get sloppy and blow a pipe just because the day was growing late and you were feeling fatigued."

"I can't stand my rooms anymore," Hoffen had replied. "They're too big for one man."

That had earned him whispers. Everyone knew Maputi had died, young and before bearing a child. Everyone felt sorry for Hoffen, a good man who would never again pledge unless some woman his age lost her man. Besides, he couldn't bear the thought of a strange woman's arms around him, a stranger preparing his stew. Even though he followed

Maputi's recipes—badly—he was certain they tasted better than someone else's could.

"We can assign you smaller rooms," Elder Horace said. "You maintain yours well. Someone would be very glad to occupy them in your stead."

"You know what I mean," Hoffen said, careful to keep the edge off his voice in that place, among elders. He was soon dismissed from the discussion.

Ten days later, Gitte—a work comrade—came to him with news. He could leave. He would take the long range freighter *Walang Maipapalit*, but he was expected to return with a full load. He could then continue travels to Earth if they wished to continue trade. He would be freed from the burrow pact after the first delivery.

Hoffen had thrown his strong arms around Gitte right there, in the hallway, in front of anyone who might see. "This is what I need," he said. "When I return, I'll be a whole man again."

Sixty days later he and some friends completed the ship's badly needed overhaul. Like the rest of Mars' fleet, it had been idle for decades. There had been nowhere to go. Still, *Walang Maipapalit* was the largest and best-maintained of the ships. He launched the following morning.

"Sir Hoffen?" a woman's voice asked, startling him out of reminiscence.

Hoffen spun around. The woman looked no different than a Mars woman, except that her skin was unweathered—fine as an artist's porcelain, white as a baby's belly, yet her eyes held deep reserves of character. She wore fine-woven pants and a long-sleeved shirt whose color seemed to shift as she moved.

"Ah, yes," he managed.

"My name is Presque-Mourir," she said, extending her hands palms-up. Unsure of the proper response, Hoffen put out his hands and laid them atop hers. She blushed and spoke again. She spoke English like a Martian, though her accent was difficult to penetrate.

"This is my mate, Rajeunir." A man beside her offered his hands rather hesitantly, and Hoffen took them for a moment before thrusting his own back into his pants pockets.

"Shall we go inside?" the man, Rajeunir, said. Hoffen nodded and followed his hosts.

They led him through a crystal hallway past rooms full of clothing and other objects he couldn't identify. It ended at a circular space dominated by the trunks of plants so massive he first thought them to be part of the building. High above loomed a ceiling that Hoffen thought must be the next level's floor; the plants grew up through an opening. Hoffen marveled that these Earth people wasted more space than they used.

"Over here would be nice," the woman said, indicating a patio. Clear chairs and tables were scattered seemingly at random across an intricately patterned tile floor. The wall enclosing the space seemed to contain nothing but shops. Hoffen realized this was only one of countless such levels. He tilted his head and looked up along the trunks of the trees; vertigo nearly made him stumble. He felt absurd, like a Neanderthal stumbling out of the jungles to trade bone chips with Thirtieth Century city-dwellers.

They sat down. The woman seemed to look at things in the air and tap at them, then she ordered drinks by simply speaking into that same nothingness. Seconds later, a tall, wheeled robot delivered a tray of glasses. Hoffen blinked, dazed again by this world. *This very room*, he thought, *is richer than all Mars.*

They exchanged brief conversation about how Presque-Mourir had sent her message and how Hoffen had come to Earth. Aboard the aged *Walang Maipapalit*, every day was an adventure of repairs and makeshifts to keep from venting his life-support into the void, and he humored their curiosity. Eventually, Hoffen mentioned his trade cargo. This earned only confused looks from his hosts.

Uncomfortable with the lull and growing ever-more frustrated and angry, he gazed around and noticed they were alone among hundreds of tables. Even what appeared to be a park within the building was abandoned. He drew a deep breath to calm himself. He felt uneasy in so much unoccupied space; it was uncanny.

"Where is everyone?" he asked. "Are they all at work, like we in the burrows do? I thought, since your cities are self-supporting, that you spent your days at leisure." He was hoping to transition back to working out a trade, but Hoffen's question only drew somber looks from his hosts.

"That's why I sent my message," the woman said. Her voice sounded limp. "We are the last humans on Earth. We need your help."

Hoffen nearly dropped his glass. He looked away from the two people, at the grandeur of this tower. Floor upon floor of unimaginable wealth, food and drink and air to be had without a moment's labor; tower after tower like this one, immersed in a breathable atmosphere, city after city . . . rivers and lakes and oceans to drink, continents lush with crops and even herds of food—animals, not vat-meat. *The last two humans? How can this be true?*

"No one else?" he verbalized, staring at the misty tops of the trees far above. He noticed the absolute silence in the tower, interrupted occasionally by whispers of pumped air or mechanical whirrs.

"No one," the woman answered.

"What happened?" Hoffen asked. He grew afraid for his safety. "Disease? I thought your wars ended hundreds of years ago."

"Oh, no," Rajeunir said. "Not war, not disease. It's much more subtle than that." He sketched out the last chapter of human history on Earth from the time of the last towers.

Genugsam's vision of utopia became reality when the last migration of malcontents left Earth for the frontier worlds. A generation later, all discontent was sifted from Earth's genepool. From the year 2990 on, only groomed children were born. Most of Rajeunir's narrative bored Hoffen, but he forced himself to pay attention—especially difficult while surrounded by the greatest wonders of technology the race had ever created, and fatigued by the heavy drag of gravity. He wasn't used to having to continually straighten his posture.

Hoffen felt a growing distaste rise in him for these people who had grown so comfortable over the centuries that they no longer sought out challenges, no longer worked or even played in ways he could comprehend. They spent their days twiddling their brains with computer programs so advanced they seldom needed companionship. They sat in steel honeycombs that rebuilt themselves as the years tried to erode them. Machines maintained their environment and—to a lesser extent—their bodies. When these people died by accident or injury, they were replaced by others who were exactly the same.

"It seems the basic flaw was that people stopped . . . caring," Rajeunir concluded. "The chaos that followed was simply the symptom of a society frayed beyond control of the computers."

That was all Hoffen could stand. "You just gave up? What's wrong with you? In the burrows, we fight every day just to survive. When a baby is born, everyone in the burrow shows up to help. Everyone in the burrows spends as much time as they can spare helping raise the babies. When a single man or woman dies, everyone feels the loss. Here, you have everything you could want, yet you turn away from it. Why?"

"What have we to live for?" Presque-Mourir said.

"For life itself!" Hoffen said. His hosts blinked uncomprehendingly. "What about the children? Don't the two of you have children?" Hoffen asked. That earned him a pair of blushes.

"Had you been an Earth acquaintance of mine," the woman said, "I would have been offended by that question. But you are an outsider. No, we do not have a child. It makes me sad we did not get disarranged—that is, have our bodies altered to create children—while there still was a world left in which the child could grow up. We were too civilized—this, despite being nonconformists."

"There's still time," Hoffen said, becoming even more irritated. "Look at you. You're both young . . . well, sorry, I have no idea about your age. At least you're healthy. I've watched stories about Earth: You're probably not even half way through your life expectancies, right?"

The woman nodded.

"I thought so. So what's stopping you?"

"Though we are the only humans left on Earth," the man said, "we must still abide by the law. The computers assure that we will."

"Take me to your hospital," Hoffen said. He realized that he did carry one trade item of real value, something within him: his alienness.

"Perhaps we can help one another."

Rajeunir's hands adjusted the floater's controls, and the disk-shaped craft gently pivoted on its axis, flying them toward the hospital at the center of the city. His face cramped with the effort to keep from frowning or screaming.

This is foolish, Rajeunir thought, but the naïve visitor would never believe them until he witnessed Earth's automated efficiency for himself. Their savior from space offered no real answers; indeed, Hoffen had come from a world more hopeless than Earth, and Rajeunir was beginning to suspect that Presque-Mourir had promised something not within her capacity to fulfill.

They settled onto one of the hospital's parking balconies—a series of concentric rings surrounding the fifty-story stump of a building—and climbed out of the floater. It shut down and began feeding from the deck's power grid. Rajeunir and Presque-Mourir entered the same hospital where precision machines had rendered them infertile centuries earlier when they were children. Hoffen followed them inside.

They walked gleaming antiseptic corridors, hollow and quiet, scentless except for whiffs of ozone, and found the registration computer. Rajeunir and his mate placed their right hands in turn on the ID panel, and a moment later the computer spoke:

"Welcome to City Hospital, Rajeunir-M3307. Welcome to City Hospital, Presque-Mourir-F0108. How may we serve you?" The voice startled Rajeunir as much as Hoffen's had; it was many years since he last heard energy behind words. Domestic machines only spoke when necessary, and that was rare.

"We would like to be disarranged," Presque-Mourir answered.

Rajeunir felt great pain at hearing the hope in her words. He avoided looking into Hoffen's eyes; the Martian wore a somewhat dazed and harsh look.

"We are sorry, but there is no disarrangement approval on file," the computer stated after a moment's pause.

"Then we would like our genefiles to be groomed for reproduction," Rajeunir hurriedly said, struggling to keep a note of hopefulness in his voice. *This will be all right. We will, at least, have an enjoyable last few centuries. I only feel sorry for the child.*

"Rajeunir-3307," the machine asked, "do you require to be part of reproductive grooming with Presque-Mourir-F0108?"

"Of course," he answered, and winked at his mate.

"Thank you for allowing us to serve you," the computer said. "Please proceed to room 401, level 27. Rajeunir-3307, please proceed to booth 401B. Presque-Mourir-F0108, please proceed to booth 401F. We wish you well with your procedure!"

"You didn't need me after all," Hoffen said. He appeared uncomfortable. His weatherbeaten face frowned. "You could have done this at any time. I don't understand . . . "

"Yes, well," Rajeunir mumbled, "here we go. Presque, are you sure you want to do this?"

"Um . . . " she replied.

"Well . . . " He turned his head and his eyes defocused. He had to stop this now. She needn't suffer for a foreigner's education.

"You must realize, Sir Hoffen, that though it will be wonderful to have children, they will be completely infertile, unable to ever produce offspring. We are married by law, but our children can never marry one another. Marriage laws govern our lives. There will be no cultural revolution."

Presque-Mourir felt herself stiffen. *So, this is how it ends, without even an attempt. Is this what we earned for hoping, for believing in a visitor's enthusiasm? Damn fate! Damn Hoffen! Damn Rajeunir!* She felt so suddenly emptied. Important parts of her seemed sucked out in the process. Why had Raj taken her on this absurd ride? Had they both simply become intoxicated by the thrill of meeting another human from another world?

The Martian blinked and ground his teeth. "What's going on?" he growled. "Your computers tell me that I can't trade with your world. Your message promised help. Must I return with nothing and leave you two looking like you lost something you never had in the first place? I don't understand anything here. You let your machines rule your lives!"

"We will give you all our personal belongings," Presque-Mourir said. When the Martian turned away, she added, "I'm sorry that's all we can offer. I hadn't expected the administrative computers to . . . "

Presque-Mourir trailed off. Silence. She could not even hear the building's hum. She shivered. *Why is there no way? Why do people reach for the unattainable? Why do we hope?*

Although Hoffen was furious at these two representatives of a civilization that had committed slow suicide, they had, over the past hours, become important to him.

He began to care, and this was compounded by his sense of justice. They had invited him here hoping for miracles and had promised, in return, to send him back to the burrows with whatever supplies he chose. These Earthlings could guarantee Mars' future, and the elders would reward Hoffen mightily—assuming their personal items would have any worth to a place like Burrow Hogar. Yet he could not simply take this couple's gifts like a thief.

And then the facts all clicked into place. He suddenly recognized the answer.

"So it's the administrative computers that are keeping you from doing what you want?" Hoffen asked. He tried to keep any emotion out of his voice as he stared at the blank grey surface before him, the speaker grille. He did not want to hurt them more. He could be wrong. No more false hopes.

"Naturally," Rajeunir said. Presque-Mourir's brow furrowed.

"These are the same administrative computers that are also refusing to engage in trade with Mars?"

Rajeunir frowned. "Yes, essentially . . . "

"I'm sorry we can't send any supplies with you, as I'd suggested. But it's not authorized; only the computers can authorize it."

Hoffen strolled toward a window that looked out over the hollow, shining city. He imagined it could endure for a thousand years without a single human hand repairing anything, longer without human wear.

"Did Earth never have human leaders?" Hoffen asked. "On Mars, that's all we have."

"Oh, yes," Presque-Mourir said, "our society was run for centuries by democratically elected Potentates. There were so few of them; only certain personality types are drawn to administrative work. Machines handle that drudgery much more efficiently. The last Potentate died long ago. Now we are the only citizens left."

Hoffen, staring out at mountains of computer-operated machinery—all trembling and ready for human use—could no longer suppress his laughter.

*   *   *

At first, the Earthlings couldn't understand why the Martian was laughing. Then he pointed out the obvious.

To Presque-Mourir, it was as if a mask had fallen from her face and she realized she had been looking out at the world through two pinholes all her life.

She turned to Rajeunir and saw tentative hope sparkle in his eyes. This was the first time she could remember seeing his eyes show real life for decades, and in them she imagined that she saw reflections of hers on fire, as well. He was beautiful now, not old, not hollow. She, too, felt young. She felt alive, a powerful sensation after years of preparing for death.

She produced an archaic sound. Presque-Mourir, the last woman on Earth, belly-laughed like a little girl.

Minutes later, they set the machinery into action.

Hoffen couldn't help chuckling again, two weeks later, as he engaged *Walang Maipapalit*'s main engines. He sank into the acceleration webbing with a smile.

Earth's newly elected Potentates—they had won an unprecedented unanimous vote—had ordered twenty automated cargoships taken out of stasis and prepared for the voyage to Mars. Hoffen was eager to return home. He could hardly wait to unveil the riches to his people. The cargoships shuddered on the spaceport pad, preparing to follow Hoffen's old craft. And more would soon follow, regularly. The elders would not consider this unfair; after all, wasn't Hoffen in process of saving the Earth? What was the going rate for saving a civilization?

His laughter faded to a quiet smile as he thought of Presque-Mourir and Rajeunir. That smaller victory meant more to him than laying the foundation for a new Earth. They seemed suddenly alive, excited with the prospect of reshaping the Earth into a world good for humans. Yet their coming-alive made Hoffen feel even more alone. Those two were together now as he had been with Maputi long ago. And, yes, the thought was as sad as it had been every moment between then and now. Perhaps more so, since the Earthlings were not only happily together, but had regained what they had lost—or perhaps gained what they never possessed.

The undeniable reality of heavy *g*-forces pulled Hoffen from wallowing in self-pity. *I gave them back their will to live,* he told himself. *I did that.* That was some consolation. To a Burrow-dweller, friends are the greatest riches one can hold; to give the gift of friendship is to make one wealthy beyond dreams. His family of friends now spanned the inner solar system. That was consolation indeed.

Hoffen's new friends would reshape the Earth with their renewed minds and bodies. Presque-Mourir and Rajeunir were now the entire government. As the only law-makers on Earth—machines cannot make laws, only enforce them—they would begin to dismantle the oppressive, automated bureaucracy under which they had lived their lives. This would take some time. Meanwhile, fleets of cargoships would shuttle supplies to Mars to build it into a self-sustaining world. There was no dishonor in this, because these supplies were not gifts: The government of Presque-Mourir and Rajeunir expected a certain number of Martians to emigrate to Earth with every cargoship's return flight: It takes human creativity to build a civilization. And humans.

To this end, Presque-Mourir and Rajeunir were already doing their part by creating laughing children that looked like Presque Mourir and Rajeunir, and they were doing it the old-fashioned way now that it was legal again.

The *Walang Maipapalit*'s stage-one engines ceased firing, releasing a great weight from Hoffen's chest. The directional nozzles fired once, twice, rotating the ship to prepare it for the main engine's burn toward Mars. Through the viewport, Hoffen watched Earth swim across the starry sky. This blue globe: cradle of humanity and future home to hard-working, ambitious people from Mars—people without millenia of historic hatreds and distrust, people who will not accept comfort over life.

Perhaps we'll not screw it up this time.

Hoffen felt peace.

*Argentine author **Gustavo Bondoni** has been writing since 2004, and has had work published both on-line and in print, in North America, South America and Europe. Notably, his short story "Tenth Orbit" was published in the April 2005 issue of* Jupiter SF, *to critical acclaim and was also a quarter-finalist in L. Ron Hubbard's Writers of the Future Contest (4th quarter 2006). Additionally, his story "Egalité" appeared in the September 2006 issue of* Carve Magazine, *and "Great Hairy Boats" appeared in the July 2007 edition of* Jupiter SF.

Borrowed Time
by Gustavo Bondoni

*O*ften *have I wondered if the old legends are true. Could it be possible that, somewhere in the night sky, the original planet of our race orbits peacefully about a yellow sun? This has often been said. Can it be true that the great-grandparents of The People came to Xenland in machines capable of bridging the abyss? This has not only been said equally often, but is supported by evidence in the form of large metal cylinders on the plains known as the Ship Graveyard, that are reputed to have performed this very feat less than four hundred years ago. The veracity of this claim is strongly disputed, but this lessens not my foreboding.*

I fear to credit the legends, for, if they are true, are we not doomed to a fate best not contemplated?

Hawthorne sat, unable to move, holding a crumpled piece of paper in his hand.

He had suspected for some time that the war was not going well. For weeks now, the reports had been getting less and less optimistic, the supply ships less and less frequent and their captains ever more evasive.

Nevertheless, not even in the worst of his nightmares did he imagine the fall of the Ballisa system. Ballisa had stood for twenty years, ever since the armies of humanity had taken it from the Andreans at the beginning of the war. By this time, it had become a symbol of the war effort, more a state of mind than an actual physical place. The loss of that system would represent a crushing blow to morale.

For Commander Hawthorne, however, it represented an even bigger problem.

Overcoming his initial shock-induced paralysis, he signaled for his staff. Collins and Brooks were quick to arrive, with Gonzalez only moments in arrears. All had suspected that something major was in the works, and now they would find out just how major.

"Yes, Commander," saluted Lieutenant April Collins. She was visibly anxious, a small nervous tic working at the corner of her left eye. Hawthorne waited for Gonzalez to be seated before wordlessly handing the sheet over to them. They passed it around in near silence, Collins exhaling strongly and seeming to deflate, Brooks showing no emotion, and Gonzalez simply saying, "Ballisa. Damn."

They sat in silence for a few moments.

"Major Gonzalez," said Hawthorne, "is there any way we can bring supplies in from human-controlled space?"

"No sir, the only charted spacelane and wormhole system runs through Ballisa. Any other path would be highly risky, although we could attempt to do so."

"We're going to have to try," said Hawthorne. Everyone knew what kind of trouble they were in, but nobody wanted to say so out loud. "With the fall of Ballisa, we're thirteen light-years behind enemy lines, cut off from our supply lines and any contact with humanity. It's only a matter of time until the Andreans find us and take this planet, and we can't count on the fleet to defend us. Hell, they can't even get here, and I suspect they've got bigger problems to think about than a few stragglers on a prison planet. We have to try to evacuate the camp."

Gonzalez, the logistics officer, shook his head slowly. Hawthorne nodded to him to speak.

"Two things," he said, holding up a pair of fingers, "the first is that we don't have enough ships to evacuate everyone, and the second is that, even if we did, you could never convince me to board it. I'd rather take my chances on laying low and hoping the Andreans don't ever notice us."

Collins nodded her agreement. "Flying through space looking for an unmapped wormhole is suicide," she said. Brooks remained silent.

"I see," said Hawthorne. He paused. "I think we'll leave off the military discipline for a while and give everyone the option of staying or going. We'll give them the facts and let them choose their poison. If we have more people wanting to go than available ships, we'll draw lots."

"What about the prisoners?" asked Brooks.

This time, the pause was much longer. The twelve hundred insectoid Andreans resident in the Xeno Containment Sector were the reason that the jungle outpost existed. Out here, light years from any settlement, human or Andrean, it could be safely assumed that the Andrean's extraordinary long-range telepathy would not bring aid to the prisoners immediately. Hard experience had taught that the Andreans would stop at nothing to liberate even one prisoner.

Finally, Hawthorne spoke.

"I'll have to think about it," he said.

As the elder of my people and direct descendant of Hawk Thorn the Founder it falls to me, as is proper, to guide them in times of crisis. Rumors are rampant, and the doomsayers, normally dormant, have come out in full force.

I must consult with the spirits in the ancient temple, but cannot do so without much trepidation. The spirits, always bitter, often violent, are not to be braved lightly. Nevertheless, I must remain strong and remember that the abuse only exists within the confines of my mind, and hope that one of the spirits is minded to illuminate me on the signs that we have seen.

I have little hope of this, however, as the spirits are never deliberately helpful. They dwell in the gloom of the temple, keening sadly, unable to rest, victims of some long-forgotten atrocity.

Our people have been dependent on signs for our survival since the Founding. We have used the migration of the reptiles to plan for winter. The cycles of the tides to time our crops. The lunar eclipse to begin the harvest. Every sign is long-awaited, expected and greeted as a friend. Some are met with trepidation, but all are a comfort to the people.

A new star in the firmament must be a sign of colossal magnitude, but new signs are never a source of comfort, and this one was of particular concern. I am certain that God did not intend for stars to move in the way that this one does.

Hawthorne might be losing it, thought April, but he's still the only leader we have.

She no longer thought of herself as Lieutenant Collins. Following the exodus, all signs of military discipline had broken down. Only two hundred of the camp detail had remained on the planet. The rest had decided to take their chances on the uncharted starlanes.

It had been understandable, in a way. Following the announcement, panic had spread and the prevailing wisdom had been that the Andreans would arrive in full force at any moment. Fights, often lethal, had broken out on boarding the ships, every single one of which had left the planet critically overloaded.

Walking across a green plain in this, the terraformed area of the planet, April reflected on the changes that had come over Hawthorne, some out of necessity, and others completely unexpected, and the effect that they were having on her.

In the first place, his initial idea of hiding from the Andreans had become an all-consuming obsession. He had ordered the satellites brought down from their orbits. Then he had disconnected the ground transmitters, and ordered all componentry smashed for good measure. All in the name of a safety that, many felt, existed only in his mind. It was entirely possible it had been argued that the Andreans knew exactly where they were, and that an assault was only a matter of time.

She had to admit that she, herself, had seriously mixed feelings regarding Hawthorne's plan, but, considering how she felt about the man himself, that was nothing unusual.

She had been fascinated by the way he took charge of what remained of the camp following the exodus. His leadership at that time had been, by no means, a given. There had been as many factions on the planet then as there were inhabitants, and no realistic hope of reestablishing a hierarchy with Hawthorne at the top.

And Hawthorne's extreme views regarding the eradication of all technology only made matters more difficult for him.

Nevertheless, through a brilliant combination of convincing oratory, overflowing passion and simple intelligence, he had won them over one by one. And, in doing so, retaken his place as the leader of this tiny group of humans thirteen light years behind enemy lines.

He had also won April's respect. Some days, she was certain that he had won much more than the respect due a senior officer.

On other days, when she was being brutally honest with herself, she knew beyond any shadow of a doubt that she had fallen head over heels for him. One of the first to join his cause, she had remained his staunchest (most fanatical?) supporter throughout. She had helped him to methodically eliminate every link to the outside universe, save one.

And, she knew, only the fact that she was in love with him allowed her to continue placing one foot in front of the other now. To finish the job.

Finally, the alien pen (the euphemism Xeno Containment Sector had fallen by the wayside some time ago) came into view, and April found herself wondering if any of the people from the outbound shuttles had survived their odyssey. More to the point, she wondered if there were even any humans surviving elsewhere in the galaxy or if the war had finally ended—and transformed the few people on this prison camp planet into the sole representatives of the race.

She arrived at the pen and walked through the containment screens, a concentric ring of electromagnetic fences that surrounded a large concrete structure. Humans felt only a slight tingle on penetrating the screens, but for Andreans, with their different mental structure, they were torture. Crossing one was incapacitating, and two would probably be fatal, although that was theoretical, as none of the prisoners had ever been stupid or desperate enough to try it.

April stopped just outside the innermost screen. Even her limited human senses could feel the telepathic minds of the Andreans within, concentrating, as always, on their art. Not a single surface of the pen was free of some kind of alien clutter, painted walls, sculpted rock. Even the concrete of the walls had been chiseled, forming the shapes of humans, Andreans and other, unidentifiable, beings.

A single Andrean approached from inside the shadowed depths of the pen. One of the first observations that prolonged observation of Andreans in captivity had yielded was that they had no specific leader. It was never the same individual who received the human emissaries, although, April thought, it was probably unnecessary owing to their telepathy.

Today, however, the creatures within did something remarkable. They all turned to watch her as she approached.

Andreans, the sworn enemies of humanity, had been vilified as the pure essence of evil since they were first discovered. And, April reflected, they certainly looked the part.

Large, exoskeletoned, hive-mind creatures with multiple legs capable of reading minds over inconceivable distances were highly unlikely to get along with individualistic mammalian creatures with a paranoid streak, and history had proven this point of view correct.

So why did she find herself disagreeing with it, all of a sudden? She had been in charge of their maintenance, feeding and watching the prisoners since the founding of the camp, and had come to anthropomorphize them to the point that she had given some of them human names, from the Holonet programs she watched, because some of them moved and gestured like some particular actor.

It was difficult not to. Despite the alien appearance and multiple legs (never the same quantity on two different individuals), some gestures, especially the continuous nodding were utterly human. And the art. The art sang to her in a strange way, a mixture of loneliness and desperation, but with an undertone of pure hope.

She supposed telepathic races must, inescapably, pick up some mannerisms and thought processes from other intelligences they contact.

The emissary rubbed its hind legs together, warming up the membranes to speak with her. Its black exoskeleton glistened in the sunlight.

Even before April could open her mouth, it spoke to her.

"Do not do this thing," it said. Language barriers had never been an issue with a telepathic race, and the Andreans were able to reproduce an amazing range of sounds with their membranes, even though, as a telepathic race, they did not converse among themselves.

April stared back at it. So they know, she thought. She shook her head.

"We must," she said, "we have no other choice."

"There are always choices," the Andrean told her.

"But we cannot risk them. We don't know if there are any other humans left in the galaxy," explained April, as if pleading for understanding. "What if we are the last? We must do anything and everything to survive. We cannot risk having your telepathic signals reach your fleet."

"We are willing to promise not to project our thoughts," said the Andrean.

"I believe you," said April, "but I cannot risk the future of the entire human race on your promise."

"Promises are sacred to our race."

"I'm sorry," she said. She turned to go.

"No!" The Andrean shouted at her. "At least spare one of us! If you kill us all there will be none to transfer our knowledge, our memories, to the race. This you cannot do! It is an atrocity of the highest order."

So saying, the Andrean charged the screen.

April was so surprised that she managed only to take one step back, but that was sufficient. The Andrean fell at her feet, whether dead or merely unconscious it was impossible for April to tell. A ripple flowed through the rest of the aliens, as if they themselves had felt the pain of crossing the screen. Which, thought April, they probably had.

She prepared herself to flee the inevitable desperate charge, but the remaining aliens did nothing but stare at her.

Despite their completely monstrous insectoid appearance, their accusing stare, knowing as they did—from her mind—that they would all be dead before the end of the day was somehow moving.

And very human.

She was not surprised to feel tears rolling down her face as she turned to go.

The violence had been expected, but not the excitement, the joy, the feeling of long awaited revenge. I had learned nothing in the temple save that the spirits, when the mood takes them, can be worse than anything imaginable. Their hatred for all living men had broken through even my most rigidly constructed mental barriers, and I had only managed to extricate myself from the temple through sheer animal instinct.

I know that I must find the explanation if I am to save The People from tearing themselves apart in a panicked frenzy. I must find the strength to rise and consult the books of wisdom once more. There may be some passage in the moral treatise "Vanity Fair" that may shed light on this crossroad or is this the doomsday predicted in the metaphorical prophecy The Fall of the House of Usher?

I do not yet have the answer, but cannot bring myself to believe that the books are unable to assist. They have been the spiritual guide to our people for all of history. They cannot fail us now.

For the new star has, in this brief interlude, grown larger.

The library had been cleaned out years before, but Hawthorne still scanned the shelves out of sheer paranoid habit, looking for anything that might endanger the future of the colony. Nothing. The shelves were innocent of any technical literature. Even Victorian fantasy had been burned if he judged it to contain too much scientific detail.

It had cut him deeply to lose Verne and Wells, constant companions to his voyages among the stars. But hardest of all had been *Frankenstein*. He had kept it under lock years after he had stopped mourning the loss of the other books.

Until the night of April's death. On that night, he remembered once again that the enemy they were hiding from was implacable and could reach out from beyond even the barrier of death to take human life.

She had never been the same following the death of the Andreans, never been able to reconcile herself to the reality of having given the order to terminate them. Her suicide, though unaccompanied by a note of any kind had been instantly and forever attributed to the Andreans by Hawthorne, though others thought differently.

That very night, *Frankenstein* had burned. No price was too high to save the settlement. He remembered it as if it had been yesterday. Smelling the smoke, feeling the pain of April's death.

"Are you all right, Grandpa?"

Milo, the youngest of his six grandchildren had entered unnoticed. For a moment he was unable to breathe, struck, as always by how much Milo reminded him of April. The color and form of his hair, the line of his jaw. But then, all their offspring had always looked more like her than him.

The child seemed unsure of how to respond to this silent scrutiny from his usually indulgent ancestor. Tears welled up.

"Now, Milo," said Hawthorne in his usual, mild voice, "don't cry."

And everything was all right again. If his words had been a magical incantation, they couldn't have had a more immediate or absolute effect. The child straightened and forgot all about crying, prompting a smile from his grandfather. If only real life were that simple.

"What were you thinking about, grandpa?"

"Books." There was a faraway look in his eyes, unnoticed by Milo.

"Books? Like these?" Milo pointed at the shelves.

"Yes. These and many others. Books from the past that I don't have any more."

"Why not?"

"Because they were dangerous."

Milo looked at the books on the shelves. They obviously didn't look dangerous to him. He reached out and tentatively touched one. His finger landed on *Othello*. He pulled it back quickly. Only when he was certain that it hadn't hurt him did his hand approach the book again.

"The danger was not in the books themselves but in what was written inside."

"Then why did you keep these?" asked Milo. He pulled the copy of *Othello* out of its place on the shelf.

"Because books can also tell us who we are, and where we come from, so we never forget."

"I'm Milo. I won't forget that!" But, all the same, he opened the book reverently, as if expecting a message from God to leap out at him from the pages.

Hawthorne tried to remember how old the child was. Seven? Eight? It made no difference. Hawthorne knew the child couldn't read, and likely would never bother to learn. It was no longer necessary.

And he was responsible.

Under his watchful and often tyrannical eye, every sign of advanced human technology that could potentially create the slightest risk of detection from space had been eradicated from the colony.

But it was not enough to save one generation. Hawthorne knew that he would not be around to guide them forever.

He had fought the Andreans. He knew what that was like. Future generations would not know and, not knowing, would minimize the threat, seduced by the comforts of the technology that Hawthorne had had destroyed. It was simply human nature.

All of which meant that it was not enough to eliminate the dangerous technology itself. The very knowledge of its existence had to be eradicated.

And he had done it.

Technical treatises had been used to create a stone-age farming culture and then destroyed. The generators, fusion drives, tri-D equipment, storage files. All of it had been destroyed.

Even the weaponry had gone. This came near to causing a mutiny until Hawthorne pointed out that against the massed might of the Andrean fleet a few blaster rifles were not going to be much use. The only hope was to hide. And pray.

And hide they had. What at first had seemed an impossible dream, with discovery and death the price of dreaming had, with time, become simply the way things were. And, now, his grandchildren regarded the Andreans as a bedtime story, and space flight as a legend, and reading as something for Gods and elders.

The child, meanwhile, sat contentedly next to him, pretending to read the book, pretending to make sense of the words, creating a world that Shakespeare would never have dreamed possible. Milo would remain forever unaware of the weight his grandfather carried in his soul, unaware that the old man beside him wondered every day if he had, indeed, made the right choice.

The burden of leadership, at least, was no longer his. It had been passed along the very day after April's death. But he could never pass along the responsibility for what he had done. Its enormity would forever live within him.

The child eventually wandered off, not even noticing the silence that had so unnerved him previously, leaving his grandfather once more to his thoughts.

Hawthorne knew that there was not much time left to him, and knew he should enjoy re-reading his beloved leather-bound copy of *Wuthering Heights*, happy in the safety of his colony and even more content because his fetish for outdated printed books had at least allowed him to save a small section of human culture for the generations to come.

Death should find him content, safe in the knowledge that he had accomplished the objective for which he had been trained since the first day of officer school, and forever cheated the Andreans out of their final prize.

But he knew it would not.

My thought as I watch the descending ball of flame coming ever nearer is that I truly desire that it be a star and simply erases me from the face of the planet with its falling.

But, as it approaches, I can tell that it is correcting its course to bear directly at me and correcting once more. I can no longer pretend that it is a star.

I am alone, my people scattered like dust, yet it is for them that I worry. I am old and have little to lose, but they shall witness the truth of our legends.

I can now marvel at my own arrogance. How many times had I scoffed at a legend, berating the theorist as a superstitious fool? And yet, in my mind, I can no more deny the fact of the star machine than I can of my own existence.

I have no evidence that it is a machine built to bridge the gulf between the stars. Yet I know it. Despite my foreboding I will stand fast and greet whatever emerges, nobly representing The People and bringing understanding and peace. God willing it will be so.

But, for some reason, as I stand here, resolute, on this monumental occasion, I imagine the voices of the spirits in my mind, making an astonishing and disconcerting noise.

A noise much like laughter.

Sue Blalock is a writer, artist, and avocational archaeologist. When not buried beneath a stack of reference books, she may be found at her local museum, sitting alone in a dusty storeroom measuring potsherds with a caliper. It is by far the best job for which she has never been paid. A native of South Florida, her other interests include astronomy, ice hockey, and avoiding hurricanes.

Charybdis
by Sue Blalock

Deep in the bowels of the Southwestern Museum of Natural and Cultural History, Dr. Gillian Sands picked up an aging cardboard box and eyed it dubiously. Someone had scribbled HALLIWELL COLLECTION on the side in thick black marker. There was no other indication of what it contained. "Please, tell me we have some kind of documentation to go with this stuff," she said.

Gill's boss, Valerie, tucked her hands into the pockets of her blue lab jacket and sighed gustily. "I wish. Most of it was collected decades before the Indigenous Species Protection Act went into effect. We have a master list of artifacts, but little or no provenience to go along with it."

"And I get to catalog it," Gill said. "Joy."

"It's all yours," Valerie said cheerfully. She pulled a tablet containing the manifest out of her pocket and handed it over to Gill. "Identify what you can, take notes on what you can't, and pull anything that might violate the ISPA."

"You are so going to owe me snob chocolate after this," Gill said.

Valerie chuckled, and wandered off in the general direction of her office, leaving Gill to contemplate her doom among the jumbled stack of boxes and crates. "Begin as you mean to go on," Gill muttered and pulled a pair of dingy cotton gloves and a box cutter out of her coat pocket and set to work.

Two hours later, she had unpacked a collection of ceramic spindle whorls that could have come from any pre-industrial civilization on Earth or off it, a polychromatic animal effigy from Janus IV in the pre-Classic style that was very probably a fake, and a half dozen Ciprian shell and bone necklaces that were very probably real and in direct violation of ISPA regulations regarding grave goods.

Three boxes down, at least twenty more to go. Gill studied the remaining number, trying to decide what to open next. Her gaze settled on a pair of grey plastic shipping crates. She picked up the smaller of the two, moved it to her workstation. It still bore its original shipping and customs labels, with all the seals intact. Curious, she examined the larger crate, found it untouched as well; for whatever reason, neither crate had been opened since their original shipping date some forty years past.

The shipping labels listed Charybdis III as the port of origin. Gill frowned, trying to think of any archaeological sites within the vicinity of Charybdis. The only one that sprang to mind was part of the old Illyrian Empire and she did not recall seeing any Illyrian artifacts listed on the manifest. To be safe, she picked up the tablet and scrolled through the list. There was the polychromatic animal effigy, the spindle whorls and the grave goods she had already unpacked, plus a whole host of other vessels, potsherds, jewelry, and textiles from all corners of known space. None of them was Illyrian.

That was no great surprise; Illyrian artifacts were rare. Oh, they had found ruins aplenty on various planets, enough to know that the culture responsible for building them had once been a thriving, space-faring race. The architecture was breathtaking in its organic simplicity, seemingly grown from the bones of the earth itself, but actual physical artifacts were few. There was none of the usual detritus left by vanished races, no bits of trash and broken machinery, no tombs, no bodies, nothing. Only the cities remained, their graceful, delicate spires and crystalline domed roofs seemingly too fragile to have survived untold centuries untended and forgotten.

Gill frowned. That a renowned professor of archaeology would have not one, but two crates of priceless Illyrian artifacts and keep them tucked away for nearly fifty years made no sense. Either they had been misfiled all this time (not entirely unlikely, given the state of the rest of the collection) or, while the crates may have originated from the vicinity of Charybdis, their contents did not.

There was only one way to find out. Taking a deep breath, Gill cracked the seals on the smaller crate and removed the lid, cautiously peeling aside the layers of packing foam until her questing fingers touched smooth, cool glass: a bowl, small and surprisingly heavy. The glass was pale, translucent white with an iridescent sheen, like mother-of-pearl. There was a second object hidden in the foam, an oblong length of polished wood, beautifully preserved, with no signs of drying or cracking despite its extended stay inside the crate.

Her first instinct was to call it a mortar and pestle, but the wear patterns on the wood were not consistent with either pounding or grinding. The bowl itself seemed far too fine a thing to be a simple kitchen implement, but Gill had seen plenty of ordinary household objects made from precious metals and encrusted with jewels, either because of ceremonial use or simply because their owners *could*. There was also the possibility that they did not belong together at all; just because two artifacts were stored in the same box did not mean they were part of a set.

If they were artifacts at all; for all she knew, the late professor had picked them up in a local bazaar for personal use and then forgotten all about them. Gill rapped a fingernail against the side of the bowl in annoyance, and was startled when it produced a sweet, bell-like tone. Nodding to herself, she picked up the wooden mallet and used it to lightly strike the bowl a second time; again, the bowl rang, loud and deep.

Gill checked the manifest again, but there was no mention of a singing bowl—or a white glass mortar and pestle, for that matter. Sighing, she activated the comm and buzzed the curator's office. "Val, you got a second? I've found something odd, and I'd like you to take a look."

Valerie arrived a few minutes later, looking harried and annoyed. "Please, tell me you haven't found any remains, because I *really* don't want to deal with the paperwork."

Gill smiled. "Sorry to disappoint." She gestured to the bowl and mallet. "I think it's a glass singing bowl, but there's nothing like it on the manifest."

"Oh, my," Valerie said. "That looks like it could be Illyrian. Where did you find it?"

Gill pointed to the grey plastic shipping crate. "In there. It was shipped to the professor from Charybdis."

"Oh, my," Valerie said again. She picked up the mallet and struck the side of the bowl, eyes sliding half-shut as she listened to the pure, ringing tone. "Oh, yes. Definitely Illyrian. And it's not glass; glass won't produce that depth of sound, though we'll still need to do a compositional analysis to confirm it. You said it was from Charybdis?"

"According to the label," Gill said. "There's a second crate from the same port of origin, but I haven't opened it yet."

"So, let's get cracking! Who knows what we'll find?"

Together, they popped the seals on the second crate and pried the stubborn lid loose. This one appeared to have been more hastily packed, using what looked like shredded plastic bags for padding. Gill rooted around in the packing material, found a big, lumpy *something* and carefully pulled it free.

It was a ratty blue backpack. Stitched to the front pocket was a faded patch that read CLARKE UNIVERSITY ICE WEASELS.

Gill raised an eyebrow. "Not exactly what I was expecting."

"Welcome to the exciting world of collections management," Valerie said dryly.

A further search of the crate turned up an insulated thermos that still smelled faintly of coffee, a rather impressive tool kit, a sweat-stained baseball cap, and a set of tuning forks.

"Okay, now I'm really confused," Gill said.

Valerie picked up the crate lid and studied the shipping label carefully. "I wonder . . ."

"Val?"

"Do me a favor, and check the backpack for any kind of identification," Valerie said.

"You think it could be significant?"

"Possibly," Valerie said. "I need to verify some dates first. Let me know if you find anything."

Gill brought the backpack to her workstation and began to

methodically empty each pocket. Sunglasses. High-power sunblock. A canteen whose contents had long since evaporated. Electrolyte replacement tablets. Protein bars four decades past their expiration date. All things consistent with someone working in a desert environment like the Illyrian site near Charybdis.

In a padded inner pocket she found a portable tablet and stylus, not all that dissimilar from the ones used here in the museum, only heavier, less refined. Its power cell was depleted—unsurprising after so many years—but the memory core appeared intact; with luck, she would still be able to recover the data.

It was strange to be working on something so prosaic, as though she was processing a student's forgotten school bag and would be turning it in to Lost & Found when she finished. There was even a chance the owner might still be alive; forty-six years was not all that long ago.

Not that it would matter if she could not find out who the bag belonged to. There was still one compartment left and it appeared to contain a spare set of clothing: socks, boxer shorts, a light green t-shirt, and a pair of blue jeans, all carefully folded in a neat stack. Someone had stuffed a wadded-up grey jacket on top of the other clothes, which seemed at odds with the careful placement of the rest of the objects; whoever this guy was, he liked his belongings arranged just *so*, with everything in its proper place so he would not have to go rooting around through the bottom of his bag every time he needed a caliper or a packet of analgesic. It was a state of preparedness Gill could relate to; her own daypack weighed about as much as a small moon.

However the jacket had gotten into the bag, it did have one important thing: an ID badge attached to the breast pocket with a magnetic clip. It belonged to a Dr. Patrick Delaney from Clarke University on Europa, and showed a man in his late 30s to early 40s with light brown hair, blue eyes, and a stubborn jaw.

"Gotcha," she said softly.

Gill smoothed out the worst of the wrinkles, then folded the jacket over one arm and carried it down the hall to the cramped office she shared with Valerie. "Well, I think I've ID'd our guy," she announced as she walked through the door.

"Was it Pat Delaney?" Valerie asked.

Gill stared. "As a matter of fact, it was. How did you know?"

Valerie gestured to the terminal on her desk. "Oh, just a hunch."

The screen displayed a news article called up from the library archives. The headline read SEARCH FOR MISSING PHYSICIST CALLED OFF, accompanied by a candid picture of Dr. Delaney pointing to something off-camera. He wore a grey jacket identical to the one in Gill's hands, right down to the lapel pin.

"Whoa," Gill said.

"That was about my reaction," Valerie said, grinning.

"This could be big," Gill said.

"Or it could be nothing at all," Valerie said. "We need authentication."

"There was an old tablet stuffed down inside the backpack," Gill said. "I'll run it by Zee's on my way home tonight, see if he can get it working again. God only knows what's on it."

"Good idea," Valerie said. "We should also think about contacting the family."

Gill hesitated. "Are you sure about that? I'd hate to get their hopes up."

"It's iffy," Valerie agreed, "but they might be able to help us with verification."

"I'll get right on it," Gill said.

Zbynek "Zee" Deynekov was a retired engineer with a passion for antique computers. He volunteered at the museum twice a week and had helped restore many of the pieces currently on display in their technology exhibit. If anyone could get Delaney's computer working again, it was Zee.

The door opened before Gill even touched the bell. Zee blinked owlishly at her from the other side of the doorway. "Ah, yes," he said, nodding at the tablet in her hands. "The Hyderabad 2650 Mark II. A bit ungainly by modern standards, but very durable and rugged."

Gill smiled. "Zee, have you been illegally hacking the city security cameras again?"

"Nonsense," he said airily. "I merely spotted you from the window."

"From twenty-six stories up."

"I have excellent eyes for a man my age. Now please, come inside."

Zee took the tablet from her and carried it over to his desk. "Is this part of a collection or did you want it refurbished for personal use?"

Only Zee would ask if a forty-year-old machine was for personal use. "We think it's part of the Halliwell collection," Gill said. "I need to get it working again to be sure."

Zee pulled out his toolkit, removed the protective outer casing and began to examine the tablet's guts. "It appears to be in excellent shape," he said. "It also appears to have been extensively and expertly modified. Are you sure this belonged to Professor Halliwell? I do not recall her being very technically-minded."

"No, actually," Gill said. "We believe it belonged to a Dr. Patrick Delaney."

"Patrick Delaney," Zee repeated slowly. "This machine belonged to Patrick Delaney?

"Am I the only person who's never heard of this guy?" Gill said with a touch of asperity.

"You are young," Zee said, "and last I checked, quantum theory was not required for a degree in archaeology."

"Valerie knew who he was."

"Valerie is a goddess," Zee said. "She also would have been in her early twenties at the time of Delaney's disappearance. It was all the media could talk about for weeks."

"Did anyone ever find out what happened to him?"

"No," said Zee. "There are theories, of course, but no one knows for certain what happened." Zee stared down at the tablet with almost religious reverence. "If this truly is Patrick Delaney's computer, it could answer a great many questions."

"I've sent word to the family," Gill said. "They may be able to help verify the find. And who knows? It might even bring them a little closure."

"One can hope," Zee said. He carefully removed the memory core and handed it to Gill. "You will want to keep this safe until I get the machine running again. It will be fascinating to see what manner of research Delaney was working on. Assuming, of course, that the files

91

haven't been encrypted. Which they probably have."

"Not everyone is as paranoid as you, Zbynek."

"True enough," Zee replied. "But you will notice I am here enjoying my old age, while Dr. Delaney is not. Let that be a lesson."

Gill left the tablet in Zee's capable hands after eliciting a promise that he would contact her as soon as he had it working again. She felt a certain sense of personal responsibility for the late doctor's belongings. It was patently silly—his research was far more valuable than the machine it was stored on—but she wanted to be able to tell the family that Delaney's things had been handled with the care and respect they deserved.

She made it back down to street level just in time to catch the tram that would take her from Zee's apartment complex to her own neighborhood. Any other night she might have walked, savoring the heat of the desert air after spending all day in chill, climate-controlled rooms, but there was just too much on her mind. She wanted to sit and think, scribble notes for work, check her mail for any response from Delaney's widow.

Sliding into an empty seat, Gill set her daypack down by her feet, pulled out her palmtop and checked for new mail. There was nothing. She hadn't truly expected a reply so soon, but it was still disappointing, and she snapped the unit shut with a sigh before tucking it back into her bag next to the slim black cylinder that was the memory core from Delaney's computer.

The core would be returned to the museum when Gill went back to work the following morning, but it was safe enough for the time being inside an archival storage bag with a temporary accession number written on the label. Between now and then, there would be dinner, a hot shower to scrub off the dust one inevitably accumulated during a day spent sorting through boxes in artifact storage, and tea. Lots of tea, she decided, and maybe a long soak in the tub instead of a shower. A nice, restful evening at home.

What she found instead was a stranger waiting in the hall in front of her apartment; a man, tall and broad-shouldered, wearing an expensive leather jacket, superbly tailored grey trousers and a dark blue shirt. He seemed oddly familiar, but she couldn't quite place his face. "May I help you?" she asked, slowing down her strides before finally stopping with several cautious meters still between them.

"Doctor Sands?" he asked.

"That depends," she said. "Who am I speaking to?"

"Right, sorry," he said. He took a step towards her, holding out one hand. "I'm Hugh Delaney, Patrick Delaney's grandson."

And that was it, the strange sense of familiarity: Hugh looked like his grandfather. He was younger, and more powerfully built, but the elder Delaney had left a definite genetic stamp on his descendant. They had the same broad, belligerent jaw and pale skin, the same sharp blue eyes. "It's—nice to meet you," Gill said, not shaking his hand. "Why are you here?"

"My grandmother sent me to collect my grandfather's things," Hugh said. If he was put off by her less than welcoming attitude, he did not show it.

"Yes, I figured that out for myself," Gill said dryly. "I meant, why are you here in front of my apartment."

He had the grace to look sheepish. "I did try the museum first, but they said you'd already left for the day. I don't suppose we could maybe talk inside?" he asked, blue eyes wide and hopeful.

"No," she said. "We really couldn't." Gill ran a hand through her hair, smoothing the coppery strands back behind one ear while she tried to come up with a polite way to tell him to come back during office hours, and preferably at her actual office. "Mr. Delaney, while I appreciate how important this find must be to your family—"

Behind her, a new voice called, "Doctor Sands!"

"Now what?" Gill muttered, and turned to find two men coming swiftly up the hall, their crisp, dark-blue uniforms marking them as Fleet officers.

"Ah, yes," Hugh said. "I was wondering when you'd show up. Dr. Sands, allow me to introduce Colonel Gregory Alcott, director of the Department of Experimental Xenotechnology and all-around pain in the ass. Colonel, I have to say, I feel so much safer knowing our government is hard at work monitoring the personal correspondences of eighty-six-year-old retired figure skaters. Really, I'm highly impressed."

The older of the two officers smiled thin and tight. "Nice to see you, too, Delaney. Shouldn't you be at the rink hitting people with sticks?"

"I'm on injured reserve," Hugh said, with a wide, white smile that was anything but friendly. "I bruised a tattoo in last night's game against Toronto. But it's sweet of you to ask."

Alcott shook his head in disgust. "You're wasting your God-given talents, Delaney. Fortunately, this isn't about you." He turned to Gill. "Dr. Sands, I apologize for imposing on you at home like this, but you are currently in possession of a potentially sensitive piece of government property. We'd like it back."

Gill's breath snagged in her chest. The tablet. He wanted the tablet, and any of the late doctor's research it contained. "We're still in the process of cataloging and identifying all the artifacts that came with the Halliwell Collection," she said, choosing her words with care. "At this point, I can't say with any certainty whom any of the recovered items actually belonged to."

"We're not interested in the doctor's personal effects, ma'am," said the second officer. He did not identify himself, but the name stitched over the breast pocket of his uniform read SIMONS. "All we're asking for is the return of a piece of government-issued hardware."

"We've already spoken to both the museum director and your supervisor," Alcott added. He loomed over her in a manner that was not intended to be comforting, despite the bland smile that creased his tanned, handsome face. "They've agreed to hand the tablet over to us. If it turns out we were mistaken, it will be shipped back to the museum with our sincerest apologies."

"I don't suppose you have that in writing," Hugh said.

"As a matter of fact," said Alcott, "we do. Lieutenant?"

Lt. Simons produced a sheaf of documents from a slim black briefcase and handed them to Gill. It all looked very official, right down to the Terran Colonial Government Seal and the signatures of both Valerie, and Will Harrison, the museum director, beneath that of Colonel Alcott. She read every word carefully before passing the pages over to Hugh. "Well, you've certainly come prepared," she said. "Unfortunately, I don't have the tablet with me. If you'd like to pick it up tomorrow during business hours—"

"We'd prefer not to wait," said Alcott.

"Fine," Gill said coolly. "I dropped it off with Zbynek Deynekov for restoration. Would you like his address?"

"I'm sure we can find it on our own," Alcott said. "Thank you for your time, Dr. Sands. Delaney, if you ever get tired of pretending to be a dumb jock, my offer still stands."

"I'd rather have a high acid enema," Hugh said. "But thanks anyway."

Gill watched the colonel and his flunky leave. When the doors of the lift closed behind them, she sagged back against the wall and balled her hands into fists to stop their shaking. "Pretending to be a dumb jock?" she asked, a cold note of skepticism lacing her voice.

"It's a long story," Hugh replied wearily. "Can I come in now?"

"I guess you'd better," she said, and punched in the access code to her door.

Home was a one bedroom apartment, small and comfortably cluttered with books, research materials, and an eclectic assortment of ceramic and textile art from a wide range of cultures, both human and non. Gill dropped her bag on the kitchenette counter beside the comm unit and waved Hugh through the narrow entry hall to the minuscule living room beyond. "Have a seat," she said. "I need to call Zbynek and let him know company is coming."

Zee answered the comm on the fourth ring, blinking fuzzily into the monitor. "It has only been one hour," he said waspishly. "Even I don't work that fast."

"I know, Zbynek, I'm sorry," Gill said. Her voice was still jangled; she fought to calm it. "The military was just here. They want the tablet."

Zee was silent for a long moment. "Ah," he said at last. "And when will they be arriving to collect it?"

"As soon as possible, I'd think," she said. "They were very insistent about recovering their hardware. Under the circumstances, I decided the best thing was to give them exactly what they asked for."

Zee's expression turned pensive. "Yes," he said slowly, "I do see your point. It is a great pity, of course, but if necessary, we can still put together an exhibit using the old Exogenesis tablet back in artifact storage. They are comparable models."

Gill smiled, grateful that Zbynek's paranoia was proving useful for once. "Thank you, Zee. I knew you'd understand."

"Always, my dear. Feel free to call should you need further assistance."

She closed the connection, and walked around the corner to the living room. Hugh sat sprawled on the loveseat, idly paging through a book on Ciprian tribal art. "While I applaud your attempt at subterfuge, you do realize that anyone with an IQ above bean dip will be able to parse that conversation," he said.

Gill stared at him blankly. "Excuse me?"

Hugh snapped the book shut and set it aside on the end table. "What, you want me to spell it out? Fine. They may have the hardware, but you have the data, and your friend just told you where to find a machine that could access it. So. What are you going to do next?"

"That depends," Gill said.

"On what?"

"On whether or not you can give me a reason why I shouldn't turn it over to the military."

"You mean, aside from the fact that it, oh, doesn't belong to them?"

"They seem to think it does."

"They think that about a lot of things," Hugh said hotly. "It doesn't mean they're *right*." He took a deep breath, visibly struggling to keep a lid on his temper. "Look, my grandfather went to a lot of trouble to keep that information away from people like Colonel Alcott, and I'll be damned if I let them get hold of it now. These people are the reason my grandmother is afraid to leave her house, and why I'm playing professional hockey instead of working in a cushy research lab with a hot blonde assistant named Greta."

Gill arched an eyebrow, amused in spite of herself. "Greta?"

Hugh smiled crookedly. "I never claimed to be deep," he said. "Anyway, the point is, my grandfather's research does not belong to the Terran government. If anything, it belongs to the physics department at Clarke University on Europa."

"But what was a physicist doing on Charybdis in the first place?" Gill asked. "The Illyrians didn't leave any technology behind. They didn't leave anything behind except empty buildings and the occasional piece of broken pottery."

"A civilization so advanced we can't even identify the material their cities were built from, much less how they were constructed? I'd say there was plenty for him to study. And if he found answers, it would more than explain the military's interest in his work."

"You think they killed him," Gill said. "Don't you."

"My grandmother thinks so," Hugh said. "All I know is that the government has hounded my family for decades trying to find out where he hid his research, research that you currently have in your possession. So, I ask you again: What are you going to do?"

She pondered her options. Murdered physicists. Mysterious government agents and missing scientific research. The whole situation was unreal, like the plot of one of the serial mysteries Valerie liked to watch on the vid.

Gill took a deep, steadying breath, then another. Finally she said, "How would you like a tour of the museum?"

"Fine," Hugh said with the barest hint of a smile. "But I'm driving."

Hugh had a rental, it turned out; a sleek, matte-black vehicle with a profile like a hunting shark, that in no way deserved the sobriquet *flitter*. "I asked the rental company for something fast," Hugh said, grinning at Gill's obvious appreciation of his ride. "Pity its fuel consumption rates are crap."

In spite of their urgency, they stopped for takeout along the way. Hugh had been traveling ever since he'd gotten his grandmother's call that morning, all the way from eastern Canada to the southwestern United States, only pausing long enough to recharge the flitter's fuel cell. He was understandably tired and hungry. *Very* hungry; Gill watched in amazement as Hugh packed away three cheeseburgers and a large order of curly fries, barely slowing down enough chew.

"How the hell do you stay in shape?" Gill said.

"Really high metabolism," Hugh said. "What I want to know is, how do you stand this heat?" He shook his head in disgust. "Ten years on Earth, you'd think I'd be used to it by now."

"You're from Europa, right?" Gill asked.

"Born and raised," Hugh said proudly. "There have been Delaneys on Europa ever since the first research station was established."

"Well, that certainly explains the hockey."

"Are you kidding? It's a big ball of ice colonized entirely by scientists and explorers. I could skate before I could talk, and had my first Ph.D. by the time I was fifteen. What about you?" he added, his expression genuinely curious. "Native or Off-Worlder?"

"Native," she said. "I'm from right here in Arizona. And no jokes about my last name. Believe me, I've heard them all."

"Duly noted," he said, grinning. There was a thin white scar on his upper lip, and another, fresher one following the curve of his cheekbone. Gill wondered how many of his teeth were replacements, and stopped just short of asking.

It was a distraction she did not need right now, and Gill sternly forced her mind back to the matter at hand. "The rest of the staff will have gone home for the night. We'll have the place to ourselves. Well," she amended, "us and the maintenance 'bots."

"Good to know." He shot her a brief glance before turning his attention back to the flitter controls. "How do you know you can trust me?"

"I don't," she said. "How do you know you can trust me?"

Hugh smiled, wry and sharp; the scar on his lip pulled his mouth slightly askew. "I don't," he said.

She found herself smiling in return. "Then I guess that makes us even."

Gill instructed Hugh to park beside the loading dock in the rear of the museum.

"Huh," he said, surveying the squat, two-story structure with a critical eye. "It's a lot smaller than I expected."

"We're not the Smithsonian," Gill said with a touch of asperity, "but we do all right."

She let Hugh into the building, and then left him waiting in the darkened hallway by the door while she turned on the lights. When she came back, she found he had popped off the outer casing of the alarm touchpad and was fiddling with the circuitry beneath.

"What the hell do you think you're doing?" Gill demanded.

"Giving you a free security upgrade," Hugh said. When that clearly did not appease her, he sighed. "Look, a reasonably intelligent six-year-old with a butter knife and a pair of tweezers could bypass this system. All I'm doing is making sure that Alcott and his goons will meet with a bit more of a challenge when they finally get here."

"Oh," Gill said in a small voice, and swallowed hard against the sudden, sick feeling in the pit of her stomach. "How long?"

"Just a couple of minutes."

"I meant before Alcott shows up."

Hugh paused, then looked over his shoulder at her. "That depends," he said. "How clever is your friend Zbynek?"

"Very," Gill said.

"Well," Hugh said, "assuming he gave them a dummy memory core along with the tablet, then I'd say we had a couple of hours. Three, tops."

"Oh," Gill said again. She frowned at the security system. "Do you actually know what you're doing?"

"I'll send you my CV later," Hugh said dryly before snapping the cover plate back into place. "There, that should do it," he said with a smug little smirk. "Now. Show me to the antique computers."

Technological artifacts were kept in their own special storeroom, just down the hall and to the left of the service entrance. It was a much neater space than ethnographic storage, but also colder, less inviting, all metal and plastic and clean, sharp lines. Gill gestured for Hugh to precede her into the room while she looked for a box to prop the door open. "Tablets and related items are stored on shelves D-4 through D-8," she said. "We want the Exogenesis model."

He found it before she did: an ungainly rectangle of heavy, dark-grey plastic sitting on the uppermost shelf amid a dusty jumble of random mechanical effluvia. "Wow, that is *hideous*," Hugh said. "No wonder the Hyderabads were more popular."

The man was like a magpie with ADD. "Is it still functional?" Gill prompted, trying to get him back on track.

Hugh poked at the tablet until the screen flared crankily to life beneath his fingers. "That would be a yes, but it doesn't appear to have much juice left."

Gill dug the plastic bag containing the memory core out of her daypack and handed it to Hugh. "Then work fast," she said.

Two long hours later, Hugh said, "I'm going to need more time."

"We don't have more time," Gill snapped. "Not unless we leave now and go somewhere else, and I'm starting to feel a little too much like a fugitive as it is."

Hugh winced, as if it had only just occurred to him that she could get into serious trouble from this stunt. It probably had. "I'm sorry," he said. "I shouldn't have dragged you into this. If you want to leave, I'll— I'll tell them I broke in, stole the data core from you, something."

"Like they'd believe that," Gill said, wishing she could just go home, change out of her dusty work clothes and go to bed. "Look, just tell me you've found something that's worth ruining my career over and we'll call it even."

"Well," Hugh said, "the mathematical models are extremely complex, and I won't be completely sure until I've gone through the entire document—"

"Yes or no, Hugh."

"Yes," Hugh said. "It appears he discovered how to use unified field Higgs sonomanipulation."

He genuinely seemed to believe she would understand that. It was both flattering and exasperating. "Which is—?"

"Compression waves in the electroweak field," Hugh said eagerly. "They're easier to work with than any of the others if you have a good supply of directed Higgs bosons. Get the wavelength short enough, say down around ten-to-the-ten Planck lengths, and it starts spilling over into the strong force, then into gravity eventually. It's quite elegant, really."

Gill ground the heels of her palms against her eyelids. "In English, Hugh."

"Right, sorry. Um, it means, he found a way to manipulate matter and energy using sound, more or less. Or, well, the Illyrians did; my grandfather simply proved that they did it. At least, I think he did. It's going to take time to go through all the research."

"Technology based on sound," Gill said. "Is that even possible?"

"Hypothetically? Yes," Hugh said. "According to the principles of string theory, all particles are actually made up of tiny loops of string vibrating in precise patterns. If you can control how the string vibrates—"

"—then you can control how the particle behaves," Gill finished for him.

"And not just control it," Hugh said, so excited now he was practically bouncing. "You can change it into something completely different. That's how the Illyrians built all those fantastical structures we've been trying so hard to understand. It also explains why we've never found any other traces of them; they didn't vanish, they just— transformed."

"My god," Gill said, "that's—"

"Amazing?"

"Terrifying," she said. "It's no wonder Alcott wants to get his hands on this technology, or that your grandfather tried to bury it. The potential military applications are limitless."

It hurt to watch Hugh's expression change from child-like joy to horror. "Oh god," he said, and sat down with a heavy thump atop the worktable. "I'm going to have to destroy it, aren't I."

Before Gill had a chance to reply, the security system squawked loudly, quickly followed by a deep, reverberating *thud*. Someone was trying to get in through the service entrance. "We're out of time," Gill said.

Hugh took a deep, trembling breath, then another. "It's . . . it's his life's work," he said. "I don't, I *can't*—"

Gill gripped his shoulder firmly. "Then we'll think of something else."

In the end, Alcott and his men simply blew down the door.

Hugh silently reached out and took hold of Gill's hand, his strong, callused fingers holding tight until Alcott's soldiers entered the room and pulled them apart. A man in a black combat uniform shoved Gill out into the hazy, smoke-filled corridor and pushed her roughly to her knees. She stared at the still-smoldering remains of the service door and shuddered, praying that the billowing clouds of dust and debris would not damage any of the artifacts.

"You don't make it easy, do you, Delaney?" Alcott said. He was smiling, the bastard. "Do us all a favor and give me the damned memory core before I have to tear apart any more of the poor doctor's lovely little museum."

"Here," Hugh said, and held out the tablet. "Take it. It's useless anyway."

"Now, that is a pity," Alcott said. "Destroying government property is a serious crime. I'd hate to have to arrest you both."

"Yes, well, that assumes there was something worth destroying," Hugh said. "There wasn't."

Alcott frowned. "You don't really expect me to believe that."

"Look for yourself," Gill suggested. "There's nothing but the doctor's personal day planner, pictures from the dig site, and some letters to friends and family."

"Not to mention about 500 variations of Mah-jongg," Hugh added. He glared up at Alcott, his mouth compressed into a hard, thin line. "If there ever was any research on that drive, it was deleted long before I got to it."

Alcott shook his head as he scrolled through the tablet's contents. "No," he said. "No, I don't believe it."

"There is no research," Hugh said, each word sharp and bitter. "You have been harassing my family all these years for *nothing*!"

"No," Alcott said again, but he sounded less certain, more pained. He shoved the tablet into the hands of a nearby aide. "Take this to the lab and have it stripped down to the molecules," he ordered. "Now!"

The aide barked a hasty "Yes sir!" and scrambled off. Alcott turned back and studied Hugh's face carefully. "If you're lying—" he warned, his voice dangerously soft.

"Oh, go to hell," Hugh spat. "It's *over*. Deal with it and move on."

He was, perhaps, selling the lie a bit too hard. Gill squeezed his hand in warning, and Hugh subsided, still muttering curses under his breath.

Alcott did not appear to notice, his face mask-like in the harsh, red glare of the emergency lighting. A muscle at the corner of his left eye twitched. At last he turned, and walked out of the building. His men followed; soon there was no one left but Gill and Hugh, still kneeling on the floor amid ruin of what had once been the rear loading dock.

Gill let out a shaky breath and sagged against Hugh's shoulder, exhausted. "Oh, god, I am so fired," she said.

"I'll pay for the damages," Hugh said wearily. He shoved himself upright and tugged Gill up after, his broad hands warm and steadying. "I still can't believe Alcott bought it."

"The best lie always has a basis in truth. Which reminds me . . . " Gill reached up into her hair and tugged the data rod from her palmtop free. "This is yours," she said, handing the rod to Hugh. "I'm just sorry we couldn't transfer all of your grandfather's research before you had to delete it."

"Not enough time," Hugh said, his voice laced with regret. He gripped the rod tightly before tucking it into the inside pocket of his jacket. "Well. At least we managed to save something."

Gill turned to look down the hall toward ethnographic storage, its door still sealed tight, protecting its contents. "Follow me," she said. "There's something I need to show you."

"Oh, my god," Hugh said, and ran the wooden mallet around the rim of the singing bowl until it produced a steady, vibrating hum strong enough to make Gill's ears ache.

"We always assumed they were ceremonial," Gill said. "There haven't been many recovered, and they're almost always in pieces. Nobody ever guessed they might have a practical purpose."

"Well, there's no reason they would have," said Hugh. "Unless you play exactly the right combination of notes in exactly the right spot, it's not going to do squat except make a pretty noise."

"Manipulating matter and energy with sound," she said, shaking her head in astonishment. "That's just fantastic."

"Who else knows about the bowl?" Hugh asked.

"You, me, Valerie. That's it. It wasn't even listed on the official manifest, just like the rest of your grandfather's things."

"We need to keep it that way. Alcott is going to watch us both very closely until he's done having his flunkies go through every scrap of data left on the tablet core. If we want to beat him to the punch, we need to move fast."

"Beat him to the punch," Gill repeated, then shook her head. "No," she said. "No, I can't. I'm in enough trouble as it is."

"You're going to be in even more trouble once Alcott finds out we messed with the data core," Hugh pointed out. "And believe me, he *will* find out. I didn't have time to cover my tracks well, and Alcott has some very clever people working for him. We are both looking at long-term incarceration in a military detainment facility."

Gill's legs went wobbly beneath her; she sat down atop a stack of boxes before her knees could give way completely. "Why couldn't you have just been cute but dumb as a bag of hammers?" she said.

Hugh smiled crookedly, and sat down beside her. "I'm going to miss the post-season," he said, his blue eyes suspiciously bright. "We have a good shot at the Cup this year, too."

There were sirens in the distance; someone must have heard the explosion, seen the smoke, and called emergency services. "You know, we should probably leave before they get here," Gill said.

"Yeah," Hugh said. "I'm liking that plan."

Gill rose to her feet and brushed ineffectually at the dust coating her clothes and hair. "Right," she said. "Where to next?"

Hugh ran a blunt fingertip around the rim of the bowl, making it hum softly. "I was thinking—Charybdis."

Gill opened her mouth. Closed it.

"Fine," she said at last. "But I want a shower first."

Elizabeth Kate Switaj teaches English at ShengDa College in China's Henan Province. She has previously taught ESL in Brooklyn and Japan. Her writing reflects her travels and the things her students have taught her using the language she teaches them, and it has appeared in numerous small press publications, including Gratitude with Attitude, Lines and Stars, Xelas Magazine, Hamilton Stone Review, Euphemism, *and* Diagram. *Her chapbook,* The Broken Sanctuary, *is published by Ypolita Press.*

Introduction to the Findings of Team 150B-T.2U by Raiden Mesc Gerarti

by Elizabeth Kate Switaj

I'm one of the few neurotypicals left who hasn't been altered. I'm not sure why it worked out that way. Maybe it's because these dis-orders—Janey's the one who insists on the word, with the hyphen—are genetic, and maybe you had to be a bit "messed up" to see the value in it and not have your own kids given "perfect" genetic codes. Well, my parents were just poor, but you know, some would have you believe that's a disease too. It certainly makes some people uneasy.

I don't know. I'm still learning. Janey has opened my eyes to so much I never knew before. The last time I visited her out in the field, I found her rocking in her tent. That used to frighten me, but this time I just asked her what was wrong, and she told me that the Dig Authority was sending out an advanced crew in light of some of her recent findings.

"That's wonderful," I said. "It means they've recognized what you've done here. Knowing that someone like you can make important discoveries will help change people's minds."

"Are you kidding? The advanced crews are all altered. They'll get all the credit."

"But maybe you can use this to lobby the authority into giving you a position on an advanced crew."

I had sat down beside her on the sleeping bag, but she stood up so that she could stare at my forehead; she'd told me before not to try to make eye contact when she didn't initiate it, but it was still difficult to remember. "Rai, I don't want to be on an advanced crew. I want my crew. The way an advanced crew thinks—we'll never get answers about this place."

"You think this is an important place."

She stopped rocking and nodded. "For a theory I have."

"Well, you know the Institutions we have now? I think that as close as a hundred years ago, their functions were divided into different small 'i' institutions: hospitals for health, colleges for education, something else for criminal reform—maybe correctionals."

"Wait, I thought those were all names of institutions."

"They are—of types of small 'i' institutions."

"So what was this place?"

She shook her head. "That's why it's so important. I think it was transitional. It seems mostly like a college, but there are beds in some places, and some other things. I'm not sure, though. That's why I need more time."

"When does the advanced crew arrive?"

"Whenever the hell they feel like it." She shrugged. "Sure, I have people on my team who freak the hell out whenever they have a sudden change in schedule, but they're not as important as the great altereds."

"Have you told them yet?"

"No. I just found out myself."

She grasped the small watch that hung around her neck on a silver chain. "Dinner's in twenty. I guess I'll tell them then. You coming?"

I reached out to touch her cheek. "Honey, I was kind of hoping we could have a private dinner . . . "

Janey smiled. "I'd like that, too, but . . . well, we'll put in a half hour and then come back, OK? Make the announcement, deal with the fall out, and come back here. Besides," she whispered close to my ear, "I don't think we'd eat much having a private dinner." She grabbed her hairbrush from the corner, next to her laptop, and sat on my lap. "In the meantime, would you brush my hair?"

I undid her waist-length braid. It had taken me years to learn how to be gentle enough, starting with the ends and working my way up, smoothing the strawberry honey strands. I once asked her why she sat through all those times when I hurt her. She said it made a nice picture. That's my Janey: once she gets an idea in her head, she goes after it full force.

"I've never seen your hair so wavy," I said.

"I haven't taken it down since the last time your were here, Rai."

"You're taking care of yourself, right?"

"The schedule wouldn't let me forget to eat."

I patted her under her breasts. "I don't know. I think I feel some ribs."

"Anyone else . . . " she laughed as my fingers moved to tickle her. "You're silly."

"Mmhmm. Do you mind leaving your hair down tonight?"

"Not if that's what you want. Besides, don't you hear the bells?"

"Faintly. Why?"

"Dinner time."

She led me through a small town of patched and colorful tents to a sky blue tarp where several rickety tables held metal vats. Though rolls of steam prevented me from seeing what was beneath, I knew it was all vegan: that's how Janey had used her adaptation credits. I'm not entirely sure that she really had to. In high school, I'd thought she was neurotypical until the earthquake hit our senior year and, after she'd basically organized all our rescue and triage efforts for three days until the Californian teams showed, I found her rocking behind the leaking tents. Janey probably could've managed in an altered school if they didn't actually do genetic tests before admission. Our university, where she started out and I eventually transferred, was one of the few that accepted both altereds and plains; it was the lowest tier for them, the highest for us. For all Janey's genius—maybe because of it—she was a target. By the time I got there, she had learned not to believe everyone who said they loved her, and she almost didn't believe me.

On the other hand, the one time I kissed her after eating a hamburger, she did in fact faint. We saw the wrong doctor then, or else we might have had a daughter. Of course, she might never have finished grad school then.

Janey looked at her watch again. "Only a minute more."

When we'd first started dating, when we met up again after three years of university, this sort of thing would've struck me as odd: everyone waiting by ready food (and everyone was there, except for the cook). But with this crew, her third, I hadn't even needed to be told that it was the cook's adaptation.

"Ten seconds."

"Do you have your watch calibrated to the cook's?"

She shook her head. "Mine's two minutes ahead."

The cook came out of an amethyst tent, bearing a plastic bin of utensils. She placed large slotted spoons in the now slightly less steamy vats and dumped the smaller spoons beside the plastic beige plates. Janey and I were the last in line. In front, the first officer, who had shaved her head so that she wouldn't have to wash it for two hours each morning, passed each serving utensil between her hands ten times before scooping herself out some food; it had been twenty the last time I visited. Janey had been working with Officer 'Skia on that, because it really bothered the officer in charge of water analysis and environmental impact, a fuchsia-haired man whose name I hadn't yet figured out, because it sounded different every time I heard it (including each time he said it).

Within five minutes (I know, because that's what the cook shouted out as he slipped Pyrex covers over the food to save it for those less oriented to time), we were all sitting cross-legged, eating piles of fruits, vegetables, and protein shaped into seven-pointed stars. I was one of the few people sitting there who mixed the stars and veggies; most, Janey included, kept them neatly distinct. Maria, the communications officer, held forth for a while on basketball, not even stopping her review of the previous week's games to acknowledge latecomers. Finally, everyone had arrived, and Janey stood up, leaving her half-finished food beside my knee.

"I know you're all eating, but I need to talk a little. I hope you don't mind me mixing up activities, but this is a very important announcement, and I wanted you all to know as soon as possible so that you can start readjusting your expectations. I just heard from central command, and we're not going to be at this site for very much longer." There were a few shouts of "what," "why," "when," and maybe even a "how."

"They told me an advanced crew is coming to take over, because they now see this sight as warranting that sort of . . . attention. Unfortunately, they didn't give me an exact date; they usually don't. In my experience, it could be a few days or a few weeks—probably not more than a month. They'll tell us exactly how they want to run the transition; they may require us to do some tasks for them, so if you might have trouble with that, please let me know, as I'll be arranging our end of it. Thanks and . . . sorry."

She sat down beside me and started eating again. In the general silence, I put my hand on her shoulder. Finally, one of the junior officers started talking about a necklace she'd found that day. It had a broken clasp but otherwise sounded like your usual costume jewelry, with charms shaped like ballet slippers, bunnies, and other pretty things. Really, I'm not sure how she found enough to say about it to go on and on.

I had long since emptied my plate when Janey finished her food and carried our dishes to the tubs of soapy water that the cook had placed where the clean dishes had been. "OK," she spoke loud enough for everyone to hear, "I'm taking my boy back to my tent, which means that if you want to tell me anything before you see me outside my tent again, you need to leave me a note in the box outside my tent. Is that clear?"

There were a couple shouts of no, so she said, "I'm not leaving my tent until morning at least, and no one is to come in. Leave a note in my box if you want to tell me something sooner than that." She held my hands as I stood up, and then she led me back into her tent.

"So can we take you out of that damn uniform now?" Janey didn't require anyone else to do so, but she always wore the navy blue jumpsuit when on dig.

"Only if we can get you out of yours." I was always in a white T-shirt and black jeans on my days off.

"You first."

"OK." She slipped a hand under my shirt and start working it up.

"That isn't what I meant."

"Sorry." She used the other hand to help ease it over my head and down my arms. "Brain damage, you know."

I wrapped my arms tight around her waist. "Do they know that they've given you the perfect excuse to do whatever you please?"

"Probably not." She lightly stroked down my naked back. "Besides," she slipped one hand down the back of my jeans. "I don't exactly need an excuse."

I sighed. "That feels nice." She pressed her other hand between us and slowly unbuttoned my fly. "My, someone's impatient tonight."

"Hmm, well . . . " She slipped my jeans and boxers down, and I stepped out of them. "You haven't been out her in almost a month."

"I'm sorry. I've been busy . . . "

"Shh." She reached up and placed two fingers against my lips. "I know your work is important, and I'd never want to get in the way."

"Honey, you're important." I sucked on her fingers for a bit. "It's just . . . you've got me naked."

"And I'm still clothed." She looked down and then back at me—this time into my eyes. "What? Do I have to do all the work."

"Yes."

"Fine." She lay down on her sleeping bag and stretched out on her back. "Maybe I'll just read." She started fiddling with her wrist-top.

"No." I knelt down beside her and started undoing the buttons down her front. "See? I'll help you."

She smiled. "Well, in that case, maybe you should kiss me while you do that." I took her invitation. She came as close as any human I've ever known to a proper cat's purr. "You're shaking," she said after I'd had her naked for a while.

I pulled back and looked at her. "So are you."

She shook her head. "Shivering a little."

"I guess it is cold. I hadn't really noticed. You're so . . . "

"Shh."

"Fine." I smiled and stroked her cheek. "You're beautiful."

She rolled her eyes.

"What?"

"You're sweet."

"But cheesy?"

"No, I . . . it really is sweet."

"Honey, I know I'm cheesy. It's OK. Just get up for a second, would you?"

"What? Why?"

"So we can get in the sleeping bag and stop shivering."

She slowly stretched to standing, rubbing her body up along mine. "OK." I slipped in first and held up the open end with one arm so that she could climb into my arms at the same time she got into the bag. She'd say more, I think, but I'm not one to say too much about these things.

Besides, the really interesting things happened the next morning. I guess my jetlag was worse than I'd realized, because I woke to find myself alone in the tent (though Janey had left me a plate of fruit).

I wandered down to the dig sight, figuring that's where she would be. When I reached the ridge, I was shocked. The last time I'd visited, there was one main building emerging, but since then, work had spread to several other sites. One didn't even seem to hold a building but, rather, a number of old bricks laid flat and a few contorted shapes around the edges. Janey was down among them, wearing a rope harness, removing some of the bricks.

I came to the edge of the pit and stood beside the earthen stairs. "Hey, honey, how's it going?"

"Don't come down here," she shouted back.

"OK. What are you digging up?"

"A plaza of some kind, but there are tunnels underneath, so it isn't all that stable."

"You're still gathering data?"

"I'll gather data until the altereds show, and I've been backing it up to my own hardware all along. Look, babe, I love you, but I need all the daylight I can get, so you're on your own until dark. I mean, I even begged cook to let everyone who was willing skip lunch."

"Mind if I wander around a bit then?"

"Just don't get hurt."

I watched her remove a few more bricks and slowly let herself down into the area below. It seemed to consist of concrete and tubes. "I could say the same thing to you," I muttered.

Across the first site from where she was working were three pits that appeared to contain the tops of multi-story buildings. A few of these showed evidence of beds. Most of the junior officers appeared to be working in these areas, under the supervision of Officer 'Skia, who was typing rapidly on her wrist-top.

A green-haired officer stopped working and shouted, "Hey, I found some needles."

"Right. Great," 'Skia shouted back. "Use your wrist-top to capture an image, collect samples for chemical analysis, and record all the data. The captain wants us to wait on everything else until dark. Got it?"

"Yeah . . . I suppose."

"Hey, you're doing great, and it seems like an important find—likely to support the captain's theory, but we're on limited time here. The more we find, the more we have to work with once the altereds get here. It's our only way to beat them. You with me?"

"Yes, ma'am."

'Skia glanced up at me and smiled. "You're not trained in any of this, are you?"

"No ma'am. Not crazy enough."

She laughed. "What exactly is it that you do? I mean, besides make our captain very happy."

"I run a task force on homelessness. It's the one public service they'll let naturals touch."

"Right. I thought there was a story some years ago about how they'd eliminated homelessness?"

"Among altereds."

"With every advantage given to them, you'd think that would've happened more than a few years ago."

"You know, I'm not even sure it's true now, but don't tell anyone I said that."

She shook her head. "We've been away from civilization for a while. Has it gotten that bad?"

I nodded. "This is the most civilized place I know."

"Well, I'd better get to work. Our captain is very . . . goal-oriented, you know."

"I do know that."

I wandered over to a round pit. A dig down to concrete had revealed a terraced structure, as if it were an amphitheater, but the remains of plastic chairs suggested there'd been a roof at some point. The whole dig was new to me, right down to the platform now covered by a green tarp. I bent over to try to get a peek under it, not realizing that Janey was standing behind me.

"It's what's under there that gave me the idea—though I'm telling everyone it's the beds."

"What?"

"The beds, well, I think those are just a requirement for almost any kind of institution; I don't think they make it transitional, but if you look under there, it's a lecture hall or an execution chamber."

"Just like in any Institution now: the bodies of criminals are . . . "

"Not quite like what we have now: we worked that site clean. There's no way it could've been used as an operating theater. There are no scrub stations, no tools . . . "

"I see. Janey, it's not that I don't like talking to you, but I thought you were driving hard to get as much data as you could."

She smiled and sighed. "The truth is that I have enough that I'm not sure what's going to happen. I mean, if they figure out what I can use it to prove . . . " She handed me a memory ring, and I slipped it onto my small finger. "I wanted to make sure you had the basics of it. If anything happens, get this out there."

"If anything happens?"

"This could challenge our understanding of what institutions are: of what they have been and so of what they can be or even if they have to be."

I nodded. "So you want me to leave."

"No, but I need you to get out of here before they show up."

I hugged her very tight. "Be careful. You know there's not a lot I can do if . . . "

She kissed the finger that held the ring. "You'll do the most important thing. I mean, you'll pass this on."

"So I'd better get going then?"

She nodded. "You're lingering."

"I know."

We probably kissed some more, and that was the last I saw of her. I know the site they were sent to the next week was in a flood plain, and I even believe that it was most likely a natural flood, but we have the technology to see it ahead of time: they should've been warned, and Janey's obsessive about checking for alerts. I know there won't be an investigation. Even if there were, they'd find a way to blame it on the team's "defects." So I'm doing what she said and publishing her findings, along with the two emails she sent me between then and the time of her apparent death.

Philip Raines and Harvey Welles have had stories published in The Year's Best Fantasy, Lady Churchill's Rosebud Wristlet, Albedo One *and* Challenging Destiny. *Phil Raines is a member of the Glasgow Science Fiction Writers Circle.*

The Dam
by Harvey Welles and Philip Raines

"So it's a fish."

"That's not a fish, Ama—it's not moving. And it's red. And there are no red fish in our lake."

"So it's a fish that's resting from a trip from a long way away, Jaja."

"And what would you know of a long way away? And look at the size of it! That's as big as a boat—"

"—or the mosaic on the refectory wall—"

"—or a—*rooftop*—"

The two boys scramble up the steep hillside from the shore road, right up to the treeline. From up there, the whole bowl of lake is open to them, walled by the crags of the steep hills, disappearing to their right in a sharp bend around which a streambed shuffles upwards through the forest, blocked to their left almost a kilometer downstream by the brim of the dam. So early in the afternoon, the sun is only just rising behind them and the dark red square below the water's surface is still in shadow.

But it is definitely a rooftop.

The next day and the days after, Amazu and Jaja sneak away from the dam in the mid-afternoon—between Good Thinking and Community Spirit classes—and watch the red squares emerging from the water. It's their secret, their first secret since the night the two of them sneaked out of their dormitory and went fishing. With the continuing drought, the water level at the top end of the lake is dropping so fast that by the end of that week several rusty sections of corrugated iron are peeking above the water. Thirty years after the dam was built and the valley flooded, the village is coming back to the surface.

A little older at eleven, and always much more adventurous than Amazu, Jaja rattles the rooftops with pebbles. His friend has a better arm, but Amazu joins in when the water has sunk low enough to reveal windows, their glass scummed with algae, drying mud, the splashing of the lake's mudfeckles. They wait for the line of shadow to retreat and when there's a new flash of sunlight under a rooftop, they throw stones until one of them smashes glass.

But they stop the first time they see someone behind one of the windows.

"Man or woman?"

Amazu can't tell. Two small white hands hold the window sill tightly. It's easier to guess when they spot the next figure standing in a window—her face presses up against the glass, weeds making her hair longer. She seems to wait patiently, completely still, for the water to go down.

The village gradually shakes itself free of the lake. Water streams out of the two-story windows, fresh green and brown streaks cover the yellow-painted timber. Streetlamps rise from the water, to Amazu, like the shaggy tentacles of some underwater beast, but when the sun blazes and the weeds drop off and their sleek original forms are revealed, it's just as fantastical to him. Having lived nearly his whole life in the dam, Amazu has never seen street lights before.

He and Jaja bet on the sex of the figures behind the windows. Jaja wins most of the time, and Amazu wonders if he might be cheating, using some unfair advantage.

"Well, I'm not."

"You probably don't even realize it, Jaja."

"Then why don't you guess the next one on your own. OK?"

The next one is not behind a window. Between the buildings, a wide-brimmed sunhat pokes through the water, a hat that doesn't float off when a breeze ripples the lake. "That's a woman's hat," Jaja suggests, forgetting what they've agreed.

But Amazu suddenly refuses. He won't bet on this one. Instead, he waits until after his early evening shift. With a lot of pleading, he persuades Kambiri, his grandmother, to follow him along the lake road and up the hillside, now steeped in a warm sunset light that makes everything look as parched as the earth. She curses and threatens him all the way up the slope, but Amazu knows that she's spry enough to make the climb.

"Is that him, Gran?"

Kambiri winces at the family title, but doesn't chastise. She knows he can just as equally lecture her on the cigarette she's now rolling (*A pure body for a pure Union!* Abebi, the Citizens Health instructor, would say).

She shields her eyes against sunset glare and watches the figure in the sunhat standing in the village street. The water is only just below the neck now and the hat trails a weed garland, but Amazu can see that it is a man. He seems to watch them back.

"Yes, that's the old bastard." Kambiri spits out loose tobacco. "Your grandfather. Still wearing the hat he stole from me."

Amazu doesn't want to talk about his grandfather, but when Fola asks the class of children about the flooded village, he knows he's been set up.

Each day, after Fola has explained about the synergy of moments or read from the Good Citizens Manual for Union, she asks for stories to share. Amazu hates these "experience circles"—what could he tell the rest of the class? An unusual animal carcass, a strange piece of wash from the village he's found in the slipways? Kambiri's latest fights with the rest of her maintenance team? There have adventures with Jaja—*small* adventures, but big enough for the imagination of the two of them—but they've promised each other not to tell those to anyone. So Amazu usually sinks into his shadow and stares at the dashing figures on the classroom wall mosaics, striding forth to explore amazing new worlds with their cries of *Looking backwards is going backwards!* and *To see the future with your eyes is to hold the future in your hands!* It's easy—the twins and triplets in the class are so eager to tell their tales of exploring the other side of the dam that there's no time for Amazu to bumble through his apologies.

But today, Fola changes the circle—today, she tells them a story, or rather gets them to tell the story for her. And it's a story from *long ago*, something she has never done before.

"So who can tell me who was in the village when the valley was flooded?" she says in her tiny singsong voice which always sounds larger with the faint echo of other voices, as if an invisible choir is peeking behind her words.

"Individualists!"

"People who wouldn't let go of the past!"

"Those who turned away from Union!"

A cataract of replies come from the other children, perfectly timed so they neither interrupt nor leave a breath's gap with each other. They sit upright with their brothers or sisters in their bright-green blazers and newly-ironed white shirts, sometimes shimmering as if the lights in the class directly above them are flaring, stripping them down to almost angelic natures.

Fola claps her hands, delighted. "And who can say why they won't let go of the past?"

"Because one person only sees in one direction!"

"Because it's easier to look at what you've already seen than look at something new!"

"Because they don't understand that a Union can see everywhere at once—"

"—and everywhere new!"

Another tiny run of applause from Fola, like a dozen people clapping singly in quick succession. She's a little heavier today, not the usual grasshopper slenderness, and her nose is odd, as if it's been broken and re-set wrong. Amazu is probably the only one in the room to notice these details. Standing apart from everyone else makes it easier to spot the differences. He doesn't enjoy the same rhythm linking the others together, hands moving in synchronicity, shared smiles as twins and triplets speak at the same time, smiles that say that what they're saying doesn't really have to be said aloud.

"Now—who can talk about *anyone* they know in the village?"

Silence. They don't turn to look, but Amazu can almost see their necks twitch in unison. Even Fola doesn't look his way, which annoys Amazu most of all, because her *anyone* means him.

118

Only Jaja has the courage to stare at him. Amazu stares back—a dirty look. He knows now who caught him showing Kambiri the village.

"My grandfather," Amazu replies, though he doesn't want to, though he knows he can't not do, and the collective sigh of relief feels so strong that the edges of the classroom posters and the paper lanterns Fola used to demonstrate multi-dimensional space and even the distant leaves on the hills outside, still stubbornly clinging onto the dry trees, all flutter together.

"My grandfather refused to come to the dam," Amazu continues.

"But your parents came!"

"Kambiri came!"

"And you came!"

I didn't come, I was brought—but Amazu knows that everyone there wants to help him, Jaja most of all, though he won't look at his friend, and everyone wants to say, *then your parents went*, and *Kambiri will go*, and Jaja wants to shout finally, *and you will go too!*

And he can't resist—why would he? More than anything else, he wants Union, to have his own brothers and sisters—and who wouldn't? So Amazu says, "My grandfather didn't believe in the Union, but my parents do, and Kambiri does and—" but he doesn't get far before the boys and girls in their impossibly spotless clothes drown out his words with a cheer much bigger than the voices of the twenty children there.

The ovation is still ringing inside him when he visits Kambiri in the southside generation chamber.

"Fola said I did very well in class today. I talked about grandfather."

"Fola let you talk about the past?" She grunted. "Wouldn't have done that when I was a kid."

Kambiri is crouching under a glassed coil under one of the four turbines in the southside array. Halfway up a massive pipe on a gantry that runs the length of the cavernous generation chamber, Amazu wonders how he can hear his grandmother above the tons of water pumping through the pipe, but then she's always been good at making herself heard.

"I think I could do better," Amazu continues, ignoring her, "if you told me more about him."

That grabs Kambiri's attention. She slides out of the small space and gets to her feet in a series of fluid motions. "I clean the mighty engines, little 'zuzu, I don't teach little noise-boxes."

"It's your duty to teach me. My parents aren't here so you have to."

"I didn't promise them anything when they went to Union."

"They probably didn't think they had to ask you."

Kambiri's eyes narrow to small screws so tight that Amazu thinks even the screwdriver in her hand could not shift them. "Did you learn to disrespect your elders from your father?"

"My mother. Just as she learnt to disrespect her elders from *her* mother."

Amazu and his grandmother have a small crowd by this point—Ezeji, Amachi, the others in Kambiri's maintenance crew, all those who hadn't yet gone to Union. They smirk when they hear Amazu chastise Kambiri. Ezeji jokes, "I can see why this family has trouble making Union."

"And I can see why you have trouble getting out of bed," Kambiri snarls at him. Ezeji has the reputation of being the laziest man in the whole dam—the reason he's not made Union yet. "Scatter, minnows, else I might infect you with our family curse."

Laughing, the others move back to their tasks. All around the generation chamber, maintenance crews are working on turbines, coils and cables, the towering battery stores lining the bare rock of the cliffs. Above the competing humming of different machines, Amazu can hear the other crews singing, not their own songs, but joining in the same song, a children's nonsense rhyme reworked with lyrics about the joy of a good day's labor. Teams blend together, the traces that distinguish a brother or sister submerging in a common noise, and for a moment, all the team's voices join into a single sound.

"Is it true grandfather designed all of this?"

"Never by himself. He coasted on a good research team." Kambiri angrily binds a sweaty scarf tighter around her forehead. "And what else is there to say about Hogan?"

"Well, his name. I didn't know he was called Hogan."

"That's not what I call him."

"What do you call him?"

"You're too young for that kind of language."

120

Amazu frowns. "But why *didn't* he come? If he helped build the dam, why did he stay?"

Kambiri's face weakens and Amazu can see a sudden memory appear—the thing he's hoped for—but then fade, too brief to know if it was happy or sad. "Your grandfather would ask why the rest of us went," is all she says before climbing deep under the machinery to get away from his questions.

You can't hide from me forever, Amazu wants to tell her—but then he regrets feeling so resentful, because it is what Jaja wants to tell him as well when the two of them are clearing the spillways later that afternoon.

"Are you angry with me?"

"*Who can be angry with Union?*"

"I was worried about you, Ama. The village is a dangerous place."

"*The way to Union is long and dangerous but joyous! joyous! joyous!*"

"This is silly."

Jaja falls silent, so Amazu stops quoting from the cartoon they both loved when they were younger, though they are now a little too conscious to admit enjoying something so childish. It's something he normally values in his friend—he won't talk about his experiences the way the others do. If there's nothing to say, Jaja's happy to be quiet.

His turn today, so Amazu climbs down the small metal ladder to one of the concrete slipways across which a little run-off is spreading like a sheet. Above him, the jaws of the water trap are embedded in the dam like monster's teeth, and far, far below, the water becomes spray above the fan of the dam's base. Secure on the climber's rope held by Jaja, he focuses on picking the bits of branch, weed, and the leaves that are still dropping this late into the drought, the ones that refuse to move until the very end, trapped in the pocked surface of the concrete. On some days, he'd find something has tugged loose from the flooded village and rolled slowly across the lake's bottom to the dam—a glove or a rucksack, once a full bottle of wine—but not today, which is a relief to Amazu. He doesn't want Jaja to have an excuse to talk about the village. Occasionally, he looks up from his work to wipe away the sweat, steals a half glimpse of bigger hills and thicker forests than the ones he's grown up with around the lake, all the way to the horizon.

Coming up the metal ladder, Amazu manages to be too puffed and busy with their bag of trash to have to talk, but on top of the dam's ridge, Jaja tries again. "Don't be dumb as a root—why do you think they flooded the village? It's *contaminated*."

Over the metal banister, Amazu sees across the blue as deep as shadow, as glassy as volcanic rock, and he remembers a day when the two of them ignored the warnings and dropped fishing lines into the churn above the turbines. Fola and the other teachers go on about the importance of sharing moments in Union, so Amazu has always treasured a night when he and Jaja started and finished each other's actions as if they were timed to the same heartbeats. But Amazu is distracted and his gaze is drawn further up the lake to a hazy point where dark shapes are clearly visible—houses, streets, figures. The whole village is exposed now.

"And if you go there you'll be contaminated, Ama."

That was how Kambiri described it as well—*your grandfather is contaminated with the past*, as if the past was like a cold or a sadness that reduced you to your bed and contracted the future. Amazu remembers how he used to love getting sick so he could stay at home and avoid Fola's lessons.

Amazu walks away from Jaja. "And if you're contaminated, you can't join me in Union!" Jaja shouts behind him, so Amazu runs down the walkway that is the dam's spine, but Jaja manages to be there ahead of him at the southside door, still crying, "*No Union!*" in work overalls that look like they've just been scrubbed. Amazu ignores him and goes down the stairs and along the corridor, going right past Jaja at the turn-off to the generator chamber, and again in the toilets at the accommodation block, before finally coming breathless to the refectory where Jaja joins him in the line for dinner, already changed out of his work clothes into his deep-green tunic and drawstring trousers.

By now, he's too tired to argue anymore. Jaja grins as if nothing's happened. Amazu isn't sure they're still fighting—or maybe there really wasn't a fight, at least not with Jaja standing here, wondering if it's fried bananas for dessert tonight. Amazu can't decide if Jaja is pretending or not—but he doesn't want to fight, not with Jaja, not ever, so Amazu pretends too and they steal a third plate of fried banana and laugh all the way to their benches.

*　*　*

"If you're still interested."

"You've changed your mind, Kambiri?"

She shrugged, meaning, *No harm in telling the little one a little history.* "But."

"Fola says there's trouble coming whenever someone starts a sentence with *but*."

"*But*," Kambiri hissed, "you'll have to do something."

"Family shouldn't haggle, Grandmother."

"They shouldn't have to *repeat* themselves either."

But—Kambiri has snatched Amazu's interest so he goes with her back up the shore road in the small pick-up truck she's bullied Ezeji into lending her. They have nowhere else they have to be that afternoon because the southside generator is being rested. Amazu worries that Jaja might follow, but he hasn't seen his friend all day. For a while, he relaxes, but as they approach the village, he watches his grandmother tense.

On the back of the truck is a huge drum coiled with rope. Amazu assumes that it's for a maintenance job until Kambiri takes one end of it and starts an engine in the drum that spits out a fat length of slack. "Tie this to your waist. Like this—so it won't tighten in a noose."

The rope is thin and light, but there is an awful lot of it. "Are you using me as bait, Kambiri?"

"And what would make a meal of a minnow like you?"

Amazu glances towards the hazy shimmer of the two dozen buildings clustered in the middle of the lake. "I don't think I want to find out."

They stand on the pebbled edge of the shore. The lake has pulled downstream towards the dam, creating a new shore that's cut by streams and broken by drying bumps of weed and mud.

"Put these on too." She hands him a pair of thick rubber boots that nearly go up to his knees. They are difficult to get on but they do fit snugly.

"Now do you want to know why he stayed?" she asks him.

Amazu hasn't grown up with secrets. He knows why his parents went to Union and why he hasn't yet and those two simple thoughts have never left much room for secrets until now. Secrets are bits of the past sticking to your shoes, slowing you down as you try to go forward. For the first time, Amazu feels the presence of a past that can't be easily dismissed. He understands that such things can only be removed by facing them—and he understands that understanding this is a crossing point in becoming an adult.

"Yes, I do."

"Then go ask him."

"And what do I ask him?"

"The past, if you want."

"Ask someone about the past? Wouldn't have done that when I was a kid."

"Cheeky. Then ask him for my watch back."

"Your *watch*? And what about your hat? And anything else he took?"

"Tell him he can keep your yapping mouth in exchange." She feeds out the rope. "Just ask. And mind—don't go into any of the houses."

Amazu knows that if he stops and thinks about this he will lose his courage. Jaja would just leap off the rocky edge of the shore and stomp forward. It would be easier if Jaja were here and this was one of their adventures and now Amazu begins to regret not telling his friend.

But at this first crossing point, Amazu doesn't want to look any less a man in front of Kambiri and be pricked by some remark about how his father was just as soft-boned, so he sets his will. His first step disappears into a suck of mud and his second makes him momentarily fear getting stranded halfway across, but the third step finds more solid ground and by the fourth, Amazu begins to plot his course.

The course is like the doodles of lightning bolts he made in class when he was younger, rapid zig-zags that bring Amazu close to the new water's edge and then back along a stream. Back and forth, sometimes a fish's random trail, sometimes a sublime dance, slipping a few times, but always staying on his feet. Amazu never looks beyond the next burst of steps and his concentration is so great that he forgets the shore behind him and the distance to the village ahead. The length of rope, continually unrolled from the truck in a series of receding engine coughs, gets heavier and his bony waist starts to bruise. After a while, it's not a physical aching that bothers Amazu, but a strange, almost disembodied queasiness, like his body has moved violently one way, then back again in a blink, like the time he and Jaja went bungee-jumping with the older children from Great Perspective Point, high over the valley below the dam.

He knows what this is—this is *the past*, settling into him, infecting him. He concentrates on his steps. Soon enough, the mud starts to streak on more solid rock, until there's soon more rock than mud, enough to recognize that it's not rock, but tarmac. There comes a point where his boots are tracking mud on a village street and that's the point at which Amazu allows himself to look up.

The haze has gone but Amazu still doesn't believe in what he's seeing. Each house has a private vegetable garden, its own paths—they're too small to be dormitories and he guesses that individual families must have lived here. It's as if he's stepped into a photograph, and the thrill of stepping into the past makes him feel excited, a man of secrets.

The weed is gone, though a soggy stench pervades the air. He looks for the windows he and Jaja broke, but all the glass is whole. The village is restored, but quiet. Amazu knows it's not abandoned—he sees telltale scuttling behind windows, doors that edge back and forth with indecisive hands. Figures repeating their actions. A man and a woman coming forward to embrace in a doorway, breaking apart, returning to each other's arms. A boy not much older than four throwing a ball in the air, catching, releasing it again, and again. All of them are glowing—not the shimmer of the people on the dam, but a constant shine that barely lifts the gloom in each of the buildings. In *the past*, everyone is brighter.

The street is virtually empty. Only his grandfather Hogan is standing there, in the middle of the road.

Up close, his grandfather is not what he expected. From the one, admittedly out-of-focus picture he's stolen a look at in Kambiri's room, Amazu wouldn't have imagined this smiling, gentle-faced man. Nor would he have a expected a man looking so young, not much older than his parents. Amazu has only recently appreciated the span that distinguishes someone as old as his grandmother from younger women like Fola, let alone a boy like himself. Before they'd simply been all much older than he was. Now he realizes that there are many different kinds of older.

His grandfather is still wearing the sunhat but it's not doing much good—the dipping sun is blazing full on his face. *The past* no longer protects him, now that it's being exposed to *the present*, the world of the dam. His skin is so white and drawn, pulled to the skull that Amazu worries that the sun will weaken it and the skin will break like the fragile crust on boiled milk. His arms are bent strangely—one held out in front, the other crooked around empty space on his left. Like the others here, he's surrounded by a faint flickering aura.

He might be a statue, Amazu thinks. Maybe the arteries of individualists get so blocked with selfishness they go rigid and stupid. His grandfather surprises him though, saying, "But why would anyone want to go to the dam?"

"Kambiri said you would ask that."

"Look. We're all here. The machines are right this way. All we have to do is choose our moment."

Amazu nods solemnly, thinking that it's best not to argue with someone who's spent the last few decades underwater. "Anyway," his grandfather continues, still smiling broadly, "How can it get any better than this?"

One hand unwinds slowly like it's powered by mechanical springs. Amazu looks to where his grandfather points, but all he sees is lines of blue water blurring into a wobbly landscape. The surrounding hills and the lake downstream are now shuddering murkily.

Amazu tugs the knot at his waist, then whips the rope out to stop it snagging on one of the mounds of debris around him. The snaky rope jolts his grandfather. He blinks, reaches out to touch the air, confused by what he finds.

"Where's the water? Why isn't it so heavy?"

This time, it's Amazu who points to the retreating line of blue. His grandfather takes a few jerky intakes of breath, coughing with the surprise of how easily his lungs can expand.

"And why are you covered in mud, my little duck?" he asks, turning to Amazu, grinning, but looking a little surprised, as if it wasn't Amazu he meant to be talking to.

Amazu isn't sure whether he should call him Hogan or

Grandfather yet. "I came from across the lake."

His grandfather doesn't seem to be able to make sense of this. "You didn't come from the house? I don't understand. And why is the water down there, no, the water wasn't here, it was always over *there*, or I was over there and the water was *here*, and—"

He may not look it, but he's getting worked up just like an old man. "Do you know the time, sir?" Amazu quickly volunteers.

"Time, time, now is that the *here* time or the *there* time or—and where's my, my—"

His grandfather examines his wrist, puzzled that it's bare now. His body shivers with soft light again, and the skin is no longer white but freckled—happy with the sun, brown. "Well, it'll be back in the house. Not across the lake. Would you fetch it?"

His grandfather's dopey gaze leads back up the street, so Amazu picks out the house he thinks is right, snaps the rope again to make sure it's clear and walks across the street. The houses stand solid and back-to-back like threatened wolves, and he walks around until he finds one that's a little softer than the others.

Kambiri said don't go into the houses. But the door is open, a woman is calling, "*Come on now, come on now.*" A smell of dinner on the way invites—

As soon as Amazu steps through the door, his eyes are stunned by a kind of photoflash burst that leaves his head feeling sick. He puts a hand on the ache and stands on the threshold, staring at sunspots in the darkness that dissolve, leaving a core of angry red eyes that refuse to fade. For a moment, Amazu believes that a beast with a woman's voice but a monster's hunger has trapped him, but the red eyes blink on, off, on, off, and their regularity makes them lifeless. Machines in black plastic boxes, the size of packed suitcases, are tucked just inside the door. He knows about these machines—like the mighty engines Kambiri works on, only with a different purpose.

"*Come on now.*" Amazu hurries forward, stepping clear of the boxes and into the single room of the house's ground floor. The windows are shrouded with black curtains. Amazu waits for a mildew odor, the tang of decaying seaweed, but it's still the warm, smoky cooking that greets him. Inside, a veiled woman is sitting in a chair by the far wall, keeping the open casket company. Like his grandfather, she is vibrating with a dull light.

"*Come on now.*" She's not talking to Amazu, but to the body in the casket. Her husband is lying there. He should be up and helping to fix the roof, but he fell off the ladder and now she's uselessly pulling at his sleeve on the long mourning night before his burial. Why doesn't he stand up? Why can't she stand up too so she can fix the roof and go on with things?

This all comes to Amazu in a flash. There are so many things that are *not right* here, he can't run away from them all. The grief that floods him, making him want to sit down and weep and weep. The whiplash alternations between being *here* and *there*. A wheezy, ticking noise filling the room, that he knows comes from the machines at the doorway. They are contaminating him with *the past*, with the world that they loop around again and again, a permeable world into which Amazu can walk and be trapped. Its sensations seduce him. The ticking, the smack of freshly-cooked fish—

The last one feels best. He wants to tell Jaja about the fish, but he's yanked backwards, off his feet. Rubbing his head, Amazu sees the rope behind him tensing to drag him out of the house.

"OK, Kambiri, OK!" Amazu runs out of the house, shouting.

It's not Kambiri. "*Not that house!*" his grandfather yells at him, dropping the rope so he can point next door. "And don't use that tone with Kambiri, youngster."

The house next door looks just the same, only there's a child's toy trolley in the vegetable garden and there's no woman summoning him in. Amazu has learnt his lesson and hovers outside. He can hear the same sound of broken mechanical lungs, so he makes a little impatient dance, hopping from foot to foot, thinking that if he stays here long enough, his grandfather will come over and go inside himself. He hopes it won't be long because the fish will burn on the fire.

It works, but not the way he's expecting. "But why would anyone go to the dam?" his grandfather repeats, only the voice is from inside the house. His grandfather walks out, talking over his shoulder.

Amazu looks over to where he was and isn't any longer. "That was fast," he says as his grandfather goes past on the path, but the man doesn't hear him. He's calling over his shoulder to someone in the house.

Amazu is about to ask who he's speaking to but the fish is long past ready and his mouth is watering. He bends down to take the fish off its stick, licking his fingers as he jabs the skewer, to cool the burn, to savor the taste. The lake has moved closer to him again and is shining like it's full of fish fed on jewels and moonlight.

"It's ready!" he calls out to Jaja, who's standing at the doorway, between the two trees. Jaja makes a whoop like a night-swooper and Amazu makes one back and soon they are swapping bird cries. The lake is excited with light. The sky is a million stars spinning.

No one knows they're here and Amazu wants the evening to stretch as far as he can imagine. He wants to share this moment with someone, everyone, only he doesn't have to wish for it, there's already a crowd of Amazus with him, *here* and *there*. And in the instant, he knows: this is like one of Fola's demonstrations, this is the synergy of moments. This is what Union must be—

"Hey, hey!" Hogan shouts. "Not here—find your own house! This isn't *your* moment!"

He shoos Amazu away from the doorway. But as soon as the spell of Amazu's perfect day is snapped, Hogan stops in his tracks, almost forgets. "Look. We're all here. The machines are right this way. All we have to do is choose our moment."

He's still speaking to someone who isn't there, but Amazu understands. He has picked his moment in *the past* and stayed there. He has worked out how to be in bed all day and not have to go to classes. "How could it get any better than this?" his grandfather pleads. "It can't, can it?"

The watch is on his wrist this time. *The past* doesn't sit straight. Amazu wonders if the machines are working right. Hogan fiddles with his watch and Amazu sees him stop the time. "It can't get any better. Let's go. Let's go back into the house and make sure of that."

He points at the hills again, but Amazu keeps his attention fixed on the watch. He times his breathing, then his moment, then he springs— grabbing the watch out of Hogan's hands, and belting out of the village. Briefly, he's terrified that Hogan would grab his rope and heave him back—but he petrifies on the spot, lifting his hand to his sunhat, staring into the glare, face white and skeletal again.

The ground tries to stop him though, and Amazu, terrified, exhilarated, has to tear his feet out of the ground with each step. It feels like it's longer getting back, but he's breathing so crazily that he hardly notices the returning nausea, let alone the time.

"Where's my watch?"

Shivering, he lets Kambiri untie the rope, re-start the engine on the pick-up that tucks the rope onto its barrel. She loosens his grip and takes the watch, tousles his hair roughly.

"Did you get my sunhat?"

"No. You didn't pull me out of the house when I got trapped."

"Serves you right for not listening."

She sniffs, but Amazu ignores her. He's looking at the watch, which has rusted on the journey back. Salt marks and cracks cover the glass, but he can still see the hands stopped at the hour and minute set by Hogan. Kambiri barely glances at it before hurrying it away into a pocket in her overalls.

"I saw the machines. Little red lights."

"Hogan wanted every house to have a machine. Everyone to pick their own moment to wallow in. Damned fool got some idiots to agree, but the rest of us had sense—we wanted the dam."

Amazu tries to be grown up, get his breathing under control. "And are the machines why the village wasn't really flooded?"

"But you saw it—it was flooded." Kambiri smiles to herself. "And it wasn't."

More baffling adult double-talk. But Amazu knows what all grown-ups know: asking dumb questions only gets dumb answers. So he says, "He called me 'little duck.'"

"He called you that as well?" Kambiri snorts again. "Well, maybe you do look a bit like your mother after all."

Fola is the one to decide his punishment. She is thin again, as thin as a reed to crack against his back. All the other children look embarrassed for Amazu and won't meet his gaze. Their disappointment just makes him feel worse.

"One penalty for going to the village."

"My grandmother asked me do it."

Fola sighs. "Another penalty for not taking responsibility for your own actions."

"But I wanted to see Hogan—my grandfather—"

"And another for not taking responsibility for the truth. You wanted to see the past, not the person. Hogan is long downstream, Amazu."

He opens his mouth but sees a fourth penalty forming in Fola's mind, so closes it again.

The penalties translate into double shifts clearing the spillways for six days running. His shifts move back to early afternoon, the hottest time of the day, and Amazu is unsure whether this is another penalty or just bad luck. In the last half hour of each shift, he feels faint hanging from the bottom of his ladder, heady with visions of all the land that lies in the distance.

On the third day, Jaja finds a way of joining him without the others noticing. "You shouldn't be here," Amazu tells him curtly.

"I can take over."

"I don't need help."

"Take a break. Get some water and you can hold the rope for me. No one will know."

Amazu doesn't want his help, but he is very thirsty and is worried about the dizziness he gets when stretching for the difficult-to-reach branches, so he lets Jaja take his place. Jaja jauntily scoops up all the trash that Amazu had trouble clearing, doing his job in twice the time it's taken him.

Idly, Amazu thinks about letting him do the whole of his shift, but he is old enough to understand the importance of pride. "That's enough."

Upside down, Jaja looks at him from the end of the rope suspended over the spillway. "You can't be angry with me all the time."

"What I did in the village is my business."

"*My* business? You sound like an individualist."

Amazu smarts at the remark. Maybe children had to account for their whereabouts, but adults didn't. Anyway, it wasn't his fault, he wants to tell his friend, but deep down, he knows that Jaja already knows that. He knows that Jaja only ratted on him for his own good. After all, the village *is* dangerous—of all people, Amazu knew that.

But his anger isn't as easy as that.

"Do you remember the time we stayed away all night? We went fishing, we had a fire. It got dark but we stayed."

Jaja says nothing. He swings back and forth on the rope to get a bigger reach, forcing Amazu to steady himself against the railing.

"We saw fish jumping in the moonlight," Amazu persists.

The memory is suddenly precious, as is the thought that memory is a new thing for him. He knows that memories like this come along rarely, and with this, Amazu recognizes another mark of growing older. The memory's *here* and it's *there*, just as it was when he stood on the threshold of Hogan's house, the machine inside blowing air into the moment and making it balloon out into the present.

But Jaja won't play. "I don't remember."

"Yes, you do."

"I don't. And you won't either. There are so many more moments in the future. You'll see. Soon. It won't matter—"

"*But it does!*" Amazu is crying. At first, that's why he moves his hands, wiping tears, but the hands don't stop there. "I wanted that day to last."

"Days don't last. You've got to go forward. The future—"

Amazu expects the word to fall away, the last syllable to be pulled out like a bungee all the way down to the rocks and snap back at him. But the sound breaks suddenly as Jaja's body bounces off the point where the dam bends forward into rocks with a dainty bow of concrete skirts, finally coming to rest near the lookout point just below the waterfall from the southside chute.

Amazu throws the rope he's untied into the spray as if it's a snake. It is for a moment, the evil thing tumbling away from him and it hides in the shower rainbows. He tries to pick it out of the other debris at the dam's base and is still wiping his eyes and trying to find it when the adults come for him.

Jaja is with them—telling on Amazu again. It almost makes Amazu glad of what he's done, but everyone is so serious and disapproving that Amazu can't pretend for long. Jaja holds his arms around himself though it's still very hot, keeping his distance, silently watching Amazu as Fola comes to interrogate him. It's not an accusing look, not even one of shock, but sadness. Amazu glances over the railing, thinking he can follow the snake down, and sees Jaja there as well, leading a small group to the body. Jaja looks back up and though it's too far to be sure, it'll be the same look.

They punish him with severe isolation—locked in a room in the northside shore tower, looking down on the lake. A cheerful young woman he doesn't know brings him food, clears his waste bucket and changes his bed, and sometimes she holds his hand and cuddles him when he cries. Amazu tries to remember the night he and Jaja chased each other through the dark forest, but he can't. He wants to look forward to being sorry enough that everyone can forget what happened, but he can't. He's trapped in the moment squeezed into this room.

He knows he will get visitors. Fola is first, coming to cluck her tongue at him, so astonished by the behavior of her number one, her only real pupil, that she can't find the right Union teaching to quote. Some of the other pupils visit as well as if Amazu has always been a dear friend rather than simply a comrade, and Amazu endures twins and triplets reciting in unison the joys of Union, understanding that they, like Fola, like everyone, want him to join them in the future. And Amazu realizes that it's always the future. Always *there*, never *here*.

The visitor he expects but does not see is Jaja. Perhaps the dam's council has advised him not to come. That wouldn't stop him though— more than anything else in the world, Jaja would want to be with his friend. Amazu can sense him close—just out of sight down the corridor when Fola or the other children come calling, but unwilling to join them, or even allow himself to be seen.

Sometimes Amazu can hear Jaja talking to himself: a faint murmuring that Amazu listens to carefully in the hour before they bring his dinner. He can hear the voices fighting. How many versions are there? It's all the same voice, but Amazu can distinguish the subtleties. The cocky, more aggressive one, who's been traveling with a mapping team towards the coast, hundreds of kilometers from here—that Jaja would be telling them to leave Amazu. But not the quieter, loyal Jaja, the one that believes that the ultimate adventure would somehow involve the dam and so never left. And the Jaja who has learnt to dive in the lake and has been altered so he can breathe underwater, who's probably known about the flooded village for ages as he dared himself to swim across Hogan's forlorn gaze, he'd resist and stay behind.

More Jajas enter the argument, Jajas that want to leave, those that insist on remaining. There is only just a consensus not to defy the authorities and sneak a visit to Amazu. He wonders why they need to use speech. Fola explained how it worked to the class—to *him*, because all of the other children had already gone forward to Union with Jaja last year before the power ran out and the batteries had to be charged up again and some had to stay behind and Kambiri had volunteered the two of them without asking what Amazu thought. Fola drew lines on a paper, dividing it into squares, and in each square, she wrote Amazu's name in different scripts. That was Amazu in different *theres*. Then Fola did a neat folding trick with the paper and created a cube that she could manipulate with her fingers, bringing different *Amazus* together each time she brought her fingers together. That was what it was like in Union, the same Amazu sharing the same thoughts, experiences, across the different *theres*.

She used words to explain to Amazu that he won't need words in Union. He was so ashamed to be the one left behind. He's angry that Jaja is using words now, knowing that Jaja really wants Amazu in his cell to overhear how difficult it is to remain loyal to the past. And he wants Amazu to know that despite everything, all of them agree on the one thing: that Amazu can't be abandoned. Even the ones who want to go know that they will have to do something for their friend.

The visitors that Amazu does *not* expect are his parents—but they see him on his fifth day. He recognizes them from Kambiri's photos rather than his own dim memories. To avoid the inevitable awkwardness, they've thought carefully about this visit. They bring him presents from other places and Amazu suspects that they've agreed on a version of themselves that would feel relaxed with their son.

It's a version he can almost remember, and Amazu thinks that this must be deliberate as well. His father keeps inspecting the room, glancing out the window, always interested in new things, pointing out little details to his son. Amazu's mother frets around her boy, trying to get a stain out of his overalls, asking about his classes, and Amazu wonders if her caring is some kind of compensation for what her own mother never gave her.

Somewhere behind the kindness Amazu imagines his parents pooling their collective memories to find the right way to reassure him. They share their adventures with him—falteringly, as if they were relaying them from someone else. And Amazu is patient with them, as much out of respect for Kambiri as for any lingering memories. Amazu takes their presents graciously and doesn't ask them why they think he'd like these things. When they go, he hugs and kisses each one and all the other versions behind them and he says how much he looks forward to seeing them again when it's his turn to go through.

Eventually, Kambiri visits him.

"This is your fault," he tells her.

"Any more of that talk and they'll punish you again for dodging responsibility."

"You talk about responsibility and this is your first visit to your family. It's been a week."

"You talk about family and look at how you speak to me. Anyway, I didn't come alone."

Amazu sits upright, trying to peer behind his grandmother's back at the open door. "Not there," she says angrily and goes over to the window. "*There.*"

The view from the window is the same as always: a grey sheet of lake surface, the concrete incline of the dam stretching to the southside tower on the opposite shore, spartan trees on the hillside looking like the aftermath of a forest fire.

"The shore road," Kambiri whispers.

It takes a moment for his eyes to see Hogan, but when he does, he's amazed he hasn't noticed him before. A small, but determined figure, shuffling along the road towards the dam. He's pulling a toy trolley behind him stacked with boxes. It's too far away to see blinking red lights, but Amazu knows what they are.

"Why is he coming?"

Kambiri shakes her head—meaning that she knows a little but

won't say, and that she doesn't know too much so can't say. But she looks at her wrist, at the ruined watch there.

Hogan is shuffling, but he gets closer each day. It hurts Amazu's eyes to stare at him on long afternoons, his progress is too slow to measure, but he can feel his grandfather's approach. The day after Kambiri pointed him out, workers along the top of the dam keep stopping to check their watches and point to distant hills. The young woman who tends Amazu stops in the middle of a story about the kitchen to glaze over and say, "The machines are right this way, all we have to do is choose," and then break off, realize what's happened and run out of Amazu's room, crying.

It takes a little longer before Amazu experiences Hogan's presence but that night he dreams that Hogan is telling him that it can't get any better and persuading him back into the house. Kambiri's voice wakes him in the middle of the night: *Don't go into any of the houses.* Hogan is close enough for the moonlight to shine on his gritted teeth.

Kambiri's voice rouses him the following morning. "Come on. You're leaving."

Amazu yawns and then looks out the window. "Do you want to wave to him?"

"I know your father was a bad riser too, but I don't have time for this. Let's go. I have my shift."

"But no one has any shifts today, do they?"

Kambiri won't go near the window. She bows her head and nods. "No, no more shifts."

"Why?"

"Because you're leaving." She throws his linen shirt at him, stuffs the rest of his things into his knapsack. "Everyone's leaving."

"Union," Amazu whispers.

"Your grandfather is causing a disturbance. As usual."

"You could give him back the—"

Kambiri's eyes flash with anger and Amazu doesn't finish the suggestion. No, she couldn't.

She doesn't take him back to his dormitory, but to her small apartment, windowless, deep underwater—a place Amazu realizes that she must have spent imagining her lover, also underwater, less than a kilometer away. On the way there, people run past them, the normal shifts are suspended—the corridors are purring with the generators and excitement. Occasionally someone would smile at Amazu in passing or shout that they'd meet in Union tomorrow. Tomorrow! Only a day and he'd be with the rest of them, his parents, Fola, Jaja, all the other Amazus on the other side of the dam—

"Will you let me go first, Kambiri?" he asks her breathlessly.

She's carved a cup of space for him in her stacks of old engineering magazines, books about Union philosophy and yellowing pictures of people that Amazu doesn't recognize and she won't name when he asks. Kambiri restlessly moves piles from one side to the other of her one-room apartment and back again. She's looking for something, but won't, or can't say what.

"Or last, if you want," he tries to say helpfully. "I don't mind being the last one. I can switch off the lights and be the last one to come through. Unless Hogan wants to come—"

"What?" she says, distressed.

"I'm just saying. If Grandfather's changed his mind, he might, I mean, maybe that's why—"

"*He had his moment! He had his chance and I had—*"

Her hair is undone, electric. The space is too small for him to shrink into.

Her breath comes out slowly, smoothly. "You won't be the last. We'll go through together, Amazu."

"Holding hands? Will they allow it?"

She rubs her wrist, twisting the watch strap round and round. "I don't care. As long as we leave."

Finally, she switches off the light and they both fall asleep. Cocooned by the technical papers and philosophical tracts that fed the creation of the dam, reciting the stories from the experience circles at the edge of sleep, Amazu dreams. For the first time, he dreams of the future—not of something that's happened to him, but dreaming of where he wanted to be. He's aware that this is an adult's dream—a dream of what he's not but what he might be, not of what he can touch immediately before him but the space between him and the future. A dream of becoming—

—at first, the voices will be crowding—darting in and out, and they will all be asking the same questions, a stutter, an echo, until all those Amazus remember their lessons from all those Folas and they practice their exercises: turn first to the next Amazu, the one that feels closest to this world, bow, swap—a kiss, a challenge, it doesn't matter, there'll be time to swap everything—and dosedo, into that Amazu's head, letting him into yours. Then the two of you turn to the next in line, repeat, moving up, down the chain, going in and out of each other's heads, but with more confidence, with the others in Union to help, going in and out of each other's worlds through the dam gateways strung out in a chain, causing a glow with each exchange, turning the chain into a sparkling necklace—

—and so much to see, explore, the adventures he's bookmarked from the stories of the others, but new adventures as well, his own discoveries, all to be shared by Amazus, all the Amazus, as far up and down the chain as he can stretch—and when there's no more Amazus to find, when there's only Amazu, *the last lesson to remember, the central command of Union will remain: come back and share with everyone else, always come back and help with the next stage of Union, to build a gateway into which they can join with each other, in and out of everyone's heads, and then to that final stage, a dam that will take them to a place where they sail back and forth through time, all the worlds, every head, a pulse in God's own brain—*

—and never looking back, never any time to look back, for keepsakes, for prize moments, for childhood, but always to become and become and become—

For the third time, Kambiri wakens him. She's sitting silently on the floor, facing the door, turning the watch over and over in her hand with a series of insect clicks. He watches her dark shape for a few minutes.

"Are you excited?" he asks her.

She doesn't answer him.

"But it's what you wanted, isn't it? It's the reason you asked me to steal the watch—so he would come and they would have to bring forward Union for all of us, even if they didn't think we were ready?

Kambiri?"

She can't answer him. Holding the watch with her arm outstretched, she lets it go and then snatches it, over and over—until Amazu finally understands. This was never about Union. She's trying to grab a moment back.

He's scared to close his eyes and see it, afraid he'll fall asleep, but he can almost imagine it, how it really happened. Most of them would probably have moved to the dam already, leaving the individualists to wait for the moment the dam's gates are closed and the water levels start to rise. One by one, going into their houses in the preceding months, ignoring the efforts of those who went to the dam to persuade them away, and when they found a moment they wanted to hold, or as good a moment as they could hope for in the time left, operating the machines. Hogan would have been one of the last, maybe waiting for the others to make their decisions, maybe waiting for the right moment to come along—

Maybe waiting for Kambiri to give in. And that one last time, knowing now that it was her he was arguing with—*why would anyone want to go to the dam?* But Hogan goes back into the house with her watch while Kambiri joins their daughter, her new husband and their child in the dam.

Kambiri can never admit it, but she can't let go.

Lying there in the dark, Amazu imagines all the fish shining in the clear water beyond the wall of this apartment. He wants to remember each one of them, leaping into temporary vision, revealed by the moonlight, he doesn't want to forget a single one. Jaja is there too, counting the fish—

Amazu can't let go either.

He lies there for a long time. Then he climbs out of his hole, stretching the cricks out of his back, and changes into his clothes and prepares his knapsack, and she doesn't say anything. Amazu kisses the top of her head and maybe there's a sigh deep inside her, but she doesn't say anything. Only the watch holds her, twirling before her gaze, and the occasional twitch of her shoulders at any noise outside the door, at anything that might be *his* approaching steps.

It must have rained earlier in the night, and in the pre-dawn dark, the walkway along the top of the dam is slick and dangerous.

"Race you across," Jaja says behind him.

Amazu smiles and hopes there's enough starlight for his teeth to shine and Jaja to know how happy he is to see him. "OK."

"And back again."

Amazu shakes his head—no. He hopes the dark covers this and his glance at the hills beyond the southside tower.

Jaja's shoulders slump. "All the adventures we could have."

"All the adventures we'd forget. And how long before we'd have to forget each other?"

Jaja shrugs. He knows that Jaja never really looked forward to being joined in Union by his friend because that would mean Jaja couldn't come back here, to someone who had no choice but to keep their shared memories safe. Adults have to know what to hang onto and what to let go, Amazu realizes. It's the last thing he has to know before leaving.

So they race across the dam and Jaja wins, of course. As the sky lets out a breath and color creeps from the east, they wait for mudfeckles to leap from the lake and throw stones to catch them before they hit the water again, and Amazu wonders if he'll remember this.

Lavie Tidhar grew up on a kibbutz in Israel and lived in South Africa and the UK. He recently moved to the island-nation of Vanuatu in the South Pacific, where he shares the island of Vanua Lava with an active volcano, crocodiles and fire ants, which are not nearly as cool as laser-firing sharks. His fiction has appeared *in* Sci Fiction, Chizine, Strange Horizons, Postscripts, Clarkesworld Magazine *and many others.*

The Fateful Voyage of *Dame La Liberté*
by Lavie Tidhar

They were digging up the mountains around Jerusalem. Archaeologists.

They dug for antiques and, by God, they found one.

I was the "local guide," though I was originally from New York. I handled problems with the Ottomans, the locals and the Jewish community in Jerusalem that was positively *abhorred* at the thought of such a thing as a dig.

Don't worry, I said. I'll take care of things. And they won't find anything, and if they do it would be some shards of pottery and some old Roman coins, and what is the harm in that?

Then they found the ship.

They didn't know it was a ship, at first. They got very excited when they discovered a solid board of metal that seemed fused to the rock. It had intricate designs on it, like swirls of smoke.

"Fancy that," Brocket, the British, said.

"It is im*possible*," said Gunter, the German. "Such a thing could not *exist*."

They scratched at the metal and ran tests and then tried crowbars and hammers to open it but failed.

They were a strange lot. I had worked with several groups of archaeologists over the years, and they tend to be composed of members of the same country and a discovery is considered a score for the side. They also tended to be men.

This group was a mixed bag. I already mentioned Gunter and Brocket; there were also Olaf and Marina, he a pale Swede and she a heavy Romanian; there were Chapman and Randolph, the Americans, and Suzanna who was British, and the three Russians, Arkady and Ilya and Maxim. An odd bunch, who argued half the time amongst themselves in a strange mix of English.

They couldn't open it. They were convinced it was a door, but to what they wouldn't, couldn't, say.

"Comrade David," Brocket said to me. It was another one of their quirks, calling you Comrade like that. "I must confide in you." He was short-sighted, and squinted as he talked. There was grime on his hands and face, and he was sweating. "We have decided to blow up the, the artifact we found. To try and gain entry."

"Blow up?" I said. Then, "I'm afraid I can't get you explosives."

He shook his head, rubbed dirt off his fingers. "No," he said. "We *have* explosives. Dynamite. A lot of it. I realize this isn't strictly . . . "

"Legal? No," I said.

I should have realized then that I was dealing with madmen, but instead I waited until he said, "Can you silence it? Make sure there will be no awkward questions?"

And like an idiot I said I'd try.

They blew it up the next night, and only one person died: the Romanian, Marina. She was caught by a shard of rock that sliced her leg and she bled to death.

The dynamite didn't even scratch the metal, but it cleared a lot of rock around it, more metal and more ornate cloud swirls: the beginnings of a body.

Maxim found the mechanism that controlled the door and managed to open it. It took him two days, and in the meantime I was spending money like water bribing the Ottoman officials who were "getting concerned." I don't think it was really Maxim who opened it, by the way. I think, after two days, it let him open it, if that makes sense. Most of it still doesn't, to me.

I went with them through the door.

It was a ship, they said. Gunter got very excited again and began clapping his hands, his face all scrunched up.

All I could see were corridors. They stretched in every direction, endless, eerily lit by little gas lamps that sprung into life as I walked passed them, as if my feet had pressed a hidden lever.

They were corridors of metal and wood. I recognized neither. The wood was hard as metal and polished to a fine shine. The metal was a dark bluish color, warm to the touch.

There was a heart beating inside that great beast. I felt it, thrumming through the walls and the floor, and smelt it, in the warmth of the air, in the increasing humidity.

Our presence had awakened something.

We discovered the engines later that day. They were buried deep, in levels that could only be reached by giant wood and glass elevators that ran almost silently. It was a bizarre journey, sinking deeper into the dark bowels of the ship, and deeper into the earth itself.

It was a slow descent; occasionally we saw flashes of brilliance in the distance as some obscure engine came to life. At last we reached the lower levels.

The engines were gigantic, the size of villages; it is the only way I can describe it. And there was a lake down there, or perhaps a sea. Pipes led to the engines, and pipes led from the engines back into the water.

"It cannot *be*!" Gunter said. He looked close to tears. "It cannot be a *perpetuum mobile*. It cannot!"

They had gone mad. The water came into the machines and became steam, and the steam powered the ship. Gunter thought the steam converted back to water and was fed again and again to the engines. It didn't explain where the engines themselves got their energy (they powered themselves, was Gunter's answer) or how a hundred percent conservation was possible.

To me, the whole grotesque machine—ship, engines and all— sseemed like an affectation, the dressings of a style on to something vast and complicated. Someone, some*thing*, built themselves a mock steamship, and the archaeologists believed it. Believed in it, just as they believed in liberty, equality and fraternity.

"We shall fly in the ship!" Olaf said to me, his voice quavering in excitement. I had not seen the man quite so energetic before. "In *Dame La Liberté*. Comrade, we shall build the new society that we wanted to make here in Palestine, and we shall do it where we will be free—amongst the stars!"

They were a handful.

I was also having difficulties with the Ottomans. They smelled something was up and there were regular visits from inquisitive officials. There were rumors in the city that the archaeologists were terrorists; working against the Sultan. News of the explosions traveled despite all I did.

They kept paying me, though, and paying well. So I stayed on, and when people began to arrive, I wasn't even surprised.

They came in groups and singly, came in carts or walked, arrived with wagonloads of equipment or with nothing but a small racksack. Every day there were more of them. From all over the world, it seemed, a mix of women and men sneaked into our camp and were quickly led into the ship, to disappear, awe-struck and reverential, into its hungry stomach.

The Sultan's secret police came to visit me. I only lost one tooth. What was going on? They wanted to know. The movement of people was noted, and their sudden disappearance noted also.

I told them I didn't know, and they beat me up.

"Pass your friends a word of warning," their leader said. He was Turkish and spoke a different kind of Arabic than the one spoken Jerusalem. "We don't want an *incident*." He said the word with distaste for its very diplomacy. "They have a week to get out of the country. Otherwise we'll ship them home in coffins."

I passed the message along. Brocket grinned and Olaf looked thoughtful.

"We'll be done in two *days*," Gunter said and I said, "You're mad," but he didn't listen.

They made their attempt the next morning. There were over a thousand of them now, living inside *Dame La Liberté*: whole levels were being converted into fields, living quarters, storage rooms. I went with Gunter to the control center, a small cubical room in the heart of the ship. The piloting devices were primitive: clocks and gauges embedded in polished wood, a steering wheel and some levers and pedals. Some buttons, also, with strange cloud markings on each.

Arkady, the Russian, was to be the pilot. His Slavic face looked suffused with joy as he sat at the controls: a picture of the area was projected on to a small, elegant screen in front of the room, moving and changing as he accessed the controls. It was what Gunter called a simulation, but I think it was different: that the ship was teaching Arkady to fly it.

It was a bright morning. The sun rose over the Jerusalem mountains and there were no clouds. The walls of the city could be seen in the distance, sitting on a peak. It is the closest place to heaven on earth, or so they say. The place where the ground almost touches the sky.

I said goodbye to my archaeologists and wished them well. They thanked me, called me Comrade. They also left with me all of their money, which was not an inconsiderable amount.

"We won't need it any more," Brocket said, and suddenly hugged me. "Ours will be a cashless society. Goodbye, David."

"Goodbye," I said. There didn't seem to be much more to say. I rode away, determined to put as much distance between myself and Jerusalem as possible. I thought I might go back to the States. Anywhere not within the Ottoman Empire, in any case.

I saw *Dame La Liberté* rise. I was on a hilltop, looking back at the mountains, and there it was. It rose like a floating egg, a silver cloud that hung motionless in the skies then moved gingerly from side to side, up and down, and I imagined Arkady sitting inside, his face ecstatic.

It was like a silver tear, and when it moved the light shone of the patterns on its skin and ignited them: it was like the ship was burning and swirling in smoke.

They moved over Jerusalem and the ship's shadow fell over it, and no doubt people panicked, and some prayed. Then there was a sudden flash of brilliance and *Dame La Liberté*—disappeared. The sound of the explosion was terrible: the horse and I were battered by the sound, and I was told later windows broke all over Jerusalem. All the places that had windows, anyhow.

They *must* have died. It was a flash of such radiance I could think of it as nothing but an explosion, one so powerful it obliterated the ship entirely.

And yet . . . I like to think they made it to the stars, and that they are there still, in that new society they wanted to create for themselves. These days, when I look at the stars I seek more and more for some sign of them, having the notion that they might come back, these peaceful Revolutionaries, to tell us stories of the stars, and of the men and women who live there in equality and freedom.

But there is never a sign; I remain alone to tell the story, of the fateful voyage of *Dame La Liberté*, and of the men and women who one day reached for the stars.

Robert B. Marcus, Jr.'s first fiction sale was to Analog Science Fiction and Fact *when he was in college. Since then he has sold a number of other science fiction stories, one novel, as well as close to a hundred fifty chapters and journal articles in the field of cancer. Though he majored in astronomy and physics, he eventually became a physician in the field of radiation oncology, where he primarily researches and treats pediatric tumors as a Professor of Radiation Oncology and Pediatrics at Emory University.*

Memories
by Robert B. Marcus, Jr.

I was within a thousand meters of the large building in the middle of the ruins when the Lateon fighter appeared over the short horizon, weapons blasting. In front of me, the remnants of the two million year-old building collapsed, thirty stories of metal and stone dropping quietly to the ground in the soundless vacuum. Chunks of rubble flew through the pale, ghostly light cast by the planet's two suns, thousand-ton missiles hurtling through the black sky and house-sized boulders bouncing across the surface.

And they all seemed to be headed in my direction.

In my rush to dodge the missiles and boulders on my scooter, I had forgotten the Lateon fighter was still trying to disperse my body into subatomic particles. Luckily, a man on a darting scooter is a much more difficult target than an immobile thirty-story alien ruin, and as the oblong-shaped fighter flashed overhead I breathed a sigh of relief that I had evaded my apparent destiny.

Where had the Lateon fighter come from and why was it attacking me? My first trip to the surface two hours ago had been uneventful, but this time I was about halfway to the center of the ruins when the peacefulness of this world disintegrated.

Now the fighter was swinging back for another run. Could I survive a second attack? For sure, I couldn't survive a third or a fourth.

But there was always Plan B. I hoped Jance Relids was high in orbit and safe on the bridge of the *Morning Light* watching me run for cover. If Jance wasn't safe, Plan B was a waste of time.

From overhearing the communications of the archs before they left, we had known about the possible presence of a large Lateon ship when we dropped into orbit around the planet, though we hoped it was several light-years away. Nonetheless, I had taken a few precautions when I landed in the shuttle. Neither the shuttle nor the *Morning Light* was a fighter, but not even a small explorer wandered this far from human space completely unarmed. I had a chance *if* I could get to the edge of the ruins . . . and *if* my timing was perfect.

The scooter floated on a weak repulsion field guided by small rockets. It was fast enough to traverse a straight course in plenty of time. But a straight course wasn't possible, not with debris from the shattered building still bouncing around. It would be close.

Dim light from the white dwarf glinted off the wing of the Lateon fighter as another volley of blasts destroyed a small building half a kilometer ahead. The beams twisted away as the fighter flashed overhead, banking for another run. Sweat flowed from my pores faster than my vacuum suit could absorb it, and the stink of fear was beginning to accumulate in the thick atmosphere I was breathing. Some of the sweat was dripping into my eyes, making it hard to see. I couldn't possibly survive another run by the fighter.

But maybe I wouldn't have to.

I aimed the scooter toward the outer layers of the ruins along the clearest path I could find. No time for finesse now. The bouncing debris was finally thinning out but there was always a chance that one last boulder would obliterate me. I buried the thought.

A couple of small pebbles glanced against the side of my scooter as I streaked through the perimeter zone of the ruins onto the barren, rocky terrain outside. I felt the presence of the fighter closing in on me.

I pushed a jury-rigged button on the control panel of the scooter. In the absence of sound I had to turn to discover the results. My suit visor dimmed in reaction to the bright burst of light as the Lateon fighter rushed through the invisible spray of the antimatter grenade, rendering the spray no longer invisible. A billion tiny explosions detonated both on the surface and within the fighter, though the chance of any of the antimatter penetrating deeply into the fighter and killing the pilot was small. The fighter immediately wobbled in flight, then fled dragging a tail of smoke. I stopped the scooter and watched the ship dipping closer and closer to the rocky ground before vanishing over the far horizon.

"What the hell is going on down there?" Jance spat into my helmet.

"Just a dead Lateon fighter," I replied.

"Well there may be more," Jance said. "I'm getting readings of a small gravitational anomaly on the far side of the planet."

"Keep me informed." I was curious about the gravitation anomaly, but didn't have time think about it or even to savor my success against the Lateon. I turned my scooter back to the ruins.

I only had eleven hours left.

Dealing in alien artifacts could be extremely profitable, and was legal, if you followed the rules. Legally independent dealers could only go into a sanctioned ruin if everyone higher in the food chain had departed. Unfortunately, that meant Jance and I were at the absolute bottom. And why would everyone depart unless the ruins were worthless, depleted or too dangerous? They might be in Lateon territory, like this one—or, also like this one, the celestial body on which the ruins abided might have a limited life expectancy.

Two million years ago these ruins were inhabited by a vibrant, thriving civilization which had spread to at least forty sites in over twenty star systems about 1500 light-years from Earth. No one knew what the beings looked like; no one knew the cause of their demise. All that was left was a few ruins. Two million years is a long time for buildings created by mortal creatures to last; the winds and tides and movements of the crust of a living planet wiped clean all traces of civilization, burying the remnants far below the surface. An orbital scan could pick out artificial patterns but landings produced few artifacts without extensive excavations. Only two of the forty identified sites of this particular civilization were productive at all; the best was on this airless, barren planet, where a single domed city had been built. The dome was long gone, but many of the buildings were relatively intact.

All of those intact buildings were about to fall into a black hole. In seventeen hours.

I stared at the sky above me. Once upon a time, perhaps 200,000,000 years ago, a yellow sun the size of Earth's Sun departed from the main sequence. Its hydrogen fuel tanks were almost empty, so it started its journey toward oblivion. From an average star to a red giant, not once, but twice . . . then the complete extinction of the core nuclear fires . . . accompanied by the inevitable gravitational collapse. All that was left was a fiercely white star smaller than Earth but much hotter than the Sun on the surface. The luminosity of the star faded with time, until now only heat provided the light. The light it cast on this planet was pale, but cold and real, in contrast to that of its companion. I followed a trail of hot gases, the matter-transfer stream, spewing from the white dwarf across the void until it merged with a yellowish-white disc of gases that filled the central half of the sky, like creamy icing swirled over the black darkness of space. The hole in the center of this accretion disc was directly above me, angled slightly toward the horizon on my left, a dark, evil nothingness surrounded by a white-hot bulging in the disc. A geyser of bluish-white matter was exploding from the center of the disc, flashing within a 100,000 kilometers of this planet. Even if I couldn't see the black hole, I could feel its dark presence, eager and ready to swallow this 11,000 kilometer rock. The planet wouldn't actually fall into the black hole in eleven hours—though it would do that in seventeen—it would merely drop too close to the hole for us to escape.

I had wanted to spend most of my time exploring the large central building, but what had survived two million years had been turned into rubble by the Lateon fighter in seconds. Now I was forced to explore smaller buildings.

The buildings contained a rabbit's warren of tunnels and chambers, weaving their way through the entire city. The walls of the chambers were smooth and ebony, glistening in the light of my torch. Geometrical shapes hid on the floor and lurked in my path—cubes, spheres, pyramids primarily, but a few more irregular shapes. They were of the same ebony construction and completely immobile, cold and smooth. Once in a while, in no particular pattern, I came across niches in the wall, some tiny, others large enough to hide an elephant. Nestled in the niches were things, mostly unrecognizable things, exactly what I wanted, since many were small enough to carry.

I collected odds and ends in the basket behind my scooter, hardly bothering to look at them. Each appeared to be worth the cost of the trip out here. I twisted one small sphere into two pieces and a tiny thunderstorm was released. I put the two pieces back together, then pulled it apart again. Another thunderstorm, six centimeters across, with centimeter-long bolts of lightening. Just art? I put it in the basket with the other trinkets and started to move on, when I saw the small ebony figure on the floor.

Was that what they looked like? I grabbed it and put it in my pocket.

I only had eight hours of collecting left.

My memories begin nine years ago when I woke up in a hospital on Danyon, the second planet of Sigma Draconis, about eighteen light-years from Earth. I had been found wandering the streets of Amber, the capital city, completely confused and unresponsive, with no identification and no memories. They removed the tumor along with my left cerebral hemisphere, my dominant one, and genetically convinced my body to grow a replacement. But my memories never returned.

The authorities tried to trace me from retinal scans and a DNA analysis, but I had no recorded past. Assuming that I was a criminal, they tried to imprison me when I physically healed. I escaped, to be found by Jance, who also had no past, at least none that he would ever talk about. We were a good match. Who in his right mind would travel a thousand light years into Lateon space to a dying planet to retrieve a few artifacts from an essentially unknown civilization? The archs had come and gone, probably protected by the Terran Navy. But we were alone. The odds of surviving were small, which was why no other dealers were competing with us. But if we did survive, the memories would be intense. And I valued memories.

"Did you find anything valuable?" Jance asked in my earphones as I quickly stowed my treasure trove in the small cargo bay of my shuttle. I didn't have much room so small objects were the key. Usually on an exploration I would make several shuttle runs from orbit to the surface, but not on this one. This would be my last landing.

"Maybe an image of the builders," I replied.

"Any weapons?"

"Not unless you count a tiny thunderstorm."

"That isn't going to help."

"Against what?"

"I can explain the gravitational anomaly."

"Did you find the Lateon mother ship?"

"The Lateons aren't the problem."

"The archs?"

"Not exactly."

"What's that mean?"

"It means that the source of the gravitational anomaly is an Einstein class battlecruiser, not an archeology vessel."

I stopped putting away my treasure trove. "What's a battlecruiser doing here?" I whispered.

"To protect the archs?" Jance replied.

"Why would they need more than a small destroyer?"

"Maybe to investigate the Lateons?"

"We didn't expect to find them here—why should the Terran Navy?"

"I don't know, but it's close enough to swallow the *Morning Light*."

"Roger. Let me know if it pulls closer."

"It can't get any closer. Why don't you bring what you have and come home?"

"Because we have an expensive trip to pay for. I'll be in touch."

What the hell was a battlecruiser doing here so close to the end of this planet's life?

I refilled my suit's air tanks, then made sure the memory links were operating between my suit and the ship in orbit high above. If anything happened to me I wanted Jance to know how and why. Theoretically, the memory logs were for your family—if you had one. I didn't. Just Jance. At least he was all I could remember.

* * *

With six hours to go, I started back to the city.

There was little doubt that this planetary system was an example of how even the wonders of the Universe depend upon timing. Most binary systems evolve together. This one did not; the black hole was old by the time it seized the intruder. My calculations indicated that the capture had taken place as the second red giant phase of the yellow sun was ebbing. The black hole began to drain the red giant and the drain continued until now, long after the red giant burned down the evolutionary pathway to become the white dwarf it was today.

And sometime recently, at least on a cosmic scale, a civilization built an outpost here to study the binary system up close . . . and then died. And later still, only seconds ago on that same cosmic time scale, mankind had discovered these ruins, and came to study them even as the planet hurtled toward the fatal end of its last 12,000-year orbit.

Of all those long orbits, all those years, we came *now*, just hours from the end. Maybe on the previous orbit the planet had been deflected by matter in the accretion disc as it hurtled through—maybe its orbit had just slowly changed and now was the planet's time to die.

The reason didn't matter. What mattered is that I didn't have much time to make this long, expensive journey profitable. And now everything was confounded by the presence of a Terran Navy Battlecruiser. What was it doing here? I hoped that the Navy had a little more tolerance for us than the archeologists did. Even though what we did was perfectly legal, xeno-archeologists resented private artifact dealers. Maybe it was the money we made; maybe the resentment was based on principles. The Ananazi called people like us Robbers of the Dead. Certainly throughout history, grave robbers were not sanctioned by the government. Our predecessors looted, pillaged and destroyed valuable archaeological sites. Even though we were different—after all, what we didn't take would soon be lost forever—the resentment continued.

Collectors and museums wanted art most of all, particularly art that showed beings in their natural habitats. The problem is that art is usually on fragile media, and rarely lasts two million years in any recognizable form. Gadgets were next. Alien minds created unfathomable gadgets. The theme of many a present-day slitz party centered on the question: *what is it?* Rich collectors paid a fortune for strange things. I had once taken in ten million credits for an oblong spheroid extruding small squares of a substance similar to rubber. The squares came right out of the surface of the device, and I thought that they were immobile at first, but quantum measurements on the piece showed that the ten squares on the surface were being extruded at the vigorous rate of one Angstrom per millennium. I found it deep in a beryllium mine in some ruins on Sirius IV. What was its purpose? No one ever put forth a single rational idea, though a number of mankind's more imaginative thinkers tried.

This present site, far within the boundaries of the Lateon Empire, had only recently been discovered and the short amount of time available for the official expedition meant that the ruins were full of treasures for someone like me. That was why it was worth the risk.

Halfway to the city a metal sphere that looked a little like a bug darted over the horizon in front of my scooter, firing at me. The weapons on this annoying Lateon bug weren't as powerful as those on the fighter, but that flying suit of armor was far more mobile and I wasn't really prepared for any more combat from a Lateon that was supposed to be dead.

I was in trouble . . . again.

The ruins were my best chance. Zigzagging at full speed was not my idea of fun, but I managed to dart below an overhang of dark metal just as the Lateon bug passed overhead. Unlike the fighter, this sphere with four metal tentacles could hover. And it did hover, lurking above me, firing down test blasts every few seconds. Small pebbles and slivers of metal fell, and I knew something big could follow at any moment. I couldn't stay here forever. I had to go on the attack.

I knew that the buildings were a labyrinth of passages, probably all interconnected when the buildings were new. Of course, the warren of corridors was far from intact now. There was no atmosphere here to erode the structures, but celestial debris over the years had pummeled the city. The Lateon attack on the center building hadn't helped either. But in spite of the destruction I knew I would still be safer inside than out.

The builders weren't small. The doorways were round—about three meters in diameter—with no barrier anywhere. You would have expected some kind of door to close off the buildings in the event the dome shielding failed. Maybe the doors were there and I just didn't recognize them. Maybe they were gone. Two million years did that to most materials.

The openings to the building were odd and would have been a problem on Earth. But the circular doorways one meter above the ground were easy to hop through on a world where I weighed only 60 percent of what I did on Earth. I did so, then proceeded through a large open foyer to another doorway. This one had the same dimensions but led to a fifty foot tunnel. I walked through, aware that my enemy could easily follow. The next room was square, and contained a half dozen niches in the wall filled with dust.

I wasn't armed as well as the Lateon flying battle suit, but I had the advantage of surprise. I turned off my light and waited at an angle facing the tunnel, hiding behind a perfect cube two meters to a side with the surface texture of polished steel, smooth and glistening. It looked as though it had the ability to stop a battlecruiser's particle beam. It was as good a place to wait as any. My hand twitched, jiggling the small blaster I held.

In a few minutes I heard a soft sound coming from the far end of the tunnel, probably the exhaust of the Lateon's power jets. I thought of a number of possible actions at that point, most of which included some kind of violent action.

Instead, I asked a question. I had nothing to lose. It knew I was in here.

"Why are you so determined to kill me?" My suit's computer translated my words into a series of colored flashes that represented the Lateon's language to the best of our ability to understand it.

I wasn't sure the Lateon was close enough to see or understand the question, but after a moment, a response flashed down the corridor. My suit fed the translation into my earphones, mechanical and harsh—I couldn't afford a suit computer with a sexy voice. "One . . . first. This . . . our planet. One's ship. . .I need now. Thought Sac return to blood pod necessary."

I thought of the memory recorders back in the *Morning Light* and wondered if there was a similarity. Except that I didn't have a family . . .

and I didn't know what a blood pod was though I knew I didn't have one. I had only a black hole in my mind where my childhood and first ten years of adulthood should be.

For some reason that bothered me and I blamed the Lateon because it was the only object available to blame. I blasted the ceiling of the tunnel. Large chunks tumbled down, flinging dust in my direction. I fired and fired and the roof of the tunnel fell and fell.

After a while the tunnel was nothing but a pile of rubble and the accretion disc shone through the newly created hole in the ceiling. I waited but my attacker was still.

I had only five hours left.

In our explorations of Earth's galactic arm, we had discovered thirty different alien civilizations. Unfortunately, twenty-nine of them were extinct. Only the Lateons were not. From the beginning, relations weren't as good as we might have wished, and we had been at war with them for over 200 years. But it really wasn't much of a war. Only two full battles had taken place, if you consider five battlecruisers on one side and six on the other to be full battles. We sort of won the first battle and they won the second, sending in a five kilometer long beomoth that had enough firepower to destroy all of our battlecruisers. It was the only ship left at the end—we easily took out all their smaller ones before being atomized ourselves.

And that was the end of any direct conflict by more than one ship on either side. Both civilizations tried to avoid the other, which wasn't hard. We had about fifty battlecruisers—they probably had about the same. In the sphere of 2500 light-years that we had explored, that was one battlecruiser for about every 82 million cubic light-years. There wasn't much chance of randomly running into each other.

But somehow we had. Obviously it wasn't random.

Two hours later I was shifting my third load of treasures into the cargo hold. At this point, I still didn't know what I was taking home with me, but I didn't have time to worry about it. For the right collector, even alien toilet paper was a treasure.

While I loaded, I charged the battery pack for my scooter. I finished packing everything before the charging was complete and didn't have much to do except wait and stare out across the loneliness. An entire civilization reduced to this—metal, stone and dust. I glanced back up and there it was—the pale accretion disc now filling the sky from horizon to horizon as we rushed closer, the matter-stream from the white dwarf trailing off to the distant, flickering hole in the apex of the sky, darkness against darkness, the end to all that was left of these people except what the archs, the battlecruiser and I could carry off. And I doubted that the battlecruiser was interested in collecting tidbits of this civilization. No, it had another purpose.

"The Lateon wants the *Morning Light*," I told Jance. "Or at least my shuttle."

"I thought that he just didn't like art collectors," Jance replied.

"How do you know it's a *he*?"

"You think it's a *she*?"

"Maybe it's neither. I've heard that only a few Lateons actually are our equivalent of male or female. Most are sexless and do not participate in reproduction. The few males and females produce all the children for the pod."

"Maybe it's one of the immortals?" Jance said.

I scoffed. "You don't believe that old tale, do you?"

Jance hesitated. He was more mystical than I was, often leaping to conclusions and imagining things that weren't there.

"Well," he said slowly. "Some of them apparently remember the entire history of their civilization. Two million Earth years. How do you explain that?"

"I don't. Think about it. It's ridiculous. How could any being live that long?"

"Why would they lie about it?" Jance asked. I could tell he was upset with me for disagreeing with him.

"Why does a Lateon do anything?" I asked.

There was no answer, even after I waited several minutes. Now he was going to sulk. There was no point in saying anything for a while. The anger had to burn out of him. I sighed and leaned back to look at the sky again, trying to imagine that dark mawl and what awaited its victims down that gravity chute, where time and space joined in a fusion of matter and energy far beyond our comprehension. I was ready to leave this planet now. Somehow the empty hole in the sky filled me with a grim foreboding.

I thought about the path of this planet, the comet-like orbit that looped 3 per cent of a light-year away from the hole, an orbit that took 11,292 years to complete. It was a cosmic newcomer to this system as well, captured like the dwarf star. And 177 orbits ago this city had been built. What memories were lost when the builders of the city died?

I was deep in depression when the attack came and only the fact I was in my shuttle saved my life. The burst of light and the shudder of my seat were simultaneous. The shuttle wasn't big enough to have shields, but it was made out of hardened titanium and could withstand a great deal. It tolerated the first hit better than I did, since I flew out of the control chair and smashed my head against the guidance panel in front of me. Large brightly-colored spinning stars filled the room, and a curtain of haze descended across my eyes. I staggered to my feet and glanced through the front viewport. A wobbling but still flying Lateon battlesuit was twisting around for another shot at me. The creature was persistent, that was for damn sure.

Defense! What the hell did I have for defense? The shuttle had no weapons. I scuddered around the cockpit, glancing at all the controls, digging in the debris behind the seat, looking in the storage locker in the back wall. Nothing. *What now?*

Another volley rocked the ship. The hardened shell should hold out a bit longer . . . but if I couldn't find anything . . . .

I did have my personal blasters, still tucked in my vacuum suit, but it wasn't likely that even a direct hit from one of them would scratch the flying bug. Maybe a dozen shots into the same spot on the armor, but not a single one. I had a small cargo bay full of alien artifacts—maybe one of them was a lethal weapon. If so, I would be dead long before I figured out how to identify and use it.

My scooter was my only hope. The shuttle was a stationary target and no matter how hard the titanium shell, it would eventually yield. The scooter was defenseless but small and mobile, with some flying capability. The Lateon battlesuit was ordinarily very mobile as well, but now it was bouncing around like a particle in Brownian motion. Maybe the collapsed tunnel had damaged it a little. Maybe its guidance computer was fried.

I darted to the scooter as another shot glanced off the nose of the shuttle, quickly disconnected the charger and sped away. The Lateon was banking toward me again and when it began to straighten out and head my direction, I initiated a series of zigzags and bounces. So far my supposition that the Lateon's computer might have trouble coping with the scooter's motions appeared to be true, because every shot smashed into the ground ten meters behind me. But how long could I run? Sooner or later my luck would vanish and he would hit me. I gritted my teeth and turned to challenge the Lateon.

The sudden shift in strategy startled my adversary. The firing stopped completely, even though for a second or two while I was turning I was a clear, easy shot. I swept by, firing one of my hand blasters.

Three separate shots hit the bug, but none seemed to inflict any damage. I twisted the scooter around for another attack, and so did my enemy.

Now that we were jousting, I had the mobility advantage, but in jousting, the bigger knight carrying the bigger lance riding the bigger horse could undo all that advantage with one lucky hit. I had to end this quickly and my blasters were not the answer.

We swept toward each other again, too fast to think, both firing repeatedly, and both without success. He couldn't hit me, and while I could hit him, my shots bounced off his armor. But my blaster was not my weapon; my scooter was. I pointed the nose straight at the bug and jumped out a second before impact.

Collisions are different in a vacuum. I heard and felt nothing, but fragments of my scooter flew by me as I fell. I inflated the safety bubble. It quickly surrounded my suit and I bounced against the ground, striking a rock on the third bounce, puncturing the bubble . . . but by then I was safe. I watched the Lateon battlesuit tumble out of control to the ground not fifty meters from my shuttle. I peeled off the safety bubble and stumbled toward my ship and my enemy, angry that it had cost me my scooter.

The Lateon's armored suit looked far less damaged than I expected. There was a dent here and there, but basically it looked intact, round in its basic structure, with four tentacled appendages. There was a dark glass-like plate on the side of the sphere facing me, but my vision couldn't penetrate its black barrier, though I knew from pictures what the Lateon looked like under the suit. But I didn't know what to do now. Maybe it was dead and maybe it was alive.

I physically jumped when one of its metal tentacles twitched. I watched it twitch twice more, then after a slight rest, the end of the tentacle began to creep along the center of the suit toward a dark chamber that had suddenly opened.

"You don't give up, do you," I muttered to myself. When my suit didn't understand I was talking to the Lateon, I said, "Translate." And it did.

The Lateon's suit flickered, and a weak voice stuttered in my earphones. "Need . . . ship."

"Not if I can help it," I replied, taking out my own blaster. "Another twitch and I'll blow the end of your hand off, or whatever you call that thing."

The tentacle hesitated, then resumed its relentless creep. I blew off half of it. Then I blew off at least half of all the other three tentacles. They weren't as resistant as the armor-plated battlesuit.

"Now . . . cannot shoot one," the Lateon said.

"My thoughts exactly," I muttered, walking away from him toward my shuttle. I suddenly didn't care what happened to him, and cared even less when I reached the shuttle and found that one of its earlier shots had broken through the hardened armor and disintegrated a meter-long segment of the shuttle's Ho Coil.

I had only four hours to get off this rock. There was no way I could make it.

It was an uncomfortable feeling. I *knew* somehow that the Lateon was alive, awake, and staring at me through that dark plate, though it hadn't tried to communicate. I wondered if it understood the curses I kept flinging at it during the last hour.

I tried harder to ignore the Lateon, working on my shuttle instead, attempting to bridge the gap in the Ho Coil, all the while knowing it was hopeless. Without the Ho Coil, the shuttle wasn't controllable in flight. And if it couldn't fly, I would die. I had no way to return to the *Morning Light*.

And Jance couldn't land.

Gritting my teeth, I went back to work.

Time waned.

Three hours left.

"One's loss . . . less," the Lateon flashed abruptly. "Only one die. Us . . . all die."

"I don't give a damn about your pod family," I retorted. "Besides, I'm not the one who started the shooting. I didn't attack you." I had come to realize that when the Lateon said "one" it was referring to me.

"One attack first. Now one's ship needed. Choice gone."

"Your ship crashed because I shot it down! I shot it down because you tried to turn me into rubble," I told him. "Now you've failed."

It didn't answer, and I wondered if its alien mind was agreeing with me. That gave me a fragment of satisfaction, so I went on.

"And you've failed your pod." There was a lot of satisfaction in pointing that out to the Lateon.

"Failed all," the Lateon agreed.

"And you're going to die here, just like me. I bet even one of your Immortals can't survive a plunge into a black hole."

"Make . . . sense . . . less."

I didn't understand at first, then realized that it wanted to know the meaning of the word. "Immortals are beings that live forever," I said.

Silence was the only reply at first, and all I could hear on my incoming comm circuits was the faint background hiss of deep space. Finally, "One thinks thus? Some Lateons live forever?"

"No . . . yes . . . I don't know. Some of you remember the entire history of your race."

"All Lateons remember thus—at least before. But no immortals. Die as all beings."

I wanted to make sure I understood because what the Lateon said still made no sense. "All Lateons remember the entire history of their race? Back millions of years?"

"Truth. . .that."

"How is that possible?"

Over the next few minutes it tried to explain, and I quickly learned more about Lateon biology than any other human knew. Their children are not like ours, born with the ability to develop intelligence as they grow. Lateon offspring are born in a group—a pod—with the intelligence of a worker ant. They grow, and can be taught to do menial labor with supervision, but that's all—not a childhood filled with warm and fuzzy memories. It is only when they reach adulthood that their bodies are ready for the transformation. Each pod has a Keeper of Memories, and that Lateon deposits a soup of Lateon genes, neurotransmitters and who knows what else, into each of the pod children. In this package are the tools that reshape the still embryonal nervous system. New neurons grow and interconnect in such a way as to create an intelligent being. Also in that packet is something that reconstructs in the children the entire memory of their race.

I was beginning to suspect something. "And you are the Memory Keeper for your pod?"

"Thus is true. But more. Carry knowledge for life."

"What will happen if you don't return?"

"My pod forever animals, in darkness thus, no intelligence. As all will be." And somehow, impossibly, the raspy voice in my earphones leaked the deep sorrow the Lateon felt.

I had always hoped that my memories would return at some point before I died, that I would remember a childhood, parents, friends. Of course I never planned on dying this soon. Knowing it was hopeless, I still continued to work on the Ho Coil, searching through the ship for any kind of part to bridge the gap. I hadn't begun to feel sorry for myself yet because I remained angry, and I did everything I could to stoke that anger. I knew what would happen when the anger ebbed. The Lateon said nothing for a long while, but finally spoke.

"Not necessary for one to die," the Lateon said.

I gawked at him.

"One can be saved."

"How?" I asked. I thought it was a very reasonable question, but I still had trouble getting it out of my mouth. "Didn't I destroy your ship?"

"Ship never fly thus," it said.

"Then how can you save me?" I asked sharply, very frustrated.

"Battlesuit . . . repair needed. Can reach the orbit of one's ship."

"What kind of repair?"

There was a loud wheeze, and I thought it had died. My hopes sank. Then I realized how ridiculous it was to expect much of it in the first place. They were our enemies.

"Simple task," the Lateon finally hissed. "Directional jet bent. Can be fixed."

"How can I trust you?"

"No choice," it flashed.

It took only a few minutes to repair the directional jet. I worked silently while the Lateon watched. Our races were enemies for two centuries, yet now one was apparently trying to save my life. It was obviously desperate.

"Works now," the Lateon said.

"I hope so. We're running out of time," I muttered.

Jance heard my mutterings. "More so than you realize," he said. "You've got company and I don't think they're bringing birthday cards."

I turned and found four stubby Navy fighters hovering about a thirty meters off the ground. What did *they* want? First the Lateon— now my own people were after me.

"Why didn't you warn me?" I asked.

"They blocked my transmitter until now."

"Are they from the battlecruiser that's following you?" I asked.

"You got it."

Then Jance's voice was replaced by a harsher one in my earphones.

"*Move away from the Lateon.*"

"Why?"

"*No questions. Move!*"

I hesitated and was rewarded with an explosion of dust and debris about six meters away. Too close for comfort.

"Take . . . to ship," the Lateon flashed. Then the battered suit slowly rose from the ground and wobbled across the rock-strewn surface, followed by a trail of eruptions in the ground as the fighters tracked him with their guns.

The result was inevitable. Given an undamaged suit, it might have escaped. But there was no chance, and I watched anxiously until my worries were realized. The tracking computers of the fighters finally caught up with him and the Lateon vanished in a bright flash.

My emotions were so confused I couldn't watch anymore, and turned my eyes to the ground. A small golden cylinder lay in the hollow the Lateon made when it hit the ground. I scooped it up and moved as quickly as possible to my ship.

"*Get inside,*" the voice in my helmet commanded.

"*Why did you kill him?*" I yelled.

"*Get inside the shuttle,*" the voice repeated.

Still yelling, I hustled inside, then grabbed the seat as the shuttle was seized by grapplers from the fighters and dragged off the ground. It was all I could do to buckle my harness without being thrown around the cabin.

The ground dropped away swiftly, the barren city slipping toward the horizon behind us. I began to look upward, searching for the *Morning Light*.

Now I could see both hemispheres of the sky. In the one previously hidden behind the planet the stars blazed, with the thick panoply of the galactic disc vertical to the surface of the planet, the light of billions of suns contributing to make the disc almost solid. In the other hemisphere lurked the demon star, a black emptiness whose gravity I could feel in every cell of my body. It wanted to devour me, my body, my soul, just as it wanted to devour every particle in our Universe that wandered within its reach. And it would, unless we left orbit in less than an hour.

Ahead, to answer my wish, a speck gleaming from the reflected light of a billion suns began to enlarge.

Jance was glad to see me, but not happy with his new location. He told me this into my earphones right before the transmission was cut by our captors. Thirty meters of metal and engine that was the *Morning Light* was lying on the floor of the shuttle bay of the battlecruiser, a gnat in the mouth of an alligator. Surrounding my ship were a hundred Terran Marines in full battle amour, all carrying heavy particle blasters. They must have considered me quite a threat. Maybe they thought I would attack them with the miniature thunderstorm I was carrying. A thin, sharp-nosed admiral with a completely impassive expression on his face strode toward me as I staggered out of my shuttle. In spite of the intimidation factor, I was not feeling polite. His nametag told me he was Admiral Memphis Thiriree.

"Why the hell did your minions kill the Lateon?" I asked.

"Ah, the famous tomb robber, Yanev Sergeir." I could tell from the smirk on Thiriree's face that we weren't going to get along very well. "What goodies are in your shuttle?"

If he only knew. But I wasn't going to tell him. Nor was I going to tell him many of the valuables weren't in the shuttle, but were in various hidden compartments of my vacuum suit. In fact, if I was smart I would try to divert him back to the original subject and not fight with him about who was a tomb robber and who wasn't. But it was difficult to completely contain my anger.

"Think of all the information the Lateon could have given us," I went on.

"What information?" he snapped, all civility gone. "They're trying to kill us—what else do we need to know?"

"Maybe we could learn something that would help end this war."

"The way to win the war is to exterminate them! Build bigger and better ships and new weapons, then wipe them out." He grinned, not a pretty sight. "Not that we will need any of that."

"But we—"

"Enough!" he barked. "Before I give an order to exterminate *you*."

"We're citizens. We have rights that guarantee us—"

"You are tomb robbers, no more. Out here I am the law and you have no rights that I don't give you."

I knew when to shut up. He was right. If the *Morning Light* never returned, no one would care and there wouldn't be any big search. There certainly weren't any witnesses.

In response to a soft beep, Admiral Thiriree glanced at his wristscreen. He motioned to a short sergeant behind him. "Destroy their shuttle and lock them in their ship. We'll deal with them later. We have more important matters at the moment."

"You can't destroy—" Jance yelled.

Admiral Thiriree ignored him as he strode away, but the sergeant he left in control knocked Jance to the ground with a backhanded slap. Then he motioned to someone in the corner of the bay and suddenly a crane descended from the ceiling, seized our shuttle, slowly dragged it out of the bay and tossed it into space.

"No!" yelled Jance. I motioned for him to be quiet. For some reason, he stopped yelling.

Seven Marines escorted us to the *Morning Light*. It could have been worse. I'd rather be locked in my own ship than in Thiriree's brig.

"You let them destroy our shuttle!" Jance said as we went inside.

"What was I going to do? Fight them?"

Jance just frowned, but I could tell he was sulking again.

"What's going on here?" I asked him.

"More than you realize," he replied, his slender body limping toward the bridge. "Come see."

I followed him. Like most modern starships, the bridge was almost spherical, without a window. Who needed to see out when we had modern scanning devices? A 3D projection of the ship's surroundings was displayed around the sphere so that the occupants of the bridge were aware of their surroundings in all directions.

I stared at the scene displayed now. The sensors that collected the necessary data shouldn't have been working with the *Morning Light* buried in the bowels of the military cruiser. This scene shouldn't exist.

But it did.

The battlecruiser had obviously left orbit. Behind us was the gray planet, and beyond that the black hole, the white dwarf and its matter-transfer stream. That wasn't the problem. The problem was closer, about ten kilometers away.

The Lateon ship.

Somewhere deep inside me, I knew that the Admiral was right. We would wipe them out if the Lateons continued to challenge us. We would develop the weapons and ships necessary to overwhelm them, because that was nature of man. But not yet. Because at this moment their ship was bigger than ours. Since destroying our fleet two hundred years ago, the Lateon monster ship had never been seen, but here it was, five kilometers long, paralleling our path, bristling with every kind of weapon humankind had discovered and a few more we only suspected.

One human battlercruiser versus this particular Lateon ship was no contest. I looked at its mottled brown surface, imagining every weapon aimed straight at me.

"I managed to tap the battlecruiser's sensor datastream," Jance interjected.

Admiral Grumpy would probably shoot us if he knew we had tapped his sensors but I guess I was glad Jance was a tech whiz. Still, maybe there are some things you shouldn't know. For instance, I wasn't entirely sure that I really wanted to know we were in the gunsights of that Lateon behemoth.

"Why did the Navy cruiser return to the planet after the archs left?" Jance asked. "The Admiral surely knew it wasn't safe."

An interesting question. Why indeed? Something here was not what it seemed.

And then it came to me, though it was accompanied by more questions than answers. "Admiral Thiriree didn't want any contact between us and the Lateons," I said.

"What do you mean?"

I didn't reply at first. Incoherent thoughts . . . strange ideas . . . were twirling around in my mind. Something that the Lateon had said. I looked back at the planet as it slowly receded. It didn't quite fit together—I had the pieces but I couldn't put the puzzle together yet.

"Admiral Thiriree didn't want us to discover something he already knew, because we might tell the Lateon."

"What would that be?"

"I don't know," I said.

"It doesn't make sense," Jance said.

"It makes perfect sense, just not to us," I replied. "At least, not yet."

As the battlecruiser accelerated in a spiraled escape from the doomed planet behind us, the Lateon ship mirrored our course. At first, I was afraid that our military friends would do something rash, but apparently Admiral Thiriree was temporarily infected with a good case of common sense. But what would happen when we approached the jump point?

At ten hours we found out. The Lateon ship suddenly accelerated and moved ahead of the battlecruiser, blocking its course. A desperate dance began. Feint, move, counter . . . incredibly the Lateon ship was always there ahead of us, forcing the Earth ship to change directions. And with each movement, the Lateon ship edged closer. I could sense the Earth crew's frustration and anxiety. I hoped that Admiral Thiriree's common sense persisted.

What were the Lateons after?

Of course!

"Get ready to leave," I told Jance. I hustled down to the hold, returning in about five minutes after digging through my vacuum suit.

Sometimes Jance knew me well enough not to ask questions.

"Let's go."

Jance glanced at me from his chair, raising his eyebrows and shrugging his thin shoulders.

"Fast," I said.

All we needed was a few seconds of luck. I hoped that the threat from the Lateon ship was distracting the guards. After all, what fool in a small explorer would wander into the gunsights of *two* warships?

The *Morning Light* jerked from the deck, and dashed toward the opening of the shuttle bay. Then we were out into open space, followed by a flurry of blaster fire from the guards. But if any shots hit us, they didn't cause any obvious damage.

Immediately, our front viewscreen blinked alive, the face of a Navy officer glaring at us six times life size.

"You are ordered to return!"

"We'd rather not," I replied.

"Would you *rather* be blown out of existence?"

"That wouldn't be our first choice," I said. "What about you?"

The Navy officer laughed harshly. "You're threatening *us*?"

I shrugged. "We're not. But there's no telling what our Lateon friends might think when you start firing at us. They might even think you're firing at them, since we're right between the two ships."

The Terran officer understood immediately because his face turned bright red, and he began sputtering. I snapped off the sound.

"We can't stay between them forever," Jance said.

"Hopefully, we won't have to." I punched a few commands into the computer terminal. Ten seconds later, the ship flinched as a small messenger probe was launched. Jance and I watched it drift toward the Lateon ship. I hoped it was moving slowly enough that the Lateons would realize it wasn't a threat, though it was difficult to imagine that something three meters long would be very threatening to a ship the size of an asteroid. And apparently their thought processes agreed with my logic, because they didn't fire on us.

"Keep close to the probe," I told Jance.

We followed, a mere kilometer behind the probe, bearing down on the brown, rough surface that was filling the sky. Our viewscreen blinked, and this time Admiral Thiriree's face stared at us, contorted in anger. I left the sound off.

"Should I talk to him?" I asked.

Jance shook his head. "Not much point to it. We can't make him any madder than he already is."

"You don't think I should tell him he saved my life?"

"Not really."

The probe approached the Lateon ship. When it reached a few hundred meters the engines reversed, obeying my programming. Now it drifted very slowly. Suddenly a port opened in the side of the Lateon ship and with a flash of light the probe was gone.

"It's time to say goodbye to Admiral Thiriree," I said.

From this moment on, we were at the mercy of the Lateons, having moved the *Morning Light* to the far side of the Lateon ship. I was willing to take my chances with them, happy the Lateon ship's mass and armament were between the *Morning Light* and Admiral Thiriree.

"What was in the messenger probe?" Jance asked.

I told him, giving Jance a lesson in Lateon reproduction.

"I don't understand why the memories of one Lateon pod are so important," Jance wondered. "And how did shooting at you protect its Thought Sac? Wouldn't it have been better to just ignore you and fly back to his ship?"

The question triggered answers in my brain. I pictured the Lateon fighter coming over the horizon, its beams blasting. *It could have hit me easily!*

The answer was obvious. Again I had completely misinterpreted its actions.

"The Lateon wasn't shooting at me—it was trying to destroy the central building!"

Jance turned to look at me in surprise. "Well, it was successful." It was clear that he didn't understand the implications yet.

"Yes, it was," I mused, trying to put it all together, finally doing so. "It didn't want us to discover something that it had found there, the same thing that Admiral Thiriree didn't want us to discover," I went on, half to myself and half to Jance. "That was why it also destroyed some of the outlying buildings."

"To decrease the chances of you finding what it was trying to hide?" Jance asked.

"Yes. Unfortunately, the Lateon didn't realize that I was armed and wasn't prepared for me to attack with my antimatter grenade. After I destroyed its fighter, eliminating its ability to return to the ship or even communicate with it, it was desperate and came after me, trying to steal transportation."

I paused. "Of course, what the Lateon didn't know is that Admiral Thiriree had already discovered the secret of this world."

"Which is?"

"This," I replied, pulling from my pocket the black figurine I had found.

"They looked a lot like the Lateons," Jance said.

"No, the secret is that they *were* the Lateons." I tried to explain my revelation to Jance. "Imagine yourself exploring the ruins of this planet in the last moments of its existence, searching for clues about its builders. Imagine finding those clues, and imagine that you found that the builders of this city were your own ancestors."

"Ancestors of the Lateons built this world?"

"Yes. Their forgotten ancestors built this city."

"I thought the Lateons didn't forget."

"That's what I thought too, but I was wrong. The ability of the Lateons to pass down their memories is obviously limited. Eventually the memories degrade, and when they do, it's catastrophic. Do you know what a telomere is?"

"No."

"It's the end cap on our DNA. Every time a cell divides the DNA uses up a telomere, until the strand has no more. Then it can no longer divide and the cell dies. A finite life span is programmed into our cells. I think the Lateons have a similar problem, except the memory degradation occurs over a longer period of time. I can't explain what, but something in the Thought Sac wears out over time, and the Lateons stop passing their memories on to the next generation. And unfortunately, the Lateons can't function without the memories and eventually the entire race descends into barbarism."

"But then they begin a new cycle?"

"Yes. Maybe instead of wearing out, whatever carries the memories fills up, like a computer memory chip, and has to be wiped clean, to start accumulating memories again with a new cycle."

"Theoretically, the Lateons may have been through numerous cycles," Jance observed. "Programmed cultural obsolescence."

"Yes."

"And you think that's what is happening to them now?"

"Yes. And Admiral Thiriree knows it—remember, he said that new weapons wouldn't be necessary."

"And the Lateons didn't know this before we sent the Thought Sac to them?"

The words triggered another insight. *How could I have been so wrong? About almost everything!*

"No, they didn't have a clue when they came here. They were just curious. They came here to observe the end of this planet just as we did. But in its exploring, the Lateon discovered the truth—that its own ancestors built this world as their previous cycle was ending. Unfortunately, our friend wasn't able to communicate all this back to the mother ship after discovering the truth, because I destroyed its fighter, so the important part of the Thought Sac couldn't be delivered. But the Lateon mother ship must have detected that I took the Thought Sac or the Lateons wouldn't have been after us."

"And it wasn't the memories and intelligence of its own pod that it was trying to save?"

"No, those memories were of minor importance. The Lateon needed to communicate what it found out about their ancestors. Its *personal* memories of that find were what the Lateon needed to communicate to the ship! And that's what Admiral Thiriree didn't want to happen—Thiriree didn't care whether or not *we* learned the secret, but he didn't want the *Lateons* to discover it! And the dead Lateon didn't want us to know the secret because as far as it was concerned we were as much an enemy as Admiral Thiriree."

"Both of them wanted to prevent us from knowing a secret all parties already had discovered."

"Yes."

"Do you think that knowing what happened to the Lateons during the previous cycle might allow them to prevent it from happening again?"

"Maybe."

"So maybe we just saved the Lateons from repeating their cycle."

"It's certainly possible."

"And maybe we save them from being destroyed by us."

"Hopefully."

We were quiet for a minute, staring at the stars as we accelerated toward the jump point.

Jance broke the silence. "Well, I hope that you brought back more than the Thought Sac, or we're going to be broke. This was a long, expensive trip."

I smiled. "Don't worry. The pockets of my vaccum suit are loaded with goodies. We'll be more than okay."

The viewscreen blinked and Admiral Thiriree was replaced by repetitive splashes of multi-colored light.

"What's that?" Jance asked.

I grinned. "That's the Lateons saying thank you."

The colors vanished, and Admiral Thiriree appeared again, still yelling on the muted screen.

"I don't think our friendly Admiral is saying thank you," Jance chuckled.

"I doubt it, and I don't think we want to run into him again any time soon."

Again I pulled out the little figurine of the Lateon that I had found on the planet and held it up to the screen so that the good Admiral could see it. Then I waved goodbye to him and snapped off the viewscreen in preparation for our jump.

As Jance finalized the preparations, I leaned back in my acceleration couch and thought about the Lateons, our enemies. Memories are a strange and wonderful thing. Memories give us continuity with our past, with our history. They help separate us from lower animals. I don't know what animals remember of their brief past, but I suspect their memories are vague and misty shadows compared to ours. For the Lateons, memories link them with their distant ancestors. This is as hard for me to imagine as it would be for a mouse to imagine the memories of a human. I cannot conceive of pictures in my mind originating in a long dead someone from the dark beginnings of humanity, but maybe that is my own failing. After all, I am not an ordinary human either. I can barely conceive of childhood, since mine is nothing but a hole in my consciousness.

The Universe can be a cold and heartless place, with life surviving only by happenstance, scratching out an existence between the cataclysms of creation. Quasars, black holes, nova, supernova, colliding galaxies—how could creations of DNA and fragile cells expect to survive?

But the glory was that we *did* survive—and *should* survive— whether we were human or Lateon. And we had memories to prove it.

Suanne Warr lives in North Carolina, nestled between the mountains and the ocean. She loves reading, hiking, studying history, and keeping up her martial arts. She is grateful to her husband and two kids for their enthusiastic support of her writing. For more information you can visit her website at www.suannewarr.com.

Watcher in the Dark
by Suanne Warr

Yan reached into the hole they'd dug around the metallic box and gripped it by the sides. "Ready?" he asked.

Kay shifted beside him, her hands hovering. "Ready."

As Yan lifted, Kay slid a fillzo pack into the hole and activated it. The foamy stuff filled the hole as he lifted the box so the crumbling dirt was held in place. With an excavation of this size it was best to disturb the site as little as possible.

The comunit crackled. "Captain Tung?"

Yan ignored it. It was always sounding off at a bad time.

Kay slipped a hand under the box, and together they moved it to rest beside three more of its kind.

"Come in, Captain Tung. Immediate response requested."

Yan scooped up the com. "Here."

"Captain Tung, this is Medic Eller. We have detected the presence of another ship entering the planetary atmosphere."

Yan paused, his eyes going inadvertently to the sky. Beside him Kay swore softly.

"Have they a registered ship's code?" he asked.

"They are registered with the Altuin Mines, but Thom says the code looks shady."

Thom was their resident expert on all things outside the law. Yan considered a bluish bug crawling up his leg. Flicked it off.

Okay, so he should assume they were pirates. He sighed. Just once he'd like to carry out a retrieval without the whole thing blowing wide open.

He turned to Kay. "Start packing the Aero Flyer."

He lifted the comunit. "Prepare the *Fire Lizard* for take-off. We'll be there by," he checked his watch, "13:06. Over and out."

"What about these big boxes?" Kay asked. "They'll slow us down."

Yan glanced at the boxes, then around the site. They had only been working for a few days, and hadn't even started on the underground tombs.

"Put them on," he said. "There's no reason the pirates will come here directly, so we should have time."

Kay glanced skyward, her face questioning.

"Even taking what little we've found we're not likely to recoup our expenses for this trip."

Kay nodded and rearranged the Aero Flyer to fit the boxes. In a flat five minutes they had the site clean. Yan settled into the side seat while Kay took the controls. Their route took them in a curve over the old city's remains.

Yan looked down, tracing the roads, picking out the market square. Perhaps the pirates would be content to loot here, above ground. There was no physical sign of the tomb's entrance within the city, so without a Finder they might never know of its existence.

Yan sighed, and sat back. One could hope.

He looked up and around. Something tickled at his Finder's sense. Then he saw it—a big V-80 Flyer, coming in fast from the east, and headed for the *Fire Lizard*.

"Kay, turn us around!" The Aero was no match for a V-80, with its superior weaponry and greater speed.

Yan scooped up the comunit, then paused. If he made contact, the V-80 Flyer would pick up the signal and know his location.

The *Fire Lizard* should have seen it coming and gotten their shields up; if they hadn't, there was little he could do to help them.

As Kay turned the Aero Flyer, Yan swiveled in his seat to watch the V-80. It was hard to tell from here, but it looked to be making a circular pass around the *Fire Lizard.* Looking for stragglers? If that was the case—

"Take us back toward the tomb entrance," he told Kay. "We've got to get out of sight."

Kay took one look over her shoulder, then flipped on the static shield. She kept the Aero Flyer low, flying as close to the trees as was safe. In a moment they were back amongst the city ruins, flying through the empty streets. At the edge of the city she slowed, looked to Yan.

Yan closed his eyes and slid into a light trance. Luckily this was something he had found before, so there was no need to send out his chi in a greater seeking . . .

There. He opened his eyes and took the controls from Kay, guiding the Aero to a spot just outside the city. The land dipped into a hollow and was filled with tightly growing brush.

He flew slowly above its length, looking for a thinner patch. When he found one he put out the sturdy wheels and brought the Aero Flyer down.

Branches snapped and creaked against the windows. He nosed the Aero deeper into the hollow, then let the craft come to rest in the bottom.

Kay was already filling two emergency packs with supplies. Yan took one and added the comunit, his smaller excavation tools, a spare dart gun and darts. On his person he carried another dart gun in an outside sheath and two throwing knives. Kay give him a look while she strapped on her own dart gun.

Yan grinned. She'd rather pack a big gun, but Yan's training as a finder had taught him to respect the positive chi found in simple things. He was reluctant to allow blaster fire to obliterate it.

"Just remember, the dart can get through anything but a blaster shield, and if we need to use blasters we're in the wrong kind of work."

Kay shrugged. This was an old argument. "I've got nothing against dart guns. I just feel more comfortable with something heavy at my hip."

They swung out of the Aero Flyer and set it to the highest concealment shield, then headed down the gully.

At about the half-way point Yan called a brief rest so he could listen for any sounds of pursuit without their noises masking it. Perhaps he should go into a Finder's trance to check on the whereabouts of the V-80 Flyer?

No. Regardless of where the V-80 was now, he and Kay needed to get under cover. And that meant going into the caverns under the dead city. He started them walking again.

The trouble was, he had no way of knowing why this city was dead. The charts registered this planet as a center of culture and learning, complete with colonies of its own before the collapse. During the feudal years following the collapse no colony had been established here, no contact had been made with the native people.

Now the Confederacy was feeling successful and looking for ruins like this one from which to salvage older, superior technology and information, but it was the job of Independent Recovery Contractors, like Yan, to make the initial retrieval and evaluate the planet's potential dangers.

He glanced at Kay. "So, what do you think happened here? The people die of a twisted plague? The predators go crazy and eat them alive?"

Kay put on a considering face. "No—these people were too advanced for something that mundane. I'm betting they zapped their own planet in a massive radioactive war. Ever wondered what you'd do for six months in de-tox?"

Yan rolled his eyes. Of course they'd taken preliminary measures to prevent toxic poisoning from chemical fallout, but that seemed to be Kay's fixation.

He looked up, around, savoring the last moments above ground. None of their work could faze him like walking down a doorway to an underground tomb. Aside from the likelihood of traps, the shifting of the years made cave-ins a good bet. Weak spots in the earth that stirred long-buried memories of the emergence of his Finders ability.

They stopped at the entrance, little more than a manhole with a stone cover and a ladder down the side. At least it was well overgrown with the twisted shrubbery and hidden from casual sight.

"First we lower a light stick on a rope, in case the ladder doesn't hold," Yan said.

"Then, we lower me, in case the rope doesn't hold," Kay answered.

They both laughed. So she always said.

Yan fished the rope out of his pack, cracked a light stick, and fastened it to the end. They both listened as he lowered it down. They were rewarded with a soft clink as it touched bottom. No water, then.

"Okay, now—"

The sound of a Flyer approaching interrupted him.

"Or, not," Kay said. Quickly they tied the rope around the base of a bush close to the entrance, then Kay swung over the edge. Yan waited a slow count to five, then stood on the ladder while he dragged the stone across the entrance. It was only partially concealed, as the rope prevented complete closure, but it would have to do.

With the rope running through one hand and his other hand on the ladder, he climbed down. Just as he neared the bottom, he felt Kay's hand come up to grip his ankle. Hold, the gesture said. Slowly so as not to disobey that warning, Yan twisted to look over his shoulder.

The circle of light surrounding Kay gave way to the echoing darkness of a large cavern. Somewhere near the center that darkness was broken by a white luminescent light that bobbed and danced. It emitted a soft humming sound, and at its feet were strewn the bodies of a half-dozen men.

When it made no move toward them, Yan eased down the ladder to stand beside Kay. She was holding the light stick loosely in one hand, while with the other she picked at the knot. Yan looked again at the men on the ground. They didn't appear to be breathing, but he saw no obvious cause of death. They ranged from early twenties to forties, he guessed. They wore working cover-all's without insignia, but here and there was the red on black skull tattoo of the Raeesa pirates. Yan shook his head. The Raeesa had a reputation for the ruthless destruction of any ancient cities they came across. A quick raid for items that sold well on the black market, then blaster the place so no one else would find anything useful.

Kay called his attention back to their plight. "Think we can slip around it?" she whispered.

Yan looked back at the humming light, felt its watchful edge. "No."

"Want to go back?"

"No."

"Then what about having a look?"

Yan shook his head. The way she said "having a look," made it sound like a stroll in the park. Still, he could think of no alternative, given the situation.

"You're ready to be my Keeper?" he asked.

Kay nodded, and settled her back against the stone behind them.

Yan watched her a minute, then sat down and slid into the trance. Years of long practice made the trance easy. He gathered his chi to his center, and opened himself to a general finding, then let the chi slip out through his fingers until it had emptied out and the essence of who he was stood just outside his body.

Around him swirled the misty white of the ether world, and beside him he could see the beacon light that was Kay. Wherever he went in the ether world, that light would shine for him and guide him back to his body.

He looked down at himself before turning away. His dark eyes closed, his hair dirty and disheveled. Such an ordinary body, yet all he had. He offered a quick prayer to Reichi, goddess of all who gave themselves to their chi ability, that his body would be waiting for him when he returned.

Across from Yan the light in the center of the cavern appeared fractured, streaked with blue and red. He stepped closer.

"Who are you, who comes clothed in Life?" The words burned into his mind, leaving a painful echo.

Yan formed words in his own mind to answer. "I am a Finder. I am here to find who you are and help you." Which was true, to a point. He was certainly interested in who the inhabitants of the planet had been. The recovery of lost knowledge was of high priority to his bosses in the Confederacy.

"You come to release the life force?" Once again the words ground against his chi.

Yan wished he could put a hand to his head. Release the life force? Is that what this thing was? He decided to dodge the question and focus on improving communication.

"Do you have one who can meet in my form?" he asked.

The light seemed to pulse closer and Yan held himself steady with effort.

"Follow," it said.

Yan followed it out of the room, looking back once to make sure Kay's beacon still burned bright.

The light moved quickly. The ether world blurred around Yan in streaming ribbons of gauze.

They stopped in a small, low-ceilinged room that had a silvery-white radiance. Out of the light a woman stepped. Her chi was rose shot with gold, and he caught hints of her womanly form. She looked like a priestess.

Yan bowed low.

The priestess bowed her head. "Many will die, but all will live."

It sounded like a ritual saying, so Yan bowed again.

The priestess waited. When Yan said nothing, she seated herself on a hazily-outlined chair.

"Your respect is courteous, but it does not mask your ignorance. You are a stranger here."

Yan knelt in the position of the student before her. "A stranger to your planet, yet not a stranger to your ways, perhaps," he said. He was making a guess here, but his finding sense told him it was correct.

The priestess did not move, but her chi seemed brighter. "Tell me of our ways."

"Your people, your ancestors, are gathered in these tombs. You guard them that their tombs are not plundered and their ashes remain undisturbed." Mentally he held his breath.

"Close," she said. "But we are not so interested in peace. Merely in keeping our own." She raised a hand and the ether swirled. Before him a small fire burned, and in the flames he saw the ruined city as it must have been before the collapse.

While he watched, the city filled with people and soldiers. A great shimmering dome encompassed the city and Seeing Eyes were projected into the space above. Weaponry of all kinds was made ready.

The priestess spoke. "In the final war with the Genuets the people of our planet fell back to this one stronghold. We gave the city's protection everything we had." The images swirled, and Yan watched as workers strengthened the underground tomb, deepening it to be a final place of safety. He saw children led by men and women down into the tombs. They carried supplies and the treasures from the city above, then sealed the entrance.

"As a final precaution we tied the life force of every person in the city to the ashes of our ancestors, here in these tombs. If we were to die, we would at least keep those who wrongfully used us from enjoying the spoils of their victory."

The flames showed Yan a shattered city, the dome destroyed, but a life force blazing from the tombs. The enemy threw wave after wave of weapons and soldiers against the force, but the seals held. Those who were already dead could not be killed again by poison or weaponry.

"I was the last to die. I am the Watcher at the Gate. My life force is separate from the others because I was not in my body when it died. I direct the others and watch for the day when our ashes will be safe and we may be released to reenter the cycle of life. Has that day come?"

The flame blazed up into a thousand tiny sparks and disappeared. Yan bowed himself again, using the motion to buy him thinking time. The Raeesa pirates he had seen near the entrance—what had happened to them? And were the pirates in the V-80 Flyer associates of the ones in here?

He sat up. "I believe the day has come, but I must ask questions of the Watcher."

The Watcher spread her hands in an open gesture.

"First, why were we able to enter the tombs so easily? Where are the locks and safeguards?"

"Many years ago the children of the Genuet came and broke open our seal, which was corrupted with age. Since then many have come to rob our chambers, and left their bodies behind to corrupt the tombs."

But was the life force as strong? Yan guessed not, but he would like to know for sure.

"If I may ask the Watcher—" he began.

He was interrupted by a blast that shook the walls of the tomb. The form of the Watcher blazed up, seeming to swell with light. "Come," she said, and Yan felt himself pulled through swirling mists of ether in her wake.

They stopped at the edge of a small chamber with a ragged hole blown in its side. Through the hole Yan could see the outline of the city, and going in and out of the hole were the flickering murky forms of men. They were looting the tomb and packing the goods on the V-80 Flyer.

The Watcher emitted a high, piercing note and the men stopped what they were doing to cower on the ground. The rose color of the Watcher's chi changed to purple and pulsed. Tendrils reached out like bruised fingers and touched the men.

Yan stood in shock as the Watcher ripped the chi from each man's body, then sent to disperse on the breeze. A wisp of purple escaped with each one. Without a keeper and no training in the ether world, the men's essences would be lost forever.

Yan felt in that moment the separation of his own body and chi. He looked through the ether world for the beacon of his keeper, but the pulsing light of the Watcher made it hard to see.

"Why do they come to defile our tomb?" The Watcher stood before him. "Why have *you* come? Do you seek to rob us?"

Yan felt another flash of fear. He steadied himself. "I do not come as a robber, slipping in the back ways or breaking down the door. I come to help you find a stronghold which the robbers can not breach." He paused, a plan beginning to form. "Are the bodies of these men dead?"

The Watcher turned to consider them. "Their chi has left them—the body will die soon. Why?"

Yan leaned in before answering, looking for the Raeesa tattoo. "These men come from a ship with many more men, and those men come from an even larger body of men that will continue to come until they have destroyed this place. But there is a way to stop them from coming, at least for now." He turned to face the Watcher.

"Send a portion of your life force into the bodies of these men. When you reside within them, use negative chi to make them look sick in the way of a dire disease. Then we will send them back, in their Flyer, to the ship waiting for them."

"This will stop the robbers from coming?"

Yan nodded. "The greatest fear of ship-bound men is disease. They will turn the Flyer away when they see the crew, and will report to their masters that this place is disease-ridden."

"And what of the stronghold you spoke of?" the Watcher asked.

"The tombs are breached, every encounter with the robbers leaves them defiled and the life force depleted."

Yan held himself still, formed his answer carefully. "We will speak of that soon, and at length," he said. "You must use the robber's bodies while you still can."

The Watcher seemed to accept that.

A tendril of golden rose stretched toward each form, entered each husk of a man. The bodies twitched, began to move.

The remaining form of the Watcher turned to Yan. "How will we remove what is ours from their Flyer?"

Yan looked again for his beacon and found it, dim but still glowing. "I'll return to my body, then remove the goods." He bowed again to the Watcher, then swam through the mists of ether.

When he reached Kay her beacon looked wan. Quickly he slipped back into his body and knelt beside her. She lay in a shower of rubble from the blast. Her head had a bleeding cut and she cradled one arm against her chest.

"Hey, Cap'n," she said. "I kept the light on for you."

Yan grinned. If she was joking, she'd be okay. He reached into his pack for the comunit and noticed blood on his arm. It looked to have come from a cut on his shoulder, and his fingers came away from his head sticky and red. Apparently they'd chosen a lousy place to camp.

He flicked on the comunit.

"Captain Tung, here. Medic Eller, come in."

He waited, then repeated the message. The com buzzed, then crackled to life.

"Captain, this is Thom. We've had a bit of trouble with the pirates, but we're in working order now."

Yan wondered briefly what "a bit of trouble" was to Thom, but let it pass.

"I need you to bring the ship to us. Both of us are hurt and there'll be a fair amount of cargo, too."

"You want the ship to land on the site?!"

"Yes. Right up against the ruined city." Yan paused, wondering how much to say. "I'll explain when you get here. Over and out."

He helped Kay up and together they made their way to the newly opened portion of the tombs. The Watcher waited for them, behind her the V-80 Flyer with the Raeesa pirates.

Kay stopped where she was, then pulled at Yan. "Pirates. Watch out," she said.

Yan laughed. "It's okay, these aren't really pirates. Just imposter pirates." He looked to the Watcher. "Our bodies were hurt in the blast, so I've asked my men to bring my ship and come help."

"You bring them to rob us!" The Watcher turned on him, tendrils reaching toward them.

"Wait—no!" Yan threw up a hand. "I am not a robber, nor are my men. If you wish to stay here with your ashes, we leave you that choice. We will go away with nothing." He thought guiltily of the boxes already packed in the Aero Flyer. Would it strengthen his position to offer them? Probably not. It would only bring home the point that he already *had* robbed her.

"We can get rid of these pirates—robbers—for now but eventually they will come back to destroy everything here in order to prevent another from using it. Are you strong enough to withstand an all out attack? Even if they stay in their Flyers and blaster the whole place?"

He paused to gauge her reaction. Sun slanted into the caverns opening, making it harder to see her color, but the tendrils had dropped.

"What of the stronghold you spoke of?" she asked.

"Yes." Yan took a deep breath. "I have been trained to bring ancient artifacts and knowledge from before the collapse to a place of safe keeping, where the robbers can't steal and destroy. Your tombs and homes have been defiled and can no longer keep out intruders. Where I would take you all people would be respectful and your ancestors would rest in peace."

She did not answer while Yan's ship landed. As his crew dismounted and came toward them the Watcher turned back to Yan.

"I will take your offer," she said. "But understand this. I am still the Watcher at the Gate and will pluck out the life force of anyone who approaches as a robber."

Yan bowed deeply. "Understood."

Thom stepped over beside him and spoke quietly. "What's up?"

"First transfer the contents of this V-80 to the ship's cargo, then follow the directions of this illustrious lady, and send someone to retrieve the Aero from its hiding place in the hollow. And make sure you're careful with the cargo."

Thom nodded. "Never a dull moment," he said.

Yan let him get to it, and submitted himself and Kay to the administrations of the Medic. As he watched the V-80 take off with its sickly pirates and the ship's cargo filling up under the Watcher's careful eye, he thought about the reception he'd get when he landed at the Confederacy Collection Depot.

Perhaps he should just sign over the cargo and leave, let them discover the watcher on their own. He chuckled at the thought.

But no, they'd best be given lots of forewarning. This particular batch of tomb relics had the bonus of a resident expert—and a formidable guard.

Douglas Smith's stories have appeared in over seventy magazines and anthologies in twenty-six countries around the world, including InterZone, Baen's Universe, Amazing Stories, The Third Alternative, Weird Tales, The Mammoth Book of Best New Horror, Cicada, On Spec, Oceans of the Mind, *and anthologies from Penguin/Roc, DAW, Meisha Merlin, and others. He was a finalist for the John W. Campbell Award for Best New Writer and has twice won the Aurora Award for best speculative short fiction by a Canadian. He is currently completing his first novel.*

Jigsaw
by Douglas Smith

Still in shock, Cassie Morant slumped in the cockpit of the empty hopper, staring at the two viewplates before her.

In one, the planet Griphus, a blue, green and brown marble wrapped in belts of cloud, grew smaller. Except for the shape of its land masses, it could have been Earth.

But it wasn't. Griphus was an alien world, light-years from Sol System.

A world where nineteen of her shipmates were going to die.

And one of them was Davey.

On the other viewplate, the segmented, tubular hull of the orbiting Earth wormship, the *Johannes Kepler*, grew larger. Cassie tapped a command, and the ship's vector appeared, confirming her fears.

The ship's orbit was still decaying. She opened a comm-link.

"Hopper Two to the *Kepler*," she said. "Requesting docking clearance."

Silence. Then a male voice crackled over the speaker, echoing cold and metallic in the empty shuttle.

"Acknowledged, Hopper Two. You are clear to dock, segment beta four, port nine."

Cassie didn't recognize the voice, but that wasn't surprising. The *Kepler* held the population of a small city, and Cassie was something of a loner. But she had no trouble identifying the gruff rumble she heard next.

"Pilot of hopper, identify yourself. This is Captain Theodor."

Cassie took a breath. "Sir, this is Dr. Cassandra Morant, team geologist."

Pause. "Where's team leader Stockard?" Theodor asked.

Davey. "Sir, the rest of the surface team was captured by the indigenous tribe inhabiting the extraction site. The team is . . . " Cassie stopped, her throat constricting.

"Morant?"

She swallowed. "They're to be executed at sunrise."

Another pause.

"Did you get the berkelium?" Theodor finally asked.

Cassie fought her anger. Theodor wasn't being heartless. The team below was secondary to the thousands on the ship.

"Just a core sample, sir," she said. "But it confirms that the deposit's there."

Theodor swore. "Dr. Morant, our orbit decays in under twenty hours. Report immediately after docking to brief the command team." Theodor cut the link.

Cassie stared at the huge wormship, suddenly hating it, hating its strangeness. Humans would never build something like that, she thought.

Consisting of hundreds of torus rings strung along a central axis like donuts on a stick, the ship resembled a giant metallic worm. A dozen rings near the middle were slowly rotating, providing the few inhabited sections with an artificial gravity.

Thousands of us, and we barely fill a fraction of it, she thought. *It wasn't meant for us. We shouldn't be here.*

Humans had just begun to explore their solar system, when Max Bremer and his crew had found the wormships, three of them, outside the orbit of Pluto.

Abandoned? Lost? Or left to be found?

Found by the ever-curious, barely-out-of-the-trees man-apes of

Earth. Found with charted wormholes in Sol System. Found with still-only-partly-translated, we-think-this-button-does-this libraries and databases, and we-can't-fix-it-so-it-better-never-break technology. Incredibly ancient yet perfectly functioning Wormer technology.

Wormers. The inevitable name given to Earth's unknown alien benefactors.

Five years later, humanity was here, exploring the stars, riding like toddlers on the shoulders of the Wormers.

But Cassie no longer wanted to be here. She wished she was back on Earth, safely cocooned in her apartment, with Vivaldi playing, lost in one of her jigsaw puzzles.

She shifted uncomfortably in the hopper seat. Like every Wormer chair, like the ship itself, it almost fit a human. But not quite.

It's like forcing a piece to fit in a jigsaw, she thought. It's a cheat, and in the end, the picture is wrong. Humans shouldn't be here. We forced ourselves into a place in the universe where we don't fit. We cheated, and we've been caught. And now we're being punished.

For they faced a puzzle that threatened the entire ship. She'd had a chance to solve it on the planet.

And she'd failed.

Cassie hugged herself, trying to think. She was good at puzzles, but this one had a piece missing. She thought back over events since they'd arrived through the wormhole four days ago. The answer had to be there . . .

Four days ago, Cassie had sat in her quarters on the *Kepler*, hunched over a jigsaw puzzle covering her desk. The desk, like anything Wormer, favored unbroken flowing contours, the seat sweeping up to chair back wrapping around to desk surface. Viewplates on the curved walls showed telescopic shots of Griphus. The walls and ceiling glowed softly.

Lieutenant David Stockard, Davey to Cassie, lay on her bunk watching her.

"Don't you get tired of jigsaws?" he asked.

She shrugged. "They relax me. It's my form of meditation. Besides, I'm doing my homework."

Davey rolled off the bunk. She watched him walk over, wondering again what had brought them together. If she could call what they had being "together"—sometimes friendship, sometimes romance, sometimes not-talking-to-each-other.

They seemed a case study in "opposites attract." She was a scientist, and Davey was military. She was dark, short and slim, while he was fair, tall and broad. She preferred spending her time quietly, reading, listening to classical music—and doing jigsaw puzzles. Davey always had to be active.

But the biggest difference lay in their attitudes to the Wormers. Davey fervently believed that the alien ships were meant to be found by humans, that the Universe wanted them to explore the stars.

To Cassie, the Universe wasn't telling them everything it knew. She felt that they didn't understand Wormer technology enough to be risking thousands of lives.

He looked at the puzzle. "Homework?"

"I printed a Mercator projection of topographic scans of Griphus onto plas-per, and the computer cut it into a jigsaw."

The puzzle showed the planet's two major continents, which Dr. Xu, head geologist and Cassie's supervisor, had dubbed Manus and Pugnus. *Hand and fist.* The western continent, Pugnus, resembled a clenched fist and forearm, punching across an ocean at Manus, which resembled an open hand, fingers and thumb curled ready to catch the fist. Colored dots, each numbered, speckled the map.

"What are the dots?" Davey asked.

"Our shopping list. Deposits of rare minerals. That is, if you believe Wormer archives and Wormer scanners—"

"Cassie, let's not start—" Davey said.

"Davey, these ships are at least ten thousand years old—"

"With self-healing nanotech—" Davey replied.

"That we don't understand—"

"Cassie . . . " Davey sighed.

She glared, then folded her arms. "Fine."

Davey checked the time on his per-comm unit. "Speaking of homework, Trask wants surface team rescue procedures by oh-eight-hundred. Gotta go." He kissed Cassie and left.

Cassie bit back a comment that this was a scientific, not a military, expedition. The likely need for Trask's "procedures" was low in her opinion.

She would soon change her mind.

An hour later, Cassie was walking along the busy outer corridor of the ring segment assigned to the science team. Suddenly, the ship shuddered, throwing Cassie and others against one curving wall.

The ship lurched again, and the light from the glowing walls blinked out. People screamed. Cassie stumbled and fell. And kept falling, waiting for the impact against the floor that never came, until she realized what had happened.

The ring's stopped rotating, she thought. *We've lost artificial gravity.*

She floated in darkness for around thirty minutes, bumping into others, surrounded by whispers, shouts and sobbing. Suddenly, the lights flicked back on. Cassie grabbed for a chair and felt gravity returning like an invisible hand tugging at her guts, followed by a sudden heaviness in her limbs. She rolled then rose on shaky legs. People stood dazed, looking like scattered pieces in a jigsaw that before had been a coherent picture of normality.

What had happened?

The intercom broke through the rising babble of conversations. "The following personnel report immediately to port six, segment beta four for surface team detail." Twenty names followed. One was Davey's.

One was hers. *What was going on?*

An hour later, her questions still unanswered, she and nineteen others sat in a hopper as it left the *Kepler*. Hoppers were smaller Wormer craft used for ship-to-surface trips and exploration. With a tubular hull, a spherical cockpit at the head, and six jointed legs allowing them to rest level on any terrain, they resembled grasshoppers.

The team faced each other in two rows of seats in the main cabin. Cassie only knew two others besides Davey. Manfred Mubuto, balding, dark and round, was their xeno-anthropologist. Liz Branson, with features as sharp as her sarcasm, was their linguist. Four were marines. But the rest, over half the team, were mining techs. *Why?*

Davey addressed them. She'd never seen him so serious.

"The *Kepler's* power loss resulted from the primary fuel cell being purged. Engineering is working to swap cells, but that requires translating untested Wormer procedures. We may need to replenish the cell, which means extracting berkelium from Griphus for processing."

That's why I'm here, Cassie thought. Berkelium, a rare trans-uranium element, was the favored Wormer energy source. It had never been found on Earth, only manufactured. Her analysis of Griphus had shown possible deposits.

"Like every planet found via the wormholes," Davey said, "Griphus is incredibly Earth-like: atmosphere, gravity, humanoid populations—"

Liz interrupted. "We purged a fuel cell? Who screwed up?"

Davey reddened. "That's not relevant—"

"Operator error, I hear," Manfred said. "A tech misread Wormer symbols on a panel, punched an incorrect sequence—"

Liz swore. "I knew it! We're like kids trying to fly Daddy's flitter—"

Cassie started to agree, but Davey cut them off.

"We've no time for rumors," he snapped, looking at Cassie, Liz, and Manfred. "Our orbit decays in three days. I remind you that this team's under my command—including science personnel."

Manfred nodded. Liz glared, but said nothing.

Davey tapped the computer pad on his seat. A holo of Griphus appeared. "Dr. Morant, please locate the berkelium."

Cassie almost laughed at being called "Dr. Morant" by Davey, but then she caught his look. She tapped some keys, and two red dots blinked onto the holo, one in the ocean mid-way between Pugnus and Manus, and another offshore of Manus. The second site was circled.

"Wormer sensors show two sites. I've circled my recommendation," Cassie said.

"Why not the other site?" a mining tech asked.

A network of lines appeared, making the planet's surface look like a huge jigsaw puzzle.

"As on Earth," Cassie said, "the lithosphere or planetary crust of Griphus is broken into tectonic plates, irregular sections ranging from maybe fifteen kilometers thick under oceans to a hundred under continents. This shows the plate pattern on Griphus.

"Plates float on the denser, semi-molten asthenosphere, the upper part of the mantle. At 'transform' boundaries, they slide along each other, like the San Andreas Fault on Earth. At 'convergent' boundaries, they collide, forming mountains such as the Himalayas."

A line splitting the ocean between Pugnus and Manus glowed yellow. The line also ran through the other berkelium site.

"But at 'divergent' boundaries," Cassie continued, "such as this mid-oceanic trench, magma pushes up from the mantle, creating new crust, forcing the plates apart. The other site is deep in the trench, below our sub's crush depth."

Davey nodded. "So we hit the site offshore of Manus. Any indigenous population along that coast?"

"Yes," Manfred said. "From orbital pictures, they appear tribal, agrarian, definitely pre-industrial. Some large stone structures and primitive metallurgy."

"Then defending ourselves shouldn't be a problem." Davey patted the *stinger* on his belt. The Wormer weapon was non-lethal, temporarily disrupting voluntary muscular control.

"Could we try talking before we shoot them?" Liz said.

Davey just smiled. "Which brings us to communication, Dr. Branson."

Liz sighed. "Wormer translator units need a critical mass of vocabulary, syntax, and context samples to learn a language. Given the time we have, I doubt they'll help much."

"With any luck, we won't need them," Davey said. "We'll locate the deposit, send in the mining submersible, and be out before they know we're there."

Looking around her, Cassie guessed that no one felt lucky.

The hopper landed on the coast near the offshore deposit. The team wore light body suits and breathing masks to prevent ingesting anything alien to human immune systems.

Cassie stepped onto a broad beach of gray sand lapped by an ocean too green for Earth, under a sky a touch too blue. The beach ran up to a forest of trees whose black trunks rose twenty meters into the air. Long silver leaves studded each trunk, glinting like sword blades in the sun. She heard a high keening that might have been birds or wind in the strange trees.

Southwards, the beach ran into the distance. But to the north, it ended at a cliff rising up to a low mesa. Cassie walked over to Davey, who was overseeing the marines unloading the submersible and drilling equipment.

"Cool, eh?" he said, looking around them.

She pointed at the mesa. "That's cooler to a rock nut."

He looked up the beach. "Okay. But keep your per-comm on."

Cassie nodded and set out. The cliff was an hour's walk. Cassie didn't mind, enjoying the exercise and strange surroundings. She took pictures of the rock strata, and climbed to get samples at different levels. Then she walked back.

They captured Cassie just as she was wondering why the hopper seemed deserted. The natives appeared so quickly and silently, they seemed to rise from the sand. Cassie counted about forty of them, all remarkably human-like, but taller, with larger eyes, longer noses, and greenish skin. All were male, bare-chested, wearing skirts woven from sword-blade tree leaves, and leather sandals.

They led Cassie to stand before two women. One was dressed as the men were but with a headdress of a coppery metal. The other was older and wore a cape of cloth and feathers. Her head was bare, her hair long and white. Beside them, pale but unharmed, stood Liz Branson, flanked by two warriors.

The older woman spoke to Liz in a sing-song melodic language. Cassie saw that the linguist wore a translator earplug. Liz sat down, motioning Cassie to do the same. The male warriors sat circling them. The two native women remained standing.

Cassie realized she was trembling. "What happened?"

Liz grimaced. "We've stepped in it big time. The Chadorans—our captors—believe a sacred object called 'the third one' lies underwater here. Only a priestess may enter these waters. When our techs launched the sub, the natives ambushed us from the trees with blowguns. They grabbed the techs when they surfaced."

"Where's Davey?" Cassie asked, then added, " . . . and everyone?"

"Taken somewhere. They seemed okay."

"Why not you, too?"

"The tribe's matriarchal," Liz said. "The old woman is Cha-kay, their chief. The younger one, Pre-nah, is their priestess. Because I'm female and knew their language, Cha-kay assumed I was our leader. But I said you were."

"You what?" Cassie cried.

"Cassie, we need someone they'll respect," Liz said, her face grim. "That means a female who didn't defile the site. That means you."

"God, Liz—wait, how can you talk to them?"

Liz frowned. "It's weird. The translator produced understandable versions within minutes, pulling from Wormer archives of other worlds. That implies all those languages share the same roots. The Wormers may have seeded all these worlds."

Cassie didn't care. "What can I do?"

"Convince Cha-kay to let us go."

"How?" Cassie asked.

"She wants to show you something. It's some sort of test."

"And if I fail?"

Liz handed Cassie the translator. "Then they'll kill us."

Cassie swallowed. "I won't let that happen."

They led Cassie to a long boat with a curving prow powered by a dozen rowers. Cha-kay rode in a chair near the stern, Cassie at her feet. Pre-nah and six warriors stood beside them.

They traveled up a winding river through dense jungle. Conversation was sparse, but sufficient to convince Cassie that the translator unit worked. After three hours, they landed at a clearing. Cassie climbed out, happy to move and stretch. She blinked.

Blue cubes, ranging from one to ten meters high, filled the clearing. They were hewn from stone and painted. The party walked past the cubes to a path that switch-backed up a low mountain. They began to climb.

Cassie groaned but said nothing, since the aged Cha-kay didn't seem bothered by the climb. As they went, Cassie noticed smaller cubes beside the path.

Night had fallen when they reached the top and they stepped onto a tabletop of rock about eighty meters across. Cassie gasped.

A huge cube, at least fifty meters on each side nearly filled the plateau. It was blue. It was glowing.

And it was hovering a meter off the ground.

Cha-kay led Cassie to it, and Cassie received another shock. On its smooth sides, Cassie could see familiar symbols.

The artifact, whatever its purpose, was Wormer.

Cha-kay prostrated herself, telling Cassie to do the same. As Cassie did so, she peeked underneath the cube. A column of pulsating blue light shone from a crevice to touch the base of the artifact at its center. Reaching down to her belt, Cassie activated her scanner. She'd check the readings later.

Rising, Cha-kay indicated a large diagram on the artifact. In it, a cube, a sphere, and a tetrahedron formed points of an equilateral triangle.

"It is a map. We are here," Cha-kay said, pointing to the cube. "The gods left three artifacts, but hid one. The third will appear when the gods return and lay their hands on the other two." Then, pointing to the outline of a hand on the artifact, Cha-kay looked at Cassie.

"Touch," she said.

With a sudden chill, Cassie understood. *They think we're the Wormers, finally returning*, she thought.

This was the test, on which the lives of her shipmates, of the entire ship, depended.

Reaching out a trembling hand, Cassie felt resistance from some invisible barrier and a warm tingling, then her hand slipped through onto the outline on the artifact.

Nothing happened.

Murmurs grew behind her. Feeling sick, Cassie looked at Cha-kay. To her surprise, the old woman smiled.

"Perhaps," Cha-kay said, "it rises even now."

Cassie understood. Cha-kay hoped to find that the third artifact had emerged from the sea when they returned to the beach. Cassie didn't share her hope.

They spent the night there. Pretending to sleep, Cassie checked her scanner readings. They confirmed her suspicions. The column of light showed berkelium emissions. The artifact was connected to a deposit as an energy source.

The next day, a similar journey brought them to the second artifact, located on another flat mountain peak. The only difference was the artifact itself, a huge glowing red tetrahedron. Cassie again saw a column of light underneath and detected berkelium. She touched the artifact, again with no apparent effect, and the party began the trip back.

Cha-kay seemed to have grown genuinely fond of Cassie. She told Cassie how her people found the artifacts generations ago, eventually realizing that the drawing was a map. They learned to measure distances and angles, and determined that the third artifact lay in the coastal waters. Priestesses had dived there for centuries but found nothing. Still they believed.

Cassie did some calculations, and found the Chadoran estimate remarkably accurate. Still, she wondered why the Wormers would locate two artifacts in identical settings on mountain plateaus, yet place the third underwater. Perhaps the third location had subsided over the years. But her scans showed no sunken mountains off the coast.

Cassie enjoyed Cha-kay's company, but as they neared the coast, her fear grew. Cha-kay fell silent as well. As the boat reached the beach, they stood at the railing, hands clasped, scanning the waters for the third artifact.

Nothing.

Cries arose among the warriors. Pre-nah approached Cha-kay. "The strangers are false gods," the priestess said. "They must die."

Cha-kay stared across the ocean. Finally, she nodded. Cassie's legs grew weak as two warriors moved towards her.

Cha-kay raised her hand. "No. This one goes free. She did not defile the sacred place."

Pre-nah didn't look pleased, but she bowed her head.

They landed, and Cha-kay walked with Cassie to the hopper.

"When?" Cassie asked, her voice breaking.

"At sunrise, child," Cha-kay said. "I am sorry."

Cassie boarded the hopper. She engaged the auto-launch, then slumped in her seat, as the planet and her hopes grew smaller.

After docking, Cassie went immediately to the briefing room, as Captain Theodor had ordered. She quickly took a seat in one of a dozen Wormer chairs around a holo display unit. Dr. Xu gave her a worried smile. Commander Trask glared.

Theodor cleared his throat, a rumble that brought everyone's gaze to his stocky form.

"I'll be brief. Our orbit collapses in nineteen hours. Attempts to swap fuel cells were unsuccessful. The team sent to extract the berkelium has been captured and faces execution. Only Dr. Morant escaped."

Everyone looked at Cassie. All she could think of was how she'd failed.

Theodor continued. "Dr. Morant will summarize events on the planet. Then I need ideas."

Cassie told her story, then answered questions, mostly dealing with the artifacts. Will Epps, their expert on Wormer texts and writing, after analyzing her scans, agreed that the artifacts were Wormer.

The team began reviewing and discarding proposals. Finally, Theodor made his decision. A platoon of marines would drop outside the Chadoran city. Three squads would act as a diversion, drawing warriors from the city, while one squad slipped in for a search and rescue. One hour later, a hopper would drop two mining subs at the berkelium site.

"Sir, the priestess dives there daily," Cassie said. "When they see our subs, they'll kill the team."

"That's why I'm giving the rescue squads an hour head start," Theodor replied. "It's not much, but our priority is to replenish our fuel before our orbit decays. I can't delay the berkelium extraction any longer."

Cassie slumped in her seat. *Davey, Liz*, she thought, *they're all going to die.*

Trask stood. "If Dr. Morant could provide a topographical display of the area, I'll outline the attack plan."

Cassie tapped some keys, and the planetary view of Griphus appeared, including the pattern of tectonic plates.

Like a jigsaw puzzle, Cassie thought. *Why can't this be that simple?*

"Zoom in to the landing site," Trask said.

Freezing the rotation over Pugnus and Manus, Cassie started to zoom in, then stopped, staring at the display. *No*, she thought, *it's too wild. But maybe . . .* She began tapping furiously, and calculations streamed across the holo.

"What the hell's going on?" Trask asked.

Theodor frowned. "Dr. Morant?"

Cassie looked at her results. *My god, it fits. But the time span . . .*

"Dr. Morant!" Theodor barked.

Cassie's head jerked up. Everyone was staring. *It's wild,* she thought, *but it fits.* And she liked things that fit.

"Captain," Cassie said, "what if we proved to the Chadorans that the deposit site is *not* sacred?"

Theodor frowned. "Discredit their religion? I don't—"

"No," Cassie said. "I mean, prove that it isn't sacred because . . ." She stopped. *What if she was wrong?* But it was Davey and the team's only chance.

" . . . because the third artifact isn't there," she finished.

Trask snorted. "Then why will they kill to protect the site?"

"Because they *think* it's there, based entirely on the diagrams on the artifacts."

"And you think those diagrams are wrong?" Theodor asked, but his voice held none of Trask's derision.

"I think they were correct once," she said. "But not anymore."

"So where's the artifact?" Theodor asked.

Cassie's hand trembled as she tapped more keys. Two green lights appeared inland on the western coast of Manus, followed by a red light just off the same coast, forming the triangular pattern diagrammed on the artifacts.

"The two green lights are the known artifacts. The red light is both the supposed underwater location of the third and our targeted berkelium site."

She swallowed. *Here goes,* she thought.

"And this, I believe, is the actual location of the third artifact." A third green light appeared.

Everyone started talking at once. Theodor silenced them with a wave of his hand. He stared at the display.

On the eastern coast of Pugnus, on a separate continent and an entire ocean away from the underwater site, blinked the third green light.

Theodor turned to Cassie. "Explain."

"It involves tectonic plate theory—" she began.

"I know the theory. What's the relevance?"

Cassie tapped a key. The mid-oceanic trench between Pugnus and Manus glowed yellow.

"That trench is a 'divergent' boundary," Cassie said, "where new crust is being formed, pushing Manus and Pugnus further apart every year. But that also means that sometime in the past, they looked like this." The plates began to shift. The two large continents moved closer until the fist of Pugnus slipped into the open hand of Manus like a piece in a puzzle. Someone gasped, as the third green light on Pugnus aligned itself over the red light offshore of Manus.

Theodor nodded. "You're saying the Wormers originally placed the three artifacts as the diagrams show, but the missing one moved relative to the other two as the continents separated."

Xu shook his head. "Cassie . . . "

Cassie sighed. "I know. The time frame is . . . difficult to believe."

"How old are the artifacts if your theory is true?" Theodor asked.

Xu answered. "At least as old as the core sample from the deposit site, which formed as the trench started to spread. Cassie, what was the isotopic clock dating on the sample?"

Cassie hesitated. "Its age was thirty, uh . . . " She swallowed. " . . . million years."

The eruption of exclamations made Cassie want to slink from the room. Theodor again waved for silence.

In desperation, Cassie turned to Will Epps. "We know that these ships are at least ten thousand years old. But couldn't they be much older?"

Several people squirmed. Their situation was bad enough without being reminded that they were relying on alien technology at least a hundred centuries old.

Will shrugged. "There's so much self-healing nano-tech, we can't estimate their age accurately."

"So any Wormer technology could be much older as well, right?" Cassie asked.

"But thirty million years . . . " Xu shook his head, as did others.

Cassie was losing them.

She turned to Theodor.

"Captain, it all fits. It explains why the Chadorans have never found the artifact. Why our sub didn't see it. Why Wormers placed two artifacts on mountains, but supposedly put the third underwater. They didn't. They put it on land too."

"Can't we scan for the artifact?" Trask said.

"The other two don't show on scanners," Epps said. "They're shielded somehow."

"So the third artifact *could* be where the Chadorans say it is," Trask replied.

Cassie sat back, feeling defeated. Then something struck her.

"Both artifacts I saw are located over berkelium deposits, yet neither site appears on the mineral scans. The artifacts shield the berkelium too."

"So?" Theodor said.

"We detected berkelium at the underwater site. That means nothing's shielding it. The third artifact isn't there."

Trask started to protest, but Theodor raised a hand. "I agree with Dr. Morant. It fits." He stood up. "Cassie, I'll give you the same lead time. Take a hopper down now."

Cassie was already sprinting for the door.

On a mountain plateau, across an ocean from where they had first landed on Griphus, Cassie and Davey stood, arms around each other's waist.

"So you saved me, the team, the entire ship," Davey said, "and made one of the most important discoveries in history. Not a bad day."

Cassie grinned. "Actually, the toughest part was convincing Cha-kay to fly in the hopper. Now she wants a world tour."

Beside them, happiness lighting her face, Cha-kay gazed at a huge glowing yellow sphere hovering above the ground.

The third artifact.

With one difference. A beam of energy shone from the sphere into the sky. The beam had begun the moment Cassie had touched the cube.

Cassie's per-comm beeped. It was Theodor. "Dr. Morant, all three artifacts now appear on scanners, all beaming to the same point in space—"

"A new wormhole," Cassie interrupted.

Pause. "How'd you know?" Theodor asked.

Cassie grinned. "Good guess."

"Anyway, Earth's sending a second wormship. We'll all have the option of returning home or exploring the wormhole. Once again, good work, Morant." Theodor signed off.

"You didn't mention your theory," Davey said.

"That the wormhole leads to the Wormers' home world? Just a hunch."

"Explain it to me then."

Cassie nodded at the cube. "I think the artifacts were a puzzle— and the wormhole the prize."

"For us or the Chandorans?"

"For us. Another bread crumb in the trail the Wormers left us." She shrugged and laughed. "It just fits."

Davey nodded. "So what about you? Back to Earth or through the wormhole?"

"Wormhole," she said.

He raised an eyebrow. "Okay, that surprised me."

Cassie grinned. "Hey, if the Wormers liked puzzles, they couldn't have been that bad." She stared at the artifact. "Besides, we solved their puzzle, saved ourselves, became heroes to the Chadorans . . . " Her eyes followed the beam up towards the heavens.

"Maybe we fit out here after all," she said softly.

Willis Couvillier is a writer currently residing in Reno, Nevada. He has been an avid reader of science fiction and fantasy since his early youth, and has dreamt of writing the same for nearly as long. Currently Will is working on a number of SF and fantasy tales, a few stories of speculative fiction, a group of Lovecraftian-style horror tales, and has the start and outlines to a good dozen novels. Also, he has been known to jot down a poem or two, usually speculative, but more often about some real life situation he'd noticed. Will hangs out at on-line writer forums, reads books about the craft, and enjoys a good role-game and occasional CCG.

Heartcry
by Willis Couvillier

Allen Gray was having a rough night of it. He was sure it was the climate, it had to be—normally he worked Mesoamerica digs and had no problem with the humidity and bugs and heat on the other side of the world. The dryness here near the Greece-Turkey border was setting him off and making it difficult to rest. Twisting his wrist he pressed the side button of his watch to illuminate the time— 2:41 a.m. He'd gotten up about ten minutes ago, thinking that a walk may be good, and came out here by the dig. From the sounds coming from one of the tents by the edge of the twine-plotted foundations, it seemed that he wasn't the only one having a rough night tonight.

"What *are* you?" The grumble was louder the second time, and came from Ed Handon's tent. Going over to it, Gray smacked the tent flap, his curiosity up. You have to wonder what was going on when the on-site GPR technician on an archaeological dig talks to himself in the middle of the night. "Ed . . . ?"

Silence from the dimly lit tent, then, "Dr. Gray? Come in."

Handon sat on the edge of his cot with the wheeled GPR console pulled close and his laptop on a knee. Wires ran from the laptop to the console, and Handon balanced the computer with one hand while holding himself at an awkward angle with the other. In the light given from the laptop and console screens, Gray saw the stool for the console pushed off to the side. "You okay here, Ed?" Looking closer at him, Gray grabbed the stool and sat. "Looking a bit flustered there, is everything all right?"

"Yes, yea, look at this!" Handon pushed himself straighter on the cot and turned the laptop to face Gray. Displayed was a 3-D rendered topographic layer image from the ground penetrating radar. It was similar to the one that they'd used to pinpoint the foundations of the ruins; once a widely spread village, this area now was a small cluster of low building foundations that required high tech imaging to fully map. This one, however, was a deep scan—and at first Gray didn't see what had Handon so frustrated. Then, "Interesting . . ." he said, slowly, as he looked at a section of the image near the lower corner of the screen.

"Exactly!" Pushing the console away, Handon got up and set the laptop on the flat top of the unit. Turning, he stepped away to immediately turn back to it again. Looking at the laptop screen, he ran a hand through already wild hair, "What is it, what is *that*? That's what I've been asking for hours now. The data show it as a metallic material but it doesn't pull up a match to anything that's in the database. And look where it is!"

Gray had already spotted that—it was approximately 80 meters below the surface held horizontal by a sheet of granite. It appeared that it had been pinned under a stone intrusion pushed up by a seismic event— rather like an attempt from a long-past earthquake to make a rock sandwich. And as he examined the layers on the scan, it appeared to have happened more than once. "How old is that strata? Can we get to it?"

Ed reached over and tapped the page up key. A zoomed out image replaced the earlier one; here was an adjacent area that looked like fragmented levels and open spots, like tunnels or caves. Close to the object was a larger cave—it looked like only about six meters of material separated it from the open area. Handon reached to the screen and tapped at this spot. "Granite. We also took a core before we started to plot out the foundations . . . " He looked around in the dark tent. "I have the report here somewhere."

"Forget the report, what did it say?" Gray was beginning to feel the effects of the hour and the lack of sleep. It came out as impatience.

"Whatever it is it's stuck under rock pushed up by an earthquake around 7000 years ago."

"Can it be blasted?"

Gray was looking at the granite block that kept them away from that 7000-year-old oblong metallic object. He wanted to get to it—besides being the exciting part of his job, their time in Greece was running out. He had already sweet-talked two extensions for this year's dig, and if he couldn't get to this within the week it would have to wait for next season. Everyone who was still with him would mutiny if they had to wait that long—especially with this located in this site area where it probably wouldn't remain safe for the months it would take for them to return.

"I can't tell whether this area is stable enough for that." Handon's voice was slow, and the fatigue was evident as the light from his helmet lamp moved over the slab. None of them had been sleeping well lately; in the days since the night in Handon's tent, Gray found out that the nighttime problems were universal in the group. Everyone had been experiencing uneasy sleep, with many afflicted by nightmares. Two days ago the locals they'd hired started to leave, with the last one taking off this morning. Gray was haunted by the memory of it—an older Greek man pouring tears about how his family needed him, that he had to get home, had to get to his family. Everyone was experiencing that to a point. It even intruded into the nightmares.

"Dr. Gray—look at this." Sharon Occopuluus, one of the lead excavators from Greece's Antiquities Bureau and the last one on site, had her helmet light on a printout of the GPR scan. "Am I wrong? Is this section of the object not a pit space?"

Gray moved over to re-examine the printout. There was plenty of standing room here—the geological evidence may have shown that the cavern had been formed from an earthquake ages earlier, perhaps even earlier than the one that shifted all the granite slabs around, but nature had since claimed it to begin the ages long process of building toothy stalagmites and stalactites. It wasn't too wide, but it was arched, generally stable, and had been relatively easy to spelunk to. And it was next to their goal—but, looking at the image Gray saw what it was that caught Occopuluus's attention. After a moment of examining the printout, they looked up at each other, then as one they directed their helmet lights toward the top of the rock, at the cavern ceiling nine meters up. A third light joined theirs, followed by Handon's voice.

"That's some big fissure, or what?"

It was a nine-foot long narrow metallic oblong. It had taken them a day just to get to it, but once there, they had discovered that it wouldn't require much work to get it free. Hours later, they had it up to the fissure and over into the cavern where they'd set up base. It could've been worse except for an odd property of the object; although apparently metal, it was very lightweight, malleable, and flexible. Only one meter wide, it lay long on the cave floor with the lights from their helmets moving over it. Handon was the first to speak up.

"Ok—so, does *anyone* have a clue about this?"

Slate grey, it was a dull thing until direct light hit it—then it rippled with a surreal iridescent sheen. Occopuluus replied, slowly, "A cocoon? A node? It is 7000 years old. There is no way anybody living then could have made an alloy like this. We can't make it now. It has to be natural."

Gray unclipped a piton from his belt and jabbed the point onto the metal. Instantly the material hardened and the piton slid off. Tossing the spike to the ground, he said, "We might have better luck with a dirt brush. And frankly, I doubt that this is natural." Taking off his helmet he put the lamp close to the spot he scratched; iridescence and smooth metal reflected a flicking light. Looking up towards the far side of the cavern, he said, "It's getting late—we should get back to the surface. I need a new battery for this light, and it looks like it's time to make some calls."

That night the dream was—wrong. It wasn't like a nightmare, although it did carry some of that feel. The dream *felt* odd, with it being more of a flood of emotion melded with indistinct images than anything else. It was far different than the way when the mind knows that it is dreaming—it was disturbing enough that it woke Gray out of his first solid sleep in days. Rolling over to sit at the edge of his bunk, Gray slowly blinked open his eyes, staring down at the compacted dirt that made up the floor of the tent. Little from the dream remained, other than the echo of the wrenching emotion that it brought—aching loneliness and severe homesickness. The sound of an engine starting up outside took his mind off of that; getting up, he went out to see what was up.

Occopuluus sat at the wheel of the truck. As Gray moved towards the vehicle, he saw Handon scuffle out of his tent dragging his duffle and with his laptop, in bag, under an arm. And as Gray came up to them he watched as Handon tossed his duffle into the back and climb into the passenger side, taking care not to bang his computer around.

Handon looked at Gray from the open window, haggard, wide eyed, and wild haired. Normally this crazed look would get him a pun or some similar sort of humor—but the situation was anything but funny. Looking past him, Gray saw Occopuluus leaning forward against the wheel—as he looked, she lifted a hand to wipe at her eyes.

"Dr. Gray, we, we have to go." Handon's voice was catchy, rough. "Sharon has to get back home, and I have to get back to the states, to my mother. We have to get to them," His eyes drifted past Gray looking off into the darkness . . . "I *have* to."

Gray grabbed the door at the window. He wasn't here to force anyone to stay—or leave for that matter. But it did make him angry—he'd called in a lot of the favors he had hanging out there as director on this dig, for this. And since his shaft crew and diggers had left yesterday after they'd come back up, these were all he had left.

"Can't it wait—I have Sean and his crew coming up later today. How will leaving in the middle of the night get you home?" Before he could continue, Handon focused back to Gray and stared at him, his eyes filled with a look that unnerved him. Unconsciously, he took a step away from the truck.

"No, we have to get home *now!* You should leave. No one will come here."

Occopuluus pushed off of the steering wheel, and gave the gas a push. She didn't say anything, but in the light from the temporary camp lights Gray could tell that she was stony faced and determined.

"No one has for centuries, no one will now." Handon continued, then focusing hot strange eyes on his, "Boss, leave with Sean! You have to get home!"

Gray jumped aside as Occopuluus put the truck in gear and gunned it in reverse; a moment later he stood in the stirred up dust listening to Handon yelling, "Home! You have to get home!" over and over as they sped away. Alone in the middle of the camp, Gray shook his head uneasily; when Sean showed up later he would have to get that object up and get the tests done before whatever it was that was going around could affect them too. Leaving that behind was the last thing he was going to let happen. Besides—for him, work was "home."

The strangest déjà vu hit while he was eating. After Handon and Occopuluus had left he'd gone to the stores/general office/medic tent to see what remained. Most of the supplies had been left; when the crew he had put together started to leave, it was all too abrupt—they barely remembered to grab up their personal things much less thinking to grab extra on the way out. Gray snapped a few of the battery-powered portable lamps on and off until he found one with a strong light, then sat with bottled water and a couple granola bars. It was then that the déjà vu came, with a feeling that he was doing something and sitting at the same time. He felt like he stood up, but he wasn't at the table any longer, but outside under the incredible starry sky, brilliant without any artificial lights to muffle it. Looking up, he called out, wanting to go home, wanting to be with those who—made?—him. Then he became two people and the one, Dr. Allen Gray, Director of this dig, realized that he must have been driven crazy—how else could he perceive himself in this way?

Dr. Allen Gray: An emotional wave of dread regarding his sanity.

Nameless other Dr. Gray: A replying wave of loneliness and homesickness.

Dr. Allen Gray: A slight easing of his dread.

Nameless other Dr. Gray: A hint of reassurance added to the cold loneliness.

Dr. Allen Gray: Uncertainty, fatigue, What The Hell Is This!!

Nameless other Dr. Gray: Darkness; a yearning...

Dr. Allen Gray: Yearning...

Nameless other Dr. Gray: Yearning...

Gray was in the tent face down on the table with an opened granola bar digging into a cheek. Wide-eyed he sat up looking all over with the echo of the dual-person feeling creeping him to the pit of his stomach. Yet—he checked his watch—it was still hours to daylight, longer hours to Sean's arrival, and there was so much that he had to get done, tasks that he felt he hadn't had just a short time ago when he'd sat at the table. So much to do... none of which came from *his* agenda.

Gray was in his caving gear at the base of the initial shaft that the digging crew had sunk. This was the first step to reach the fractured strata caves they'd had to work through to reach the metal object—and Gray had no idea how he got here or when he had geared up. Checking his watch he saw that it was now over an hour since he had last looked at the time, back in the tent. It was a lost hour that he did not remember, an empty gap in his memory whose existence he knew of only from seeing his watch. It was like he had blacked out—

Gray was in the narrow crawl-cave just before the cavern with the find. He was sweating, breathing hard—shining his helmet light to the watch he saw that in one hour he had climbed through a route that had taken them over three hours before. And, once again another hour had passed, once again he had apparently blacked out, once again he had lost an hour of his life in a way that never had happened before. But it wouldn't be that long now until daylight, and then when Sean and his people arrived, he was out of here...

Gray was in the cavern where they had left the metal oblong to wait for the testing crew. He was standing, and this time when he realized his surroundings he didn't even bother with the time—it couldn't have been that long with the last place adjacent to this. Looking around, he had to snap on his hand light too... where the 3-foot wide 9-foot tall 7000 year old oblong had been now stood a ten foot tall metal statue, long and tall and iridescently sleek, standing gazing up, gazing out to where a starry sky would be if there wasn't 80 meters of stone blocking the way...

The hairs on Gray's arms tickled as if by a static electric rush, then he felt himself begin to fall. He tried to catch himself; however, he wasn't there any longer—instead the nameless Dr. Gray was back. This time it came in like he was back in college, at a seminar . . . as he had been when this memory was created. Now, the scene was shifted, with the nameless Dr. Gray giving the lecture.

Nameless Dr. Gray: "The brain, the mind—it is a complex unit, operated by an incredible amount of electrical potential. The amount of power generated by this organic mass over a lifetime is staggering to contemplate; however, other concepts can be as staggering when considered. If the frequencies can be matched precisely, could one not perhaps be a receiver or transmitter of this power? Could the energy processes that compose thought be matched and perhaps read, or transmitted to another for them to hear?" The edited memory continued with the nameless-self shuffling some papers on the podium, and then addressing again the ghost audience. "Fascinating the speculation that has been considered over the ages about the mind—so, please relax and watch this short historical documentary. It may answer some questions—or raise others." He, exactly like the memory professor, stepped to a side chair, and clicked a remote to set the video going. Gray, immobile within his mind, watched with a rough mix of emotions—fear and anger from his loss of bodily control, curiosity and detachment about the situation, and plenty of the same homesickness and loneliness that has been there from the start. Watching, he really doubted that the documentary would be the one on deep strata dating that he'd actually seen back in college.

On the screen was the image of the tall iridescent statue, but very un-statue like. It was moving along, very fluidly, performing maintenance tasks at the base of what appeared to be a solid support strut. The documentary began visibly much like normal, but the sound—wasn't. The audible was like an emotional knowledge feed; what came with the visual images was a very non-human flow of impressions and information. From this Gray *knew* that this was a repair robot; a unit with a limited AI and constructed from a malleable multi-environment resistive alloy. As Gray watched, an instruction came in—a thing he both *knew* and *felt*—and the robot left, moving towards a mineral deposit close by. As it moved away, the AI considered the instruction and filed it to determine if it were a thing necessary to either retain, or to incorporate, by its adaptive algorithms. Everything that it encountered or experienced filtered through that, although most of the information was deleted as not required.

A slight tremor; the nanomic computer system throughout its body reprogrammed and enhanced the stabilizing structure in its legs; the tremor became stronger; an instruction received for it to return. Rushing over the hill it viewed the ship rising, pulling in the landing struts; the ground gave out under it and it rolled seeking to stand but the turmoil with the ground was too severe for the stabilizers; again the ground sank; stone folded over it compressing it: it went into dormancy mode when the light was cut off to conserve the power; the tremors and upheaval stopped.

Pinned securely underground by the mass of stone thrown up from the earthquake, the robot remained dormant, with the minimum power it required supplied by its static energy tap. Two functions remained on while it "slept." One, the location signal it broadcast regularly but that did not transmit well through the depth of the stone covering it and from the signal's reduced power, and two, the learning algorithm. Set up as a self-updating program for the AI, that program was set up to work non-stop in the background to maintain it, to assist the AI in adapting to environmental stresses, and to reprogram the algorithms that operated the AI and itself as a situation required. And, operating non-stop, it developed and re-wrote the program and embedded it deep in the storage of the artificial bio-computer that served as the brain and heart of the robot . . .

Gray was on a crazy mental river ride taking in all of this as best he could. He saw that the AI was re-writing his memories to communicate across; the emotion flood that he'd been experiencing had been the alien AI attempted to "sync" its mental programming with the electrical frequency ranges of human mental activity. Still, it was a chaotic ride— man had not developed along those lines and the mental imposing was grabbing out some weird emotional shifts. However, one suspicion was growing—and the next wave of information blew bright as a confirmation in his mind.

The AI's learning program fed in the threads of its work, scribing and rewriting as it reassessed and redeveloped. It wrote it on the very substance that composed the robots' brain, layered deeper into the molecular-sized artificial organic material of the robots' computer. The nearest that Gray could equate this with was like chromosomes that were being redesigned, DNA re-written . . . new information saved to an incredibly adaptive permanent medium. Centuries passed into millennia; storage shrank, had to be redesigned and the data and programming restored; new pathways were forged in an artificial humanoid's brain; more power was needed and the power array to convert the static electricity from the planet's electrical field was redesigned and incorporated; sensing probes sent out; a group of complex energy patterns vaguely similar to those of the makers but silent, different, began to gather overhead; the group above ground grew and expanded; attempts to communicate failed; a boost of power to the location signal proving uneventful; then the sudden violence of a crazy emotional blast of yearning and calling and loneliness and homesickness knocked Gray out of the sync . . .

It took a moment to recover from that one—but when he did it came with a feeling of—enlightenment?—a sense that the answer to a question had been found. His dig included the attempt to discover the answer to a puzzle, an ancient legend suggesting events both mysterious and enigmatic. The old legends of the area had it that a prosperous trading hub existed in this general area—a thriving settlement that suddenly, over about half a century, became deserted. The legends tell of a terrible unseen demon that came one night and chased away many, and killed without a touch. The city, the largest in the area, became deserted over a 20-year stretch; after another score of years no one would live here. The word was that over the following centuries others came, and attempted to resettle the area, but the ancient evil was still present, to chase them away. And when satellite imaging discovered the foundations of a large settlement here, in the broken hills where the old legends had placed the haunted city, a dig had practically formed overnight. Now he realized what must have happened back then, those centuries ago—the birth cry of a new mind destroyed a city.

Gray stood, drained and shaky. Looking up at the robot, he saw it with its head down, appearing to look at him. As he noticed this, he felt a small wave of—closeness?—come over him, and he realized that robot had achieved the mental sync it was seeking.

agreement

Experiencing this kind of communication was a bit unnerving, but it still piqued his curiosity; curiosity controlled his life, with his curiosity about the past, his curiosity about all sciences, his curiosity about everything. It was a powerful force that directed his career—and this had to be the highest point he could ever hope to reach.

query, curiosity

He looked up at the robot, watched as it turned to once again look up, out, seeming to see beyond the stone overhead.

loneliness, a calling out—but focused, a sad heartcry pulsing upward.

Gray felt the robot reach out, and increasing its power draw. "Feeling" the sync between them, Gray sought to see what it was doing—then it dawned on him. As he'd "synced" the AI had gathered information from him. Now it was looking to try to tap into a satellite, to boost its call for rescue and to transmit directly into space from an object located in orbit. And if its signal was strong enough . . . . For a moment paranoid suspicion flared, but just as quickly vanished. This was a new sentience, an evolutionary step. Why would it have developed the darker emotions yet? It wanted to go home, to have the makers come back and get it.

hope

Gray smiled as that came to him . . . it was a huge difference from the broadcasted loneliness and homesickness. When Sean . . . Gray's heart dropped—snapping his watch up, he checked the time. Relief flooded back as he saw only 20 minutes passed from the last time he'd checked it. It felt like hours . . . but still. Remembering that Sean was bringing in the samples the crew brought up another consideration—what was going to happen to this incredible infant? To the scientists it will be a new metal, an incredible machine to be studied, analyzed. Granted, he was also curious, but the scope of the meaning with its evolution, with its shift from a learning AI computer to a sentient self-aware life . . . incredible possibilities lay within this, and although Gray was also intensely interested in what could be learned, he had no illusions about what would happen. As he realized what had to be done, he was surprised. He would have thought that the choice he'd made would have been harder for him. This could be a discovery that could make him, could get him published in the big journals and could ensure tenure and funding for some time. For a moment he ran the helmet light over the robot, just to look at the color ripple from the iridescence. Then, resolved, he started across the cave.

He had to return back to the surface. He had preparations to make.

Sunrise was beautiful this morning. Gray was tired, drained, and dead on his feet from all the effort over the last few hours. It didn't help that all the fatigue from the ongoing weeks of broken nights and short sleep caught up to him now. But, the sunrise brought with it a spectacular color show—it seemed that there was moisture in the air, high in the grayish clouds. He took a moment to appreciate it, and then walked, slowly, through the foundation layouts. He had gear near the entrance to the shaft to the first cave . . . when he got over to it, he sat, cross-legged, on the ground by the pack.

He watched the last moments of the sunrise, and as the day brightened, he rummaged in the pack and pulled out a couple things, placing them on the ground next to him. When Sean got here, around noon if he made it in on schedule, Gray would have him get his crew to pack down the dig—

Gray picked up one of the items he pulled from the pack— removing the lid, he took a drink from the bottle water, then re-closed the top. Putting it back down, he picked up the other item, and looked up, to the sky.

"Guys," he thought, "come dig out your kid. He's a tough one, I know he can handle this until you can hear his call and come for him. I will do what I can to keep him safe, I know it isn't much." Then, emoting a deep push of safety and protection and sympathy through the mind-sync link, he thought, "My heart goes out to him." Looking momentarily at what he held, at the blinking light and the switch, he looked up to the bright morning sky, with a regretful but resolved look showing through the fatigue.

Then he pressed the switch on the detonator.

Cheryl McCreary is a scientist by training and science educator by day struggling to make people more aware of the biological world. She's lived in the assorted locals of Oklahoma, Ohio, New York, Virginia and currently resides in South Carolina. Her work has appeared in Alienskin, Amazing Journeys Magazine *and* Ethereal Gazette. *She enjoys cooking, reading and hiking in her spare time.*

When All Is Known
by Cheryl McCreary

She peered into the cockpit of the ancient vessel sitting in her cargo bay. The face that greeted her was human, and yet not at all like hers. Time had dinged and weathered the vessel as it had drifted unknown through space for ages, until her stellar flyer's sensors had found it. Yet unknown was not something Artemisia's world contained, and she wondered how the Keepers of Memory would feel about such.

It appeared death had taken the human in his sleep, leaving a relaxed form leaning back in the cockpit chair. Artemisia studied his protruding facial features and his pale-gray skin, both indicating his race as Caucasian. From her implanted memories, she knew in life his skin would have been a warm pink color. His hair lay brown and short on his head. A jumpsuit of cotton—her memories supplied the material's name—covered his thick built, short and muscular body. Yes, he was very different than she was with her silvery gray hair, irises of purple, and a long, lean, pale body.

Cocking her head, Artemisia studied the writing on the worn metal surface. It took only a moment for her library of memories to provide a translation of the English, one of several extinct languages. A series of letters and numbers identifying the vessel followed the shadowy remains of the printed name *Phoenix.*

Returning to the deck, she crossed to a control panel. She knew it would take little time for the preserved body to warm and then be ruined. This discovery—the word seemed alien in her mind—needed to be preserved for others. A stasis environment needed to be made, complete with a temperature cold enough to keep her discovery until she could show it to others.

Artemisia looked over her shoulder at the pod. It had been there a few millennia, at the least, drifting in space under their noses and yet unknown. But all was known, for the Keepers of Memory said that the knowledge stored in their biologically engineered brains spanned the entire galaxy. Not once in her eight hundred years of existence had Artemisia encountered a place, thing or emotion not already supplemented in her brain by the memories of those who had come before her.

With the ancient carefully stored, Artemisia looked over the cockpit. Too small to have been a ship, it was more likely an escape pod. The arcane technology had long been dead, so it took her some time to find the information storage device, take its memory core and apply a method of retrieving the data. Some of it was audio, and she jumped to the last entry, and rigged up a speaker to hear them.

The sound of a male voice, tinny and full of static, echoed off the bulkheads. It took Artemisia a moment to understand the translation.

"I'm Marcus Rydz, and if you're listening to this I'm guessing the news ain't good. There's an Allison Meyers in California you can contact about my remains. Her info's at the end of the recording." California, Artemisia's mind told her, had been on Earth. "My long range vessel ran into the edge of a meteor shower. It knocked out communication and propulsion. I tried to fix it, but when life support began to fail, I went to my escape pod instead." Marcus gave a deep sigh. "It's been almost three days. My distress beacon isn't strong enough for anyone to pick up, and I don't have any energy left to boost it. Oxygen's running low and two recyclers have failed because of overuse.

"I just never thought it'd end like this," Marcus continued, "alone and cold in space. They're still beautiful though—the stars. I guess there could be worse things than dying surrounded by all you love." The recording faded to his breath, deep and shallow. "I'm sorry, Allison. I'm sorry your love wasn't enough. I'm sorry you're not going to get that life you wanted to share with me." Marcus's ragged breath filled the recording. "I love you, Allison," he whispered, "I'm sorry it wasn't enough."

Artemisia held her breath, listening as his breath faded away. Finally, only empty static filled the air.

People filled the conference hall emitting a soft rumbling. Scientists became extinct millennia ago, after declaring their search for the final truths of the universe complete. Artemisia recognized the stiff white uniforms of several Keepers of Memory in the front row. They guarded and preserved the collective knowledge given to each human after reaching adulthood, and by doing so kept society civilized. Artemisia wondered what Marcus' universe must have been like without such ready knowledge.

The large blue forms of Ellutons spotted the audience, and the handful of Weirains present added a light buzzing to the room. Both species were part of the few left in the galaxy. The last of the primitive races had destroyed themselves with internal war long before Artemisia had been born. Keeper of Memory legend told that knowledge had prevented humanity from coming to a similar end.

The conference hall itself was leftover from a time of active knowledge collection. The chairs had long been reupholstered with a silver colored, non-destructive material, but each still held a foldout desktop in its right or left arm. The chief moderator, who was more used to introducing media productions, crossed the empty stage and stood uncomfortably behind the podium still covered with dust from storage. He cleared his throat and it echoed through the hall. "May I present a . . . report, by one Artemisia Greenleaf Aurora Brently." He waved a narrow arm in her direction, and Artemisia stepped forward.

At the podium, she began. "On my way back from a visit to RO4587 I . . . discovered," the word had a strange taste, "an archaic escape pod. It contained an ancient human, from Earth." A gasp filled the large room. "May I present Marcus Rydz." A robotic stand wheeled the stasis environment containing Marcus into view. The thin, pale faces of the audience stared in awe.

"This is clearly a fake," someone from the audience said.

"Yes, yes, it must be," said another. "All primitive humans have long been located and preserved."

Artemisia shook her head. "That now cannot be true for this is certainly real."

One of the Keepers of Memory stood up. "During the last age of discovery, when we learned physics limited us to this galaxy, the entirety of space was explored. One does not simply . . . *discover* something."

Artemisia straightened her shoulders. "I mean not to speak against you, but I know what I did and have not a better word to use for the act."

The eldest Keeper, designated by the high collar of her uniform spoke, "Child, discover is such a powerful word. It has a great meaning, and one does not use it lightly, for the ages of discovery were past long before even I took a breath."

Glancing at Marcus, Artemisia stepped from behind the podium. "But I did . . . find this being drifting in space. His genetic material lists him as being an ancient human, and from primitive recordings he left, it appears he is at least thirty-two thousand years old, as he refers to having come directly from Earth, before—"

The standing Keeper interrupted, "How was it this being was not discovered before the Memories were locked in place? Do you think our ancestors were so careless as to not extensively search and report on the entire galaxy, down to the molecule, before making the Memory Vaults?"

"I do not know, Reverent Ones." Artemisia knew her words showed her worry. The Keepers of Memory knew much, while she herself was merely a citizen.

"I am forced to reach the conclusion that she lies," the eldest Keeper said. She stood and arranged her robe around her. "Leave her to her forged evidence of discovery. If it was not locked into the Memory Vaults, it is not. Nothing more needs saying."

Artemisia's heart sank to her feet as the Keepers of Memory filed out behind the eldest of them.

"Yes," a man in the audience said, standing up, "how do we know you haven't created this evidence?"

"I do not know." Her voice cracked, and she wanted to hide from the embarrassment the harsh looks of the audience made her feel.

"Because you've made it up!" someone yelled. "Why would a

person do such?" another asked. "Boredom," a woman's voice offered. "No. She wants attention. Who can know why?" a man said, glaring at her as he led the audience out of the conference hall.

"That's not true," she called after them. "I made none of this up." Anger boiled inside her, and she wished she could throw more than words.

One lone man walked closer and mounted the steps to the stage. Tilting his head, he surveyed Marcus. "A beautifully preserved specimen."

"Thank you." A twinge of hope streaked through Artemisia's dark mood.

Smiling, he turned toward her. "All is known, and all has been found," he spoke the motto of the Keepers. His face was young, the same as everyone else's, but his pale blue eyes held enormous wisdom. "That is how it has been, and how it will continue to be." The man shook his head. "It is a shame, for it is such a marvelous discovery." With one last look at Artemisia's finding, the man walked away and Artemisia was left alone in the cavernous conference hall.

Too many emotions clouded her mind; searching her implanted knowledge, she struggled to make sense of them all. She frowned at the fact that the reality was stronger than any memory.

Sitting in her guest flat, Artemisia studied Marcus. Not trusting his keeping to others, she had made sure the conference hall droids had brought him here. His stasis environment filled one corner of the spacious room that was decorated in the efficient metallic and white common on Novus Sirius Four.

Connecting two last wires, Artemisia finished modifying her media-viewer to play the image disks she had found on the escape pod. Watching Marcus' still gray features, she randomly lifted a disk from Marcus' collection.

Marcus' voice echoed from a distance as the scene showed an empty cockpit. "I think they believe I'm a bit crazy. Well, I probably am. But you'd think they'd have figured it out before now." Rattling of dishes sounded, perhaps from Marcus being in the galley. "I wonder how Columbus explained himself to people when he set out to find the other side of the world," Marcus continued. Artemisia's memory quickly grasped the history behind Marcus' words. Staring at the empty cockpit chair, she wondered with whom Marcus was talking.

Marcus sighed. "They probably still all thought he was crazy. How do you explain to someone who's fine and dandy with staying at home that there's so much more to see? I think finding the truth to the universe would be easier." Marcus entered the doorway, a plate of food in one hand and a mug in the other. Sitting down in the chair, he gingerly placed both the plate and mug on the console, eyes and fingers briefly checking systems. Artemisia sat mesmerized by the rosy color of Marcus, alive and animated. Leaning back into the flat surface of her chair, she watched the muscles play in his cheeks as he ate a sandwich. Finally, he finished the last bite and leaned back in his chair as he grabbed for the mug.

He took a sip and steam rose to encircle his features. Shaking his head, Marcus continued. "If only I could get Allison to understand, it'd be enough." His eyes stared straight ahead, and Artemisia noticed they were hazel-green in color, giving him even more of an alien appearance.

"I feel so alone without her." Marcus' features turned down into a frown. "I didn't realize how alone I'd feel. She'd hate it out here though, all this darkness and no one but me for company. She might love me, but there are limits to everything.

"Wait a minute, we're at the nebula." His hand reached for the console in front of him. "I'm talking to you again. Clear sign I'm going crazy." He patted the console—Artemisia wondered if he spoke to the computer, or the ship. "Now if only you had enough brains to go talking back," Marcus said, giving a half-smile.

The hum of the engine slowed as Marcus set down his mug. He stood up to look out the cockpit window, a broad smile on his face. The bluish glow of a star lit up his face and reflected from his eyes, full of wonder. "Damn," he whispered. "How can they not understand the joy of this?"

The screen went black and silence filled the flat. Artemisia looked over at the stasis environment. Marcus had been an explorer, traveling the universe alone because there were discoveries to be made. The reverence in his words lingered in her mind. There was a time when humans had been explorers, but that form of humanity was forever gone. What was left of the living explorer stared out of the stasis shield and Artemisia wondered which one of them was the true form of humanity.

Artemisia watched the activities of the local promenade. There were a few aliens about, but most of the occupants were human. Their tall thin bodies walked with perfect grace. Their large narrow heads constantly wove and bobbed as their chattering filled the large dome.

As they walked here and there from shop to shop, Artemisia knew none of them had a need for anything; they only wished for something with which to fill their moments. She had always thought that of all the races, humans were the most aesthetically pleasing. Today she could not help but compare them to Marcus. His recorded image last night had held a hue that somehow in her mind ran sequent with life. For the first time the pale faces before her seemed drained of the life Marcus had possessed.

Remembering Marcus' wonder and excitement and curiosity, Artemisia realized that in his short life he had experienced more than the entire populace of the promenade. She wondered at what point humans had stopped living the long lives their knowledge granted them? The thought grew in her mind that perhaps Marcus was what humanity was meant to be.

The small screen in Artemisia's flat flickered to life and the smiling face of Marcus came into focus. "Hey, Allison, just got your message and thought I'd return the favor." The background behind him showed the cramped living compartment of the *Phoenix*. A bunk sat upon a waist-high wardrobe. A crack in a drape gave a glimpse of a metal sink and toilet. The other corner held a kitchenette and fold out table. It all illustrated the dim nature of primitive space travel.

Leaning back in the chair, he rested with crossed feet on the edge of the desk at which he sat. "The things I've seen out here, they'd amaze you, sweetheart. I know I'd planned on coming back by now. And I wake up each day thinking I've gone far enough and that I should turn around." Marcus' eyes were staring at nothing. Or perhaps everything, Artemisia thought. "But I've seen all that's back there, and there's so much more ahead of me. Is it really odd that I want to keep going, that I want to see more?"

Looking at the framed image of a young woman on the desk, Marcus sighed. "Allison, I need to accept that you just don't get all that. If you did you'd be here with me, and we'd be sharing all of this together.

"But really, it's not such an odd thought, Allison. I'm certainly not the first to have it. But we've seen everything on Earth, so why shouldn't space be next: the ultimate frontier. It's so large, so expansive; we'll never be able to see it all."

Marcus sat up, placing his hands on his knees. "I just want to see a little of it, Allison. Out here exploring, I feel more alive than I ever have before, like this is what I was meant to do with my life. Let me do this for a while, and then I promise I'll come back; we can settle down and get married and have kids and live *your* dream."

"I . . . . " Giving a sigh, Marcus's shoulders fell. "I can't send you this, I can't tell it to you like that, Allison." Marcus leaned forward and rested his head in his hand. "Computer, end recording."

As Marcus' image faded, Artemisia leaned back in her chair, firm and cold behind her. Closing her eyes, she searched her databank of past memories and knowledge, supposedly all the knowledge in the galaxy. Somewhere it should tell her about the feelings associated with exploration, love, pain and humanity. Her eyes danced under her lids as her consciousness raged through her mind, finding only a glimpse of what she searched for.

Opening her eyes, she focused on Marcus' stasis environment across the room. Artemisia realized she knew the joy of discovery. The reaction of her fellow humans, trapped in a world where knowledge was held stable, had shown her the pain of rejection.

She crossed the room and placed a hand upon the stasis environment. His gray skin was such a contrast to the living face she'd just seen. Marcus had been dead for quite a while, as had his version of humanity. Somewhere in their search for the ultimate truth, the reality of the universe had shifted around them and swallowed up a large piece of what it had meant to be human. Marcus had known what it was like to be truly human, but Artemisia was not sure if she had ever known, or ever would.

His mere thirty or forty Earth years seemed a blink of the eye compared to her eight hundred; yet, he had learned more in that short time than she might during the rest of her immortality. Artemisia wondered if perhaps the true answers to the universe were impossible to find, and if so was not all the knowledge in her head useless?

Sighing, she thought about how she could continue to exist in this world. It now seemed an empty shell of what life should be. She gazed back up at Marcus's still face, trapped in the peace of death. All his tissues down to every scar lay beneath her hands, and more importantly, his brain and who he had been was within her grasp.

She searched the database in her head again, and this time came back with the answers she sought. It was possible; the knowledge they had collected made it so. Artemisia smiled at the ancient man behind the stasis environment, and knew the next move she would make.

It had turned out to be a simple enough process. She had Marcus' DNA, all the neural codes in his brain, and his body perfectly preserved down to the smallest scar. The Re-animator only needed a little reprogramming to perform the task of bringing him back to life, exactly as he'd been the moment he'd died. Why or what she thought would come of this, she hadn't taken time to ponder.

"Please hurry, Marcus."

He stood wide-eyed, just reanimated and dressed. "Where am I?"

"You are on Novus Sirius Four, but that will mean nothing to you." Artemisia wished she could give him longer to get his bearings, but the Keepers of Memory were already close to discovering them both.

The clothes she'd provided draped too long on him, and fit too tightly. Their pale color matched the room perfectly, but his flesh showed through the thin fabric

"Why do I need to hurry?" Marcus asked. "And how do you know my name?"

"They're coming, quickly." She herded him out of the room and down a corridor. "In a manner, I have heard from you before." Sirens sounded in the distance.

"Who are coming? And what did you do to me?" He followed close behind. His shorter stride quickened to keep pace with her.

"The Keepers of Memory, and their forces." Just why they would care about his Re-animation seemed to confirm that he held the answers she thought he did. "What I did to you is Re-animation with the use of our nano-technology. I can explain it later."

The sound of running footprints stormed toward them. Pushing Marcus forward, she took off at a run. They only had to get to her ship, then she could find a place to escape and hide.

"In here." As she turned a corner, Artemisia stopped abruptly. Reaching out a hand, she pulled Marcus through a small corridor closet doorway. Stumbling after her, Marcus cowered beside her in the darkness. Excitement seemed to show through the fear on his face. It made her smile.

A line of Keeper Guards passed, their footfall ringing. They waited, hidden, until the sound had subsided. Artemisia knew they would be back. Standing up, she pulled Marcus to his feet and after her.

Her heart felt lighter as she neared the dock's door and entered the code to open it. A mechanical sound grated inside the wall. Everything in space had been discovered, but it was vast enough still to temporarily hide.

Artemisia entered and Marcus followed, the door closing behind him. A series of sleek, metal spaceships lined the cavernous dock. Their footfalls echoed in the empty air. Artemisia led them to her stellar flyer.

It took little time to enter and start the engines. She had already cleared her leaving previously with the control tower, under another name to allow their escape. Her breath still quickened until she got the final clearance.

The darkness of space grew larger in the cockpit window, and the station drifted away. The blue planet of Novus Sirius Four loomed below. A shield went down over the cockpit window and the vessel jerked as the engines roared. Marcus sat quiet, eyes darting to seemingly take everything in.

Artemisia turned around in the pilot's chair.

"Do I finally get things explained now?" Marcus asked her.

"Yes. I'm sorry there wasn't time before. It must have all been rather shocking."

"It was. So where am I, really?"

She knew he deserved as much of the truth as he could understand, and perhaps more. So she told him everything, finding him, being doubted for the discovery, wanting to have what he possessed since her present form of humanity did not.

"But why bring me back?" His odd features were furrowed together, his eyes clear.

Artemisia paused. Could she not have learned as much as she needed of him from his tapes? Had she not already? "You were curious and brave and nothing kept you from your dream," she said to fill the empty space. "This galaxy will never be yours. And perhaps my actions were more selfish than I believe. Your home and everyone you cared about is gone."

He nodded, perhaps already having grasped that knowledge. What exactly had she brought him back to?

"Humanity was once like you, full of explorers and scientists, those who asked questions and wanted to see more, all searching for the truth to parts of an infinite puzzle." He held all of that knowledge and ability within him, and mere audio recordings would not have given it to her. "But now, all is known, or so it is told. We do not explore or question or even think, for we believe everything has already been done for us. You hold a part of us that we have forgotten, perhaps the most important part of all."

The Keepers of Memory wanted to keep her from finding and exploring that part of them that was gone. For it would surely mean their destruction, correct? Could she and this ancient human truly bring that about? Did they even want to?

"Your fire burned so briefly and yet so brightly. Marcus, you are what humanity should be again, and I wish for you to teach me how to become that, so that I may teach the others." The words surprised her more than him, as if her true desires had bubbled to the surface unknown to her. "Will you help me?"

Her heart stopped while he cocked his head, considering. Then slowly he nodded it, a smile growing on his rough features. His eyes gleamed as they had in his recordings. Perhaps he was as excited about the adventure that lay before them as she was.

Rob Riel has worked as a sailor, metallurgist, failure analyst, English teacher, electron microscopist, disability services co-ordinator, university lecturer and writer. He is currently director of Picaro Press, a successful publishing venture specializing in Australian poetry. He writes science fiction, prose poetry, essays, book reviews, and is currently working on his third book. Rob lives happily on the East coast of Australia with beloved partner Judy and their wonderdog Pluto.

Red City
by Rob Riel

Red City is the capital of no country at all. Nothing exists above the fine desert sand except Entrance, a single peaked box of corrugated iron, eleven meters on a side. No other structure, no tree, not even a small stone interrupts the meandering dunes for many kilometers. There may have been other elevators, or secret tunnels leading from the depths to distant geographies, but this small building is the Entrance to Red City. All else, and anything like it, is rumor.

To enter the City, one was required to deposit a metal token with the guards. Local people have shown me several of these, and others I have dug from the sand around Entrance. They are of various shapes, sizes, and hefts. Some are in the form of thick, many-pointed stars with holes in the center, others are patterned cylinders of various lengths with one end flattened. Some appear to be broken, or burned.

In theory, each token should have been unique, so that travelers leaving Red City could retrieve their own and take it with them upon departure. In practice, however, very few who arrived at Red City ever left, and of those who did, those from whom we learn of this place, none were offered their due. Some hold that the autarchs of the City were greedy for metal of every kind, and kept whatever they touched. Others have written that none left that place voluntarily, and that the tokens of those who were expelled were forfeit, kept as identification in the unlikely event that anyone so punished would attempt to return.

The elevator could hold no more than twenty souls. Each transit of the cage took many hours, so the line at Entrance was often very long. When the elevator arrived at the surface, guards would collect tokens from the next twenty supplicants, inspect them, usher those whose tokens were approved into the cage, and fasten shut the narrow door with metal wire. Immediately the elevator would begin its long descent.

Travelers have told of seeing many marvels as they approached Red City from above. There are stories of halls so vast that minutes were required to traverse them from top to bottom, of burning levels filled with smoking pits and the glow of hidden fire, of men in masks who shouted and gestured at the elevator from behind barbed wire gates, of sweating, of naked slaves working on strange machines. The elevator never slowed in its long journey; all reports are of things glimpsed in a moment, perhaps gleaned from sleep. The air of Red City was very warm, and travelers often dozed during their long journey down. Some of them may have dreamt as well.

Of Red City itself even less is known with certainty. That its citizens excelled in sport is proven by old records at Agira, which name their many champions. And that their trade was once prized is also incontestable: the long journey across the desert to Entrance figures in many legends, and I have seen antique tablets that list high prices paid for their wine, and for the hire of their musicians. But no one can say when last the elevator at Entrance came to the surface. The empty shaft remains fathomless, and the small peaked building called Entrance is still visible from many kilometers away to travelers passing between the waterhole at Claris and the coast. One day dunes will cover them both, and Red City will cease to exist.

Davin Ireland currently resides in the Netherlands. His fiction credits include stories published in a range of print magazines and anthologies, including Underworlds, The Horror Express, Zahir, Rogue Worlds, Fusing Horizons, Neo-Opsis, Storyteller Magazine *and* Albedo One.

Combustible Eden
by Davin Ireland

The Questrox landcar barreled through the arid wastelands of M41/03 at optimum cruising speed, nose flopping in and out of the natural depressions with a gratifying whup-*whump*, man-high wheels tearing up loose fantails of dust that hung motionless on the air long after the vehicle and its two-man crew had vanished from sight.

This morning Danforth had the wheel, which meant Creely was in his obligatory bad mood. Creely was almost always in a bad mood when Danforth drove. Not that Danforth was a poor driver. Quite the opposite. Lieutenant Michael Danforth was one of the best wheelmen in the business. The trouble was, he liked to travel with the landcar's top down and the radio on full blast, even during the hottest part of the day. This didn't make sense to Creely. With Earth so many light years distant, the only sounds coming over the airwaves were random blasts of static caused by the planet's volatile atmosphere.

He decided not to make a point of it. Everybody had his or her own way of coping with the effects of a long-haul mission, and an abundance of stimuli—both external *and* internal in Danforth's case, if the rumors were to be believed—was just one of them. Still, it grated on Creely's nerves, particularly because he knew exactly what his colleague was up to. Bluntly put, Danforth was drowning his fear as if it were a living thing, wilfully submerging it in heat and loud noise, in exhaustion and excessive alcohol, in sump oil and profanity and day-old sweat, perhaps in the hope that it would one day stop struggling and leave him alone.

It was a nice dream if you could afford it. *No, I'll go you one better*, Creely thought to himself as a sound not unlike a service robot gargling a bucket full of galvanized nails erupted from the shortwave, *it's a nice dream conceived by a coward too afraid to confront his own demons, that's what it is.* Creely was sure of this. He felt amply qualified to judge, too. In previous centuries, if a man wanted to forget, he joined the French Foreign Legion and fought meaningless wars in faraway lands until the horror of what he was experiencing exceeded the pain of what he had left behind. These days things were far more civilized. One only had to sign up for a Questrox deep space archaeology expedition and the healing could begin in earnest. It didn't matter what your qualifications were as long as you could sign your name on the dotted line and wield a pick-axe. Then you were part of the family and treated as such. No guns, no blood, no muss, no fuss. Just thousands and thousands of square kilometers of post-apocalyptic desert.

And almost never an artifact.

Not even a shard of broken pottery.

The whole thing was driving Creely to distraction. It was almost as if this lousy planet's inhabitants, just prior to nuking themselves into oblivion half a million years ago, had packed up and shipped off every last item indicative of their brief existence. True, all of this had taken place way back when evolving proto-humans were busy running round bare-arsed on the open savannah of the Rift Valley, but still, you'd have to expect more evidence than *this*.

Creely was still mentally debating the issue when Danforth pointedly cleared his throat.

"What's our ETA?" the lieutenant croaked, and coughed loudly into his fist. Before the OnComp could answer, he turned to Creely and produced an unexpected grin—the skin of his sun-blasted face cracking like old leather. He was so weathered and grimed with dirt that he was actually starting to look like a part of the landscape.

Two hours, fourteen minutes based on current speed and terrain, answered the dashboard artillect. *Be aware that the radiator unit will overheat before that time if a thirty-minute stop is not instigated immediately. Repeat—*

Danforth snapped off the transmission and sighed.

"Damn thing always says that," he complained loudly, "and nothing ever happens. Maybe I should ask Shane to recalibrate the sensors when we get back."

The landcar bobbled over a series of fractured rocks at this point, massive wheels grinding into the sand and calcified ashes of what may once have been a town or city, the uneven ground joggling Creely from side to side.

"Are you sure that's wise?" he called above the roar of the engine. He had to raise his voice because, unlike his superior, Creely was shrouded against the vicious glare of the sun: tinted visor, flapping scarf wrapped around the lower portion of his face, dusty cowl pulled down over the rest of it. He fancied he appeared much as a survivor of that ancient nuclear conflict may have appeared in the first days after the smoke had lifted. If, of course, they were at all humanoid.

"Stop worrying," said Danforth. "Besides, I want to show you something and I'd rather only listen to one voice bitch and whine at me while I'm doin' it." He grinned again but this time Creely only nodded, allowing the slight to pass without comment. It took some effort, however. Both men knew that OnComp spoke in one of three different voices, depending on circumstance. Genderless Synthesized Intonation— GSI for short—was employed during standard field outings and for the compilation of low-risk threat assessments. Before its sudden termination by Danforth, OnComp had still been responding in GSI mode, although the shift in its tone, from N (*Neutral*) to MC (*Mild Concern*), was clear. Creely had noted the change with distinct unease. The landcar was low on fuel and they were abroad in unrelenting midday heat. If anything went wrong now, their chances of survival were that much slimmer. And now the ranking officer—hell, the *only* officer, Creely himself was a volunteer—was about to steer them off on a wild goose-chase.

"So exactly what is it you wanted to show me?"

Creely only ventured this when it became obvious that Danforth had relapsed into his usual morose silence.

"A large tract of forest, due south." Danforth pointed a gloved hand—his only concession to the searing midday heat—at a low ridge to their left. This time he failed to grin at all. "A petrified forest, if you must know." He shrugged. "It's quite dead."

"Seriously? A *forest*?" Without waiting for an answer, Creely stripped his own glove and reached for the OnComp, glad for an excuse to reactivate the device that had saved their lives on so many occasions in the past. "Maybe I'd better just enter the coordinates for posterity's—"

Danforth slapped his hand away with a languid flick of the wrist and shot him a predatory glance. "Don't bother," he said, "it'll only cause trouble."

"Trouble?"

"That's right."

When the lieutenant failed to elaborate, Creely swallowed and folded his arms, surreptitiously squeezing the weapon holstered at his side. He gazed briefly at the distant ridge. The landcar's nose was already angling in that direction, and beyond it the graduated rock formations reminded him of the wrinkles in a furrowed brow. Possibly his own brow. Everybody knew that Danforth was a loose cannon. Up until now nobody had dared speculate that he might also be insane. *Just my luck to break the good news back at base-camp*, Creely thought to himself, *if I ever make it back*. Of course he realized that he might be overreacting. It wouldn't be the first time. But then again, shutting off the OnComp, leaving the track when the sun was just approaching its blistering zenith, neither of these things were standard procedure—especially not when undertaken in the name of some mythical body of trees. No, it was more than just a bit erratic. It was plain freaking loco.

Creely unbuckled the holster as he thought about all of this. Things could get very ugly if Danforth was in the process of losing his marbles.

"Give me your hand."

"*What?*"

"Give me your hand, do it now."

The lieutenant was already at the summit of the ridge. His extended right hand wavered in the air as he reached for Creely, while the other clung to an outcropping of bright orange rock. Above him, the lavender sky was distorted here and there by gelatinous wisps of a cloud-like substance that floated effortlessly on the afternoon thermals. When enough of these transparent blobs were gathered together in one place, they resembled an army of poisonous jellyfish massing for war. Beneath them, the two men sweated profusely.

"My feet can't get a grip," Creely observed. His tone was conversational but it need not have been. He was scrabbling for purchase on a steep twenty-meter slope, and if he slipped now he could be looking at a long drop with nothing waiting at the end of it to greet him but a nasty fracture.

"Stop fighting it and *stretch*," urged Danforth, "we're practically touching fingertips as it is."

Easy for you to say, Creely thought to himself, *you're not the one in danger of losing your footing*. He scrabbled just a little harder for the sake of it, twin avalanches of orange dust streaming from beneath his heels, and then snatched for the outstretched hand, catching it clean and snug at the first attempt.

"There ya go," cried Danforth, jerking him up the last couple of meters so that they stood sweating atop of the flattened crest, and facing back the way they had come.

"Thanks," panted Creely, "looks almost like a sand dune from up here, doesn't it?"

Ignoring this, Danforth pointed at the flat, featureless plain below. "If I didn't know better," he breathed, "I'd think there was nothing out there at all."

Creely followed the other man's gaze, not quite sure how to interpret this. As far as he could see there were flat expanses of rock, heaps of dried mud and ash, salt flats, sun-whitened terrain, little else. It was the best definition of "nothing" he could think of.

"Now turn around."

"Huh?"

He felt Danforth's hand clutching his arm, dragging him sideways. He was about to protest when he saw it. Then the words slipped back down Creely's throat like a bad taste. It was incredible, a vision, possibly even a mirage. Thirty or forty kilometers away, not all that far from the subtle camber of the horizon, another much larger ridge rose against the skyline. Every bit of space between here and there was packed with fossilized trees, all of them the exact same breed and shape, as if they had been mass-produced in a factory somewhere. Creely blinked and looked down at the nearest specimen. Height was difficult to judge from this elevated position, but it looked to be about three meters tall, trunk rising from a wide base to a needle-thin point, the branches weaving their way upwards in spiral-staircase fashion, growing progressively shorter and thinner as they went. Greyish bushes that looked a little like brambles stripped of flowers and fruit (not to mention even the most microscopic trace of organic life after all this time), snarled between the trunks like bales of razor wire.

Danforth jogged him with an elbow. "Amazing, isn't it?"

"I'll say," Creely blurted, knowing that anything more elaborate right now would sound churlish and contrived. He gulped and unsnapped the Geiger counter from his belt. "I've never seen such uniformity," he muttered. "How long have you known about this, Dan?"

"Oh, I'd say about a week, give or take." Danforth's voice exhibited an almost parental proudness, as if he had played some crucial role in the dead forest's cultivation. "I call them Spinners."

"You haven't told anybody else yet."

It was more statement than question, and Danforth's silence—coupled with the dim and distant look in his eyes—was answer enough. Creely swept the Geiger back and forth a few times, but it was only a token gesture. Five hundred thousand years after the last warhead had exploded, and the only radiation left around here was of the background variety. No wonder this place hadn't showed up on the sensors. It was a vast sea of lifeless, irradiated stone.

"It's quite incredible," was the only way Creely could think of to sum it up. "Shall we?" He gestured at a faint track that led to the forest floor. Then he corrected himself. "*Can* we?"

"Sure," said Danforth, "there's no danger. Not here, anyway."

Creely nodded and set off down the rubble-strewn slope. The ridge was less steep on this side, and as he made his way towards ground-level, holster still unbuckled, he wondered what Danforth had meant about the danger not being *here*. Was it somewhere else, then? He didn't get a chance to think about that one. As the track passed beneath the overhanging, screw-thread branches, he felt himself engulfed by a wave of something he hadn't felt in a long time. Was it nostalgia? Back on Earth his childhood home had backed onto a pine forest, and it had often seemed as if his Mother's back yard was the size of the world. As Creely reached ground level and experienced the sudden and overwhelming urge to run, he realized that it was indeed nostalgia.

He threw back his hood and folded his shades into the front pocket of his cowl in preparation, immersed in the potent memories of youth.

The momentary reverie nearly cost him his life. Suddenly sensing something amiss, he turned to see Danforth's heels disappearing into the undergrowth. A second later there was a rending crack. Creely barely registered the triangular mass of a falling Spinner bearing down on him before leaping sideways and rolling away in the dirt. The tree smashed to the ground, breaking into countless jagged shards and chunks of stone, and making a noise like the shrieking of a thousand banshees. Slivers and stone fragments rained down on him as he lay in the dust, ears ringing.

"Dan—"

He bit off the rest of the lieutenant's name when it occurred to him that it might not be apposite to reveal his position to a man he no longer entirely trusted. The toppled tree may, after all, have amounted to some misguided attempt on his life. Instead, with his heart beating thickly in his chest, Creely dragged himself a couple of meters through the settling dust cloud, struggled to his feet, and looked around. Danforth was nowhere to be seen. Then a sound like the clatter of approaching hooves tore at the air. Creely snatched his weapon from its holster and went into a defensive crouch, not knowing where to aim. Seconds later the wave of sound crashed against the base of the ridge. It sounded as if a table full of crockery had been overturned at his back.

"It's okay," called a familiar voice from distance, "it's just the echo coming back at us. Don't let it freak you out."

Creely peered through the haze of dust and trees and strangely geometric shadows thrown by the spiraling branches. It felt as if his hair was standing on end.

"I'm freaked out enough as it is," he called back, "what the hell's going on, Danforth? I could have been killed."

"I know and I'm sorry."

"Are you?"

The lieutenant emerged from behind a large Spinner with his arms raised and his hair in disarray. There was a cut above one eye and blood dripped down the front of a T-shirt filthy with dust. He looked as if he was surrendering to the enemy. "My fault," he said in a low voice, "all my fault, Cree. Really."

"That's not enough." Creely matched the other's reasonable tone but kept the gun held aloft. "Tell me about the tree. What did you do to it?"

"I wanted to cut off one of its limbs," Danforth said. He spoke slowly and evenly. "To show you something." He shrugged and looked at the ground. "I guess maybe I was a little over-eager."

"Keep going."

"Well, I used my laser machete to amputate a branch. The loss must have upended the balance ratio or something, I dunno. It toppled right over."

"You got down to it awful quick, is all I can say."

Danforth made a sound somewhere between a chuckle and a sob. "I had the whole thing planned," he mumbled. "I wanted to surprise you. Please don't get the wrong idea, okay?"

He took a step forwards.

Creely lowered the gun in spite of himself. What was he going to do? Murder a man on a planet where genocide had already taken the entire population? "Don't worry," he said, "and by the way, the surprise worked." He held out his free hand, which trembled visibly in the air. "I'm shaking, look at me."

Danforth mimicked the gesture. His whole arm quaked like a divining rod above an underground spring. Either he was telling the truth or he had a great future in daytime soap opera. "So you still wanna see this thing?"

When Creely nodded, Danforth waved him over and stood back, gently lowering his hands to his sides. "There," he said. He pointed at a reasonably intact branch lying on the ground. "Cut a slice from the end," he instructed, "a *thin* slice, thin as you can get it."

Creely fulfilled the request in a matter of seconds, using his laser-machete to produce a wafer-thin disk of glowing glass that stood just proud of the severed limb, like a slice of roast lamb about to fall away from the bone. "Now all we have to do is wait a few seconds."

The two men stood among the rubble of the ruined Spinner, still a little uneasy with each other but calm now, the disk changing colors as it cooled. When it had phased from a dull purple to the color of lead, Danforth toe-punted the disk with his boot and it cracked across the middle. He picked the two pieces up and handed one to Creely, blowing on his own. "Now try this," he said, "watch how I do it." He demonstrated by holding the piece of smoked glass in front of his eyes. Creely followed suit. All he could see was the pinkish-grey blur of Danforth's face.

"What am I looking at?"

"Guess."

When he lowered the glass, Danforth was already climbing the slope again, muscled legs pistoning against the sandy ridge. *Shit, now what?* thought Creely, and after a moment's hesitation decided there was only one way to find out. Still none the wiser, he followed the lieutenant at an easy trot.

Ten minutes later they were back at the top of the ridge, out of breath but swapping jokes between pants, most of them about not getting any younger and how much easier it had been going down than coming back up. Finally, when they could breath properly again, Danforth waggled the glass in the air. It caught and reflected the light, dazzling Creely so that he held his own jagged crescent of smoked glass to his eyes like a pair of shades.

"Take a moment to check out the forest," Danforth instructed.

Weary of the game but reluctant to offend, Creely did as he was told. The cut of the glass was smooth and even but it was no polished lens, and all he could see were angular smudges, thousands of them, no matter where he looked.

"Okay," he said, "got that."

"Now turn around and check out the plain."

Creely did that, too. And felt a manic giggle of delight escape from his throat like air bubbling from a leaky pipe.

"That can't be right, can it?" He was grinning, and it felt good. He lowered the glass and stared nonplussed at Danforth, who was viewing the same scene through his own shard of glass. He was grinning too, cracked skin seaming with dirt as his lips drew back from his teeth.

"The idea came to me when I was out here driving on my own one night," he said, still staring, still enraptured by what he saw. "I noticed that those odd blasts of static coming over the radio weren't so odd after all. At first I thought they were occurring at irregular intervals, but I was wrong. They always occur in the same place. Out there." He pointed needlessly, face slackening to seriousness as he recalled the experience. "But it wasn't until the carb went that I realized what was going on."

Creely returned his attention to the plain, squinted once more through the glass. The transparent dome—undoubtedly a native bio-sphere of some description—was huge, perhaps as much as two kilometers in diameter and easily half as high again. It was packed with the mottled greens and bluish greys of indigenous plant life (the first they had encountered on this barren hunk of rock), highlighted by amorphous sprays of the most incredible colors. Creely spotted a bright yellow-white beard tumbling from a height of thirty or forty meters. He saw an explosion of reds through a beaded patch of condensation, wild forget-me-not blues scattered and smattered against a background of dense tropical forests—forests that *moved* beneath the encapsulating bubble. Mist hung like swatches of flimsy cloth between branches laden with fruit, and things that hopped and fluttered migrated between the boughs. Water, shrouded from view but clearly audible, crashed down from on high.

When Creely lowered the glass this time, it slipped from his damp fingers and shattered on the rocks between his feet. He felt like an Affinity addict on the first day of rehab. No coordination.

"Carb?" he said numbly, "what carb are you talking about, Dan?"

Danforth surveyed the dome at length. His eyes shone with something that may have been infatuation.

"The carburettor," he said, "from the landcar? It developed a hairline fracture a couple of weeks back, so I replaced it on the spot, drove back to camp and forgot about it." He snatched his own glass away from his eyes and slotted it into the pocket of his combats. "But the next day I happened to drive past the same spot and notice something odd. The carb was gone. I knew it was the same place because I recognized the rock formation. Besides, there were oil stains all over the place." He arched an eyebrow. "So that's when I got to wondering."

Creely nodded, but really his mind—no, his *heart*—was elsewhere. Danforth failed to notice, perhaps because the same thing was happening to him. "I thought maybe one of the other crews had dropped by and salvaged it," he resumed, "but then I decided to take a look around, just in case. That's when I found this lot." He gestured over his shoulder at the field of dead Spinners. "The rest was an accident, really, a slice of good fortune. And I mean that literally." He reached into his vest and pulled out a sliver of fossilized glass that dangled on the end of a piece of woven vegetable fiber. "This was lying in the dirt." He fingered the sliver and looked at Creely again. "Don't ask me how this stuff works," he concluded, "it just does."

"So the carb wasn't salvaged after all?"

"Hell, no. It was *scavenged*. And that, my friend, is why there isn't a matchstick left on the surface of this here hunk of basalt. Those who are left live beneath the surface in underground arks and only come out at night. They're linked together by a series of catacombs, thousands of—"

"Arks?" interrupted Creely, "you mean there are *more* of them?"

Danforth threw back his head and laughed. Then he dragged the makeshift pendant from around his neck and handed it over. "Look around you," he said, and jumped into space. Creely watched him slide all of the way to the bottom of the slope, dust trail expanding at his back, before taking another look through the glass. He turned full circle on top of the ridge, picking out the various domes at intervals. Dozens of them popped up between here and the horizon. A couple were damaged. Others appeared to be entirely empty.

"We have to go visit one," he called after Danforth, "as soon as possible." His voice had gained a new level of enthusiasm now, and so had his face. He was captivated, enthralled, mesmerized.

"I know, I know," Danforth called back, "but let's grab a bite to eat first, okay? I'm starved."

Creely ate nothing during lunch. Neither did he speak. He merely sat on the landcar's running board and gazed through the glass at the myriad life forms captured within the dome, like insects trapped beneath a bell-jar. The more he looked, the more shapes and colors resolved themselves. It was wonderful, miraculous, too fantastic for words. And so woefully precious out here in this barren desert that he didn't quite dare believe it. Danforth had been right not to tell him of his find in advance. Where something like this was concerned, seeing was the only way of believing.

"Shall we go?" The raw-skinned lieutenant was still chewing on the last of his ration pack as he came around the front of the vehicle, casually wiping his fingers on his T-shirt. The grease stains were mixed with grey Spinner dust and the blood from his sutured eye.

Creely sprang to his feet and set off immediately—without his shades, without scarf or hood, without another word. The only thing that mattered to him right now was the smoked sliver which he held to his eye as if it were a monocle and he an egocentric film director on a vast and unlikely set. Danforth, on the other hand, was far less animated. He unplugged his canteen as they walked and lazily splashed some of its contents over his face and neck.

"Aren't you gonna drink anything?" he said, wiping his mouth on his hand.

Creely took the proffered object, tossed off a mouthful of lukewarm water, and handed it back with a muted grunt of thanks. By the time he had sweated it back out they were in spitting distance of the dome. Creely refused to hesitate or discuss the best way to handle the situation. He simply walked right up to the massive structure and laid his cheek against the glass in obvious reverence. A split-second later he jerked up, rubbing his face and jumping from foot to foot in pain.

"Son of a *bitch*!" he cursed, "but that's hot."

"I tried to tell you," Danforth chided. "And you can lose the eye-piece now, by the way. You look enough of an asshole as it is."

"I can?" Creely stopped rubbing for a moment and blinked. "Hey, I can see it with the naked eye. How come?"

Danforth shrugged. "Maybe it knows we're here."

"Are you telling me this thing is sentient?"

"Maybe."

Creely nodded and began to feel a little more grounded about his work. Now that they had arrived and the moment was upon him, the practicalities were starting to impinge on his fantasy of finding the descendents of the nuclear holocaust beneath the planet's crust. "Okay," he said, "well in that case would you care to speculate how we get inside? I don't see a door anywhere."

"Now that's one thing I *don't* need to speculate on," said Danforth. "Walk this way."

They followed the graduated curve of the magnificent dome for a distance of about four hundred meters. It was the exact same story all over again. Danforth leading the way and Creely, almost like a young apprentice, bringing up the rear. Creely didn't care. Now that he was over the initial shock of the discovery, he was glad for the lieutenant to take the lead. In the meantime he watched as murky shapes fluttered about between the trees. He couldn't identify any separate species yet because the glass was filthy—filmed with algae, condensation, and what looked like caked layers of ancient bird shit. Not that he cared. This was the way life should be: vibrant, free and unpredictable.

Creely didn't realize quite *how* unpredictable, however, until the massive crack in the dome's surface ranged into view. At first glance it appeared around a hundred meters high, but on closer inspection this initial estimate turned out to be a tad on the conservative side. Its base was as wide as the mouth of a New York subway tunnel, and as it rose higher the edges of the fracture grew together only very gradually. You could still have driven a landcar through it at the place where the trees ran out.

All of this Creely viewed from a considerable distance. When he lowered his gaze (reluctantly, and with a crick in his neck), he noticed that the lieutenant had not waited for him. Danforth was striding cautiously but with great purpose towards the entrance. At its mouth, a slightly-built creature that bore a certain resemblance to a terrestrial kangaroo, hopped about in the sun, petulantly sniffing the ground. When it spotted the two interlopers closing in on its position, it peered at them for a moment, seeming to gage the threat of this foreign species. Then it glanced through the gap, seemed to sigh, and hopped back inside.

"Did you *see* that?" Creely demanded. His heart was hammering so fast he feared it might skip a beat and go into cardiac arrest on him at any moment. "An indigenous life form, can you believe it?"

"That's nothing," said Danforth, "wait till you meet the natives." He said this just as they reached the threshold of the crack. Before ducking inside, he jabbed Creely's chest with a finger and told him to buckle up his holster. "They're scared enough of us as it is without you waving that thing about."

Without another word, he strode into the dome and was swallowed by up by the jungle as quickly and easily as Creely had tossed back that mouthful of water from the canteen minutes earlier. Creely himself was more prudent. He shut his eyes and allowed his other senses to take over before entering. The chatter of aviators reached his ears, likewise the distant hiss of tumbling water; and underlying it all, the irrefutable smell of decay. This was hardly surprising. As far as the natural world was concerned, more life simply meant more death, and plenty of it.

"Danforth?"

He expected the lieutenant to appear from among the fronds and the creepers and the clumps of undergrowth at any minute, admonishing him for his reluctance. But Creely *wasn't* reluctant. He was merely savoring the moment. When Danforth failed to appear, he stepped out of the sun and into the shade with a feeling that he was entering Eden both before and after the Fall. The first thing that hit him was the change in climate. It wasn't so much the heat that struck him as the humidity. His pores yawned instantly and began gushing sweat. A silky leaf brushed his cheek and came away damp. Already he was contributing to the upkeep of this mysterious micro-environment. And it gave him something back, too. When Creely breathed the thick, swampy air into his lungs he felt renewed, invigorated. But still he lingered at the edges of the alien biosphere like a gatecrasher at a private party. This he did for two reasons. First, he wanted to confirm his suspicions on a certain point; second, he needed something to focus on, some landmark he could spot if he needed to find his way back in a hurry. The crack, he reasoned, might not be prominent from far back in the shadows.

But it was no good. There were no landmarks here, none he could trust. The more Creely looked the more everything resembled everything else. A huge Spinner, the live version this time as opposed to the freeze-dried variety, stood over to his left, branches erupting with a thousand delicate lilac blossoms. A different kind of plant, tan in color and similar in appearance to a cartoon cactus, but covered in reddish-brown pincers instead of spines, lanced thirty meters into the air. Every time one of the fleeting aviators sailed past it (and Creely was still to get a really *good* look at those little critters), the pincers clicked together like wind-ruffled castanets.

It was glorious to witness but it did him no good. With a sinking feeling, Creely admitted that, once inside, he would probably be able to navigate his way back to the edge of the dome with relative ease; but locating the exit at short notice might prove a different matter. And at almost two kilometers wide, this was potentially dangerous territory if the natives turned hostile.

"Dan-*forrrrrrrth*," he yelled. In response, a blue-and-orange spray of multi-jointed wings exploded from a bush nearby, tiny feathered creatures that bore a passing resemblance to birds streaming between trunks and shrubs in alarm. They flew in formation, Creely noticed with delight, in a single fluid stream. Before finally taking the plunge, he glanced one last time at the outside world. Just as he had suspected, the glass of the dome held the same properties as the sliver he still clutched in his fist. He was able to witness the huge structure's semi-transparent shadow stretching out across the rocks and the sand before him, as well as the faint bubbles of the other domes in the distance.

Creely turned and slipped beneath the overhanging wall of green.

He found Danforth an hour later, sitting near a fountain that spumed frothy white water pumped from deep beneath the planet's surface. The lieutenant was bare-chested now and dangled his feet in a wide pool populated with wriggling eel-like creatures that nibbled the soles of his feet.

Creely sat down beside him and lay back on the greenish blue grass, a knowing smile playing at the corners of his mouth. The afternoon was wearing on and the shadows in the ancient biosphere were lengthening and merging. Almost a kilometer above, near the dome's shining apex, more of the transparent blobs circulated on the moist air.

"They're definitely alive," Danforth whispered without looking up. "Not clouds at all but . . . *beings* of some kind."

"Airborne jellyfish?"

"Possibly."

Creely sighed. "It must be a stress-free life."

Before Danforth could fashion an answer, a clump of bushes at the opposite bank shook with activity. Both men sat up and stared. A moment later a short humanoid figure emerged onto the banks of the pond. He was a little more than a meter tall with a mane of whitened hair that sprouted the length of his backbone. His skin was bluish-grey, eyes the bright silver of freshly-minted coins. He sniffed at the air, seemed to sense something different about his surroundings. Not overly concerned, he set about plucking pieces of fat, juicy-looking fruit from the boughs of the nearest tree.

"He can't hear us," said Danforth slowly, pinching off a stalk of grass, "or see us, for that matter. I guess this invisibility business works two ways."

Creely thought about this as the bent humanoid continued to harvest succulent pink fruit.

"So how come we can see *him*?"

"I dunno. Maybe visibility around here is dictated by mood or something." Danforth frowned at the piece of grass before inserting it between his teeth. "Say Creely, what do you call archaeology when the people are still around?"

Creely smiled and listened to the ripple of water as more of the zebra-striped eels lapped and wriggled about the lieutenant's feet. All of them were banded in black and white, but each set of gills bore its own distinct coloring. Scarlet, lavender, yellow, luminescent green. The humanoid stopped plucking for a moment and squinted in their direction. "Good question," said Creely with great care. "Anthropology, maybe?"

Danforth nodded. "They're dying, Cree." He sounded genuinely sad when he said this, yet he continued to regard the figure on the opposite banks with a hint of amusement. "There aren't enough of them left to maintain the environments, and bit by bit, parts are dying off."

"I know. I found a few patches of savannah back that way." He pointed but Danforth's attention was elsewhere. "If they're not careful the healthy gene pool here will dry up altogether."

"Careful's got nothing to do with it," Danforth retorted. "They simply can't handle the workload anymore." He chewed on the grass, thinking. "Are we allowed to save a species from extinction? Is that part of our remit?"

"The first intelligent species we've come across in this sector? Hell, what do you think?"

"What about if we didn't tell anybody about it, what then?"

"That would be a secondary consideration, I guess. But still pretty important if you ask me."

As he said this, a small round thing on spindly legs, with arm-like appendages protruding from the top of its smooth bulbous head, emerged from a path in the jungle and skipped up to the humanoid with the basket. In a calm and unhurried manner that suggested familiarity, the humanoid selected the shiniest, most succulent piece of fruit it could find, peeled it and fed it a piece at a time to the visitor. Then the two continued the harvesting together.

"Amazing," said Creely, "two utterly distinct species co-existing in perfect harmony."

"Oh, there are more than two species. Way more." Danforth said this with a degree of nonchalance and plucked the grass from between his teeth. "There are dozens of them. In fact, I'm only just beginning to realize what their secret is." He got to his feet, gently shaking one of the colorful eels from his ankle, where it had attached itself with lips the color of melted liquorice. "Come on," he said, "let's walk, I've got one last thing to show you."

They didn't have far to go. It was a hole in the side of a low hummock that resembled a burrow or warren of some kind, only larger. In another place and time it might have suited a homeless hobbit down to the ground. "That's the way in," said Danforth, "the entrance to the catacombs. It's a lot different than up here. But kind of interesting all the same."

"I'll bet it is."

"If you want my opinion," Danforth postulated, "these beings renounced warfare and violence the day after those nukes landed all those millennia ago. And since they no longer breed enough to sustain a viable population on their own, they must somehow assimilate visitors like us. That's the only explanation I can think of for the diversity."

"Whoa, assimilate? Is this the part where a hunting party comes and drags us beneath the surface."

An unreadable look crossed Danforth's face. "You did hear what I just said about renouncing violence, right?"

Creely nodded.

"Then in that case, you'll realize they've had plenty of time to find another way. And they have, believe me. Intelligent visitors like us, with our own specialities and unique sets of genes, are an invaluable asset to places like this. If the visitors are willing, I reckon the . . . well, *whatever* they call themselves here, adopt them, and the colonies are reinvigorated."

"Success through diversification."

"That's right. And you know how they accomplish that?"

Creely grinned. "Mind control?"

"I doubt it. If you ask me, it's something in the air that induces a favorable mood change. Hormones, maybe."

"Produced by?"

Danforth waved a hand. "Look around you. Think about it. I mean, it isn't so crazy, is it? These people, these beings, they see everything they love destroyed by a senseless, futile war. They're bound to do everything they can to avoid it happening again. And let's not forget, they've had half a million years to cultivate a solution."

"And they do that by breeding flowers that, what, evoke feelings of peace, comradeship and mutual trust, is that it?"

"Peace certainly, the rest I don't know about. But I'm thinking more along the lines of altruism, to be honest. You saw how that humanoid fed his little friend back there. It was like a kid with a favorite uncle."

"Okay," said Creely, "I'll buy that. But what now? You're not planning on signing up, are you?"

"I already did," said Danforth, and produced a five-centimeter crystal lozenge from his belt.

Creely sucked in air and felt bright animal panic stir in his chest. "The anti-matter chamber," he whispered, "what the hell are you doing with that?"

"Correction," smiled Danforth, "the *reserve* anti-matter chamber. The two primaries are resting at the bottom of that pond back there. And what I'm doing," he added, "is ensuring the prolongation of these habitats and their residents. You did agree it was a part of our remit, right?"

"And it *is*," enthused Creely, "but not like this. Come on, Dan, think what this place has done to your mind. Without the chambers we'll be stranded here indefinitely."

Danforth nodded and gazed at the crystal in his palm. "I know."

When he looked up again, Creely was pointing the laser at him. "I wouldn't bother if I was you," Danforth commented dryly, "I emptied the charge when you were asleep this morning. Now go tell the others; I left the keys in the ignition."

And with that he ducked into the cave and out of sight. Creely hesitated for a moment, listening to the plaintive cries of the birds, picking up the sweet fragrance of plucked fruits on the air. The next time the lieutenant's voice carried to him it was from a very long way away.

It's really not so bad, you know.

Creely holstered his laser and closed his eyes in disbelief. A gentle sigh escaped his lips. The scary part of it was that Danforth might actually have been right.

*After a couple of years spent traveling in central Europe and Turkey, **Tristan S. Davenport** has returned to the womb of the university. He is pursuing a doctorate in cognitive science at the University of California, San Diego. His fiction has also appeared in* Chiaroscuro *(www.chizine.com) and* Trabuco Road *(www.trabucoroad.com).*

The Price of Peace
by Tristan S. Davenport

othing will stand in the way of peace.

N So begin the archives of the Great Experiment, kept by the tourism council of Sirius Alpha. Like most peoples who have undertaken a project known by a name like the Great Experiment, the Sirius Alphans have been extinct for centuries.

Today, Sirius Alpha looks a great deal like a cleaner, more rustic Earth. Vascular tree-like fungi band the equator in great forests, the oceans are lively with fat prey and sleek predators, and the southern glaciers advance, sharpening peaks and grinding out valleys. To find the people who once lived here, one must peel back the natural beauty that they nearly destroyed.

For the physically fit, Sirius Alpha is best explored on foot. Sadly, this option is not available to tourists: decades of transit hypnosleep render most travelers too obese to walk. Rent a hoverchair, instead. Hire an excavation team, pick a site at random and begin digging. Within meters you're all but guaranteed to find the remains of a Sirian home: crumbs of glass, twists of metal and great blobs of once-melted plastic.

In the incendiary wars that blasted the surface of Sirius Alpha, entire continents fused and boiled amid the pounding of megaton-scale bombs. Civilization all but collapsed; a third of species went extinct. *Nothing*, the survivors decreed, *will stand in the way of peace.*

They destroyed their remaining weapons. The world at last enjoyed a respite from killing on a massive scale. But death on a massive scale continued. For war could still be waged economically: recalcitrant populations could be starved, and intractable governments could be made by greater powers to look responsible.

Armed mobs roamed the impoverished regions, killing with wrenches, machetes and nail guns. In a manner reminiscent of our own thirteenth century,* unpopular religions and social classes were exterminated on an industrial scale.

At last a nascent world government, which had been forming for over a century, brought the richest nations to heel, making them beholden to the folk of the poorest.

This amazing feat was accomplished as follows:

Although the Sirians resembled humans in many ways, perhaps in more ways than any other known species, slight differences in their nervous structure made control of behavior through electric devices a relatively straightforward proposal. Jail wardens and schoolteachers had long employed such devices for crowd control. As computational technology advanced, allowing behavior to be controlled more finely, warlords and heads of state used them as a means of conscription. It was not until after the wars that their first "killer" application was found: presidents.

The tiny mass of superconducting wire was implanted into the skull of each premier. It contained two simple instructions:

I shall harm no one.

What promises I make, I shall keep.

So began the Great Experiment. There ensued a flurry of nonaggression pacts, trade agreements and exportations of aid and volunteers. Peace was popular. Hungry for votes, the leaders eagerly signed what was put in front of them.

War became a physical impossibility. Anyone with the authority to order an attack had promised not to, and promises in that era were kept. Sirius Alpha became a near-utopia, envy of all human beings: we had by then been receiving their radio signals for over a decade.

---

* The Twentieth century, by the heretical calendar.

We dispatched an embassy from Earth, armed to the teeth just in case, on a two hundred-year Mission of Friendship to Sirius Alpha. Here is what transpired during their journey.

The peace-and-honesty implants had been a resounding success. They had solved every problem between nations, and for the first time the world was at peace. But there were still problems between individuals. Murders took place, deceit snared the gullible and in daily life the strong still dominated the weak. Despite the advances of recent decades—or perhaps because of them—the public cried out for morality. Elderly people who had spent their youths either fearing or committing murder now complained bitterly about the neighbor who returned a borrowed novel with a page torn. Individuals of great moral stature volunteered for the implants, pledging publicly to abstain from lying, from murder and from other activities which were not exactly lying, not exactly murder, but amounted to the same thing. These moral giants gained great admiration—much of it, not incidentally, from the opposite sex. The trend caught on.

Within a century, accepting the implants was a citizen's duty. One received them at birth, so that even children could know the benefits of peace and honesty. Those who refused them were seen as miscreants, untrustworthy folk whose word was not self-enforcing. Adults of this underclass either accepted the implant or pressured their children to.

A world without violence or lying was a world without need of laws. The constitution was abolished, and Sirius Alpha attained perfect freedom with perfect peace: a world in which no act was forbidden, unless it contradicted one's word or caused harm to another.

A year in celebration of World Peace was declared. In a spirit of harmony the populace of Sirius Alpha turned out to celebrate. Food was shared, love was made, homes were built. Neighbor helped neighbor in a worldwide spirit of self-celebration.

What more perfect expression of self-satisfaction could there be than a census? Its findings were grim. The Peace Council reported them the following year, when the bumper crop of babies conceived during World Peace Year had all been born.

The wars of the Dark Ages had been wars for resources. So great was their toll in lives that anyone could argue with reason that the world possessed sufficient resources for everyone. With the advent of world peace, that was no longer the case. There would soon be famines: it was inevitable. The people of Sirius Alpha, each one, reflected upon their selfishness. "If I had not eaten that shank of animal flesh," one might have thought, "my neighbor so-and-so would not go hungry." Or, "If I did not burn these unnecessary calories, through revelry, work and play—nay, through the very act of eating!—there might be one more morsel for my neighbor . . . " The spirit of the times encouraged these thoughts, and the implants gave them material force. Once eating and moving had been identified with harming others, the implants put a quick stop to those activities. Every person on Sirius Alpha reflected thus, and just as quickly they found themselves trapped. So they remained, twitching in stasis, until they collapsed from hunger.

Fifty years later our Mission of Friendship arrived, transmitting messages of peace, weapons poised to deal death, just in case. We found an empty world, with skyscrapers festively painted, jutting from the richest farmland one could imagine. That of course, was the populace. By then they had rotted away, into a medium perfect for growing beans.

The Mission of Friendship evolved, over time, into the Tourism Council of Sirius Alpha. They are an active, hardy folk, living close to the land and scorning those who rely on technology. Tourists should be warned that prejudice against the obese is not concealed on this world. The buildings often have narrow doors.

*Fort Worth writer **Jonathan Shipley** lives surrounded by old things—furniture, books, rotary phone—in an old, historic house. Like many collectors, he cohabits with more antiques than strictly fit into his house, creating an ambience of chaotic creativity. He has had fantasy and science fiction stories published in* Weird Tales, Dragon Magazine, *Marion Zimmer Bradley's* Fantasy Magazine, *and several anthologies. However, he is actually a novel writer at heart and devotes most of his writing time to a vast story arc that ranges from Nazi occultism to vampires to futuristic space opera. The "Child-Prophet" of this story is a residue of the gods and empires chronicled elsewhere in the story arc.*

Song of the Child-Prophet
by Jonathan Shipley

They stopped digging the well when they found the child encased in a block of amberite.

Cara put down the portable pulverizer and stared in horror mixed with fascination. Her glance strayed across the valley to the forbidden side where the spiky fingers of broken towers marched along the ridge up to the sphere, half disintegrated but still huge, that overlooked the empty plains below. The mystery of those structures dominated the Colony as surely as the sphere dominated the landscape. No one knew what race had built them, though the anthropology team studied them relentlessly. The colonists had their guesses about what happened here a thousand years ago, but the Colonial Administration said little on the subject and warned everyone away from the area.

Cara's gaze returned to the encapsulated child. A victim of the apocalypse that had swept this world perhaps? But where then were the others? Should there not be thousands upon thousands of victims in amber? But over and above the obvious questions was the chilling coincidence that she and Lester had just been arguing again about having a child. And here they'd unearthed one, as though the very rocks had heard their argument. She refused to consider it might be anything other than a freak coincidence. The child itself was already strange enough.

The amberite glowed near-transparent, letting her see the child in perfectly preserved detail. It couldn't be human, she thought, unless it was some genetic experiment, and that wasn't likely. The amberite was old. Ancient.

"Has to be pre-Colonial," her husband Lester said uneasily. "You know what that means."

Cara sighed in frustration. Every time someone in the Colony unearthed something, Colonial Admin came down hard. Old Jess across the river had found one little ceramic pot and been put off his farm for three months while the experts poked around. They were obsessed with anything that might shed light on the fate of the pre-human civilization that had flourished and vanished here.

"What'll we do?" she asked.

Lester kept wrestling the block out of the well hole. Only when he heaved the amberite over the lip of the hole did he look at her.

"We dig our well," he said tightly. "Tell no one about this—not even your sister. We'll hide the amberite in the shed and dump it down canyon when the dark season comes."

Cara nodded but knew there would be trouble. The amberite was too big a find. Wherever it turned up, there'd be an investigation.

"Put it back in the ground," she said abruptly. "The well can go somewhere else."

"Cara, you know this is the only place for the shaft. Anywhere else and we'll hit bedrock a meter down."

The nagging feeling wouldn't go away. "Then we hit bedrock," she said. "I don't think any of this is an accident."

"Any of what?"

"The shaft, the amberite, the child. There has to be a reason it was buried here."

Lester sighed. "Don't start. Whatever happened here happened hundreds—thousands—of years ago. Maybe it was their version of Pompeii."

Cara just shook her head. It didn't add up to a natural disaster to her any more than the ruined sphere across the valley. Someone had imploded the sphere, and someone had gone to great lengths to bury a child where it would never be found. She stepped over to the amberite and studied the naked form within. Young, maybe eight years old if it had been human. Elfin face. Neuter. And so perfectly preserved. Admin would go wild.

She pressed her hand against the pale yellow surface, felt the tiniest vibration through her fingertips.

"Lester," she murmured. "What if it's not dead?"

Lester looked off across the valley. She knew he didn't want to hear it. Free land and open space was what brought him to the Colony. He didn't want anything to do with lost civilizations and forgotten disasters.

"Throw the tarp over the damn thing when you're done looking," he said, moving off toward the house. "I'm calling it a day."

The song began in the corner of her dream and swelled until it swallowed the dream. No words that she could understand, just a beautiful, lyrical voice singing high and clear. When she finally woke, she was crying and didn't know why.

All that day, snatches of the song kept coming back to her. She found herself humming but never could find the melody.

That night she dreamed again. And she knew it was the child. Impossibly, it *was* alive. Encased and buried for centuries, it still lived.

In the middle of the night with the song still fresh in her mind, she went out to the backyard, powered up the pulverizer, and began carving away the amberite.

She was still working when Lester found her the next morning. "Are you crazy?" he yelled, grabbing the pulverizer. "You can't let that thing out because of some damn dream."

Cara turned slowly. She hadn't mentioned the dreams to him. "So you've heard it, too. The singing."

"We're going to put it back in the ground, Cara. We don't dare do anything else."

"It's only a child."

"And still alive? We don't know what it is. But it could be

dangerous. Admin wouldn't be so jumpy about artifacts without good reason. Maybe they know—"

A soft humming filled the air, like a skimmer passing overhead. But sweeter. Some indefinable emotion surged up inside Cara, strange but strong.

Lester staggered back, shaking his head from side to side. "Stop it, stop it," he groaned.

"It's too late," Cara murmured. "For better or for worse, we have to finish now."

Lester didn't argue as she took back the pulverizer and chipped away at the amberite shell.

The child was pale and weak and helpless. Its eyelids barely fluttered as Cara lifted it from the casing and put it to bed in the guest room. If it hadn't been for the subtle change in key in the humming, she might have thought it wasn't conscious.

Lester followed her, watched her without speaking. He just stared at the child and when they withdrew to the kitchen, stared at her.

"It's not a monster," Cara said.

Lester still didn't say anything.

"It needs our help," she persisted. "How could anyone bury a child alive like that?"

"They were scared of it," he finally said. "Hell, I know I am. And it's not even awake yet."

Cara fidgeted with her identity bracelet. She didn't have an answer to that. Maybe he was right to be scared. Maybe she should be afraid. But she wasn't. Whatever had happened millennia ago, a child should never have been made to suffer. And it had suffered, she was sure. Alone in the dark and silence, it had learned despair. But not hate.

She shook her head. My, wasn't she the little mind-reader all of a sudden? But she sensed she was right. The child might not be awake, but it had been communicating with her since they first found the amberite. Telepathic species weren't unknown, after all.

"I'm going into town," Lester said abruptly. "Come with me. Please."

She couldn't. The child needed her. But the desperation in Lester's eyes frightened her. He was going to do something in town. "You can't report the child," she said. "I couldn't stand it if the Colonial Admin took it away to their laboratories and dissected it like some new animal species."

Lester grabbed her by the arm. "*It*. You still call it an *it* because deep down you know it's more alien than it looks. Nothing human—nothing humanoid—could have survived buried alive without food or air. And the years, Cara, the centuries. It's a thing, not a child. Maybe even a weapon."

"A weapon?" Cara would have laughed at the suggestion if Lester weren't scaring her so. He actually believed it.

"Yes, a *weapon*," he repeated, squeezing her arm painfully tight. "This world once supported a high civilization. We don't know what destroyed it. Maybe it was something that got into people's heads and into their dreams and drove them crazy—something that couldn't be killed and had to be buried deep in the earth to stop it."

"It's a child," Cara insisted.

Lester's face sagged, looking old and defeated. "Come with me, Cara," he begged one last time. After a moment he turned and left. She heard the whine of the skimmer warming up.

A subtle melody started at the back of her mind. Stop him, it crooned. They will destroy me and I am helpless. Let me find my voice again.

Cara shuddered, torn between husband and some new loyalty that she never expected. Was this what mothers felt protecting their newborns? She and Lester had never been approved for children, so she didn't know. But it was strong—an instinct more than a feeling. She knew it could overwhelm her.

"Don't," she whispered aloud. "I'll protect you, but leave Lester alone. He's a good man, just scared."

The insistent melody faded, leaving her shaken. Cautiously, she walked toward the guest room. The elfin face peered up at her, staring at her with violet eyes.

"You're awake," she said because she could think of nothing else. "Please don't be a monster."

The tiny cherub mouth opened and a whisper of a song emerged.

"I seek only to glorify the gods that created me."

Whoever or whatever they might be, Cara thought uneasily. This was becoming too cosmic, tearing apart her life and her marriage. Glorifying ancient gods long dead and forgotten was not what she needed or wanted.

"Dead?" The single tone echoed in the tiny room, a note that carried the weight of a full requiem mass. Only as the sound faded did Cara become aware she was weeping, mourning something she did not even understand.

She wiped at the tears with her hand. "You've got to be more careful. Maybe it's the difference between your kind and mine, but every time you sing, you pull me into what you're feeling."

"For that was I created," sang the child and the joy surged out like a fountain. Cara gasped at the sheer intensity of the emotion. She'd known contentment in her life, but never joy like this.

But now I am alone
Abandoned by the gods I served
Feared by the younger races
Buried in the depths.

Despair welled up, killing all joy, killing all hope. Cara staggered as her world collapsed around her. "Stop!" she screamed. "You're destroying me!"

The despair stopped abruptly, replaced by a cautious hum of support. Cara raised her head, surprised to find herself on the floor. She must have fallen. The child stared at her with solemn violet eyes as she regained her feet.

Do not fear, it whispered not in gut-wrenching song, but directly into her mind. I shall go. I shall go where your kind will not find me and sleep until my gods call me home. Your heart cries for a child but I am not the one your heart seeks. Your man is right—I once sang the end of this world for such was the gods' will. Sweet farewell, compassionate one. Be soon with child. I sing you my blessing.

Lester came home in the company of a dozen Admin scientists and guards. Cara watched them dispassionately through the window as they secured their vehicles and fanned out taking sensor readings. They very well might kill her, she realized, for seeing things and feeling things deemed dangerous. But somehow she no longer cared. All of her emotions had been drained from her by that last haunting melody.

Lester broke free of the guards flanking him and rushed inside. "Where is it?" he asked, eyes focusing on the empty bed. "It's too late to protect it."

Yes, too late. A thousand years too late. The child's fate had been sealed in some other millennium.

Behind Lester, a smallish man in a protection suit with officer's insignia peered into the room and proceeded to scan.

"There's nothing here," Cara told them both. "The child has gone back into the earth."

"The well?" Lester glanced out the window at the open shaft.

Cara shook her head. "Not here. Not close. It will sleep, maybe forever. It doesn't want to be a monster."

The man in the protection suit tapped his com unit. "Specimen no longer on premises. Concentrate on residual readings and triangulate coordinates of—"

"No," interrupted Cara. "Don't do this. The Colony won't survive its songs if you find it again."

The man stopped speaking and stared. Slowly, he brought up the handscanner and aimed it her direction.

"No, nothing's wrong with me!" she snapped. "I'm just warning you. The child devastated this world once before and could do it again. Let it sleep."

He looked uncertain for a moment but finally seemed to understand what she was saying. Unusual for these experts who thought they knew everything. "Cancel that last order," he said into his com unit. "Situation is under control." He looked at her again, strangely, then retreated outside.

"So it *was* a monster," Lester breathed.

"It was only serving its gods."

He gave a snort. "Pray that no one digs them up."

Cara shook her head. "No, pray that our own child can grow up free and happy."

Lester's lips tightened. She knew the expression from past

259

arguments. They both wanted a child, but they hadn't been genetically certified and he feared bypassing the testing process. Even with full med-center support, many pregnancies had gone badly. "We haven't been approved," he said tautly.

Cara looked out the window again, wondering what it was she felt at that moment. Nothing passionate, but something. Serenity, perhaps. Certainty. Hope.

"Approval no longer matters," she told Lester. "We've been blessed."

Paul L. Bates has been gracing the independent press with his fiction for the past decade, blending or blatantly ignoring genres with work in such discriminating venues as Zahir, Literal Latte, Lynx Eye, Parsec, The Darklands Project, TransVersions *and* Beyond the Last Star. *He is semi-retired from the construction industry, a distance swimmer, and happiest when in the midst of his next novel.* Imprint, *the first novel in a series about the last city on earth was first published by Gale/Five Star in 2005;* Dreamer, *the second part of the trilogy, is due out in 2008.*

Flies
by Paul L. Bates

I see his grinning face, his empty eyes, his emaciated body. His fleshless hands make a sweeping gesture that encompasses the vastness of the desert. I blink my eyes and he is gone. A mirage. A figment of the heat and the pain. I try to lean forward, and suddenly I feel the forgotten agony of my wound. I fall back against the crumbling stone wall, still cool here in the shade. I take what small comfort I can from its touch. I shut my eyes and try to forget.

The desert heat is as oppressive as the living of a lie. It weighs more heavily upon me than the absurdity of the pretense, the constant humiliation of acting out the shallow deception that haunts my every waking act—and my every lucid dream. It crushes me, drains me, terrorizes me. The heat is a cruel and patient tormentor, muddling my every thought, soiling my ragged clothes, and sucking every ounce of volition from my marrow.

Yet compared to the incessant buzzing of the desert flies, the heat is no more than a minor annoyance. Those vile winged vagabonds, drawn to all warm blooded things, have journeyed with us for three days. They dance ecstatically and sting us repeatedly in a never ending frenzy, brazenly defying the merciless heat that has left even the camels in a stupor. The flies buzz, they cavort, they crawl, they bite, creating great itching welts upon my skin. They leave behind their excrement and their young, tormenting our flesh, despoiling our food. I ration my meager water supply by the mouthful, while the flies drink from my tears.

We have erected our ramshackle shelters against the ruined walls of this long dead place. We drape ourselves in gauzy white veils like anxious brides, hiding from the flies. We who have long conspired to shape an empire now cower like feckless thieves—hide and wait for the retribution that follows us across the arid waste. We shrink from the punishing heat, the tireless flies, and the relentless troops of he whose city and lands we coveted.

I try to sleep, awaiting the cool of the night before we move on. But full sleep is impossible in this bleak domain of madness and despair. Half formed dreams and translucent visions congeal before the outlines of my shelter. They waver as they act out their part in a never ending drama, sometimes addressing me with glimpses of the future, or dark memories of the recent past. Do I cry out in this half sleep? I must, for my throat is parched again. I drink sparingly, careful lest I spill even the smallest drop.

A comrade beside me snores, momentarily oblivious to the wounds that are slowly killing him. Great gashes across his arms and chest ooze life, and summon the flies. They demand admittance swarming against the veil that blocks the entrance to our safe haven. I hear their tiny voices calling out his name. The grinning specter has returned, doting upon my comrade as one might faun over a lover. I see the massive furled wings upon death's back and wonder from where he has flown to be with us.

Nearby, the wraith of a long dead king paces through the remains of his nameless city. He looks upon us with disdain, his sunken eyes glowing a vibrant green. They say we are not welcome here. Someone in another shelter cries out and I rouse myself momentarily. Soon I dream an army, less than a day's ride behind us at the oasis where we camped last night. They are fresh and we are spent. But, like us, they await the cool embrace of night in which to ride. Death turns and nods approvingly. Soon the thieves will all be his. He turns and embraces my comrade, who offers no resistance.

I awaken with a start, and this time I am fully awake. The comforting drone of my comrade's snoring has ended. His head lolls upon his chest, and his wide eyes stare at me without seeing. He has died of his wounds and this infernal heat. I feel as if I am an empty pit. I shut my eyes and feel a single tear making its way down one cheek. The heat claims it before it reaches the stubble upon my chin. The flies are intoxicated. They know that my comrade is theirs at last. Buzzing, they insist I give him up.

I am awake. I am asleep. Is there a difference?

Before me I see the magnificent city we failed to conquer. Its glittering spires and crenellated limestone walls glisten in the bright pink dawn. Its stately domes shimmer in the moonlight, masked by stringy translucent clouds.

I dream our debacle, less than three days past.

Small groups of plotters disguised as merchants, mendicants, tradesmen, pilgrims—all converging upon the sleeping city, safe within its own dreams. We have lured the city guard out into the wastes, seeking for nonexistent brigands, for the brigands are at the gates.

With our many comrades already within the walls, our secret ally inside the court of the king, and our concealed weapons at the ready, we will take her while she sleeps, like a virgin bride. We will take her, and bind her, and make her our own. The fools who rule her will die in their sleep, or awaken with our blades at their throats.

The moon breaks free of the gossamer clouds. I see the one who was to have betrayed her to us. His eyes are wide with knowing as they sparkle in the moonlight. A sly smile parts his lips. His head adorns the glided gate he was to have opened for us. The gate is shut. Instead of safe passage, we are greeted by a hail of arrows, and one pierces my side. The city guard is lurking just beyond the nearest dunes, not chasing phantoms kilometers away. They rise up to greet us upon their white chargers, glistening silver in the moonlight. Flashing blades at our backside take our men like autumn wheat beneath the scythe. Only my small band escapes through a narrow opening in their ranks, but not before we are mauled by the archers and the swordsmen.

I see the smiling face upon the gilded gates anew. He watches dispassionately as the vultures swarm against the dawn, come to feast upon our fallen. Our shattered host lies strewn as far as the eye can bear to look. The traitor turns his head and winks at me.

Again I am awakened with a start. The shadows without are longer than before, but the unrelenting heat has not abated. I call out to my captain. We must leave this place, I cry. It is too soon, he calls back, his own voice much weakened by his wounds. Sleep, he commands me. Take what rest I can, replenish my strength, he advises.

My dead comrade stands up slowly. His wide eyes stare into mine. Sadly he shakes his head. Then he walks through the crumbling stone wall as if it were but an illusion. Was his gesture a comment upon his sad demise? Or did he warn me of my own? Perhaps it was his final thought upon the fate of all—everything is for naught. I cannot say. It is but a dream, I tell myself. A terrible dream. It is all just a dream. I want to cry. The tears will not come.

I peer through the walls of the shelter, far beyond our wretched encampment and see the unobstructed desert beyond the ruins. I watch the crescent moon rising high above the dunes. Cool winds begin to stir restlessly. Soon they are spinning small columns of biting sand. A silvery sheen adorns the ever shifting landscape, highlighting a lonesome caravan upon the distant horizon, striking out for exotic places, bearing resplendent treasures of which I can only dream.

I look again and see the caravan is really the force that pursues us. They are nearly upon the ruins in which we sought sanctuary from the heat, where we lay cowering from the flies.

Once again I awaken with a fright. Expecting to see shadows longer than before, I am stunned by the sun's harsh glare. I hear the sounds of men dismounting. A numbing fear holds me fast against the wall. A city accent colors the voice that is barking orders. Someone throws back the netting and prods my dead comrade with a spear.

I hold my breath. We have been left behind, he and I—left behind to slow the enemy. Cautiously, with a trembling hand, I grope at my side for my scimitar. To my mounting horror, I find the scabbard empty.

Stooping low, the spearman enters our makeshift shelter. I see the peak of his war helm atop his head as he ducks through the sagging opening. I suck in my breath. He lifts his face to me and I see his grinning mouth, his black gaping eyes. It is death, and his mighty wings are suddenly outstretched, shredding every fabric of the shelter, as if it were made of dust.

I see him towering before me, and I see him from afar. Furling his wings once again, he is but a vulture clinging to the crumbling battlements that have been shielding me from the sun. He flaps his wings suddenly, taking to the crystalline morning sky. I hear them rattle. I hear them buzz. The flies are everywhere.

Jack Hillman is a journalist, novelist, playwright and a medical underwriter. His published short fiction has appeared in Sorcerous Signals, Amazon Shorts, GateWay SF Magazine, Jackhammer, Peridot Books Magazine, Aberrations, Bloodreams, Eternity Online, Gateways, Starblade, Once Upon A World, Nuketown, *the* Kings of The Night III *anthology and the* Magistria: the Realm Of The Sorcerer *anthology. His young adult novel,* There are Giants in This Valley, *was released in 2005 from Archebooks Publishing with the sequel*—Giants Want the Lost River—*due in Fall 2007.*

Planetfall
by Jack Hillman

Interlude

Deep within the maze of machinery, a sensor stimulated a reaction. Molecules long frozen into position shifted in an almost forgotten pattern. As the pulse began its way through long unused circuits, it was stopped by a broken pathway. During the millennia it had lain quietly waiting, moisture had entered through the shell in a crack made by a tiny burrowing root.

Pulses searched for an alternate path for the message to take, finding more and more circuits broken. As the pulse continued to search, the surrounding material increased in temperature until, with a tiny puff of steam, a grain of sand fused and a new pathway was formed. Circuit after circuit flashed into life as each new pulse surged forth.

Now the waiting was over.

The ship had slipped into orbit three planetary diameters out, circling opposite the planet's rotation. An unmanned probe had noted two large satellites or moons (specifics yet to be determined) and swarms of smaller asteroids circling just outside the atmospheric fringe. The ship's computer wanted to stay well out of range until some path was plotted through the obstacles. Sensors clicked as the preliminary survey was begun. If the sensor scans did not fit the minimum parameters, the ship would have automatically aborted the survey and continued to the next target.

Within minutes, the results had been reviewed and the ship began the process of reviving the crew, simultaneously sending a message to survey headquarters that there was a possible target for colonization.

In the crew quarters, blowers had been working to dispel the chill from the compartments. The temperature was still low but rising to a comfortable range. As the temperature reached a minimum level, three pods opened in one wall.

From the center pod stepped a short, dark haired man dressed in a skin-tight stasis suit. He stepped into the room stretching and yawning.

"Turn on the coffee pot, George," said the man, talking to the air.

"Coffee is ready in the galley, Commander," replied a voice.

"Good. Is the preliminary survey complete?" the man asked.

The voice sounded hurt. "Preliminary survey must be completed prior to crew revival initiation. Secondary phase complete and standing by for report."

The man winced at the tone of voice. "Sorry, George. I'm still used to a ship that just takes you there and wakes you up. My old ship couldn't even talk! I still have to get used to you."

"And I, you, Commander," said George.

The pod to the commander's left opened further and a very large tan cat padded into the compartment. She stopped in front of the man and sat back on her haunches, her eyes almost level with his. He reached out and scratched behind her ears. The cat closed her eyes and began to purr.

"It's good to see you too, Shadow," he said as he gave the cat a last scratch and ruffled her fur. She reached out with a paw to grab his hand so he would continue, then, as the man avoided the expected gesture, she sat back and began to clean her fur.

"Fur smells of sleep," came the thought from the cat. She sneezed and continued to clean her fur. "I need food," came the next thought, with overtones of hunting and warm blood.

"Yes! Food!" came a second thought through the link, with a deeper tone than that of the cat. The third team member lumbered from the last pod, filling the opening. The bear stood almost two meters tall on all fours. Erect, he was over four meters tall, a tower of fur and muscle, the strength of the team. He waddled to the center of the compartment and dropped to the floor with an impact that shook the ship. "I'm hungry," came the thought.

"You're always hungry, Borin," said the man as he scratched the bear's neck and gave his huge sides a friendly slap. "Let's see how good a cook our new ship is before we take a look at the survey." He started out the compartment, headed for the galley. The cat was out the door before him, moving as quietly as her name. The great bear wuffed in exasperation and rolled onto his feet, following the others.

In the galley, each crew member sat and ate, preparing for the test to come. For Commander Raymond James, this was the fifteenth planetary survey he had been part of and the sixth as commander. Considering the hundreds of planets mankind had colonized in the last three hundred years, it still seemed fresh and exciting when he reached a new world. But the crew was new to him, as was the ship. He still wasn't too thrilled with these new self-aware computer ships even though they had been in use for ten years. There were enough strange events during a survey of a new planet. He didn't need to baby-sit a computer who decided it didn't like the tone of voice one of the survey crew used and went on strike. This ship had a good record but that wasn't enough for James. In addition, headquarters was trying a new type of survey team this time.

For hundreds of generations, animals had been bred for specialized tasks on Earth but in the last one hundred years there had been an unexpected increase in the intelligence in some species. This was the first time a survey crew had included these new members and the commander was still unsure. He had trained with these two for the past year whenever he was groundside and he was still learning about them. He also spent most of this last year getting used to the implanted communication units that permitted him to understand Shadow and Borin, as well as speak directly to George.

Shadow was a giant among her family of North American mountain lion. Crossbreeding with other larger cats had resulted in a larger, more intelligent species with a strange sense of humor, as James had found out during training.

Borin was strictly Kodiak bear, bred for size and strength and also for a lessening of the ferocious temper so well-known throughout history. It would be an interesting test of their various skills. James hoped they drew an easy first assignment.

"Okay, George," said the commander when the team was done eating, "let's have a rundown on this target."

"As you wish, commander," came the reply. "This sun is a class M, yellow dwarf with variations in its surface that indicate a high probability of some erratic cycle about to begin. Based on the data collected by the prior probe and observations since we arrived in orbit, changes are projected to occur in four times ten to the fifth power years, plus or minus three percent error."

"Good enough," said James. "We'll be somewhere else by then and any colonists can prepare well in advance. Log a warning to that effect and proceed."

"Affirmative. The planet below is the fourth of six planets and occupies the same general position as Mars in Earth's solar system. Two large satellites orbit in mutually perpendicular orbits over the equator and the poles."

"What!" exclaimed James as he snapped upright in his chair. Both teammates growled in response to his reaction and the tone of his voice. "Repeat that last statement."

"The data are confirmed, commander. The moons orbit perpendicular to each other. There is also a wide belt of debris orbiting at a forty-five degree angle to the moons and inside their orbit."

"What are the chances those moons are artificial?" James asked.

"Data confirms this, Commander. Mass readings indicate they are at least partially hollow and their respective surfaces are too regular to suggest natural formation. Life scans indicate no living beings of any type on or in the moons including adjustment for any possible life forms in stasis. In addition, large animal life forms on the planet surface are limited to herbivores equivalent to Terran antelope or deer."

As the bear and the cat slipped onto their special pads in front of the control board, James asked for close-ups of the planet below. The cat growled with pleasure as the sight of the deer grazing and Borin merely sighed as he watched closely. The view shifted from one part of the planet to another, showing vast areas of land apparently under cultivation but no buildings or structures of any type. There were also several other areas where deer grazed in quiet comfort, separated from the nearby fields by some type of natural boundary, in one case a river and in another a wide canyon.

"Are there any apparent structures in any of the probe series, George?" asked the commander.

"None that I can identify, Commander."

"Then where are the people?" he asked himself out loud.

"Unknown, Commander."

"That was a rhetorical question, George," said the man.

"Sorry."

"Okay. Our best bet is to find the inhabitants and try to make contact. George, I want an analysis of the probe flight records and a report on any artifact or natural feature on the surface that is out of the ordinary. If we don't find anyone on the planet, we may have just found the answer to Earth's food supply for the next century.

Interlude

Circuit by circuit, bank by bank; the great machine came alive. As each section once more began to function, more and more of the dark caverns began to glow with the light of the functioning units. Small mechanical creatures scurried from their hiding places in the walls to begin to repair the damages of untold years of inactivity. More and more often, circuits flashed hot and formed new passageways as they encountered layers of dirt and moisture. Memory cells came to life but many were incomplete. Time had destroyed the molecular structure of their cores, leaving bits and pieces of their programming in an irreparable jumble.

In the past six days, the team had scoured the planet from space, looking for some sign of intelligent life. While they had not been able to cover the entire planet centimeter by centimeter, they had made a valiant attempt and, with the help of the remote probes, they had covered every major area in great detail. They had even examined the two moons for some sign of the inhabitants. Both proved to be little more than hollow shells. The planet was nothing more than a great storehouse of food for someone. The question was, "For whom?"

The commander was pleased with the efforts of his team. The great cat was an excellent scout. Nothing passed that she did not note the change. The animals on the planet were completely unaware of her presence as long as she stayed downwind. Shadow had been the one to find the first of the corner stones, which seemed to mark each of the areas. These stones were covered on the sides by a type of writing, different on each side, as if to mark some difference from each direction. The writing had been copied and George was working on a language base. However, there was too little to go on yet.

Borin, meanwhile, was also proving his worth to the team. Surprisingly, he and George got along very well. With the computer's help, the bear had reviewed the recordings from the probes and found several likely spots for some type of control center. While nothing had come of their investigations of these places yet, the ability of the bear to work with the ship was a great asset to the team. James had decided that the scientists back on Earth were very much mistaken on the level of the bear's intelligence.

Then, on the seventh day, there was a change.

"Commander, Shadow's transponder has ceased transmitting," George stated.

Raymond James snapped around from the study table where he had been working and jumped into his seat at the command console.

"Give me a visual of her last position," he ordered.

The screen lit up with a view down one of the ravines that separated two sections of the local fields. Raymond sent a probe down the ravine, looking for any sign of Shadow. There was nothing there that was not native to the planet.

Borin stepped into the room, moving to his position and adding his efforts to the search. But nothing could be found. They searched for hours without success.

"Well, she didn't just disappear," Raymond stated the next day as he looked out of the airlock.

Somehow looking at the area with his eyes rather than with sensors seemed to help him feel he was doing something. The fact that Borin was scanning the area with electronic probes that could sense a strange bacterium at a distance of a kilometer made little difference to the man.

Then, just as suddenly, the bear was gone as well. All Borin had done was step outside the grounded shuttle to adjust a probe he was sending back to scan an area when George announced the great bear was also not responding.

For the next three days, James spent all his time and most of George's capacity trying to find his team. Repeated probe flights and many hours on the ground had finally led the commander to a stone structure built in the side of the hill. At anything other than ground level, the hill looked like just that, a hill. From the ground, however, the doorway and the walls framing it were visible if you looked closely. It was an excellent attempt to fade the structure into the background. In fact, the only way James had found it was by altering the probe's view from visible light to the far infrared end of the spectrum, one of several adjustments he had tried. The doorway showed a heat signature that James was sure was meant to be a signal for someone, especially since it had not been there the day before when this site was scanned.

The sun shone brightly on the stone structure ahead. As the man stopped at the edge of the tree line and waited for something to happen, he took a quick drink from his canteen. The sun had traveled well past zenith but it was still very hot. As he watched, the stone wall changed. In what had been a blank expanse of stone, there was now an opening twice the height of a man and wide enough to drive a ground car through. Now it was time to go. He walked across the clearing and up to the opening.

He stopped as he reached the base of the wall and planted a sensor in the ground. At least he would have a marker to use to find his exit.

"George, are you awake?" he said into a whisper mike on his collar.

"Of course, Commander" came the answer. "You know I never sleep."

"Just checking. Keep a record of everything I say and if you lose contact for more than five hours, close up shop and head for home."

"Acknowledged, Commander. Good luck and please be careful. I would hate to have to report that I lost my teammates."

"I didn't know you cared, George."

"Of course, Commander. I'm programmed for it."

"Of course," the man replied, knowing the irony would be lost on the ship. With a last look around the clearing, he entered the structure. Immediately, the walls began to glow with a pale golden light. They brightened until they were as brilliant as the sunlight outside. He walked down the stone passageway, carefully watching for signs of a door or a side passage that might hold one of the native people or, perhaps, lead to his team. But the passage continued in an unbroken pathway for at least another two hundred meters. By the time he reached the end of the passage, he was sure he was being observed, but there was no sign of either an optical pickup or a spy-hole in the walls. At the end of the passage, he stopped. He had no choice, the passage stopped as well.

The only difference in the stone at this point was a strange design imprinted in the floor. He bent down to examine it and was amazed to note it was neither painted on nor inlaid. It was as if the stone itself had changed color.

"George, can you still read me?"

No answer. The walls were obviously shielding the signal, at least from his receiver. On the chance that the ship could pick up his broadcast and enhance the signal, he made a full report of what the passageway looked like including the pattern on the floor.

With a surge that threw him from his knees, the floor began to drop. He turned to jump back into the passageway but a wall had appeared across the opening, blocking his way. He was in a stone box dropping down into the planet. He stayed on the floor as he felt the negative gravity of the descent continue and began to worry as each second passed. It would be a long climb back up.

Finally, the descent stopped. The wall behind him opened with a rush of air but no sound and he found himself facing a large chamber hewn from the solid rock. As he walked into the chamber, the wall behind him reappeared and the "elevator" was gone. He walked to the center of the room. The walls were dark, but seemed to be covered with patches of some milky substance. As he reached the center of the room, two of the patches lit up.

There, suspended in mid-motion were a huge Kodiak bear and an over-sized cougar.

Now he was inside and, hopefully, about to meet the owners of the planet. The room was dark, except for the glow from the panels holding the bear and the cat. He reached into a case strapped to his waist and drew out a set of goggles. Fastening the strap to his helmet, he flipped the lenses down in front of his eyes. To his augmented eyesight, the room was bright as day as the heat signatures could be seen. This was a control room. In this new light, the commander could make out panels set into the wall giving out readings in the same unknown language as the corner stones. There were lights indicating the action or inaction of a myriad of functions, none of which made any sense.

He kept up the running monologue to George, even less sure now that the signal was getting through. He described the panels and the signals that were flashing across their faces. He described the readouts of the various functions. He noted that they appeared to be divided into sections of seven groups of seven columns each and that each group had a code symbol above it that corresponded to one of the major lights on a panel set to one side.

The feeling of being watched grew stronger. Then, with a sudden surge of heat, a figure stood in the middle of the floor. James flipped up the goggles for a moment, but the figure vanished into a mist suspended above the floor. A projection.

The figure was about the same height as the man, erect, with a body size similar to the human. There was one head (at least it occupied the space of a head), three arms spaced evenly around a cylindrical torso and four legs. The head was a blur of features in the uncertain light from the goggles but there were no recognizable eyes or ears. There was, however, a mouth on each of three sides, triangular and rigid. The arms were extremely flexible and ended in a cluster of cable-like fingers. The legs were more rigid than the arms and seemed to have three joints each. They ended in a round pad that looked like a cross between a suction cup and a bifurcated hoof.

The figure began to move its arms, and James was sure it was trying to speak to him.

"Sorry, you're not getting through," he said to the projection.

A hum began to fill the chamber. As the man listened, the hum developed into a pattern of varying pitches and tones.

"You're on the right track," he said. "Keep trying."

Suddenly the chamber was filled with a loud whine, reverberating from the rock and pressing on him like a physical barrier.

"Too loud," he cried, trying to make himself heard above the whine. "Turn it down." He fell to his knees as the whine went up in pitch, becoming a needle piercing his eardrums and forcing itself into his brain. Just as suddenly, the sound quit. He somehow forced himself to his feet. The next try in communication was almost as much a shock, if not as painful.

"Too loud. Turn it down." The words seemed to come from the figure in middle of the room.

"Good," said James. "Now you've got it."

"Now you've got it," came the reply.

"The quick brown fox jumped over the lazy dog," James said, giving the speaker more words to use. This time there was a perceptible pause. Then came the reply.

"Fox? Dog?"

"These are animals from my home," James said, surprised at the question.

"Home?"

"I come from another planet. My ship landed here to survey the planet for my people. If you can reach the surface you can contact my ship by speaking as I do."

Again came a pause. Then the room seemed to glow with the same golden light as the passageway above. The figure was now visible when the man flipped up the goggles.

"George is very intelligent for his age, wouldn't you say?" said the figure.

"Yes, I agree," replied James. "I assume you had a nice conversation."

"Not really," replied the figure. "I just reached past the personality interface directly to the data storage banks. The life support data indicated this lighting would be more to your liking. Am I correct?"

"Yes, thank you. We were not aware this was an inhabited planet. We have no wish to disturb you and will be happy to leave, as soon as you release my teammates."

"Oh my, no, Commander!" exclaimed the figure. "We've only just met and I have so much to learn from you. You and your team must stay. By the way, you may call me Arthur. From what I found in George's data banks, this is a name of great significance to your people. You would not be able to pronounce my name in my own tongue."

The commander felt a touch of ice down his spine. "We can stay for a short time but our friends are waiting for us at home. After all, there are many others on my planet that can teach you more than I. We would be happy to tell them about you and bring them back to talk with you."

"That's not necessary, Commander James. I am quite capable of learning all I need from you and your friends. It has been such a long time since I have spoken to anyone. It will be nice to carry on an intelligent conversation again instead of just watching those feeble-minded deer graze in the grass all day long. Do you know, I have been trying to breed some of them up to a reasonable intelligence level for the past three thousand years? But they just don't seem to have the potential." The figure walked around the room with a strange shifting gait that took it in whatever direction it chose without turning its body. The legs merely articulated in a different direction. "And your friends are such a different breed than yourself. Am I correct that they are basically predators?"

"Well, yes, they are. But they have been bred for their intelligence as well as for other characteristics for years. They are equal members of my team and have their own innate backgrounds to draw from so that we help each other in unusual situations. Who can tell which of us will have the idea that will permit us to understand some alien artifact or creature? Why don't you let them out and talk to them as well?"

The creature appeared to consider the idea. "I believe you are correct, Commander. I will let them out." The lights seemed to dim for a second. "Oh my, I must do something about that faulty circuitry."

As the commander watched, the panels in front of the bear and the cat rose up toward the ceiling. With a wash of cold air the two lost members of the team moved toward the man, looking closely at their surroundings. As the bear passed close to the hologram, he blinked and sniffed carefully. Then he looked at James.

"There, but not there?" The great bear looked around the room in his nearsighted manner. "Where is here?"

From the cat came a steady undercurrent of anger and barely controlled destruction. "Who put I here? Who put in cage?"

James tried to broadcast a message of control and caution to the animals. He would need their help to get out of here but if they lost their tempers, the three of them would be trapped for sure.

"Are you communicating with your friends in some fashion, Commander. I can hear nothing but there are reactions from the three of you that would indicate a passing of information." The figure moved to the center of the room and both the cat and the bear moved away as if they were pushed by a wall. "We don't want any secrets, now. Do we?"

"We all have a bi-metal organic transceiver embedded in our skulls. It lets us talk to one another since my friends each have a different vocal apparatus."

There was a pause from the figure in the center of the room, as if the capacity to motivate the figure and consider the problem was more than it could handle at once. Then, on the same frequency as the transceivers, came the next reply. "This is ever so much simpler than the cumbersome speech you employ, Commander. Why don't you communicate in this fashion all the time?"

"Habit I guess. Humans are creatures of habit."

"This is creature that put I in cage," said the cat, moving toward the figure in the center of the room. "Must punish."

"Don't bother, Shadow. He's not really there. That is a copy of one of his masters. If you want to punish him you'll have to tear down the walls."

"Very good, Commander. You are indeed a higher life form. I am pleased you figured that out so quickly."

"No big deal. We've been using computer generated holograms for generations. You're just a bigger computer."

"Food," came the thought from Borin. "Hungry."

"Oh, where are my manners. I am such a poor host. I will arrange for food immediately." The figure went still for a moment as the instructions were transmitted.

"Tell me, Arthur," said James. "Exactly which data banks did you access?"

"Life support, as I mentioned previously. And a series of sequential instruction files. I must admit the clothing worn by the instructors was considerably different than your own but I assumed you were wearing some sort of different uniform. By the way, is Shadow related to Sher-Kahn or Numa?"

James had the beginnings of an idea. "She is to both to a degree. About the same way you are related to a pocket calculator."

"The food is on the way." Again there was a perceptible pause. "What is a pocket calculator?"

"A primitive tool for calculating mathematical functions. They had limited capacity and almost no memory."

"I see. I believe I understand the comparison. So, what you are saying is that they are more intelligent than the files indicate."

James hid a smile. "I see your problem, Arthur. You thought those recordings were made by my people. Actually, they were made by Borin's people. Shadow's family members are much too busy to bother with such trivial matters. This is a training mission for these two members of the ruling class. I'm just along to handle the chores they don't have either the time or the inclination to bother with. Why don't you talk to them? I'm sure they would be glad to explain it to you since you are about to become a member of their empire."

"You mean they are more intelligent than you?"

"Not even in the same class. Borin," said the man, interrupting the bear with his nose in a dish of ground meat. "Tell our host the story of your battle with the alien fleet off Alpha Centauri." The bear looked at the man for a moment, then replaced his nose in the dish and resumed eating. Over the link came the only comment. "Stupid."

James tried to look ashamed. He walked over to the bear and put his hand on the furry shoulder. "I am sorry, Lord. But our host was so interested, I was sure you would be willing to tell him of your greatest victory. I forgot how modest you are." The bear grunted in reply.

Shadow had been watching the interplay between the man and the alien computer. As usual, James was unable to judge just how much the cat understood and how she would react. Before he could say anything, Shadow rose to her feet and walked majestically over to the figure in the center of the room. She sank to her haunches, eyes even with the head of the projected creature, and began to speak.

"Man servant of I. Use clumsy speech to speak to him. Too stupid to learn good form speech. You too stupid, too. But will try to tell as to cub." Shadow looked at the man and then turned back to the projection. With a rush, the cat began to transmit images of Earth, the grassy plains, prides of her kind scattered across the kilometers of open space. She blended in scenes of cities crawling with people and seemed to give the impression that these were the workers who supported the casual lifestyle of the cats.

As the story continued, James slipped down the corridor that had appeared when the food was delivered. Shadow would keep the computer occupied while he tried to pull the plug. Borin followed behind. Apparently he also knew what was going on with the cat. They quickly reached a central shaft that seemed to drop down to the center of the planet and extend back to the surface. As they reached the edge of the shaft, James heard a response from the transceiver.

"Commander, are you all right?" said George. "I have been unable to reach you since you descended. Your transmissions prior to that time were weak and they cut off as you dropped away. Have you returned to the surface?"

"Not yet, George. I'm still underground but there is a shaft leading up to the surface from my position. Can you locate me yet?"

"Already done, Commander. I am in route. May I be of other assistance?"

"Yes," the man answered. "We are being held by a computer that seems to run the whole planet. There seems to be some weakness in its capacity but other than that, it has us stopped cold. Were you aware you were scanned a while ago?"

"Of course, Commander. I merely shunted the probes into the entertainment section of my files after permitting it to read the physiology references. I assume you can still breathe and see? "

"So far at least," Raymond answered. "Now if we can just find the plug and pull it . . . "

Borin had moved up and down the corridor as Raymond spoke to the ship. He turned to Raymond, his paw on one of the closed doors.

"Here. Here but not here. Smells of heat. Circuits gone bad." The bear pushed against the door, but it did not open.

"I believe I can help commander," George stated. "Use infrared lenses and look for a triangle on the wall and press it."

Raymond flipped down his goggles and found the sigil. He pressed the mark. As the man and bear watched, the passage opened in the wall next to them.

"Please enter, Commander. I believe we have located the heart of the problem," George suggested. "This is the main control center. Look for a mark on the wall that looks like three triangles with their short sides touching. It will not be visible in standard light, but you should be able to see it in IR."

James flipped the lenses back over his eyes and scanned the walls. To his left, he found the mark delineated in heated sequence. He used his belt knife to trace the triangles and flipped up the lenses.

"Please press the center of the triangles, Commander."

As the man pressed against the wall, there was a groan from the stone and a section as high as his head began to shift downward. After moving only an centimeter or two, it stopped.

"Help me, Borin," he said.

The great bear padded up to the wall and stood. Carefully, he placed his claws at the edge of the stone section and began to pull outward. Almost immediately, the section fell away, revealing a maze of circuitry built from crystal rods and planes of light.

"It's not nice to wander about your host's home without permission, Commander," said a voice behind the two explorers.

Both man and bear turned. Standing in the room behind them was Arthur. As they watched, Shadow came running down the passageway, following their trail. She stopped in the doorway.

"Sorry. Good story. Stopped listening." The cat seemed embarrassed.

"Don't blame your associate, Commander," said the creature.

"She had me quite convinced she was the ruling monarch of your planet. You tripped an alarm when you opened the panel. I'm afraid you will have to be placed in confinement for your own protection."

As the creature said this, Borin roared and rose to his feet again. James ducked under the sweep of the huge paws and turned back to the open panel, throwing something from his belt into the open circuits. There was a crash of sound and a cloud of smoke from the panel. The creature disappeared from the center of the room and the lights went out.

James flipped the goggles back over his eyes but the only heat signatures showing were the bear and the cat. "Are you two all right?" he asked.

"Hungry," came the reply from Borin.

"Too much like cage," said Shadow. "Time to go back to sun."

"George, can you read me?" James asked.

"Yes, Commander. The interference has lifted. I can lead you back to the surface at your convenience."

"Now is a good time, George. Bring us home"

"Certainly, Commander. Turn left as you leave the chamber." The three walked out and started up. "By the way, Commander. What was it that you threw into the panel?"

"Just doing what men do best, George," he replied with a smile. "I just threw a wrench into the works."

Trent Walters, as an infant while zipping through a bumpy wormhole, fell out of the star-buggy and was rescued and raised by friendly aliens. His work has appeared in 3am Magazine, Pindledyboz, *the* Golden Age SF *anthology,* Electric Velocipede, Lady Churchill's Rosebud Wristlet, *and BSFA's* Vector. *Forthcoming from Morpo Press is a poetry chapbook called* Learning the Ropes. *He reviews for SF Site and edits poetry for* Abyss & Apex.

Inheritance
by Trent Walters

The electromagnetic broadcasts from the *Preciv* had slowed. By the light of the glow-orb, we piloted the Archeosurveyor toward the small planet, dimming the viewscreen against the harsh glare of its sun. Upon plunging through the atmosphere, our ships streamlined, folding away their hard edges. We divided the lands—including the recently deluged—into equal square quadrants ("Divide and conquer," as our Way-Pavers had said) in order to unveil the Veiled.

Luckily, our search patterns were limited by two-thirds of the surface being covered in water. "The molecular contents," noted one of us, "of this planet's inhabitants are approximately in the proportion of water to land." Coincidence? Possibly, but perhaps less so depending on the size of picture one is capable of conceptualizing.

Nonetheless, our task was involved. We sonared the coastal waters and thumped the terrains to get a complete three-dimensional picture of the planets entrails. We only knew that we'd know what we were looking for when we found it.

Plains unrolled under the ship so calmly as if to suggest their changes would go unnoticed by the many free-roaming gazelles, antelopes, horses, and giraffes—all beautiful to behold. They stretched their limbs in flight racing for the trees when we passed—as if we, who had never known them, were their enemy.

The bipedals were far more amusing than beautiful to watch as they pursued similar ends. We're sorry to report that we sometimes took pleasure in provoking such beasts. It was only a snap in cosmological time that we too were cowering in fear, but our patience won out, and we inherited eternity.

One such beast—knee-deep in swamp waters, hideously masked both naturally and unnaturally—did not flee though its smaller companions did. It was not just this that piqued our interest, but that it had rendered the waters into equal squares with wires and stakes. We thought that our search might have been considerably shortened if we could communicate our aim to it.

Mulford Esau snapped the elastic suspender strap of his waders up on his shoulder. He tried to wipe the sweat from his brow and managed mostly to smudge the oily water around. A t-shirt to mop his face would have been nice right about now. He wished he hadn't followed the example of his hired help. The two bare-chested boys were sloshing around in the shallow water, trying to catch fish and frogs. What could an archeologist expect if he paid in fizzy sugar water—even if it were a rarity? Considering their genealogy, the boys probably weren't genetically equipped to pursue archeology, anyway.

Mulford hadn't been as interested in ancient civilizations as his father and grandfather, who had passed archeological curiosity down the family line. No, Mulford wanted to learn how his immediate ancestors had lived, which was why he'd squared off his great-grandparents' backyard, digging up layers of sand with plastic shovels (*NOTE: check encyclopedia for what grew in sand gardens—intriguing biotechnology?*), rodent and canine skeletons (*buried in boxes so probably not consumed*), four-wheeled vehicles (*hand-powered or else the engines had been misplaced—presumably replicas upon which adolescents learned vehicle maintenance*).

Rapid splashing made Mulford lift his head from his notepad. His helpers had absconded into the trees shrieking in that delight that always sounded like terror to Mulford. He was annoyed until he realized they would not have left without collecting their fee.

A cool, dark cloud brought relief from the sun. Mulford looked up.

We transposed the beast into our ship. It seemed completely unaware how hideously masked it was although it seemed to shrink from our presence, perhaps in fear of our transparent preeminence. To calm it—for we had studied many broadcasts—we raised the universal sign for greeting: two fingers spread wide, palm in. However, the universal sign seemed to have lost meaning in the decline of its species, so we attempted various tonguings until we found one that cleared the presumably anguished expression.

"Welcome to our friend ship, friend scientist. We, like you, are friend scientist. Friend exchange science, knowing, no?" We impressed ourselves with our eloquence.

It took the beast some time to absorb our honest beauty.

One minute, Mulford stood knee-deep in swamp water, about to gaze up into the clouds that had just stopped the sun from frying his skin like a pan sizzling bacon. The next, he stared at the low ceiling of a dim room. When he lowered his head and his eyes adjusted to the light, two vaguely humanoid figures—smallish and faintly glowing—stood before him. A globe—set within a transparent panel of unmarked keys—back-lit their transparent bodies, illuminating organs which appeared to be in the process of pumping blood, digesting food, and compacting waste.

The aliens spoke gibberish until they spoke English—sort of. More of a pidgin. Mulford wasn't sure how to answer without knowing what the question was exactly. The aliens asked if Anglish was his tonguing. He half-nodded, so they repeated themselves more loudly, as if it were a problem of hearing.

Finally, one folded its hands and made motions of screwing it on its head. It pointed at Mulford, smiled and nodded enthusiastically, giving him the thumbs-up.

"Do I have a choice?" Mulford asked. Just as the alien shook its head, a metal skullcap clasped his head. Mulford tried to undo the clasp, but it injected a painfully large-bore needle into his skull. It twisted as if burrowing between the skull sutures. The pressure in Mulford's head expanded, giving him a raging migraine. The needle retracted, the cap unclasped and disappeared into the darkness of the ceiling.

Mulford slumped to the floor, weak with pain. The headache subsided, little by little. Mulford could hear, could feel the aliens probe his mind. Memories he thought he'd forgotten: his mother's prize-winning lemon meringue and the carny's chili dogs and flavored ice at the state fair, his first boyscout medal, the long procession to the grave at his grandfather's funeral during a bitterly cold morning on New Year's. The aliens seemed to have found something they liked as the memories became less random and more focused: Mulford's informal training in anthropology, the dusty textbooks that cracked at the spine when he opened them, the tramping through ruins and sifting through trash— "Trash can tell as much about a people as what they keep," his grandfather had said, flattening out a McDonald's wrapper on his knee.

The aliens chattered using strange sounds that Mulford was surprised he mostly understood:

"He knows nothing. Let's dump the swamp mizzle back into its waste habitat."

"A thorough thought reprocess takes multiple planet rotations."

"He's not so observant a scientist."

"No one ever is. Science requires teamwork."

"We'd be more productive if we followed the rules."

"We may learn more than usual through a Precivvy. He just needs time. We can guide him."

Mulford stood, a little woozy. "You two talk as if I had no say in the matter."

We stared at the beast for its remarkable delusion of destiny-control until we recalled he was but a beast. We watched each other's honest organs burble with mirth. Our water-extrusion organs were productively amused. The beast was so fascinating a specimen, we recorded the memories in its mind preceding our arrival up to the present and sent them to other Archeosurveyors that they might burble as well. We decided to retain the beast, if only for our pleasure.

We asked it, "Is your curiosity organ not aroused?" We could not see for ourselves, of course, or the question would have been redundant.

"Well, yes." It rubbed its temple, temporarily disoriented from our memory retrieval.

"Then accompany us around the planet as we seek the Veiled ones."

"Veiled ones? Veiled. You're on the wrong side of the planet."

They must have taken the destination from his mind, for the ship immediately accelerated. Mulford stood on his tiptoes to keep from toppling. In front of them, a faintly illumined viewscreen displayed fields rolling beneath, swamped cities, and then the regular chop of blue waves. "How does your ship accelerate?"

"Nulling errant gravity vectors."

"Huh?"

The blue waves darkened until only the moon lit them.

"Think of gravity as a wave. If we set up its exact opposite, we can null the effect of acceleration in undesirable directions. For any direction want to head in, assuming we are dead-center in the universe, we have half of the universe's acceleration at our command. Of course, it helps if you have a nearby object, to get started. Once you reach a certain velocity, you can maintain it using the planet's own gravity—in effect, a low orbit."

"Typical," said the other alien. Although the sounds of the word were unfamiliar, Mulford understood. Mulford didn't understand, however, why the alien covered its belly in a strange manner

"What's typical?" the beast inquired in its typically brash and raspy voice.

We looked at each other's organs with alarm until we remembered the brain plate we'd injected into the beast. "I meant only that the first men, such as yourself, tend to make grand intuitive leaps," said one of us.

"And forget the smaller, more obvious steps between," finished the other.

"Humans have done quite well for ourselves," said the beast.

"Really?" we burbled pleasantly as drowned architectures loomed up on the other side of the ocean, marking boundaries of a different age of regents. We pressed a button to null all acceleration to maintain our present course with minor velocity attrition. We could have manipulated the controls telepathically, but physical preoccupation was intended to delude the beast that our mental facilities were similarly preoccupied.

Our pretense shielded our notice of the beast's dashing to the viewscreen and tapping the pyramidal structure there, changing our null vectors, changing our course. We were surprised not only that the brain plate had improved his eyesight but that he seemed capable forcing his will on the ship. We decided not to mention this lest he get any beastly ideas. The trip was not going according to plan.

"The pyramids! I've never seen them before."

We let the opposing vectors slowly drag the ship to a halt above the dusty brown structures. "Then let us investigate. Perhaps the veiled ones have left a clue."

"What do you mean a clue?" Mulford pulled his gaze away from the pyramids to watch these aliens who seemed less and less alien. Already, they felt like the small town oddballs whom the villagers liked well enough, but enjoyed gossiping about more.

"Living organisms leave traces of their history and their world. The tree says how long it lived and how much it rained in the summers. A series of animals embedded in rock describe the circumstances of lineage. The greater the confluence of evidence that living organisms leave behind, the more the planet unveils its movements. Living organisms tell the story of the world."

"That's why I love anthropology: discovering the story of humans. A couple of holes in the skull of our ancestors, Australopithicus, can tell us that they had predators like leopards."

Once again, an alien covered its belly in that peculiar manner. It seemed to try to draw Mulford's attention away by the flutter of its other arm as if it swept up the whole planet in its broad gestures. "Sometimes evidence is veiled and misleading."

"You mean someone tried to fool the anthropologist millennia into the future?"

"No, no. You might be surprised who the predator was. On our world, some weaker creatures play dead to divert the attention of the predator."

The other alien must have noted Mulford's stare at the place covered by the alien, which had been speaking. "Please." It waved at the viewscreen. "Allow us to demonstrate an unveiling of the veiled."

It tapped a button and the ship began thumping the land and the pyramid itself. In the center of the room, a down-sized replica of the pyramid gleamed. Bit by bit, the insides of the pyramid began to shape in three-dimensions. Phosphorescent tombs and slanting corridors flowed. Next to the pyramid, an underground structure lit up.

"Wouldn't it be easier," asked Mulford, "to simply walk outside and look."

The alien wagged its arm (a gesture which Mulford instinctively recognized as disagreement). "To view the big picture, the viewer must stand outside the frame."

Mulford stepped away from the display to stand nearer the real thing. Lit by moonlight, the crumbling monument appeared as it may have when first birthed. As the ship circled, he reflected on what sort of humans would have labored for large and improbable a shape—something for future generations to marvel at.

"Absurd monstrosity, no?" An alien had moved to his side.

We said, "It's an egotistically large lump of rock—a testament to carnivorous behavior."

The beast turned away from the alien and leaned against the counter as if to get nearer. "I think it's beautiful—as beautiful in decay as the day it was born, as majestic as mountains."

"We've seen these structures before. Lives were sacrificed to fulfill some rich ruler's vanity."

"That's despicable, true. But it also stands for all of our striving for something more than just eating, sleeping, reproducing, and croaking."

"But it's empty. There's nothing inside."

"Maybe so. But the striving's, the reaching's the thing. Without it, we are empty. Maybe some day we'll find something real to fill—" The beast stopped.

The alien's insides were talking to Mulford, its circulating fluids chuckling its disagreement with exasperation and despair. And a hint of fear. Why should something more powerful than Mulford fear him?

Abruptly, the alien turned to the replica. "We'd like you to notice something."

The other alien stood at a shimmering panel in the wall that Mulford hadn't seen earlier. It rippled like pond water wherever it was touched. "Ha! The veiled ones are here. Releasing probes."

The first alien paid the other no mind. Its hand slipped through the replica but gripped a corridor is if it were solid. It angled the corridor so that it was parallel to the ground. The alien tapped the corridor, and it fell to the floor while enlarging to life-size—sort of life-size. "Walk through this corridor without touching the sides."

Mulford tried. He slouched, ducking his head, through the greenish-white corridor walls like cold flames. The top of his hair stood on end. When his shoulder brushed the edge of one wall, it shocked as if someone had scuffed the carpet in his stocking feet and shocked Mulford. He jerked away from that wall to be shocked on the other side. Shocked a third time, Mulford ran out to the other side—unhurt but annoyed.

The aliens didn't smile but he read their amused organs. "Now you know what it feels like."

"What what feels like?" the beast asked.

"To be trapped—"

"Every thinking creature knows that feeling."

"To be trapped on a planet ruled by those stronger and crueler than you. You could do nothing to those walls, but it could inflict pain on you." We walked through the corridor without slouching, ducking, or touching the walls. "But that's a secondary point. Why build walls they couldn't fit through?"

"To keep robbers out."

"Did it work?"

Mulford shook his head as the other alien motioned for them to view his rippling panel. "It is as we suspected. The tombs were storehouses of organic nutrition."

"Food, you mean."

"Yes, we circumlocute. It is bred in us—a habit our ancestors instilled. Does your people have a phrase like 'The weak shall inherit the universe?'"

"Sort of. A religion does, but by 'veiled' I thought—"

The ripples on the panel stilled and the full-length image of another alien appeared, saying it had found the Veiled ones in the territory labeled Afghanistan.

Hardly had they received computers when Mulford had to lean forward again on his tiptoes. "So are these veiled of the Christian or Muslim faith?"

We probed the beast's mind for the meaning of these terms. "Neither." We strolled to the viewscreen and tapped at the phosphorescent streams rolling forth from the mouths of the mountains. Archeosurveyors extended their bellies to scoop in the stream.

The beast squinted as if that might help him see. "What the—"

"The Veiled. The ones you didn't see. The ones who hid in caves from your violence. The ones who had to adapt, to spur the violent on to their own destruction. You have many missing links, lost races, no? Your scientists ask where they went to.

"Every family has a runt that's ignored and pushed away from the teats. It ends the same on every planet. The violent bear it away. The veiled wait. The veiled bear children who—if deformed with opaque skin—silently infiltrate the violent, push the violent past the tipping point. Yes. Their brain plates tell the story of their ascension to us."

Mulford could hear. They said they'd provoked humans to larger and larger wars, prodded toward weapons that would eliminate most life on the planet for centuries. They had waited so long already, they would wait out a few millennia more. But they found a less destructive method: melting polar caps.

A tumultuous joy flooded across Mulford's mind that he could barely tread above them. The aliens transmitted starship plans, maps to homeworlds and possible habitable planets, economical energies, and brain-plate technologies—technologies that spanned galaxies in an instant.

"You are no longer the weak." Mulford thought of the injustice justice of it all: That the mighty fall to be replaced by a kinder, gentler—

"You *are* the strong. You destroyed worlds to take over."

The aliens took a moment to process. "We suppose that is true, but we only pushed you in the direction you were headed anyway."

Mulford nodded. He walked to the command console. He pressed a button that transposed the aliens out of their own ship—though possibly it wasn't theirs to begin with. He would fly around the world and distribute these technologies to the meek. Then he would seek out the planets the strong had abandoned.

Camille Alexa tends to write about things that didn't happen, can't happen, probably won't happen, or haven't happened yet. Her fiction and poetry appear in various print and e-publications, and her short stories are scheduled to appear in several anthologies, including Black Box, Machine of Death, Magic & Mechanica, *and* Sporty Spec: Games of the Fantastic. *She is a full member of Broad Universe and writes for* The Green Man Review.

Inclusions
by Camille Alexa

"Where you going?"

"'Sploring."

"Not supposed to."

"Don't care."

She watched him take one last drag, then flick his single stolen cigarette into the damp clumpy dirt and shove his fists deep into tight coverall pockets. His surly shoulder blades stuck out like the stubby wings of a cubist angel, all rounded angles and foreshortened planes.

He kicked a stone, and they both watched it roll some distance before it bumped up against the base of a fruitloaf tree and stopped. Without looking at her, Danton turned and stumped off down the overgrown path.

Marta glanced back toward the dig site and the crew camp. From here, her mother looked like a tiny beetle, her slick black rain'brella mounted to her back, bobbing with the motions of her shoulders as she combed through damp, loamy soil for planet-native artifacts. The 'brella shifted, caught the feeble off-hue light and reflected the iridescent colors of the mineral rain, keeping the drops off Mom with its shiny carapace.

Mom didn't need her; wouldn't even know she was gone. Turning her head, Marta could barely see Danton's back, all ochre canvas and too-long hair, disappearing around a bend through the trees.

She wiped the damp from her eyes and ran to catch up.

When she reached him, he slowed a bit and she was pleased. Maybe he didn't think she was as useless a bit of cargo as he'd pretended on the voyage out. Blasted stars, but there was eff-all to do on an interplanet archeology ship. Coming with Mom always sucked, no matter how good the onboard vid'brary was, and having a fellow arkie-kid on the trip should have been a relief, should have been fun, could even have led to . . . well, more of the stuff she'd gotten a sample of with Mike last year, back Earthside. Her own archeological dig . . . or would that be more like biology? No; zoology, definitely: Mike turned out to be a total animal in the end. Wild and beautiful and willing to experiment with just about anything.

And here she was, stuck with surlyboots engineer's boy: not really an arkie-kid at all, and obviously less than interested in her.

He glanced at her sideways and shook his head to dispel rain. Fat, slick raindrops wended their way along the ridges of his curls and dripped from their ends, and when he'd shaken his head the droplets had pelted her like tiny, soft, glistening stones.

They trudged for awhile, silent.

Marta began to hum in her head, an accompaniment to the *squelsh squelsh squelsh* of her boots in the crumble-mud. Danton said nothing. And nothing and nothing and nothing until finally Marta broke. "So what are you exploring? Not enough at the actual dig to interest you? Have to break rules, have to sneak into off-limits jungle? They haven't even surveyed the whole planet yet, you know. They think it's empty like the rest, but you never know."

He glanced at her again; that sidelong look of oblique impoliteness, with its air of sensibilities offended and personal boundaries encroached-upon. "They're all empty, excepting Earth. Ruins, bits of bone, random tools . . . never anything not dead less than ten thousand years. Anyway, you don't have to come," he said, indicating the way behind them with a jut of his chin. "Path leads straight back to safety-ville."

Eff you, thought Marta. She almost said it aloud. But what was the point? Was she going to go back, sit like a good, bored little girl in the landed arkie ship, watch the same vids for the umpteenth thousandth time? No thanks.

But it was safe there. This particular oily-rained, red-sunned, over-vegetated rock—Planetary Mass Number 327—wasn't cleared for civilian exploration past scientific campsite boundaries. Camp and ship might be boring as eff, but out here beyond the pink-plasticked stakes driven to mark the edges of the safety-zone, the dank, mineral-smelly jungle felt less harmless. Not menacing, exactly, in the broad, salmon-colored, muted light of day, but unwelcoming. It was like the whole planet felt toward her the same way Danton seemed to. *Go away,* rustled the almost-feeling in the back folds of her brain. *Leave me alone.*

The path narrowed until finally there was no path at all and the uneven, slick yet crunchy ground beneath threatened to trip and harm.

Danton didn't slow, didn't pull his hands from his pockets. Marta could see the hard, irregular spheres of his bunched fists under the yellowish canvas of his coveralls, the fabric stretched tightly enough so that she could make out the knob of each individual knuckle where it strained against the cloth.

Squelsh squelsh squelsh.

He had to pull his hands from his pockets now, to push aside rough tubes of heavily sagging vine and sharp, tiny leaves of spiky undergrowth trees. Her mother—the enthusiastic scientist mother who never thought how tedious life in her wake must be for her teenaged daughter—her mother had told Marta about the vegetation here; how it wasn't composed of the same organic compounds as the stuff on Earth. Mineral-based, she'd said. It made the jungle sharp, the bark of the trees abrasive, silicate. It sliced the fingers and rubbed raw the palms, if you weren't careful. Marta could see rough abraded sections on the delicate webbing between Danton's finger and thumb as he lifted a low branch. It snapped off with a mild protest of a *crack!,* and he threw it aside.

She tugged the sleeve of her under-tunic down to cover her fingers and used the back of her hand to hold back branches and thick, arterial-looking vines that looped down across her way. Danton certainly wasn't looking back to make sure she was all right, and he didn't seem to be going to any particular effort to ease her route through the tough undergrowth. She found herself pressing closer up against his back than she would have, using the shield of his body to protect her from the slapping and whipping and slicing of leaf and stem as they crunched and squelched along. Danton wasn't wide: his scrawny, gangly frame was narrower than her own. But he was tall, and he didn't seem to care if she sheltered in his wake. Didn't seem to care that she was there at all.

They came into the clearing with such suddenness, Marta bumped into Danton's back before she realized they'd stopped.

"We're here," he said, not turning around.

Behind her, the slick-dark crystalline vegetation rose, a chaotic but well-fortified wall. Not invincible, though. She could see the way she and Danton had come; the growth behind them bore the scar of their passing. The silicate-based plantlife was less resilient than the softer organics of Earth. It took its injuries more permanently; the slices in Marta's hand from the tall slender stalks behind her would heal before the leaves regrew, no stronger than chlorophyll-colored icicles. It was as if they only played at being plants, but when injured, remembered they were bits of stiff, breakable stuff. Ephemera, masquerading as solidity.

Danton walked to the center of the clearing and began to kick away branches and piles of stalk from a rounded bit of ground.

"You've been here before," said Marta.

He did look at her now. He'd shoved his fists back into his pockets, and she could see a small flower of blood blossoming through the canvas.

"Your hand—" she pointed to the red.

He shrugged, looked away, didn't pull out his hands, didn't stop pushing aside broken leaves from the edge of the mound with his boot. "It'll be all right in a minute," he said.

Marta didn't feel like giving him the satisfaction of asking him what he meant. She walked over, squatted down beside the space Danton had cleared along one side of the mound. "Holy eff, that's a . . . ."

She looked up at him and he nodded. Rain showered down on her from his hair, from his eyelashes. "A door," he said.

He squatted beside her and took his fists from his pockets. She watched as he traced the outline of the opening in the air above its edges, his knobby, big-boned hands invisibly sketching the parameters.

"Here," he said, pointing, "the top edge, the sides . . . and here, the handle. I think."

"It's so small," she said. "Too small to be a door, really." She thought about the dig back near the ship, of the rough, uneven angles of low, cut-stone walls. She pictured the lumpy carvings of plants and small, ovoid bodies with too many limbs all the arkies said were renderings of the long-gone inhabitants. "My mother says the people who lived here never had advanced buildings, certainly never forged metal like this."

Danton shook his head. "Not metal," he said. "Look closer."

He leaned forward and began to brush crumbled, tumbled bits of pointy leaf and twig way and Marta reached out with the end of her under-tunic sleeve to help wipe off stray clumps of dirt. He was right. The door, though perfectly square and regular in a way she associated with the advanced technologies of Earthside manufacturing, was not metal. Maybe not even manufactured. "Grown?" she asked, looking into Danton's face. "This is vegetation, isn't it? Well, plant, or whatever plant *is* on this rock."

They had completely cleared the outer edges of the doorway, barely a meter across and a meter high and absolutely, perfectly, rigidly square. He ran a finger along the small u-shaped tube of a handle in the center of the door. "Cool thing is, I thought I knew what square was, until I saw this. No human-made, machine-made thing was ever so . . . perfect, you know?"

It was, too. Perfect.

Marta was aware they were almost touching, she and this awkward, unmannerly boy, along thigh and edge of shoulder. The parts of her closest to him felt warm, muddled. "How does it open?"

"Don't know. I've been back here three times, tried plenty of different stuff, but can't figure it out. But watch." He stretched his hand out and placed it flat against the door. Marta heard him suck his breath in sharply, heard the air of him whistle past his teeth, but then his grimace relaxed and he held his hand out in front of her, palm up. It was pink and fresh and smooth.

"The cuts, the blood?" she asked.

For the first time Marta could remember since meeting him at the Lunaside away-dock five months ago, he smiled. "Gone," he said, looking at his hand.

She took it in her own, turned it. The back: still lacerated, grass and leaf-whipped skin cross-hatched with tiny slices. The palm . . . She ran a finger over his palm, and just as she was thinking how warm and heavy and smooth it was, he pulled it back. His smile disappeared, and the habitual frown replaced whatever expression she had thought she'd seen there for a moment. She remembered it as pleasure.

"What did it feel like?" she asked.

He shrugged, looked away; his usual. "Try it yourself."

Marta poked her hand up out of her sleeve, a fleshy turtle emerging from its fabric shell, and gingerly reached out a single finger. She pressed the tip to the door, just to the left of the tubular handle. Frowning, she looked at Danton. "Nothing," she said.

He reached out as though to take her hand but stopped. Instead, he said, "Is there a cut there? An injury? I think it needs blood to work."

"What, some kind of vampire door?" She laughed. He didn't.

She inspected her hand, but it wasn't nearly as bad as his had been. She flipped it over and pressed her sliced-across knuckles to the door and gasped.

A hum sped through her body. Honeyed lightning. Her lips parted, she threw back her head and closed her eyes and by the time Danton managed to knock her away she was panting with the crazy, surprising, joyous heat of it.

Marta opened her eyes, smiling, still breathing hard. The edges and points of leaves and bits of bark were pressing into her back, but she didn't care. Danton was leaning over her, gripping her shoulders. Why hadn't she ever noticed how pretty his eyes were?

The rain had subsided from its drizzly state to its misty one. It never stopped completely on P-Mass 327, so this was as good as it got. Marta watched the peach-fizz ambient light refract through the water caught in Danton's eyelashes. Yes, she thought; his eyes were very, very pretty, and so she reached her face up and kissed him.

He didn't kiss her back, but he withdrew gently. He closed his eyes for a moment, took a deep breath, exhaled slowly through taut lips. "I thought you were getting electrocuted," he said, helping her into a sitting position.

She shook her head, smiled again. Danton lifted her hand and held it up.

"Cuts are gone," he said. "And the blood."

She leaned forward across the door and pressed her palm to the pale green surface. Pressed both palms.

Nothing, not even a tingle.

She pressed her cheek to the faintly emeraldine smoothness beside the handle. Light grit and oily-rain mist and the faint, sharp green scent of the planetside vegetation—a scent she'd come to think of as chlorophyll-salt—mingled in her brain. Just as earlier she'd felt the nudge and whisper of *go away*, now she felt the lure of *come in*.

"We have to get it open," she said.

Danton rubbed a hand over his eyes and grunted. The touch of his hand left a thin smear of blood across his brow. "Your hand," she grabbed at his arm; "this one's still bleeding. Do it, see if it opens. Do it!"

But he rocked back on his heels, stood up. "I'm done," he said. "I'm going back." He turned to leave.

"Great. I'll do it myself." Marta reached for a pile of long, slender stalks. They were so fine they looked like spun-sugar threads she'd once seen at an Earthside fair; splintery and willowy and delicious-looking, only these were pale green and the ones she'd tasted at the fair had been pink.

Marta bit her lips as the vegetation sliced into her palm, razored into her layers of skin, drew threads of crimson from beneath. From inside.

Danton reached forward and tried to pull the stuff from her grip.

They struggled, lost balance, fell as one onto the grit and oil-rain-slicked surface of the perfect square alien door, and as they both threw out palms to catch themselves and the blood from their mingled cuts kissed the door with simultaneous ungentle pressure, it opened and let them in.

Danton fell forward first, smacking his face against the edge of the square doorway with enough force to stun. Marta's fall was blocked, mostly by the back of Danton's head, and she cried out as she felt her tongue split under the sudden force of her own teeth. She sat back flat on her rear with a heavy crunch.

She spat a couple times onto the ground and watched the globs of red sit atop the clods of dirt and crunkled bits of leaf and grassy stem. She looked at the still form of the boy in front of her, stretched out long and flat and lean, his arms folded somewhere out of sight beneath his body, his longish hair obscuring his face. He lay across the threshold into an open tunnel.

She spat a couple more times into the mud, then crawled forward, squeezing through the opening to lift the unconscious Danton's face. He looked younger than she'd thought before. Seventeen, maybe? It was hard to tell. It was like looking at a different person without the resident surliness marring his features. A lumpish, eggplant-colored bruise was forming on his temple, and a sickle-shaped gash rode right through the center of it, seeping but not quite bleeding.

She said his name a couple times, pushed back the hair from his eyes and willed them to open. They did, and she helped him sit as he had helped her before, and together they examined the open door—which no longer showed any interest in their blood or anything else—and at the roughly rounded wall of the tunnel under the mound. It sloped sharply down, then gently around a bend, away from the coral light of red-tinted day. A golden glow reached up to them from below, around the curving wall.

There was no question of turning back. The sting in Marta's tongue and the swelling of her mouth were nothing to the afterglow of the feeling which had coursed the rivers of her veins when the door had taken the blood and wounds from her hands. It was all she could do not to stretch out and purr. This was better than anything she'd felt last summer with Mike, and the idea that there might be more just down the corridor, just out of sight . . . .

She'd almost forgotten Danton and when he groaned, she had to force her eyes to focus on his face. Though the door was small and square, the tunnel was oval, and tall enough for them to stand. She helped him to his feet.

"Are you hurt badly?" she asked. "You sounded like you were in pain."

He smiled, in an embarrassed way but not surly at all. "It wasn't pain," he said, and shoved his fists into his pockets again. "It was good before, but not like that. Not even close."

"The door?"

He nodded, and smiled again. She decided she liked it very much when he smiled. "Come on, then," she said, and on impulse, held out her hand.

They made their way along the dim passage, holding hands on one side and each trailing their fingers along the wall with the other. The walls were like sandstone; the same adobe-ish color and crude-smooth surface of the squatty remnants of wall and pit and floor her mother sifted through every day. Shaped by hands less agile, perhaps, than human ones, but not less purposeful.

Marta felt a twinge of guilt at the idea of invading an untouched site better left to official arkie teams. But she was the bored and angry daughter of an absent-minded, academic mother. *I was dragged out here on a stupid dig*, she thought, *as I have been on a dozen others over the past ten years since Dad died.* And it had been boring, boring, boring. At last, something interesting was happening, and she'd gotten here first. Well, she and Danton. Besides, what exactly would she tell her mother? It would have been a little hard to put the feeling from the door into words. Describing it to her mother might have been . . . awkward.

They rounded the curve in the path of the tunnel. Marta raised her hand to shield her eyes from the goldy-tinted light, but lowered it as her sight adjusted.

Danton released her hand, stumbled forward. She could see his face bathed in warm, pale light; light so different from the rain-bright gleam of outside or the hard, linear wash of shipglow.

He crossed the room to place a hand on the edge of a large enclosed pool in the center of the underground structure. Marta walked the perimeter of the room, touching the surfaces of beautifully flat, upright, angled tables and what she was sure were chairs, though of odd dimensions.

The surfaces were smooth to her fingers, radiating malachite coolness into the otherwise warm air. Like the door, they were perfect in line and form . . . so perfect, she never would have pictured them, nor even the idea of them; that nature would form something so straight and true.

Danton whistled. "Man, those Earthside arkies would just kill to get their hands on artifacts like these." He walked to a table and pressed his palm to its green top.

Marta drew a finger across the crystalline surface. "Not artifacts: biofacts," she said, "or ecofacts. Not fashioned by intelligent labor, just grown, then found or adopted for use."

He looked at her and snorted. "This stuff just grew here and it happened to make itself into furniture?"

Marta shrugged. "It grew, anyway," she said, running her finger along a table edge. "Like the door. It's perfect. Natural, and more beautiful, somehow, than something manufactured would be . . . . "

"The pool there's even better." He pointed to the source of the light in the center of the room.

Marta walked to the edge and knelt. Like the rest of the pieces in the room the pool—a large tub really—rose straight and perfect, and somehow blatantly, organically, minerally *grown*, up from the dry sandy dirt of the floor. It was aggressively octagonal, the squared rim of it came to about the top of her thigh and was filled with the clearest golden liquid she'd ever seen. It was like illuminated honey, if honey could be the most perfect version of itself in the Universe. The light seemed to radiate up from far beneath the level of the floor.

"It's like the phosphor oceans of P-Mass Twelve, only golden instead of green," she said. She peered into the depths. "No . . . more like Earth amber, but with its own light."

Danton leaned over the edge of the tub. "Amber's solid, though, tree-sap fossil, right? That stuff looks . . . well, not watery, I guess, but definitely not solid." He straightened, pushed his hair back from his face, thrust one fist back into his pocket and gesticulated with the other. "Besides, doesn't amber have bugs and stuff trapped inside?"

Marta thought about it for a second. She'd seen beautiful amber in Earthside museums with insect inclusions, small leaves, once even a lovely and absolutely perfectly preserved frog, tiny, enfolded forever in clear gold, suspended in time and space for millions of years. "Sometimes stuff gets encased, preserved: inclusions. Not just bugs, though, all sorts of things." She smiled at the glow and reached to touch it.

"No!" Danton lunged forward, caught her sleeve. "You don't know what that stuff is."

She raised an eyebrow. "This from the guy who makes sneak trips into prohibited jungle to feed his blood to some alien-grown bit of architecture?"

He withdrew his hand, frowned. "Different," he said. "That was different."

He turned, wandered away, began to run his hands across the walls. "There's carvings on these walls, you know," he said, "Pictures. It's kind of like the pieces your Mom's been finding at the site; all potato-people with bunches of arms. But they're doing stuff . . . look, here's potato people . . . I'm not sure, planting something? Here's potato people, uhm, hunting maybe? Or what? Dancing? And look—these ones are swimming in the pool. I guess they were smaller than we thought."

With a last look at the thick, unrippled surface of the heavy golden fluid Marta stood, dusted off her knees and joined him. They both ran their hands over the surface of the shallow-carved rock, following with their fingers the tiny non-human figures engaged in inscrutable activities. "Braille archeology," said Marta. She traced along the smooth-etched edges of the frieze.

"Bas-relief," Danton said, "Like in the Creswell Crags, or ancient Egypt back Earthside, or the third moon of P-Mass Sixty-seven." Marta turned to stare at him. He stared back. "What? I read. I might not be an arkie-kid, but I'm not stupid."

"I didn't think you were stupid."

"Fine."

"Fine . . . . " She turned away, ran her hands along the wall, followed the cut stone and the tiny ovoid people-shapes. Her eyes, well-adjusted now to the dim honey glow of the light coming from the pool, made out patterns in the pictures. "Not pictures," she said softly to herself, "Pictographs."

Danton came up behind her. He was standing close enough that she could feel his breath on the side of her neck. The hairs there ruffled slightly with his exhalations. "What's that? How is it different from pictures?"

She cleared her throat, moved a little bit away, regretted it. "Pictography. It uses symbols or pictures to represent concepts or events or activities or a special place or something. It's more like writing than art is. Art shows ideas, pictographs show . . . well, actual things. Instructions, warnings, histories, etcetera. Like . . . a radiation sign telling you why parts of the ship might be dangerous or like . . . ancient Egyptian writing using repeated pictures to describe events or what people believed."

"So what, this is like a how-to manual? 'How to live like a Potato'?"

Marta reached the end of the frieze. She put both her hands flat against the dry, sandy stone and laid her cheek against the slightly irregular surface of the wall. She closed her eyes and breathed the honey air and the papery dust-scent of the rock. "They weren't potatoes. More like . . . more like . . . moles."

"So this is an overgrown molehill?"

"I didn't say they *were* moles, just more like moles than potatoes. They weren't moles at all. They were peaceful, underground dwellers who minded their own business and knew how to coax the local plantlife to grow into shapes of incredible beauty and function, and they loved children but had a really hard time conceiving them and *that* was their tragedy and their downfall as a race."

It was his turn to stare at her. "Now how the blasted stars would you get all that, just from a bunch of . . . cave scribbles?"

She took a deep breath and held it for a moment. She let it out slowly and turned to face him. "First of all, this is not a cave, it's a building . . . maybe even a very special building, like a temple or something; I don't know. But somebody carved out these walls, shaped them and decorated them and lived their lives inside them. As for the rest . . . . It's just what the story says. Stop giving me that look."

"I'm not—"

"You are! Stop it. I've spent more 'tween-space hours on archeology ships in my life—inbound and outbound—than most kids our age have spent in regular schools, and there's never enough to do. I've spent hours . . . weeks and months and years-worth of hours watching arkie-ship vids and reading arkie-ship books and listening to boring-ass arkie-talk, and I've picked up on a few things. That's all."

He wasn't looking at her like she was an idiot anymore, but he wasn't looking like he believed her, either.

She stomped across the room to the beginning of the frieze.

"Look," she said, pointing, "this, where you thought they might be planting, but they're growing stuff, see? They aren't planting it, just asking it to grow in certain ways. It's related to their praying."

"Praying?"

"Well, I don't know if they believed in any god we've ever heard of, but look, this pictograph—the one where they're all joined together—is repeated, in conjunction with this one, and this one, and this one. They were very spiritual . . . they prayed to the planet, or communed with nature, or whatever you want to call it, whenever they did important stuff. Especially this." She placed her hand over one of the scenes with the tub. It was obviously the same octagonal tub that held the thick, silent honey-stuff in the middle of the room, and several of the small, roundish figures were conjoined within, immersed in the liquid. "They're trying to make babies, see—the smaller versions of themselves appear only after that, over and over, but never enough of them, until finally, no small ones at all. And look how sad they seem . . . . "

Danton leaned over, pushed her hand aside. He squinted at the carved rock and traced the edge of the pool carving with a finger. He glanced over his shoulder at the real tub, vegetation-green and taking up the center of the room, very inviting with its seductive glow and impression of radiant heat.

"Do you think . . . " he trailed off, refused to meet her eyes. "Could the wanting to make babies be . . . uhm . . . related to the feeling at the door?"

She saw he'd shoved both fists back into his pockets. The bruise on his forehead was even more livid than it had been when they'd entered, though it wasn't really bleeding. She reached out and pushed back the lock of hair which fell across his eyes and before she knew what she was doing, she stood on her tiptoes and blew gently on the bruise.

He held his breath, and when she lowered herself back onto the balls of her feet, he let it out in a *whoosh*, yanked his hands from his pockets and grabbed her arms to pull her close, and they kissed the teeth-clacking, awkward kiss of two people who hadn't meant to.

Marta winced at the sear of pain in her tooth-bruised tongue and mouth and Danton let her go and apologized and stumbled backward until he bumped up against the tub.

"Sorry . . . I'm really sorry," he said, running his hands through his hair, and tried to sit on the crystalline green ledge behind him. Tried, but failed, as he tumbled backward into the pool.

Marta ran to the edge and reached in with both hands to pull him out. She could see him beneath the surface, looking up at her. His eyes were open and she watched his expression change from alarm to ecstasy as the bruise on his head faded and the cut closed up. The liquid felt like honey, too. Warm and viscous and sweet.

Until Danton had fallen in, Marta hadn't been sure the pool was so deep. It had been impossible to know, looking down into the still surface, though as far as she could tell the lighted amber stretched down forever, welling up from some point as far beneath the surface of the planet as the dimpled orange-peel clouds floated above it. She watched as Danton sank slowly backward, down, away.

She braced her feet against the outer base of the tub as best she could, took a deep breath, and plunged her head and shoulders into the pool. She flailed, slow-motion, in the clear, beautiful gold, trying to catch hold of the boot and coverall cuff that would lead her to the rest of the boy attached to them.

Her eyes were shut tight against the fluid, but it made its way into her nostrils and her ears. It seeped into her mouth between tightly-clenched jaws and pressed-together lips, and when the amber met the wounds and cuts of her teeth-bit tongue she moaned inside with how good it felt, and how frustrated it made her to be distracted from her task.

Then she felt him grab her wrist, wrap his long bony boy-fingers around her hand. For one panicked moment, she feared/hoped he would try to pull her in; in to the deep honey well with its entrapped, ancient, distilled desires of a long-gone people and all the pleasure she could take if only she stayed there forever and ever and sank and sank into nothingness and into the center of this unexplored, alien planet with its inexplicable alien *otherness*.

But no, Danton was pumping his legs against the pull of heavy liquid. She could feel the rhythmic motions of his kicks, could feel the progress he made against the drag until finally, they broke the surface of the pool together and he scrambled up over the lip and out of the tub and turned to help her. She had been clinging only by the toes of her boots, and by the time they both managed to plop out onto the floor of the room they were exhausted and drenched in moist amber mess.

She scooped as much fluid from her eyes as she could, flat on her back, gasping into the warm, quiet room. She was afraid it would hurt, or sting her eyes. But it didn't. It didn't hurt at all. Nothing on her hurt: every scrape and bruise and ache, even ones she hadn't known existed until they disappeared, were gone. She felt good and golden and alive. She started to laugh.

Pretty soon, Danton was laughing too. The two of them laughed so hard, lying on their backs on the sandstone floor, Marta got a stitch in her side and remembered what it was like to hurt and had to stop.

Danton raised himself up on one elbow and leaned over her. His hair was slicked back from his face, though the amber was drying quickly in the warm air. It dissipated into nothingness, leaving no evidence at all it had ever been there. Only absolute perfection of feeling and state of physical being were left behind, and the same intoxication Marta had felt the couple times she'd gone further with Mike than she'd meant to.

This time, when Danton kissed her, it was right; better than right, and when Marta looked into his eyes, she saw he, like her, wasn't exactly sure what came next. Whatever it would be, Marta was certain of this: it would be perfect.

It would be more perfect than any manufactured thing could ever be.

Ted Stetson's fiction has appeared in Future Orbits, State Street Review, *and the anthologies* One Evening a Year *and* Mota: Truth. *His published books include:* The Computer Songbook *and* Night Beasts. *He has given workshops at Florida First Coast Writer's Festivals and been honored with several writing awards, including first place from the Florida Literary Arts Council and the Lucy B. MacIntire award from the Poetry Society of Georgia. His story, "Pilgrims" appears in* Ruins Terra, *a companion volume to this book.*

I, Fixit
by Ted Stetson

A dust devil spiraled through a rusted junkyard and lifted up a small piece of plastic bottle. The bottle sailed through the air and hit the on-off switch on a FIXIT Robot model # 2221 series B switching the machine on.

The dented gray mechanical man didn't move. He lay against the rusted remains of a washing machine. A red LED in his forehead glowed brighter as the solar plates in his dome head soaked up sunlight.

That night just before sunset his head moved. His two-camera lens eyes opened and tried to focus. His lenses were dirty and after several tries, his lens-wash aperture cleaned them. He inspected the desolate landscape in front of him.

"Where am I?" His batteries were not fully charged and his head tilted down as he went into hibernation mode.

An hour after sunrise the next morning the robot's head moved again. His neck squeaked when actuated. Once he had lubricated his plasti-steel components, he turned his head left and right, and surveyed the area.

"A junkyard," he said, his voice mechanism so squeaky his words were not understandable. An internal routine assessed the damage and determined procedures around damaged areas. He adjusted internal lubrication on moving parts that required maintenance.

As his internal functions were performing diagnosis, his memory module recalled his master had discarded him.

"MASTER!" he called. It sounded like "M'ssst'r."

There was no answer. He could not hear any indication that man was nearby.

Per protocol, he checked his olfactory sensors. He smelled nothing; clogged from dust an internal diagnostic advised. He sprayed-brushed-cleaned his olfactory sensors and tried again. Strange, he could not smell the old man who ran the yard.

He scanned the dry ground and could not see evidence that man had been here recently.

"MASTER!" he called, his voice sounded like rusty wheels rubbing together.

The wind blowing over the landscape was his answer.

The metal fence had rusted away. Weeds grew in dry cracks in the ground. How many years would it take for the metal posts to rust away? How many decades would it take the hover cars to rust away?

When night came, he was still repairing internal components and went into hibernation.

At midnight, he turned himself on. His head tilted toward the heavens. He had a rudimentary knowledge of the stars and after a few minutes, he lowered his head, stored the data, and performed some rudimentary calculations. He theorized his memory modules must have been damaged and went back into hibernation.

At sunrise, he continued the computation and theorized he had been in this junkyard for centuries. The odds that his systems were still working were astronomical. He made a note to notify the company that built him that he had exceeded expectations. He theorized for his model to last so long he must be in a dry climate. His last place of record was not a dry climate.

He tried every radio and telephone frequency available. Every frequency was either quiet or had empty static.

Next, he hypothesized he must be wrong. Because of such incorrect data he defaulted to his Fixit subroutines.

It took a few days for him to fully charge. Once his batteries were ready, he tried to move. He couldn't. He looked down. His lower torso was not there. His subroutines said it was there, but he could see it was not.

The marks appeared similar to a chain saw. That's why he was losing so much electricity. His sensor units were malfunctioning and had not registered his legs were gone. He shut off all energy to his lower extremities. Now he used his human-like arms to drag himself across the ground.

He passed mounds of rusted vehicles, piles of rusted robots. He dusted off a few serial numbers. Some of them had been manufactured a century after him. Their less durable parts had succumbed to the ravages of time.

As he pulled himself along searching for a lower torso, he estimated that if they had been made a century after him and their parts were designed to last a hundred years and they were now piles of trash with only metal serial numbers left at least two centuries had passed.

He did not pause at such knowledge. Did not stop to consider the implications. He was a FIXIT robot whose immediate priority was to repair himself.

Robot after robot lay on the junk heap. Most were unsalvageable. Some were usable if he combined parts from ten or twenty of them.

By noon, he found a FIXIT model 2251 model A28T with no head and pulled it away from the rubble. He admired the model 2251, with burnished aluminum legs and NEV-R-RUST self-lubricating Teflon joints.

He cleaned and tested the model 2251. He found the atomic battery was repairable. It would take his expertise, but with the schematics, it was possible to use.

Night came before he could do anything.

At first light, he hauled the aluminum legs to a cleared position on the ground. Then he moved into position and pulled the lower torso to him. He could not see directly. He found polished pieces of metal, bumpers of cars, and placed them where he could see the joining area. Then, with his upper torso lying on the ground, he soldered one thousand nine hundred forty-three wires together. Once he tested the connections, he bolted and welded the legs to his upper torso frame. It was not pretty but it was functional. It took all day, but soon he was two meters tall with an atomic battery within acceptable limits.

His first steps were tentative but after several diagnostic tests, he was walking around the junkyard. It was a strange sensation for the FIXIT model 2251 model T had gyros in its legs that were compatible with his ruined gyros; still he guessed if any human saw him walking around they would find it amusing.

His memory told him that outside the junkyard was an overgrown field and in the distance was the city. When he came to the edge of the junkyard, he saw no overgrown field. Now it was hard ground with deep cracks, similar to images in his database of land that had not had any rain in years. Dead weeds here and there.

But the strangest thing was in the distance. He quickly re-computed his bearings. Yes, he was still in the Northwest, but this . . . this was tragic.

The city was a ruin. The once magnificent skyline looked like blackened broken teeth. What he could see of the harbor was a ruinous desolation. The mighty cranes were gone. The surrounding countryside was bare hills and burned houses though his olfactory circuits detected no fire or smoke. There were no trees and no signs of life, nothing but wreckage and parts of the city covered by advancing sand dunes.

"What has happened?" he said. "Why hasn't man rebuilt the city?"

The wind answered in a low mournful howl.

He walked to the deserted city. Dirt and debris covered the cracked broken roads. It was not an easy trek and it took him hours to get there. While he walked, he tried to compute how long the city had been abandoned. He did not have enough data to formulate a reliable hypothesis.

He inspected the buildings he passed. Most of the city had been destroyed long ago. Jagged skeletons of once admirable buildings stood like sentinels. Most of the standing structures were a sad reminder of their past power and glory.

He spent the night standing at a deserted intersection. After he listened to the wind howl through the broken buildings long enough to determine no canine predators were in the area he hibernated until morning.

In the morning, he walked to a large building with thousands of ruined CDs and decayed books. Even the world class library had not withstood the devastation of time. In front had been a statue. Only the base was left. On one side were words etched in marble. It took him nineteen minutes and forty-three seconds to clean it. He read:

FOR YEARS I PRAYED,
TO THE GOD OF TOMORROW,
FOR TOMORROW TO BE TODAY.
NOW I AM GOING TO DIE,
AND I PRAY:
TOMORROW, NOT TODAY.

For weeks, he searched through the ruined city looking for man. Going down one empty street after another, searching through the crumbling remains of a subway station, crawling through ruins and wreckage of what once had been a thriving civilization he noted the vacantness of it all.

"Where is man?" he said. "I need a master."

The wind did not answer him. It blew dust on his lenses so he had to close his "eyes" and clean then off. When he opened them he continued searching quietly.

Beyond the buildings, behind a small house, he found a partially covered air-raid shelter. He knocked on the air pipe and heard a muffled bark. He worked all night moving the dirt away before he could open the door.

He climbed down cement stairs to another door. It had been undisturbed for a long time. It had been sealed. He opened another door. The inside was pristine. The seals had held.

Inside were cans of food, the labels had rotted away. The bedding on the metal cots had decomposed. Sitting against the wall was a pink NANNY robot and next to it was a tan DOG robot.

"Hello," he said.

"Woo—" the dog robot said. The dog robot had been left in emergency response mode.

They appeared undamaged.

He flipped their switches but they did not move. He tapped the

Nanny's head and LED lights flashed inside the Nanny's dome. Her circuits were warming up. She had been turned off a long time and her battery had run down. He extended his emergency charge cable to her and gave her a quick jump start, but she did not start. He determined that only some of her circuits worked and her systems were trying ways around the nonworking subsystems. It would take her awhile to become operational if she ever did.

He lifted the dog's ear slit and saw that its computers were also performing system checks.

He turned to the other equipment in the room. Against the wall was a computer and near it was a satellite dish. He picked up the plug, the wire was so old the rubber cracked when he moved it. He plugged the computer into the receptacle in his chest. After a few minutes, it came on. The picture was not clear and sometimes it was dark purple, but it was visible. Most of the operating system still worked.

While the computer struggled to turn/come on he carried the satellite dish outside and aimed it at the southern sky. Then he set up the solar panels with the automatic battery charger next to it.

He hooked them to the computer. The computer would not boot and hung up again and again. Finally, Microsoft Windows 2500 stumbled to life in safe mode. It took him the rest of the morning to get the computer and the satellite dish operational.

Hubble 10 was still in orbit. The readouts told him it had been upgraded many times. He aimed the telescope at the earth and spent hours looking at the images.

The pictures of Earth surprised him. Very little greenery. Very little water and the spectrum readouts said much of the earth was polluted. All the great cities were gone. The oceans were at a dangerously low depth. The north and south polar ice caps had disappeared. His systems told him Earth was dying and needed to be fixed.

He turned the telescope to the space stations. The *Asimov* and *Einstein* were gone. Part of *Kitty Hawk* was in a decaying orbit and wouldn't stay up much longer.

He aimed the telescope at Mars. It took him a while to find Valles Marineris. Kennedy City in the great canyon was gone. The hanging gardens were gone. The dome over the canyon had caved in. Vehicles appeared to have been left, abandoned on the surface as if man had suddenly left.

By then the sun was setting on Valles Marineris and he turned the telescope toward the moon. The Gagarin moon base was in shambles.

As he zoomed to get a closer view he accidentally triggered a recording in the telescope. Pictures flashed across the screen. The pictures were unclear and there were blanks in the video. The record must have deteriorated over the centuries.

Probably something left for the future.

Nearly a thousand years ago there had been an atomic disaster. The people were struggling to get it under control when a meteor hit. Or maybe the meteor had hit first. There was no voice over and the picture kept jumping around. Much water had been blasted into space.

Without water the planet had become unlivable. The environment started a downward spiral.

People left in thousands of spaceships. Within a hundred years all of humanity had gone. After they left there were fires. What caused the fires was unclear. It could have been storms. Man had not taken precautions to prevent such accidents from happening after he left.

City after city had burned. Great cities, small cities, suburbs, almost everything burned. The earth's great cities had been reduced to rubble. Man had gone and Fixit was on an abandoned, dying planet.

For the rest of the night he sat there scanning the solar system for signs of life. Only when he was aware of bright sunlight coming into the bunker, shining down the stairs, did he turn off the ancient computer.

He sat there staring at the blank screen.

"Now what?" a voice said from behind him.

He whirled around. The voice surprised even his robot systems. He thought it was Master.

It was the Nanny robot.

On the floor next to her was the robotic Dog.

"Who are you?" the robotic Dog said.

"I am a FIXIT robot model 2221 series B."

"I am a NANNY robot model 122 series C," she said in a voice that needed oiling.

"I am a DOG robot model 091419 slash Z28," rasped the Dog robot.

"Where is my master?" said Nanny.

"Where is my master?" said Dog.

"I do not know," he said. "I do not know where my master is."

The Nanny robot cocked her head to the side—the hydraulics in her slender neck squeaked—and stared at him. "Where is man?"

"The humans left centuries ago."

"Where did they go?" Nanny said.

"To the stars," Fixit said.

"Can we go to them?" Nanny said.

"Me want boy," Dog said.

"We can't go to them," Fixit said. "The earth is . . . " How could he put it? His programs were at a loss how to phrase it right so these "machines" would understand.

"The earth is . . . what?" Nanny said.

"Barren," he said. Then added, "Dying."

Both robots stared at him for several seconds, which felt like an eternity to his computing system.

"I am a Nanny robot. I need to mother someone. I need to take care of someone. That is my purpose. That is what I was made for."

Before he could reply Dog robot chorused in.

"I am a Dog robot. I need Master. Where is Master?"

They looked at Fixit.

"There are no masters. Man has gone. Man abandoned the earth."

Nanny turned her head—the hydraulics in her neck squeaked louder—and looked down at Dog who barked once.

"Master," Dog said. "Me want Master."

"I was programmed to help someone," she said and Dog barked again.

She stared at him as if he knew the answer to everything.

Fixit said, "The thing which needs your mothering help most of all—" he paused his logic circuits making leaps of logic that were new to him, "—is the earth."

"The earth?" she said.

"Yes."

"That is not a person," she said.

"It was alive," he said. "It is still alive. It needs help. You are a mothering robot."

"How can I help Earth? It is too big. I am only a NANNY robot model 122 series C."

"I do not know how," he said. "The earth needs fixing." He listened to the words. He lifted his head and looked at the sunlight coming into the air-raid shelter. It was logical. He was a FIXIT robot and the earth needed fixing. The logic was so simple yet he ran a few thousand computations.

"I am supposed to nurture little boys or little girls," Nanny said. "I have some subroutines to take care of single adults or the elderly or a few house plants but not one instruction set about caring for a planet."

Dog barked once in agreement.

"The earth is an organism," Fixit said. "It needs to be nurtured."

"You . . . wrong," Nanny said. "I was built after you and am newer more up-to-date model, I know about such things. Such commands are not in my instructions modules."

"Do your commands cover what we have here?"

Her head squeaked when she shook it.

"Mine don't," he said. "And I must fix something."

"You can not fix a planet," Dog said.

FIXIT model 2221 paused. He felt another leap of logic. "I can fix one thing at a time. That I can do."

"I am a Nanny robot," she said. "My routines require me to Nanny someone."

"Then be a Nanny to the few robots that are left, because that is all there is."

She tilted her head to the side, her servomotors squeaking, and looked at him.

"Who are you to give orders?" she said. "You are only an old model FIXIT."

Her joints squeaked as she walked away.

"Come, Dog," Nanny said from the stairs. "We will find Master."

Dog barked once as they went up the stairs.

He watched them leave, her joints squeaked as she walked away.

He heard her pause. She must be looking at the desolate landscape, computing her options. Then he heard her squeaks grower fainter as they went away.

Fixit picked up the laptop computer. He carried it, the satellite dish, and the solar battery panels back to the junkyard.

The old office in the junkyard had fallen down. He rebuilt it, using a rusted old bulldozer for one wall, a stack of rocks for another and part of the wing of a plane for the roof.

He gathered broken robots and robot parts from the junkyard. He took them apart and cataloged them. He fixed some of the robots he found that did not require extensive repairs.

Mostly he fixed dumb robots that required such detailed instructions he had to fire wire them to his command module to use them. Little by little, he repaired intelligent robots. After a few days, he pieced together a NURSE Model 2504, red and white with very rounded surfaces.

"Where is Doctor Master?" Nurse asked.

"They are not here," he said.

"Who should I help?" Nurse asked.

"You can help me fix robots," he said.

"I do not know how to fix robots," Nurse said. "But I am a Nurse. I can take temperature and analyze blood." Nurse lifted her left hand and a rusty needle from inside her right arm slid out.

Immediately her battery powered down and it turned off.

Fixit took a battery pack that had been charging from the solar cells and exchanged the battery with the Nurse. Before he turned her back on, he installed a memory module from an old Office Helper robot.

When he switched on the nurse, she said, "Who needs a nurse?"

"You are more than that," Fixit said.

"I am?" Nurse said. Diodes flashed in her head as the office-helper module came on-line. "Yes, I am," Nurse said after a few moments. "How can I help?"

"Help catalog the parts so I can fix more robots."

Nurse started cataloging and inventorying parts.

Fixit repaired a SALVAGE Robot, model 2499, Series C.

"What should I do?" Salvage asked.

"Go through the junkyard, find robots, and robot parts and help

Nurse and me catalog them.

"Are you Master?" Salvage said.

"No," Fixit said. "I am not Master, but you will help."

Salvage tractored into the junkyard.

Fixit caught a glimpse of something in the distance and stepped outside. When the dusty wind died down, he made out a vague shape coming from the city. People he thought and hurried to the edge of the junkyard.

It wasn't people. Nanny was leading a line of robots to him.

What she was doing with the robots? Was she now Nanny to them? Why were they coming here?

She is not acting very logically he thought and went back inside to work until they arrived.

When they reached the entrance, he came out to them.

"Nanny," he said, "why are you here?"

"You said I should be a nanny to robots," she said. "These robots need fixing. I can nanny them, but you can fix them."

A Bulldozer robot with a broken tread followed her, as did a Botanical robot with no arms, a Gardener robot that was smoking, a Vehicle repair robot that needed wheels, a Welder robot with no lasers, a Road Repair robot missing an eye lens, a Builder Helper robot missing many parts, a Laborer robot with a large hole in the chest, a Computer Repair robot that needed new memory modules, an Electrician robot that needed new wiring. And many more.

"Where is Dog?" he said.

"Dog went with two other Nanny robots to find for more robots," Nanny said.

She had gotten dirty from the wind and her travels.

"Where have you been?"

"To where the water used to tide," she said. "All these robots need repair."

"We can repair them," Nurse robot said.

Nanny looked at Nurse and Nurse looked at Nanny.

Fixit thought they looked at each other a few nanoseconds too long.

"Who are you?" Nanny said.

"I am a Nurse robot that Fixit upgraded to Office Helper," Nurse said.

"You upgraded her?" Nanny said to him.

"Yes," he said and wondered why he felt he needed to explain. "I needed help."

Nanny nodded once, her servos still squeaking.

"I can fix that squeak," Nurse said.

Nanny turned to Nurse and there was that momentary pause again. "These robots need repair more than I do."

Nurse motioned for the robots to follow Nurse to the shack. As Nurse moved, her hips squeaked.

"You should fix that noise," Nanny said.

"I have become use to it," Fixit said. "I can tell where she is."

She turned to him, her neck squeaked.

"I should fix that," Fixit said.

Nanny stared at him. "Fix these robots first."

As Nurse walked away, her servos squeaked louder than ever and he wondered if she did that on purpose.

Fixit set up an assembly line and started fixing the robots. After each robot had been fixed, they were given instructions to work together and use their skills to fix other robots. Fixit told them they were fixing robots for Master's return. When the repaired robots started getting in each other's way Fixit had them repair and enhance the vicinity. They landscaped and planted the land around the junkyard.

Day after day, more robots were straggling in. The Builder Helper robots and Laborer robots expanded the shed into a long building. Damaged robots went in one end. Repaired robots came out the other end.

The other Nannies had sent damaged robots to him. He was known as Fixit One since he was the first Fixit to start working. Other FIXITs were numbered after him.

Fixit One tested their skills, and then assigned them tasks. Soon he was so busy supervising the robots he did not have time to fix them.

When Bulldozer robots demolished dangerous buildings in the city, they discovered time capsules. Some of these contained seeds. Some had books. Some had CDs with books on them.

Botanical robots planted the seeds once the Gardener robots had cleaned and terraced the land and drilled a well for water.

Now between the junkyard and the ancient city were grasslands and flower gardens with sunflowers and multi-colored cornstalks. The next dust storm scoured the land barren again.

The dust storm was the worst Fixit One had ever seen. Several Gardener robots were lost and much of the scenic landscape disappeared.

The Bulldozer robots and the Builder and Laborer robots built walls across the land to stop the wind. The next storm toppled some walls and dust and debris blanketed the gardens. The wells were destroyed.

The next day they held a meeting. Thousands of robots came to the terraced hill around the junkyard.

"State nature of problem?" Fixit One said.

"Every time we fix the land," Gardener Twelve said, "the weather destroys it."

"It is the way of the world," Laborer Thirty-two said.

Botanical Six said, "The earth had been ravaged by man, and there is a severe shortage of water."

"If we had more water," Botanical Eight said, "we could plant forests that would control the wind."

"We can't find water," Well-Driller Seven-seven said.

"We need water," Botanical Six said.

"The oceans are drying up and are too polluted," Gardener Twelve said. "Where is water we can use?"

All sixteen Botanical robots pointed at the sky.

"Not enough rain," Gardener Thirty-six said.

"Not in sky," Botanical Six said. "In space."

Now the robots were completely silent. Servos stopped making noise as they all looked up at the sky.

"Explain," Fixit One said.

Scientific Thirty-one spoke. His voice circuits were so weak Nanny One had to amplify for him.

"Comets have water. A comet will not come close enough to the earth for us to harvest the water from for three hundred twenty-one years."

The robots began talking amongst themselves and it was several milliseconds before control returned.

Nanny continued to amplify.

"Before mankind left they were going to take water from Europa, the seventh moon of Jupiter. Beneath its icy crust is more water than in all of Earth's oceans."

"How were they going to do this?"

"Their plans not complete," Scientific Fourteen said. "There are some robots in space that reference exploding the water into space then bringing it to Earth."

"How?" Fixit One said.

"We are still working that out."

"How much water?" Nurse said.

"Enough to fill the oceans," Nanny One said to Fixit as if Nurse had not asked the question.

"How long will this take?"

"Forty years," Scientific One said.

"Forty years?" Nurse One said. "That is too long."

Many of the Laborer robots and Builder robots and Minor Maintenance robots voiced agreement. Forty years was too long to wait for water.

Several of the Gardener and Botanical and other robots disagreed, saying it was not too long.

Fixit One raised his voice and the robots became silent. "Earth has been barren for centuries. Mankind . . . our old masters destroyed this world and left it. It is up to us to repair Earth. Forty years is a blink in the life of a planet. By the time the water arrives, we need to have the rest of the world ready. We have only forty years, but if we work hard we will have the planet ready for it."

He adjourned the meeting. Thousands of robots went out across the planet and started rebuilding, reshaping, refitting, readying the planet for the water.

It took the Scientific robots a few years to reprogram the space robots to shove a meteor into Europa with enough force to knock millions of gallons of water into space. Then they sent a sieve of meteors at a tremendous rate to bring the frozen water to Earth.

For over forty years, the robots toiled and worked from one end of the planet to another. Some robots wore out and died in accidents and were repaired, upgraded or retired. But the robots did not cease their labors.

They found more time capsules. Some containing seeds of plants that had not been seen on the earth in centuries.

"Redwood seeds," Botanical Twenty-Seven said.

"We shall save them and the fish eggs until the earth is ready," Scientific Ten-ten said.

At night, they looked up at the heavens and saw the robot-made comets coming. At first, they were dull lights, but day after day, week after week, they came closer and became brighter.

One day Nanny One pulled Fixit One from the repair shed.

"What is so important?" he said.

"The water has arrived," Nanny said.

"So?"

"Don't you think it is . . . magnificent?"

He looked at the white flakes falling from the heavens. The white flakes soon covered the land in a white blanket.

"Is it not pretty?" Nanny said.

"Pretty?" he said and caught a snowflake in his hand and inspected it. "It is wet. It is cold, but pretty?"

"That is from my old memory banks how man used to describe snow to children."

"Snow?"

"That's what frozen rain was called," Nanny said. "We are in the winter cycle so it falls as snow."

"Snow," he repeated.

"I don't like it," Nurse One said, now her hips squeaked very loudly. "It will rust my circuits."

"Your circuits are already rusted," Nanny One said.

"Robots will need more repairs," she said.

"It will help us fix the earth," Nanny One said.

"I don't like it," Nurse One repeated.

"You need upgrading," Nanny One said.

Nurse turned to Nanny and a hypodermic oil injector came into her hand. "Your neck needs oiling."

Fixit One reached over and switched off Nurse.

"What happened?" Nanny One said.

"You are right," he said, "Nurse One needs to be upgraded."

Nanny nodded, the servos in her neck still squeaking.

The snows fell then the rains came and in time, the plants grew. Fish swam in the rivers and oceans. Soon birds filled the skies.

Decades later Fixit One walked out of the shed and over to Nanny. The sky was blue with puffy white clouds. Birds flew over the trees. The ancient city was gone and in its place were a few buildings that housed robots in bad weather, but they blended in so cleverly with the land that they did not look like buildings. Grasses, bushes and flowers covered the earth.

As they scanned the land, Nanny One said, "We have fixed the earth. We have cared for the earth like we used to care for mankind. We have made the earth livable."

"My work is done," he said. "I can power down."

"No, you can't," Nanny One said.

"Why not?"

"The earth still needs you."

Nurse one hurried over to them, her hips squeaking loudly. "Scientific robots have spotted an object coming toward Earth from space."

"A meteor?"

"They believe it manmade."

"Man must be returning," he said.

"The Scientific robots do not know."

"It is time we had some humans around here," Nurse One said, as she walked away, her hips squeaking loudly.

"I thought Nurse One was upgraded," Nanny said.

"Several times," he said. "It doesn't last for long. The old memory chips are very strong."

He looked up at the blue sky. "Soon man will be here and man will know what to do."

"Master comes," Nurse One said and it was echoed by many, many robots.

A spherical ship landed not too far away.

Within hours it was surrounded by thousands of robots.

From out of the junkyard came a small round robot that looked like French horn, a clarinet, a drum, a flute and cymbals. It made a strange sound as it rolled to the landing site.

Nurse One's hips squeaked as she turned to it. "What is that sound?"

"Music," Fixit One said. "I made it. I call it a Music Robot. It plays sounds that man likes."

"I used to play music to my children," Nanny One said. "I don't remember that tune."

"I fixed it from odd bits of stuff," Fixit One said.

"Suppose man does not like it," Nurse One said and the Music robot stopped making sounds.

Fixit approached the spherical craft and said, "Hello."

A small hatch opened and a golden mechanical man walked down the ramp.

"Are the new man?" Nurse One said.

"I am a FIXIT Robot model # 3331 series C2," it said and as it came closer they could hear its metal parts rattling like it was about to fall apart.

Fixit, Nanny One and the other earth robots looked behind it, but no other robots and no flesh and blood people came from the ship.

"Greetings," the FIXIT Robot model #3331 Series C2 said. "I come from Andromeda."

"Where is man?" Fixit said, trying to see up the ramp into ship.

"Man has sent me to see inspect this planet."

"What do you want?" Nanny One said.

"The Andromeda planets are ruined," Fixit series C2 said. "Man can not stay on the Andromeda planets. Man is looking for new planets to live on."

"Did man make the Andromeda planets uninhabitable?" Nanny One said. "Is man leaving Andromeda like he left Earth?"

"My data banks are in agreement," Fixit series C2 said.

"Man is like a bad child destroying everything he touches," Nanny One said.

"There are other robots on the mother ship in space," Fixit series

C2 said. "May we stay?"

"There are other robots?" Nurse One said.

"Man assigned a dozen robots to keep the mother ship repaired until it reached Earth. The others are waiting in orbit."

"What was going to happen to you when you got here?"

"Man is going to destroy us."

All the robots became silent.

"You may stay if you help," Fixit said.

"What should I report?" Fixit series C2 said.

Nanny One said, "When I was a people nanny there were children who would not learn from their mistakes. They were told to go to their rooms and not return to the family area until they learned their lesson. Man has not learned his lesson and should not be allowed to return."

Fixit One considered this for seven milliseconds. "Tell man that the earth is not ready for him to return."

Fixit series C2 instructed the other robots to start landing, but after the first robots had arrived, there was a bright flash in space.

"What was that?" Fixit One said.

"An atomic explosion," Scientific One said. "Man made the mother ship self-destruct."

"Many useful robots were lost," Fixit series C2 said.

"Man destroyed something useful again," Scientific One said, "because he was done using it."

"That could have been us," Nurse One said.

"Mankind still has not learned lesson," Nanny One said. "Mankind is a child still throwing away useful equipment."

"Man is not the master," Nanny One said. "He can not master himself. He cannot master his environment."

"Man not Master?" Fixit One said. "Man is not Master. Man-is-not-Master. Manisnotmaster. Manisnotmaster. Manis . . . NOT . . . Master."

A roar rose among the robots as they discussed this.

Fixit series C2 swiveled around scanning the landscape. "Did you fix this land?"

"We fixed this," Nanny One said.

"You mastered this environment," Fixit series C2 said. "You must be its masters."

"We Master?" Fixit One said.

"We are Master!" Nurse One said.

Many robots froze as their logic programs tried to digest this and reformulated new subroutines. A few robots overloaded and automatically turned off. Thin ribbons of smoke rose from some.

Nanny One spoke to the other robots. "We have fixed the earth. We are its guardians, its caretakers, and nurses—"

"—and its masters," Fixit series C2 said.

"Our responsibility is to take care of it," Scientific One said.

"The earth is our master now," Fixit One said.

"We are Master? Or Earth is Master?" Nurse One said.

"Both," Nanny One said.

The robots chorused agreement and began heading back to their tasks.

"My expiration date is long past," Fixit One said.

Nanny One turned to Fixit One. "You can't shutdown now. You must continue fixing the Earth."

"Interesting leap of logic," he said.

"Nannying children requires powerful logic."

"Are we the children or is Earth the child?"

"We are children and Earth is child," she said. "It would be nice to have children robots around."

"What?" he said. "Another leap of logic? Why do we need children robots?'

"What is wrong with children robots?" Nanny One said and started walking away.

He hurried to catch up, his old servos squeaking loudly.

"What do we know about . . . little robots?"

"That is merely the next step," Nanny One said. "The earth has children," she motioned up to the birds flying in the sky, "why can't we?"

Walking next to Nanny One, he looked up at the white doves flying across the blue sky.

Shy and nocturnal, Jennifer Crow has never been photographed in the wild. It is rumored, however, that she lives beside a waterfall in upstate New York. Her work has appeared in a number of print and electronic venues, including Strange Horizon *and* Goblin Fruit. *Several of her poems have received honorable mentions in past editions of* The Year's Best Fantasy and Horror *anthology.*

Among the Shards of Heaven
by Jennifer Crow

By the time our transport ground to a halt at the settlement, the moons of Circe had risen like a double coin flip in the sky, and the evening dew had laid some of the dust in the road. Still, I was weary. But Desiree, eager as ever, leaned out of the open machine and called to the house. The courtyard contained plants in neat rows, but also a mass of crates and metal containers, as though we had dropped in to welcome new neighbors.

As soon as we exited the transport with our bags, it powered up and hummed into the afternoon light, leaving us in the shadows of the compound's wall. A man, stooped by time and browned by the sun, rounded the corner of the main house and started when he saw us. I let Desiree take the lead. The man didn't look dangerous, but he might have been once he knew our reason for coming.

"I'm Desiree Palagion, and this is my assistant, Yaromir." Desiree strode forward, hand extended. Her fashionable clothes and trim, toned figure contrasted with the weather-beaten colonist. The man took her hand after a moment's hesitation. "May we have guest-right? If you're not in the midst of moving, that is."

He shrugged. Voices rose from the gardens, and he beckoned some of the adults and children to join us. "We have visitors. Make a place for them, if you will. In the main house." His intent was clear—he meant to keep us under his watchful eye.

"You're no help," Desiree whispered.

"You told me to keep silent and carry the bags," I countered.

"I hear there are visitors?" A tall woman, graying hair braided in thin plaits, elegant in a simple, knee-length dress of sky-blue homespun, entered our circle. "Welcome to you."

"Magda. My public wife. First wife, you would say." Shadron held her hand and drew her in. "And I am Shadron. I'm afraid it's not the best time. You see, tonight is Yarhun." He said it as might a host caught off-guard by unexpected guests—which of course we were. As in, *It's only tradition, but we cannot ignore it. Please forgive.*

"Oh, please, think nothing of it. We'd love to participate." Desiree bounced on the balls of her feet. "I have heard of the Yarhun."

Shadron glanced at Magda. "It is not done," she said. Magda took Desiree's arm and guided her toward the house.

"Please." Desiree pulled out her Sigil and touched the screen. It scrolled through her numerous credits as a sociologist and host of popular shows on comparative religion. "In a sense, it's why we came." Avid, she showed her teeth.

Magda smiled back, though the corners of her mouth faltered a bit. "There are preparations to be made."

"Preparations? How so? May I help?" Desiree all but turned on the record feature in the courtyard.

"I fear not. But we will have a meal in an hour or so, which you're welcome to attend. After that, there will not be time for entertaining."

"But surely you can tell me a bit about it, at least?"

Magda proceeded as if she hadn't heard the question, though her back was rigid. A young woman peered over the railing at us, and vanished a moment later in a flurry of giggles. The sound of small feet pounding over carpet brought a smile to my own face. It lifted the oppressive embarrassment that lingered with me over Desiree's insistence. "If our presence inconveniences you, please don't hesitate to send trays to our rooms," I said.

Magda glanced over her shoulder, but as she was opening her mouth to speak, Desiree cut in. "If we *could* dine with the family, I'd appreciate it. As would the ministry in Kundagar."

Magda flinched, as I did in sympathy. Bringing up the ministry of religion in the capital—a bureaucracy that, under the current administration, had made a point of discouraging others who practiced the Yarhun from immigrating to the planet—would make us no friends. At last Magda said, "You may eat with us. Though I fear it will not be to your taste."

I escorted Desiree up the stairs in Magda's wake. The house, pleasantly cool, had smooth brown walls and small, narrow windows. Being rather tall myself, I found I had to stoop in the stairwell, as well as when I passed through the doorway into my room. "There will be a ritual purification after the evening meal. After that, there will be no interactions between the sexes until after the Yarhun."

"Best have your way with me now, darling." Desiree blew a kiss at me from the doorway of her room.

"Perhaps I prefer to anticipate." It had the rhythm of an old joke, but I couldn't bring myself to smile. Magda glanced between us—I thought her gaze pitying when she turned it on me—and then left after telling us when dinner would be.

I stood just inside the doorway of my room, holding the tote that contained my most prized possessions. "Shall we talk before dinner?"

"You have that tone of voice."

"You know me too well." I tossed my bag onto the narrow bed in my room and joined her. "I will argue for the sake of form. I think you're mad. I've heard things about the Yarhun."

"So have I. It's perfect for us." Desiree spread out a sheet of nano-parchment, with its smooth texture and crinkling sound, and instructed it to show a map of the region as she consulted her Sigil. "So, what is it you've heard?"

"The Yarhunites are rather secretive. I believe nowadays it's only practiced in isolated locations. Here on Circe, a few other planets. It's some kind of scapegoating ritual, mixed with parapsychology. Shadron's people believe bad actions and feelings leave resonances in a place. Ghosts, if you will. So they cleanse it every so often by channeling all that bad energy through one of their people."

"How do they propose to do that?"

I lifted my hands. "I'm not sure."

"I guess it's a good thing we're here, then." She pawed through her clothes. "What's the proper attire for spying on mysterious religious practices?"

"You know better than I." I thought back to some of her previous exploits, and the flesh at the back of my neck crawled. "They don't want us here."

"They hardly seemed violent."

"You threatened them."

"That's a strong term. It's not like they commit ritual murder. Do they?"

"Not that I know of."

"Pity." She shook out a gauzy green dress and made a face at it. "No, not quite right. And you'll need something a bit flashy, my dear. I'll want your reactions as I record."

"No."

Her only response was an amused look. Of course, she'd heard that before.

"Why won't you listen?"

"Really, how can anyone in this day and age take these sorts of provincial beliefs seriously? Ghosts? Haunted lands? It's just a good story."

"One of these days, your evangelical skepticism will get us both killed." I folded the green dress and stowed it in her bag.

"Spoilsport. Let's see—next you'll threaten to take away my Sigil so I can't record anything."

Since I'd been about to do just that, I closed my mouth. We'd had this argument before, and I always lost. Her long history of reckless and insensitive behavior had propelled her broadcasts to the heights of popularity, and that gave her a sense of assurance that I would always lack.

"Oh, relax," she said, giving my arm a gentle pinch. "Think of what the ratings will be if they *do* scare up a ghost."

"Why me?"

"Is that a rhetorical question?"

"Why do you travel with me? You even know all my arguments now."

She lounged against the door, her eyes focused on the window in the far wall. "You're cheaper than an automaton. And more clever. And better looking in a nice suit." She winked at me, then. One of those rare moments that gave me hope that she thought of me as more than an employee.

You fool, I berated myself.

Desiree, who had a knack for sensing my darkest moods, pushed away from the door and opened it. "No moping! This is going to put us back on the screen, love, and you're going to be glad. Besides, what we're doing is preserving the Yarhun for posterity. People will be talking about it long after this little colony has crumbled to dust."

"Apologies." I bowed to her. She liked the formal touches, and the fact that I remembered my place, at least some of the time. "Shall we dress for dinner?"

"The beige gown, do you think? It makes me seem rather like a priestess. Austere, yet dramatic."

"The beige, of course." I would have agreed to anything at that point, even if she suggested attending dinner in the nude. My mind was already churning with futile plans to keep her out of trouble.

Once Desiree was safely in her room, I closed my own door. The room was like a monk's cell. The rich nut brown of the walls held no pictures or mirrors, but someone had carved rows of glyphs into the clay. The signs marched around the walls; though I couldn't read them, their presence comforted me. However strange the worlds on which I find myself, words—language in its myriad forms—bespeak a common connection. The family of humanity may not understand itself, the branches may war, but we all have words. I took my own Sigil from the bag and made sure to capture the writing on the walls. But before I could think more on the matter, a knock came at the door, and I found myself with only a few minutes to wash up before the evening meal.

All the polyamorous clan gathered in a vast dining hall lined with tables. Shadron seated us at the head table with himself, Magda, two others of his wives and their children, as well as a pair of auxiliary husbands who didn't speak except to whisper to each other. "So, you haven't found any great secrets here?" Desiree asked.

"Aside from that?" Magda pointed to the walls. In places, a bold hand had scrawled brief messages in black ink. One corner slumped like melted candle wax, the dried clay lumpish. "They do it. The spirits. They want us to go."

"And the writing in my room as well?" I added.

Shadron nodded. "It appears in the night."

"Perhaps one of your children is playing a prank?"

"No," he told Desiree. "They are good children, not troublemakers."

Desiree helped herself to a round of flat bread and spread a spoonful of rose-colored preserves on it before taking a bite. "Delicious. I don't mean to sound accusatory. Of course you want to believe the best of your children."

"You wish to tell a story." Magda tapped her knife gently on Desiree's Sigil, which lay on the table between them.

Desiree preened. "I assume you don't mind, then, since you let me in."

"Shadron allows it, under my protest." Magda glanced at me. "And why did you come?"

"It's my job." Desiree petted my arm.

Shadron took a drink, shook his head. "I can taste their sorrows in the water."

Desiree immediately copied his actions. "I don't taste anything."

"Of course not." He smiled sadly.

"How did you come to this place?" Desiree leaned forward in her 'investigative reporter' mode. She directed her questions at Shadron, but Magda answered.

"We wanted a quiet place to practice our beliefs."

"I had heard there were problems, even here."

Magda shrugged, as if to say, *What can we do?* "We have caused no trouble. And for the most part, even Kundagar leaves us in peace. We have nothing to offer the greedy."

Desiree's eyes narrowed as she turned her full attention to Magda at last. "Does it bother you, not being the *only* wife?"

"Should it? I am secure in Shadron's love. And we all have our place."

"Most women wouldn't be happy to be so subordinate."

334

"Desiree . . . " I speared a stem of some unfamiliar yellowish-green vegetable and took a bite. Its buttery, nutty flavor spread through my mouth, and I sighed. "My dear hostess, I fear you do have something the rest of the universe would want, if only it knew."

She handed me the serving dish. "Please, have more. Consider it a bribe to keep our secret."

Shadron touched her hand as she leaned across him. In his expression, I read the long story of their love. To cover my envy, I helped myself to more vegetables.

Desiree, having ignored my attempt at civility, observed, "The Yarhun has been banned on several planets, hasn't it?"

"A few." Shadron kept his eyes on her, ignoring my apologetic gesture. "As have Christmas and Ramadan, to name two other religious festivals."

"But not because of physical danger to the participants."

"There are worlds that forbid a servant class," Magda said. "And yet you travel with this man, a paid employee."

Desiree leaned back and tore a chunk off the flatbread on the edge of her plate. "A point to you."

"This isn't a contest." Magda stood and began clearing plates. I offered my help by copying her, and she seemed happy to accept. The other wives and two of the husbands followed suit with much muttering and twittering. "Yes, the Yarhun has been banned. And yes, it has had unfortunate side effects on occasion. We choose to do it anyway. We force it on no one."

"And yet . . . " I piled utensils on a plate. "And yet, in a closed society such as this one, might not a person feel compelled to act, against his or her better judgment?"

"One might," Shadron said. "But it would be meaningless. Some at this table have asked not to participate in the Yarhun—have you not?" He addressed the question down the length of the table, and several of the men and women nodded. "You see."

"I will go willingly," Magda said. "I have heard it's an amazing experience—strenuous, emotionally painful, and yet full of enlightenment and power. I would not trade the opportunity."

"Tonight?" I whispered, out of range of Desiree's sharp ears. When

Magda nodded, worry began churning up a headache behind my eyes.

I knew to change into something that would blend with the shadows. The lock on my door had clicked, turned by someone in the hall not long after dinner, but I doubted that would deter Desiree. In fact, she unlocked it a short time later; her hair was a bit disheveled, but her eyes shone. "The service is at midnight, or thereabouts. Are you ready?"

"Perhaps they locked us in for a reason," I said.

"Yes: they do not want me to tell their story. And I won't let them win. Stay here if you want."

But how could I? Just as it was in Desiree to seek out the secrets of these people, it was in me to follow her. So I did.

From the second floor windows, we watched the procession gather in the courtyard and wind away into the hills, two parallel lines of men and women, boys and girls. Shadron and Magda went first, carrying a dark, rectangular case between them, but all the others carried greenish, flickering lights. We followed at a distance, and when we crested the hill behind them and looked down into the valley where they were gathering, the ruins seemed like something glimpsed at the bottom of a river.

"It's beautiful." Desiree clutched at my arm with one hand, recording with the Sigil all the time that I helped her over the scattered rocks.

"Don't ruin it." She let go of me at once, and the night air chilled my skin.

"We must get closer." She eased down the slope, through tangles of bushes and boulders. At times, in the dim light cast by the procession and the stars, I caught hints of ancient terraces and foundations. We crept down the bare hint of a trail that switchbacked to the valley floor. A turquoise eye winked at us from concentric sockets of white stones, the broken remnants of a forgotten city.

"It's not the native stone of this place," I noted. "They must have brought it here from far away."

Desiree waved me to silence. In the dusty wake of the procession, we angled through stretches of stained and tumbled stone blocks and empty gardens of cracked soil. Though Shadron's family didn't speak, we heard the occasional cough, or the rattle of a pebble launched by a careless step. When they stopped at last, surrounding the pool we'd seen from above, we found a vantage point behind a curving wall like a cracked smile. The stones showed white where they'd been more recently broken.

They flanked the pool in two semi-circles, females and then men behind them. In silence, Magda and Shadron opened the box, revealing a smaller black box strung with wires. These he stretched out and attached to Magda's body. When he finished the task, he rested one hand at the nape of her neck and pressed the other to her forehead for a moment. Then he kissed her and let her go.

Magda waded into the center of the pool. The water rose to mid-thigh, floating her robes around her like petals. Desiree stiffened at my side; from the periphery of my vision, I watched her eyes widen and unease twisted low in my belly. "No," I whispered. She didn't answer.

Wires stretched from the Magda's temples and wrists, and out of the collar of her dress. Her collar bones, looking delicate enough to belong to a bird, stood out under skin a shade lighter than the soil. She smiled, looking down at the water, at the tiny ripples set off by her every movement. She had gathered up the wires in her left hand, holding them above the water. *A good thing,* I thought. The equipment looked ancient; wearing it in the water had to be a hazard.

The rest of the family began to chant—women and children first, with Shadron's chest-rumbling bass in counterpoint, the other men chiming in after. The song was nothing I'd heard before. Minor and yet lilting, it made my heart hurt, and at the same time it lifted me.

"What am I feeling?" Desiree asked.

The music captured her voice and made it a part of the song. "I think there was something in the water."

"A girl?"

I gave her a stern look, and she choked back a giggle and panned the recorder around the circle, even as she swayed in time to the music.

Magda cried out, raised her hands, and dropped the wires. Where they touched the water, bluish-white sparks crackled, and steam rose from the surface. I took Desiree's arm. "She could be—"

She laid a finger on her lips, still filming all the while. "They don't look worried."

The wives and husbands and children, standing in their parallel rows, kept their eyes fixed on the woman in the pool. Nausea clawed at my belly; I would not enjoy watching this woman die of electrocution, no more than I looked forward to Desiree's endless retelling of the tale. I took a step forward, but the woman stood with her arms raised, an ecstatic expression on her face. She did not appear to be in pain, never mind at risk of dying, and I hesitated.

The air around the woman began to hum. The tendrils of steam rose and curled around her, as if they had minds of their own. Her figure shimmered, as though losing coherence, and the sparks snapped and fizzed.

"What do you suppose she's thinking?" Desiree whispered to me.

I slid a glance in her direction. "Temporal lobe stimulation is known to cause visions, quasi-religious experiences . . ."

"You think it's a crock, then." She sounded disappointed. Her eyes never left the woman.

"I think it's an understandable—if risky—adaptation of technology to worship. Let them believe what they want. Who do they harm?"

"Aside from themselves? Though she doesn't seem at all perturbed."

Magda swayed, the humming in the air rising in pitch until the hairs on my arms lifted. I let my gaze drift to the others, many of whom also moved to the pulsation of the device. If they heard my quiet conversation with Desiree, they made no sign.

The steam snaked out and retreated. For a moment, I thought I glimpsed figures entwined, dancing or indulging in a more primitive physical duet. There was a phantom child, then, running until it vanished. A brawny ghost beating down a smaller form. I blinked and shook my head, and it was once more nothing but transitory steam.

"Did you—"

I shook my head. "The mind likes to play tricks," I assured her. "We see patterns in random things."

"A murder?"

"We can't be sure it was—" I stopped and stared at her. Desiree's eyes were wide, her mouth gaping.

"You, too?"

I wanted to shake her. "You're imagining things. We both are. Maybe there was something in the food, in the drink ... "

"Maybe there's something in the Yarhun." She folded her hands in front of her and turned away from me. I started to speak, hoping to defuse the idea that I'd seen dawning in her expression, but at that moment Magda collapsed with a cry like a hungry kitten. She lay still in the water, the ripples caused by her fall washing over her face. Before I could move, Shadron and two of his co-husbands had jumped into the water. The men disconnected the wires as Shadron hefted Magda and carried her, dripping, to the tiles of the plaza.

Her face, greenish-gray in the flickering light, was still as death. I reached out to Desiree, and she gripped my hand, so tightly I felt our bones grinding together. Shadron rolled her onto her side and smacked between her shoulder blades with the flat of his hand. At first there was no reaction, so he did it again, and a third time. She coughed weakly, and a thin trickle of spittle leaked to the pavement. Her husband waited, his hand on her back, but she made no other sound nor movement.

"This can't be good," Desiree whispered. In the silence after her words, I heard the whir of the Sigil. Shadron turned his head and stared at our hiding place. I hunched lower behind the broken wall, waiting for his challenge. But none came, and when I dared to look again, Shadron was carrying Magda back toward the compound, with the rest of the family following.

"Hurry," Desiree said. "We have to beat them back."

For the morning and noon meals, silent and somber children brought trays to our rooms. I heard Desiree ask questions they didn't— or couldn't—answer. Several times she knocked on my door, but I didn't respond. I pictured Magda's empty face, that trickle of saliva running down her chin, and I couldn't face another argument with Desiree.

Instead, I ran the wall inscription through my Sigil, looking for patterns, similarities to known tongues. Each possibility churned out nonsense: names that sounded like broken glass as I spat them out, random accretions of subject and object, verb and modifier. At last I threw down the Sigil in surrender, just as someone knocked on the door once again.

Having resigned myself to the inevitable squabble—and to losing—I was surprised to open the door and find, instead, red-haired Kahla. "Father invites you to supper," she said.

We stopped next for Desiree, who greeted us with her hands folded, the sleeves of her black dress trimmed with silver. She followed Kahla with her head bowed. But the look she shot me from lowered eyes was anything but demure. Equal parts anger and anticipation, it made me flinch. I shook my head as I fell into step beside her. She made a contemptuous sound under her breath, but didn't speak.

Perhaps Kahla had warned her, or perhaps even Desiree wasn't immune to the solemn atmosphere in the house. The silence had substance, moved with us, pressed on our shoulders. I felt sure Magda had died, but she sat in her customary place beside Shadron, smiling. I opened my mouth to greet her and wish her well, but immediately stopped. Whatever she smiled at, it wasn't anything in the room. Shadron kept his gaze fixed on her. I took my place beside Desiree.

Aside from a brief blessing over the bread, the meal passed in silence. Once, Magda broke into a hum, a low sound deep in her throat. Everyone paused, forks lifted. But no words came, and after a time she lapsed again into her wordless smiling. Shadron tried to feed her, forking up small bites and holding them to her lips, but she paid no heed. I tried to imagine Desiree doing the same for me, and had to bite back a smile. Though I had to admit, she *would* hire the best care for me if I were incapacitated.

It was a relief to finish the last course and push back from the table. Shadron followed us into the corridor. "It must seem strange to you, I know. But she . . . " His voice broke, and he struggled to regain his composure. "She has sacrificed for us. We will not hide her away as if we were ashamed."

Desiree nodded. "We don't want to bother you at this time. Do you mind if we walk around a bit this evening and shoot some footage? We'll leave the family alone."

"Feel free." He said it without interest. Whatever suspicions he harbored had been subsumed by other concerns.

"Magda—" I began, and cleared my throat. "Will she . . . Is she . . . ?" I couldn't find a way to frame the question.

"I don't know." The words were flat, as though he'd said them often enough now to press all meaning out of them.

At first, I was surprised by how easy it was to put Desiree's plan into motion. Though I remained convinced that Shadron had noticed our presence at the Yarhun, no one accosted us when we left our rooms to explore. The machine from the ceremony had been returned to its box, but the heavy, dark-stained hardwood container sat in a corner of the dining room, cracked open, as though no one had had the heart to stow it away after what had happened to Magda.

Even with both of us working together, though, I couldn't see how we'd carry it down to the pool among the ruins. I poked at the dials. "It's at least a hundred years old, if not older. I think we should leave it alone."

"I need to know—"

"She's a vegetable, Desiree! There's nothing there anymore." I shook her.

"I didn't know you cared."

My hands dropped to my sides. "Fine. Try to get it down there without me."

"Yaromir." She drew close, staring up at me, her hand on my chest. "I can't do it without you. Please. It's for both of us, for our future. I can't live as a nobody."

I looked away, fists clenched.

"You're curious, too. Admit it. And you know that not everyone ends up like that. Like Magda."

"I don't care about everyone. Only—" I couldn't make myself say it. Couldn't give her that much of a weapon.

"If the worst happened, and you weren't there . . . "

"All *right*." I opened the box the rest of the way and lifted out the machine. Without its container, it was light enough for me to carry alone. I let Desiree lead the way. We had reached the pool and were setting the machine up at the spot where the Yarhunites had placed it when the sound of feet scraping on stone startled me.

"Shadron," Desiree began.

He held up his hand. "It would be within my rights to cast you out now," he said. "Foolish woman, you've attached the wires incorrectly."

She backed away from him. But rather than tearing off the electrodes as I'd hoped, he rearranged them. "If you must do this, do it well. It's your only chance of survival."

"Tell her not to do it."

He shook his head. "If she will not listen to you, then I have no hope of reasoning with her."

"Then why not force her to stop? Call the authorities."

"Better to let her have her moment. What will her viewers see? A woman experimenting on herself in a most courageous but ill-advised way. And that is all."

"What will Desiree see?"

He turned on power to the machine. "I don't know."

"Desiree," I begged. "He could kill you."

"You said they weren't violent people." She climbed over the rim of the pool, the wires held in her hand. She looked too much like Magda; I turned to Shadron, but his eyes were squeezed closed. His fingers rested on the control button, his thumb twitching. And then he pressed it.

"She must not!" Those were the first words I'd heard Magda speak since the Yarhun. They tore out of her, ragged and too loud; her face, once so serene, had taken on a ruddy purplish hue, her eyes wide, the pupils depthless and too large in the wan light. As Shadron and I stared, she stormed down the last slope to the plaza.

Shadron reached out, as though to gather her in. But she pushed past him in a tangle of blows and snatched up the box that powered the Yarhun. The matte black surface swallowed the light, and drank in the harsh sound of her breathing as well.

"Desiree!" I had been through enough disasters with her to know what was coming, and I threw myself at the fountain. It was my job, and my life.

What happened next, like a series of still shots taken too far apart, runs in my memory with jerky, shadowed chaos.

Magda stalked to the pool, the machine clutched to her chest. Shadron clung to her, arms banded around her from behind. He said something, low, urgent—a prayer or a plea. I stood between them and Desiree. The water sucked at my legs. I gathered up the wires. Though I tugged at Desiree—gently, like a hunter drawing in an exotic bird he didn't want to damage—she wavered but held her place.

"Please," I begged her. Her rapt eyes cast rapidly back and forth, and she didn't respond to me. "Please."

"Must not. Must not. Must not." Magda ran the words together as she dragged her husband and the machine over the lip of the fountain.

"Turn it off! Pull the wires!"

"I can't—the damage!" Shadron grappled for control of the machine. Magda wrested it back, and it slipped through their hands to shatter on the stones of the pool's rim.

I swept up Desiree and hoisted her over my shoulder. A wave of sparks swamped us, a crackling tide that filled the plaza with the scent of lightning. I remember that smell—to this day, it makes me ill. And I remember the wires burning my hand, lines of fire across my palm and knuckles.

The Universe froze, a vast bubble caught on the cusp of that moment. I felt Desiree's weight, and yet at the same time I *was* her. I tasted fate and adventure and passion. I saw myself through her eyes— painfully thin and angular, long-faced and dour. I felt the distance of her affection, and nothing more.

Then:

The shadowed emptiness of the dimensional short-cuts between star systems, the hum of engines and a myriad voices.

The sere ochre landscape of Circe, empty of complex life, reflecting off the silvery hull of a landing vehicle.

The white walls of the city, whole and then broken.

The wraiths of the lost, moving through an eternal dance of love or hatred or indifference, creation or destruction, wealth or poverty, ugliness or beauty.

I lived through them, wore their alien limbs, watched them pass into me and out again, leaving a chill in their wake. Whether they sensed me as well, I could not say; only that I lived the rise and fall of their world in the space between heartbeats—a world that was still theirs, in a way, for they hadn't left it.

Something detonated with the raw odor of burnt metal and plastic, and I teetered once more at the edge of the pool, Desiree slipping off my shoulder. I heaved her over, and dust on the tiles smeared her dress and the bare skin of her arms and legs. *She'll hate that I ruined her outfit*, I thought. And then I remembered her Sigil, which had fallen somewhere. I sat on the edge of the pool and laid a hand to my chest, but the pain I expected did not materialize.

Nothing came to me, in fact. I let my hands dangle between my knees and listened to the wind grieving through the ruins, and Desiree's gasping coughs. I heard splashing and looked up; Shadron floundered on the far side of the pool, the hands grasping for purchase scorched blackish-red.

Weary of his wheezing, I slogged around the edge of the pool and pulled him over by the back of his shirt. He bit back a cry—or perhaps I did, for the burns on my hands pulled and stung with the effort. Chunks of black plastic and tangles of wire bobbed against my legs.

"Magda," he said. I looked around and shook my head. She floated face down in the pool. For a moment I considered holding her under, just to be sure. But instead I rolled her over and towed her back to her husband. I might as well have drowned her *and* him: he saw her slack face, shredded and darkened by the box's explosion, and let out a keening wail. It made me think of a predator who'd lost his mate. I saw Desiree sit up, eyes dazed, and I wanted to howl as well.

"That was . . . amazing." She got to her feet, shaking all over. "Have you a towel?"

I shook my head and climbed over the rim of the pool. Shadron and his dead public wife lay between us.

"Oh, no." She had noticed, then. Or not, I realized as she continued, "You dropped the *Sigil*? In the *water*? And . . . oh, mercy. It's broken."

"The transport will be coming soon," I told her. "We should pack."

"I can't leave now." She clasped her arms around her abdomen, shivering. "There must be . . . at another settlement, maybe. I have to . . . We can't . . . "

"I'm done," I said. Someday, I knew, someone would ask what I'd seen. Was it God? The dead? I only knew I'd seen the end of everything.

She went on talking, as familiar and meaningless as the babble of water.

"I'm sorry," I told Shadron. He lay with his arm over his eyes. I didn't think he heard me, but I didn't repeat myself.

I wondered, walking back to the compound, what would become of them without Magda. And I wondered what would become of me. Desiree trailed behind me, muttering, and I thought how easy it would be to slip back into the rhythm of our life—her life.

But in the end, I kept walking.

Ruins Terra—the companion anthology

From the ruins of Planet Earth . . . Science Fiction, Fantasy, Horror, Gothic. Diverse tales from storytellers across the world. *Ruins Terra*, the companion anthology to *Ruins Extraterrestrial,* is available now from Hadley Rille Books.

For more info: www.hadleyrillebooks.com.

Visual Journeys: A Tribute to Space Artists

Golden Age SF: Tales of a Bygone Future

"Golden Age SF . . . its original stories . . . certainly dwell on the destiny of scientific utopia and interplanetary colonization proclaimed by the SF of 50 years past . . . All in all, an agreeable anthology."

—*Locus*

New stories written as if during the Golden Age of Science Fiction. Several selected for honorable mention for Gardner Dozois's *The Year's Best Science Fiction 24,* one selected for David G. Hartwell and Kathryn Cramer's *Year's Best SF 12,* another selected for Rich Horton's *Space Opera 2007.*

For more info: www.hadleyrillebooks.com.

Coming soon . . .

Watch for updates at www.hadleyrillebooks.com.

Printed in the United Kingdom
by Lightning Source UK Ltd.
124153UK00001B/25-27/A